MARCHING
IN SCOTLAND,
DANCING
IN
NEW YORK

By

MARGARET M. DUNLOP

Published by

MELROSE BOOKS

An Imprint of Melrose Press Limited
St Thomas Place, Ely
Cambridgeshire
CB7 4GG, UK
www.melrosebooks.com

FIRST EDITION

Copyright © Margaret M. Dunlop 2007

The Author asserts her moral right to
be identified as the author of this work

Cover designed by Catherine McIntyre

ISBN 978 1906050 19 1

Printed and bound in Great Britain by:
Cromwell Press, Aintree Avenue, White Horse Business Park,
Trowbridge, Wiltshire, BA14 0XB, UK

CONTENTS

CHAPTER 1

William was tall, at least a foot taller than his wife, Louisa. Right now he was seated at the table, an empty soup plate in front of him. His posture as he sat, his broad shoulders rounded, his chin down, was defensive, the gaze guarded. Experience told him that his wife could easily become very angry. After some minutes, the eyes of both parents turned to the slight girl who stood working at the kitchen sink by the window. The sun shone scantily through the curtain onto her soapy hands as she dealt with the dishes. Her brothers and sisters had all found things to do when it was decided it was her turn to do the washing-up. The girl's soft blue eyes were downcast, but this did not hide the turmoil that was in her, as she faced her mother's onslaught of questions.

"Just tell me that Edward Denny's not coming round here this evening. You mind my words, Honor. He's not the one for you. There's better fish in the sea than him. You think on. And if he appears at the party this evening you watch out. Don't get yourself caught up with a penniless Scotsman. Anyway, get a move on. There's a mountain of ironing, and the small bedroom has to be cleaned out."

William interrupted the flow of annoyance, unable to bear seeing the tears spill down the face of his favourite girl. "Leave the lass alone, Louisa. She likes Edward, and he's not so bad. Just give her a bit of peace. She's washed up all the pots. She's stood there for nearly an hour. And she's done a day's work. Leave over, Louisa."

But Louisa would not be deflected from her mood. Duster in hand, she turned to poke the good-going fire in the range and added some small coal to the top of the blaze. "Time wasting, that's all it is. These Scotch folk are all the same. They give no time to looking after their houses, or attending to their own business. If they're not out drinking, then they're sitting up half the night arguing about politics, or they're going to the races and betting good money on horses. They should learn to make use of the time God gave them. What a black day it was, William Dryden, that you ever brought me to this godforsaken Scotland." Now she was getting into her stride, and she strenuously polished the shining steel of the range as she spoke. Then she stopped and glared at him. "Never to see my sister Liza or our Doris. Always to be a foreigner to these folk – folk whose talk I can hardly understand. We should never have left England. Even if we had stayed in Newcastle it would have been better than this."

At last she sat down and took up a bit of sewing, while William quietly slipped out the door to the back green where he lit up his pipe. Musing on his life, as the thick tobacco smoke rose in the air, his mind turned to consider the year, now over twelve years ago, when he had taken the offer of a job as foreman of the new glassworks being built on the outskirts of Glasgow. The children (Honor and Nelly left temporarily in England) had been trailed from the railway station to their tenement flat with Louisa carrying a bag of flour for breadmaking, thinking none would be available in this outlandish place. It had been an unbelievable twelve years of ups and downs. Three more children had been born to Louisa, making ten in all, four boys and six girls, although Willie, their first-born, had stayed in England.

As a glass-blower, the big man with his massive lungs had been a great success in the new Scottish factory. But now, worn out and retired from this fierce work, he had found peace and happiness in his garden. There, in his allotment, his vegetable crops were equalled by none in the area. Also, English William was famous locally for his singing voice, and his rendering of 'Rocked in the Cradle of the Deep' moved many a one to tears. He was a large, soft, good-living man who found fault with nobody.

Honor, escaping from the kitchen sink, slipped into her coat and made her way to the railway yard, knowing that the men would soon be making their ways home for the start of their weekend. Her heart was heavy and she felt a real ache of worry about her condition, but she had a great longing to see Edward, even if just for a moment. Anyway, she thought, if I don't see him on my walk, at least I will be near him as I pass the yard. Perhaps I'll catch a glimpse of him through the hedge, or hear his voice as I pass along.

The girl had no luck, for the men were working some extra hours this Saturday, and she carried on her way, her longing still with her, and she prayed that he would not forget the party. With a long lingering look towards the bothy where she knew her sweetheart would be, Honor walked on, leaving this male world behind.

It seemed as if the railway yard had always been there. Just down from the little local station, there were abandoned wagons, sheds full of iron rails, bolts, hammers, all manner of ironwork. Outside were engine oil spills, lurid black and purple on the springing grass of the embankments. Creosoted great railway sleepers were everywhere, and piles of coal, of cinders, and of gravel had been dumped in a seemingly disorderly fashion around the place. And then there was the workmen's bothy, a haven from the cold wind and sometimes driving rain the railway main-tenance men had to endure. The whole complex had been enclosed by a high brick wall to keep out the unkempt, wild children of the area, and the local poverty-stricken folk who would have stolen anything if they thought they could get away with it. Over the high brick walls some hawthorn bushes drooped, relics of the countryside before the iron rails and brash, smoky trains were a commonplace.

Halfway through their shift the men had a tea break. Edward, or Ned as they called him, the youngest of the crew, fresh and handsome, just back from the war, had sat himself down along with six or seven men in the workmen's bothy. There they ate their sandwiches and drank scalding hot tea from tin cans whose handles were of thin wire. The cans of water were boiled on a coke fire in an iron fire basket and then spoonfuls of black tea leaves were added to them. It was at these times that the gossiping and wisecracking began. Any story that raised a laugh was welcomed. Charlie McGowan, a wizened, comical little man, was speaking. "I tell you, Ned, he stole a swan!" There was laughter in the bothy at the story.

"Away with you, Charlie," Edward said. "Even Paddy Riley wouldn't be as daft as that. Everybody knows that swans belong to the Crown. You could get the jail for that."

"It's the truth, Ned. Honest to God! He took his little brother, Chuck, you know, and there was the swan, padding along on the banks of the loch. His wife had told him there wasn't a bite to eat in the house, and he hadn't to come back unless he brought something for her and the bairns to eat." Edward's face reddened with laughter as he listened to the story.

"Nobody could eat a swan, Charlie, pull the other one!"

"Sure, didn't they make soup with it? Swan soup!"

The bothy at the side of the railtrack rocked with laughter and one of the men piped up, "Aye, and if we don't get a rise in the hourly rate soon, we'll all be eating swan soup. I've got five mouths to feed now, and how do I do that on forty-two shillings a fortnight?"

"I've only got three bairns, but I haven't been home for my dinner, yet," cracked Charlie.

They laughed heartily. "Aye, Ned, don't get married too young. It's a soul-destroying bloody business trying to live on the wages the railway pays."

"Not me!" Edward answered. "These black curls will not turn grey so easily. I'm young and fancy-free. I'm going to a party tonight. There'll be plenty of women there, I can tell you."

"You stay lucky, son. For it's a hellish millstone around your neck – a houseful of kids and a wife aye moaning aboot something. You stick to parties. I wish I had the chance again."

That evening, the party was already in full swing when Edward arrived at the door, and Honor hurried to greet him. He saw the table piled high with good things to eat and heard the music and laughter in the background, but at once, he saw from her serious face that all was not well. The knowledge she had tried to give him on their last meeting, the words that he had tried to bury, rose up again. They sat together on a padded stool at the back of the parlour, and if they joined in the singing and laughter, they were a bit half-hearted about it.

Soon the furniture was pushed back and a waltz was played on the piano. Half a dozen couples squeezed up to dance in the crowded room, and Edward and Honor joined them.

"I'll have to tell my mother soon, Edward," she whispered. "I'm scared."

Edward's face grew pale with shock, and he did not answer. After some anguished minutes he said, "First we should tell my mother. She'll know what to do."

The music stopped, and they sat down. Edward continued, "I know my mother is more churchgoing than yours, and all that, but she's more broad-minded, too. We'll tell her tomorrow morning." Relief flooded through the worried girl's body. Scared stiff and full of guilt and apprehension, she had told no one of her predicament.

"Oh, Edward, you're so good. I love you so much." She put her arm on his shoulder and kissed him warmly.

"That's more like it!" The voice was her brother Rob's. Slightly tipsy, his red hair falling over his eyes, and with his arm around his girlfriend, he started to sing:

> "I'm shy, Mary-Ellen, I'm shy.
> It does seem so naughty, oh my ..."

The others joined in, and soon Edward and Honor were pulled up to dance, surrounded by their happy friends and relations. It was the happiest the two had felt in weeks.

Next morning, Edward returned from church to find his mother busy in the kitchen with the stewpot and vegetables. It was a small house of only three rooms, a ground-floor flat in an ancient grey sandstone building. Three of Edward's sisters had left home to take up careers in nursing, and his brother Joe had married at eighteen. So there was only Archie, the clever son of the family, that is the educated one, for he was not of as broad an intellect as the older Edward, but he was the one who was getting the chance, destined for university. Annie had been to an early church service, and now she was engrossed in her thoughts as she prepared the Sunday dinner.

"Honor is going to call in this morning," Edward announced.

"Oh, that's nice. I haven't seen her for a while," his mother answered. At this there was the noise of footsteps, and they turned to see Edward's sweetheart at the kitchen door. Unexpectedly, Edward's father was at home that morning, seated at the fireside, puffing at his pipe. Usually on a Sunday morning, he made himself scarce, to escape the nagging about the previous evening's imbibing of alcohol, or often a chastising about his non-attendance at church. Immediately Annie saw Honor's face, she knew something was the matter.

"Sit down, Honor. I'm right glad you called in. You've got fine rosy cheeks this morning," she greeted the girl.

"Yes. It's nice to see you, Mrs Denny. You're always busy at something."

"Well, I'll make a cup of tea and sit down for ten minutes. You can stay for dinner, if you like."

"Oh, my mother will have made mine by now. But, thanks for inviting me."

"Well, take off your coat and hat, anyway, lass," the older woman said kindly.

"Mother," Edward cut in. He glanced at his father. "Honor's got something to tell you." Annie sat down, but she had already guessed the position as she looked from one to the other, and sadness and joy, excitement and dread filled her, but most of all she felt sympathy for the troubled young couple.

"So, there's a baby on the way, Honor?"

The young girl broke down in tears, and Edward's father rose from his chair and put an arm around her shaking body.

"There! There! My flower, don't cry! You won't be the first girl that's been foolish, and you won't be the last. You and Edward have been courting for more than a year now. Don't cry, m'dear."

Annie rose and made a pot of tea. She poured out four cupfuls and placed some biscuits on the table. "There's a house coming empty in Greengairs Street. I heard about it yesterday. I'll see the factor myself tomorrow. I brought his last two children into the world, and they were difficult births." She paused and looked at John, her husband. "He'll oblige me, I'm sure." John nodded his response, and she turned to Honor. "Dry your eyes, girl. It'll be all right." Annie felt the tears start in her own eyes. "What does your mother say?"

This question set Honor sobbing. "She doesn't know. I haven't told her." The two older people looked at each other, anticipating the bombshell that this news would be to Louisa Dryden and the reaction that would be heard at the other end of the town. "I'm scared to tell her, Mrs Denny. She'll kill me."

"Oh, we'll see about that," was the reply. "Finish up your tea. Get your hat and coat, and go home. Say nothing. Edward and I will be there within the hour." Edward couldn't restrain a smile of relief from crossing his face. With his mother on his side, he could conquer the world.

When Annie had got herself dressed in her best coat and hat, and had prepared herself for the confrontation, John asked timidly, "Do you want me to go or will you be all right without me?"

"You stay here, John. You watch that stew. I'll no' be long."

CHAPTER 2

Enjoying his tobacco, Honor's father walked to the front of the house, clutching his pipe. Coming towards him were a couple of people who were familiar to him. It was Edward, Honor's beau, dressed in his weekend tweed sports jacket, accompanied by his mother in her Sunday best. Disquiet filled him, still he greeted them politely and led them into the parlour of the house where Louisa was already ensconced while Honor, her apron removed, the sleeves of her dress rolled down, stood beside her.

Edward settled himself, standing by the side of his mother's chair. Annie Denny had never been inside the Dryden's house, although she had heard rumours that it was very fine. And with its high-backed leather chairs and fine cushions and ornaments, its fancy fireplace displaying tiles of Diana, the Huntress, it was certainly more grand than the usual. Everyone seemed serious as they gathered in the beams of dusty sunshine which streamed through the tall parlour windows. There was a short silence, and after tea was refused Louisa got straight to the point. "This visit is unexpected, Mrs Denny. You are not working today? No call-outs today, or maybe babies don't come on a Sunday?" Her small joke fell on deaf ears.

The black feathers of Mrs Denny's best hat shook slightly as the pale and thin from overwork Annie launched into her speech. "Mrs Dryden, Mr Dryden, I won't beat about the bush. You know as well as I do that your Honor and my Edward have been going out together. Well ..." she paused searching for the words while Honor stood like a figure of stone and the tall, handsome Edward hung his head, his black curls falling over and covering his eyes.

Annie gulped slightly and continued, "Well, late last night Edward has given me some bad news. It seems that," she took a quick glance at Honor, "it seems that the two of them have got themselves into trouble." She looked directly at Louisa, who read the look and in a flash had burst into a paroxysm of tears and wailing. Her husband, with eyes burning and face ashen, stood up and moving towards the stiff figure of his daughter, threw his arms around her, muttering into her luxuriant hair, "Don't cry, love, don't cry!"

Edward cast his head down even lower, still trying to comprehend the situation, the certainty that Honor was in the family way. He blinked back the tears as he relived his consternation, and then the scene at home, when later he had told his mother of his predicament. How would his workmates react? And the rest of the Denny family, would they be scandalised, would people talk against him? He thought of the large family photograph, taken ten years before, his mother's pride and joy in its large gilded frame, her three sons and four daughters, and he, the tallest as a boy of fourteen, standing with the others, proudly wearing his fine suit bought for the occasion. His younger brother Archie, accepted by Glasgow University to study for an Arts degree, was the lucky one, the star of the family. He would never have to struggle as Edward would have to do. His mother had been adamant. He would have to marry Honor. He was caught, and his life was now being mapped out for him.

He sneaked a glance at Honor and saw that her cheeks burned with embarrassment as the truth of her condition became known. She was in shock, so that she did not dare glance directly at him or at anyone. His mother sat upright, her auburn hair spilling below her black hat, she was determined that her son would do right by this girl. Her strong religious faith and her innate idea of right and wrong were to the fore.

In contrast, Honor's mother was collapsing into self-indulgent tears. Loudly she sobbed as she pressed a handkerchief to her face to soak up the flow. And her husband stayed beside his daughter while he waited for the histrionics of his wife to pass.

Honor said in a tiny voice, "We want to get married, Mam and Dad."

"There's no disgrace here. Get that right!" Edward's mother's voice was hard and decisive. "They love each other, and Edward wants to marry your girl. I'm going to see about a house for them, and I'll see Father Niven this evening."

"Why?" wailed Louisa. "Why didn't you tell me – your mother?"

Honor hung her head. She knew her mother did not think much of her. She knew that each one of her sisters was prettier and quicker on the uptake than she was, and that any one of them would come before her, in her mother's estimation. Sometimes she wondered if it was because she was her father's favourite.

"It was Edward's idea that I should be told first. He thought I could help them." And so saying, Annie approached Louisa and embraced her. "Don't be so upset, Louisa!" and for a few seconds they shared their unhappiness. "It'll be all right. You'll see. You haven't forgotten your own young days, now have you?"

"We'll be the talk of the place, Annie. People are always accusing us of being snobs. Now they'll have something to gossip about and to throw in our faces." Sensing that she had the limelight, Louisa carried on in her wailing. "They'll say we're Godless. They'll think I let my family run wild. Oh God! Oh God! What's to become of us?"

"Listen, woman," answered Annie, shaking Louisa. "I know it seems bad for you and Honor, but who's to know? If they're married within the month then all will be well. Let's try and be happy for them. We'll announce a wedding, and let them all go and jump in the Clyde if they're scandalised."

Louisa turned to her sad, deflated husband as he sat in his big leather winged armchair, his head dropped, his eyes tearful. Her dark blue eyes burned in her face, the white of her pulled-back hair framing the reddening of her face. Secretly she thought of William as a useless lump who frustrated her in his good-natured, slow and gentlemanly manner. "We should never have left England. I've told you before we should never have come here! All my family, our Liza and our Doris, I never see them. Maybe I'll never see them again." Tears of frustration and self-pity had started now, but Honor had heard it all before. The same recriminations were thrown at her father every time there was a crisis in the house.

"We had to come here, Louisa, you know that. I had to come here for work." William looked round the faces in the room, appealing to their reason. "This is our home, Louisa. It's nearly thirteen years we've been here."

Louisa stopped snivelling. She was shocked and saddened by the morning's events, but having borne ten children herself, as she looked at her dejected daughter she couldn't help but understand the predicament and powerlessness of the pregnant girl. The baby was there, and what could they do?

"How far on is it?" she whispered.

Glancing quickly at Edward and his mother, in a low voice Honor said, "I think three months."

Louisa lifted the hem of her black linen skirt and dried her eyes. She took a couple of steps towards her daughter and put her arms around her. For a few seconds they stood together watched by the others. Then Louisa drew back and looking at the quivering face of the girl, she said, "You'll make a lovely bride, Honor."

And so it was that the preparations for the wedding began. Honor found solace in making a confidante of Susan Denny, Edward's sister who came home some weekends. They chattered and planned on every occasion that they could. "You're really quite lucky, Honor. Soon you'll have your own home, a loving husband, and a little baby to love," Susan said as they finished the hemming of the wedding dress that had been made by Mrs Dryden.

"Well, I'm a bit nervous, but yes, I'm happy now," replied Honor. "It's just a vestry wedding, me being non-Catholic, but I'm taking instructions from Father Niven before the baby comes, and then I can join your church."

"Oh, you'll be welcome, too. All the family are pleased. They're looking forward to the wedding and especially to the dance afterwards. Archie's quite excited. So many lovely girls are going to be there!"

"You'll marry some day, Susan. You and Tommy have been going together for ages."

"No, we won't marry, not till we are in a better position." Susan pursed her lips. "Some day, maybe, I don't know." She carried on sewing, lost in thought.

"Is Tommy coming to the wedding?"

"Yes, he'll be there. He wouldn't miss an excuse for a feast and a dance! Who would?" The two girls laughed together in the little parlour of the Denny's house, their heads full of excitement at the thought of the wedding day to come.

It was a happy Honor and Edward who left the church that June morning. The joy and promise in the face of the bride and the upright strength, pride and 'joie de vivre' on the face of the handsome, dark-haired groom seemed to match the mood of the people. Everything and everyone seemed full of hope and happiness as they threw rice and confetti and cheered the young couple as they walked to the church hall and the wedding breakfast.

Edward's job with the railway was a steady one, the war was forgotten, and matching the sunshine, hope was in his heart for the future. Honor smiled at everyone around. She had left her job, having saved a few pounds. Her 'bottom drawer' was full of tablecloths and bedlinen, and baby clothes, too. The trauma of the revelation of her pregnancy was over. The inevitability of the marriage had had to be accepted by both families.

The invited guests walked to the little hall where all was in readiness for the celebrations. Tables were laid and soon great ashets of steak pie and pots of steaming potatoes and of peas appeared. Village ways had not been lost, and friends and relations had helped and contributed towards the wedding feast. The two families who were now uniting were both large and well respected in the neighbourhood. Their standing showed in their easy acceptance of the duty to prepare and eat this hearty meal and to dance and be merry until they came to a standstill.

The band struck up a waltz as the big folding trestle tables were cleared away. Everyone clapped and cheered as the newly-weds danced the first dance, soon to be joined by most of the assembled guests.

"Congratulations, Mrs Dryden. Edward's a fine boy and has a good job, too." Louisa Dryden looked up at her neighbour who had spoken. She had her misgivings. Her own husband was tamed and docile, but men in general, she didn't trust. She knew her daughter was like her father, simple and naive. Edward was not much above a labourer, for all his book learning. Besides, he was popular and handsome. Would he stay true to Honor? Would he be a good man to her? She thought of his fondness for the public house and like many Scotsmen for endless discussing, arguing and carousing, and she shuddered to think of the future.

"Yes, he's fond of Honor, and they make a good-looking couple." She smiled politely as expected.

Annie Denny rose from where she was seated at the table beside her husband, who was downing the whisky in his glass, too quickly for her liking, and came and sat beside her new relation.

"Well, Louisa, that was a fine meal you provided. You can't beat the cooking of you folk from England."

Louisa, looking pleased, said, "Yes, eighty-four guests, Annie. A big crowd to feed, that's true, but I've catered for big crowds at home in England. Helped at weddings and all kinds of celebrations, and my girls are good in the kitchen. They're well trained in cooking and in housekeeping." The underlying suggestion that this was not the case in her Scottish counterpart's household was left hanging as Louisa continued, perhaps trying to soften the atmosphere, "I hear you passed your final examination, and have letters after your name, Annie."

"Yes," said Annie. "The certificate came by post last week." She subsumed the thought of the hours and hours of cold, weary reading, often by candlelight or poor gaslight, while the children slept. She would admit nothing of the harsh, long days she had endured for the past five years, when she had added the burden of entering herself for nursing examinations to her already long days of washing, cooking and cleaning for her family. "I'm relieved the studying's all over." Annie allowed herself a quiet, confident smile to this slightly superior-mannered woman. And then she couldn't resist adding, "And our Archie's won the history prize at St Mungo's Academy. He's been accepted for Glasgow University. I'm very proud of him. He's a clever, hard-working boy."

"Well, you can't beat your lot for bookishness." Louisa made it sound like an eccentric trait. She herself had never properly learned to read. Born in the 1870s, it was common for the children of her Yorkshire village, where she had been born, to be unschooled or scarcely literate. Unlike in Scotland where the authorities, mainly the church, made sure that no child escaped it.

Intelligent and extremely skilful, Louisa was illiterate. She could design and make beautiful clothes, bake bread and cakes of legendary quality, cook meats that melted in your mouth, and keep a house that shone with brass and copper and with gleaming furniture, but had not the skill to read a headline of a newspaper or the labels in the local grocer's shop. Not many folk knew of her handicap, and William concealed it from people when he could. Only her children, who used to read to her, and a few close friends from England who had moved to Scotland with the Drydens knew the truth. Yet Louisa was proud of her birthplace and of her family. She felt herself a cut above her Scottish neighbours. Wasn't that evident from her well-kept house and excellent table? she told herself.

William and Louisa were too old to ever feel totally at one with the Scots and the area they had settled in. The outlook of the incomers from the south was different. They did their work and at the end of the day, or at the weekend, they made their home a place of relaxation and entertainment. There was always someone to play the piano, and others would start up a sing-song at the drop of a hat. Also the Drydens were the first in the neighbourhood to have a gramophone, and this was played to entertain guests.

Gardening, drying herbs and making up infusions, breeding canaries, all these were part of the life of William, while Louisa baked and sewed beautifully. Their talk between themselves when the family were around them, and they were at leisure, was cultured and mannerly, and they found little use for drinking or public houses.

But for Edward's family, it was all education, books, studying, never-ending studying, and when that was done, for the men at least, there was the public house. The pub was the place where they met their cronies, where the discussions were endless. They talked of politics, of the plight of the working man and of how they could solve the problems that beset them. They would change the world, they didn't doubt it, and the more beer they drank, the quicker things would be sure to change. All they needed was a revolution and a new political system.

The wedding was going at a great pace. At the appearance of the wide expanse of wooden floor, the children took to running and dancing around, while the adults settled in seats around the room and waited for the band to start up the dance. There was an accordionist, a pianist, a drummer, and lastly a violinist. The group were sorting out moth-eaten sheets of music and making odd sounds as they tuned their instruments.

Louisa was dressed in a suit of navy blue crepe material which threw into contrast her beautiful white hair. This she had dressed in a bun on the nape of her neck. At her bosom, beneath the crossing of the bodice, she had placed what she called a fascinator, a triangle of white lace so that too much was not revealed. She had sat down next to Annie. The Scotswoman was resplendent in black velvet, so flattering to her white skin and auburn hair. Annie's expression was one of gravity and dignity as she sat looking straight ahead. A waiter came round with a tray of glasses, and they were each persuaded to take a small glass of port wine.

Louisa spoke first. "I hear your husband is thinking of going down the pit to work. It would be a pity if he left the parish school where he works alongside the priest. They say he's a great teacher."

"Aye, that's right, Mrs Dryden. It's for more money he would earn. He's a clever man, my husband, although at times you woulnae think so." She made a face to show her disgust. "Aye, it seems all the Dennys are clever. John was a very good scholar at school when he was a boy. He has beautiful handwriting, copperplate it is. I'm sure if he'd had the chance, he could have been somebody – a politician, maybe. Maybe even Prime Minister." Not noticing Louisa's scepticism at this remark, she pulled open the strings of her little black silk dolly bag and took out a folded sheet of paper. Unwrapping it, she showed Louisa that it contained a five pound note.

"Let me show you our present to Edward and Honor. It's a little bit of money and there's a letter to them from John." She held up the stiff piece of writing paper showing the perfectly formed copperplate writing:

> *To Edward and Honor:*
>
> *May you both be happy for as long as God spares you. May Our Good Lord send his blessings to you on this day of your marriage.*
>
> *From John and Annie Denny, Sunday, 1st June 1921.*

Louisa Dryden looked dumfounded at the beauty of the writing. Hastily, she said, "Could you read it to me, Annie? I've left my spectacles at home." Annie read the message out carefully. The two women looked at each other as they took in the sentiment of the letter. Hard grinding child-bearing and rearing them up through illness and misadventure had been what marriage had brought them. Happiness often hid itself in the face of the effort and will-power needed to feed and raise a large, healthy family. Without the women the men would have been greatly diminished.

The attention of the two women was drawn by their two husbands, as different as chalk and cheese, who were causing some commotion at the bandstand. William, the tall and erect, was being pulled by John, the burly Scotsman, whose intake of liquor was starting to be obvious. John Denny, the schoolmaster come coal miner, was addressing the company of dancers and revellers.

"My friends," he called out, swaying slightly and with his eyes slightly cockeyed from whisky. "Friends, I have a beautiful family," and remembering to be diplomatic, he added, "I have a beautiful wife." All turned to look at Annie, sitting beside Louisa, as she tried to hide her embarrassment and disapproval. "This man, this man ..." said John thickly, one arm around William and the other arm used to indicate to the wedding guests the subject of his speech, "is William Dryden."

A few groans and cries of, "We know."

"This," said John grandly, "is Honor's father." Those around looked with feigned patience at one another as he continued, "And William is a wonderful singer. I now have the honour to announce to you," (he hiccupped) "to announce to you on the occasion of my son Edward's wedding to Honor that her father, William ..." – he glanced up squint-eyed at William – "... is going to give us a song." Sounds of approval and some clapping were heard. The pianist started the introduction to 'Rocked in the Cradle of the Deep', one of William's favourites, and soon the true notes of the sad, old song brought a hush to the noisy party. The chattering stopped and by the end of the song they were captivated and called for more, with much applause. William was delighted to oblige the company, but first he looked around for his daughter. Modestly William looked at the bride, and sadness filled him then at the thought he was losing an ally in the often fraught and uncomfortable atmosphere of Louisa's ruling hand. He would no longer be her first love, and what would she have in store for her, after the first flush of marriage had passed?

"I'll sing one for Honor," said her father, "'Take thou this Rose'." And he sang from the heart a farewell to his beloved child, and as she stood with the arm of Edward around her, she felt a tug at her heart for an instant and a shaft of sadness blended with the happiness of her wedding.

Soon, when tears were dried and goodbyes were said and good wishes given, Honor and Edward, followed by some of their younger friends and relations, walked noisily through the streets to the small apartment that was to be the home of the newly-weds. Honor produced a large key from her purse, and to calls of "Good night, Edward!" and "Sleep tight, Honor! Don't let the bugs bite!" and other teasing calls, the pair entered the little, sparsely furnished, house to start their new life. "Look, Ned, that's the rug my Mam and Dad gave us for a wedding present, look, it's lovely, it's covered in a pattern of roses. Look, Ned, we've got roses at our feet."

Edward looked indulgently at his happy bride. "That's right, love. Roses at our feet."

CHAPTER 3

The apartment that Edward and Honor moved into was very basic. It was at the lower end of the market in this area on the fringes of the great city. One room was the combined living room and kitchen, and another was a tiny bedroom. Outside in the close was the communal toilet, shared with another two families. It was a lowly beginning for them, but plenty of people had less in their circumstances, and at least Edward had only five minutes to walk to the railway yard. They had a house, money coming in, and supportive families on both sides.

For Edward there was resignation. His mother and, through her, the social circle in which they lived, combined with the Catholic Church, were a tight vice which kept men like Edward, who got girls pregnant, held fast. It was marriage or a life as a social outcast. Get married or take flight. And flight to where was the question.

Meanwhile, life was not so bad. Edward's job was harsh in the winter, but the camaraderie at work was valued highly by the men, as were the political and philosophical discussions the men had in their breaks. Radios were few and far between, only newspapers gave them information, and that was often slanted against the lower classes. Above all, the humour they found in their close lives together, as they got through their working week, kept them going. And there was always the weekend to look forward to. Leisure began at Saturday lunchtime when they were 'loused', or loosed, from their week's labour. Then the sports jackets and flannels came out, the checked caps or 'bunnets' as they were called, the freshly ironed shirts, and off they went to the races or to the soccer matches in the vicinity. Or maybe just to the pub, to revel in the joy of a few hours that was theirs, and no foreman to look out for.

Edward was lucky in lots of ways. His wife adored him, his family, especially his mother, thought him a wonderful creation of hers, and his workmates and drinking companions looked up to him for his intellect, his interpretation of current affairs, and for his ability to speak for them in their undeclared war against the bosses. For in those days, nobody spoke seriously about much else. It was the twenties, the Great War where thousands of men had died was over. In Russia there had been a bloody revolution, and everybody wondered just where the world was going.

Honor and Edward passed their first Christmas in their new home, happily preparing for the arrival of their baby. On the 10th of January, after many hours of labour, an eight-pound baby girl was born in the tiny apartment, Mrs Denny attending at the birth of her first grandchild. They called her Louie after Honor's mother. Edward made a good father, helping his wife when he could. Cooking and the washing and drying of clothes took up much of Honor's time. Necessities were bought on a daily basis, so each day, little Louie was bundled in a white woollen shawl, while Honor did her round of the butcher's, the grocer's, the dairy and the greengrocer's. But the food was well cooked and delicious, and the table was always set with a fresh, clean tablecloth each day. The apartment was always warm and cheerful, so that Edward came home to a loving wife and a happy, contented baby.

In the evenings, friends and relations called, just to visit and have a chat. They would discuss the weather, forthcoming marriages and births, or just how the baby had slept the previous night. The best times were Saturdays and Sundays when the men were on holiday, and the endless housework was given a rest. Then people relaxed and found time to help with the nursing of the baby, and have a glass of beer and a joke or two.

Little Louie grew into a bright and beautiful baby with curls the colour of spun gold. When Honor carried her out, heads would turn in the street to see the beauty of the child. Edward, when he had a drink on a Saturday night, would puff with pride when his cronies were allowed to admire the child, and Honor could spend an age just looking at her and turning her beautiful hair into curls around her fingers.

By the time the baby was two years old, Honor found herself pregnant again. She was half-pleased and half-sorry, as children were considered a mixed blessing and finding oneself to be 'expecting' was greeted with jittery resignation. In the August of 1924, a sister for Louie, little Nana, was born, christened Annie after Edward's mother. Now the little apartment became more crowded, and Edward found more places to go, to escape from the environment of drying clothes and crying babies. He found his attendance at political meetings increasingly necessary, and most of these ended up in the pub for a pint before closing time. A small cloud had appeared on the horizon, and observers from the older generation watched the young couple, their experienced eyes troubled, especially those of Edward's mother. She knew her son's weakness for talking and drinking, and for romancing about Utopias of the future; the more he drank, the easier it became to improve the lot of his fellow men.

Edward always managed to get round his wife when she complained that he spent too much time in the pub. She was young and naive, and believed, like most young women, that child rearing was her job and not her husband's, and that she must accept her lot without complaint. Her own mother was not much help to her. They had never been close, and secretly Louisa thought her daughter stupid to have married so poorly. How could she bear to be so dominated by an opinionated man who spent so much time in public houses? Only Honor's father was solace to her, visiting often and helping her with the children, praising them in his broad, Yorkshire accent.

"You have a beautiful family, Honor. You may think your sisters will be better off than you, but you're the richest of them all with these two lovely babies."

Edward's mother was not flowery in her praise, but she thought the world of the gentle girl who was her daughter-in-law, and tried to help her with the odd few shillings when she could. Saturday afternoon was the time she usually paid a visit to see her grandchildren, after she closed up her little baker's shop, which she part-owned. She hurried home this Saturday, carrying scones and leftovers from the shop, and thinking excitedly of how she would take a walk to Edward's house that afternoon and spend time with the two children. She longed to nurse the little baby, and as she hung up her tweed coat on the hallstand, Annie surveyed her empty little house. It was two-thirty and she knew John would be back from the pub presently with much joking and fun in his head from too much drink taken. He would probably be carrying some useless trinkets, bought from peddlers who frequented the taverns, selling mirrors and combs and the like for a few pence to the tipsy railwaymen and coal miners.

The fire in the kitchen range was very low, but there was coal still in the brass coal scuttle, and she carefully stoked the fire with small pieces to get it going again. She washed her hands, then she methodically dusted the shelves of the dresser, giving a special polish to two china dogs. She had some fine pieces of furniture, carefully polished daily – a folding gate-legged table of walnut, inlaid with a lighter wood, a shining drop-head Singer sewing machine, a fairly recent purchase, draped with a chenille runner on which was placed a brass-potted aspidistra. At the heavy oak dining table she had sat most evenings with her books, studying for her midwifery certificate, while her husband looked on in secret admiration.

John Denny was Annie's second husband, but few people knew of this. Her first husband, Andrew, had been killed tragically in a coal-mining disaster when her marriage was only months old. A widow when she was just eighteen, she was heartbroken and sick with grief, and she returned to live with her family. But within two years, John, who had been best man at her wedding, stepped in and declared his love for her and that he wanted to marry her. There was nothing else for it. She and John worked out a kind of loving and mutual respect, although Annie had to convert to Catholicism to marry in John's church. When the local people saw her at church, they said, "There is no Catholic like a convert," and she proved this to be true. Each morning, when she could manage it, she was to be found on her knees at Mass in the old stone-built church near her house. John seldom was seen there, even on Sundays, and he would curse mildly in disbelief when he found her, not at home waiting for him, but lost in prayer in the church. "Prayin' like a bloody linty she is over there, and all my money in her pocket," he would lament.

Annie tidied the books on the shelves. Here were her medical textbooks, a few Dickens novels, books by Thomas Carlyle and Robert Burns, and other popular writers. There was a clutter of history textbooks and papers left there by Archie, her studious son. She had wanted to have a son grow up to be a priest, but her prayer had not been answered. "Still," she mused as she arranged his books, "he'll be almost as good as a priest some day. If God spares him," she added, as usual, under her breath. Joe, her middle son, was a wild rogue and a drinker. He was the life and soul of any party, and Annie shook her head in despair when she thought of Joe's escapades, and of his sure journey to hell as God's punishment to him. Edward, the eldest, had his own worries, but Archie would be the shining light of the family – the raison d'être of her life. Her mind switched back to Edward. On Saturdays, he often had a drink with his friends and workmates. She hoped he wasn't in bad company. The tick of the clock invaded her thoughts. Half past two. The pub would be closed now. John would be home soon. And sure enough, as she glanced at the clock, the door opened and her sheepish-faced husband insinuated himself into the parlour.

"Well, how's my Annie this beautiful day?" He sat down unsteadily at the table.

"I hear you've kissed the blarney stone again today and a few pint mugs as well."

"Oh, come now, my darling!" He could see that his intoxicated state had been judged by Annie to be not too outrageous for a full-scale row. Rising and putting his arm around his wife, he tried to steal a kiss, whispering, "By God!

You're as lovely as the day I met you. A little fuller here and there, maybe." He stroked her breasts and her buttocks.

"You just keep your hands to yourself, John Denny. Can't you see I'm busy? You may choose to waste the afternoon drinking and talking nonsense, but I have other things to do."

"Well, now, yes, Annie. You're a credit to the neighbourhood, a veritable saint!" He managed to utter these words before sinking into the nearest armchair under her scowling eyes.

"Archie and Susan will be in soon. She's coming home from the Royal Infirmary this weekend, and I've got to get the dinner made." A heavy silence prevailed. As she started to prepare some vegetables, she looked round from the table, "Did you know that Susan's written away for a job as a nanny to some family in America, New York it is."

"In the name of God, sure, we'll soon have no children left. They're a' growing out the nest, Annie. Growing out the nest," and his drooping eyes closed.

She shook her head and turned to him, vegetable knife in hand, "You're a disgrace, Jock!" using his nickname. "Just a disgrace! Look at you. Instead of being here to help on a Saturday, you're slouched there useless. You don't give me a hand, and you can't even make a decent conversation after your drinking with your cronies."

"Oh, you're a lovely woman, Annie, and no mistake. You're just a picture. A veritable picture. Just look at those slim ankles, and your hair with that auburn light to it. You look good enough to eat." She frowned in disapproval, but a smile stole over her face as she turned away. With a one-sided grin and hands outstretched he began singing:

"'Believe me if all those endearing young charms …'."

"You're such a clown, Jock. This is no' the time for singing." She handed him a cup and saucer. "Here's a cup of tea and a piece of cake. Not that you deserve it. Did you see that black-haired son of yours on your travels?"

"Yes," he answered very correctly, trying to sober up. "Edward had a jar or two with Charlie McPherson and Gordon

Byrne, and then left. Sure, he'll be home with Honor and the children by now."

"Well, you read the paper there until I get back. I've got an hour or so before Susan and Archie will be in for dinner. I'll see if Honor needs a hand with those two bairns. I'll take her some of this blackcurrant jam and a piece of this cake." She cut a large chunk of the cake, wrapped it in a dish-towel and put it with the jam in a basket.

"Right, Annie. She's a fine girl, is Honor. Tell her I'll be down to see the darlings tomorrow. And I still love her. They're beautiful children, right enough, and better than our Edward deserves. And she's made a wonderful mother. Like an angel she is with those children. Edward spends too much time talking politics and blethering with his friends. He'd do better to let the rest of the world take care of itself, and bother more about his family."

"Oh!" Annie excused her son, "he's a good boy, really, and very popular. Ned's got a good brain. You know that. He was cleverer than Archie at the school. Lack of application, that's what's wrong with him. He's a daydreamer – like somebody else I could mention," and she looked at him straight.

"Somebody's got to dream in this world, my darling." John was sinking down in the armchair, and she could see that he would soon be asleep.

As she left the house she saw, on the other side of the road, William and Louisa Dryden returning from their vegetable plot. Louisa was carrying some marigolds and gypsophila, and William had a basket filled with lettuces, rhubarb and carrots.

"A fine day, Mrs Denny!" William greeted her, lifting his hat to her. Annie smiled and crossed the road, and the three continued walking together.

Annie said, "I'm just on my way to see Ned and Honor, and the two bairns." She noticed Louisa's mouth tighten, and her heart sank. Had she heard about Edward's too frequent visits to the pub? She looked towards Louisa, trying to keep up an air of unconcern.

They both smiled and bowed slightly as she left them to re-cross the main road. Her thoughts were on the young pair she was to visit. She would have a word with Edward. Perhaps it would help. How she wished John were stronger, or a better example to her sons. The apple does not fall far from the tree, thought Annie. As she hurried on, her face lined with anxiety, lost in thought as to how best to deal with things, she reached the door of Honor and Edward's house.

Inside, the child with the tumbling, golden curls tugged at Honor's skirts as she leaned over the crib to look at her sleeping baby. Honor was saying, "Louie, my darling. Your daddy will be home soon, and he'll want his dinner." She lifted the child onto her knee and held her close.

As she spoke, the door opened. "Daddy!" she shouted, and she wriggled down to meet him. Honor heard it wasn't Edward's step.

"It's Grandma Denny," called out little Louie.

"And how's my little sweetheart Louie today? I think I'll steal a couple of these curls for my head," said Annie, entering the little living room. "I would suit golden curls. Don't you think so?"

"No!" said the child, unable to understand that she was being teased, and she ran to her mother. But Honor had heard little Nana crying, and she was lifting her out of her crib.

"Well, look at this! Another little beauty! What a size she is, Honor, you must have good milk, my dear."

"I'm trying to get her on to some cow's milk, now. Watered down. But I have to feed her at night-time myself, to get her off to sleep. Will you hold her, Mrs Denny, while I get some milk for her?"

"Come to me, my little angel," cooed the doting grandmother.

When Honor returned, she took the baby as her mother-in-law queried, "And where's his Lordship today?"

"Oh, he went out about half past one. He came home from work at midday, had a bite to eat and went out. I think he was putting a bet on a horse and going to meet somebody in the Railway Tavern."

"But it's gone four o'clock, girl. The pub closes at two-thirty. Have you no idea where he is?"

Honor held the bottle of milk to the baby's lips. "Sometimes he goes home with Gordon Byrne on a Saturday afternoon, up

Springboig way. I think they play cards or something." The admission was affecting Honor, and she felt the tears stinging her eyes.

"Play cards – and drink, no doubt! Doesn't Gordon Byrne have several sisters, who are not up to much either?"

"Yes, there's two I know of – Rose and Lizzie."

The older woman, agitated, now paced the floor in anger. "You're a soft besom sitting there. Why don't you go and pull him out o' that dump?" Honor looked up at her, her eyes big at the impossibility of the suggestion.

"Oh, Mrs Denny, I couldn't do that."

"Could you not, now? Well, you're going to. Put these two children in to Mary, next door, for an hour. They'll be fine there. You're coming with me."

They set out, one determined and quick in her manner, the other slower and reluctant to seek out the errant Edward. They passed into a seamier district, where children ran about barefoot, and half-drunk men stood propping up the walls of the buildings. Women in shawls with babies wrapped inside them stared at the unfamiliar pair as they walked purposefully along the street. When they reached the Byrne's house, Annie spoke firmly, "Go on, Honor. Ring the bell. Tell him he's to come home at once. I'll wait round the corner. Say you want to speak to Edward."

Shakily Honor rang the bell of the house. Her face was scarlet, and her stomach felt queasy. The door was opened by a woman, young and gypsy-like, who hadn't finished laughing before coming to the door. Her red lipstick flashed in the dim light. Honor, refined of bearing and manner, drew back with shock at the sight of the plump vulgarity of the other.

"Well, what do you want?"

"I'm Honor Denny. Is Edward here?"

"Sure, he is, my love. Come in, come in. I'm Madge Morrisey. I'm a friend of Rose and Lizzie." These two now came to see who it was. "Come on in, Honor. We're having a little get-together." Lizzie had a glass of beer in her hand. As the door of the parlour swung open, Honor took in the scene. Beer bottles and glasses, sandwiches and playing cards, and four half-drunk men sitting around a dark oak table, and Edward was one of them. When he saw poor, serious Honor standing at the door of the smoke-filled room, his face fell.

"What are you doing here?" came the automatic question.

"You've to come home," she mumbled. Edward was astonished. "You have to come. Your mother said it. She's very angry with you."

"My mother!" Edward was dumbfounded.

"She's waiting outside." Honor's chest was bursting in the effort of keeping the tears at bay, in front of the painted women and the beer-swilling men. Edward, worried now, left his cards and guided Honor out of the house. Outside his mother awaited them.

"So you were there, right enough!" He looked down on his mother, cringing at the censure in her voice. "Are you not a disgrace to your family, and to yourself? To think that I had to bring Honor to a slum like this, to get you out of a shebeen like that! Painted women! Whores, the lot o' them! And you with a good, hard-working wife, sitting there on a Saturday afternoon with two infants with a meal ready for you. I'm black ashamed of you! To think a son of mine could behave like this!" So saying, she slapped his face hard and the tears of shame ran down his cheeks.

"You'll go home, and you'll see to your wife and children, and give her any money you've got left. Gambling and drinking's no' enough for you. It's low women now, too. I tell you, Edward, I didn't educate you and bring you up for this. If it happens again I'll put Honor and the children on the boat with our Susan and send them to America." Unable to stand the sight of him any longer, Annie took her anger with her and marched at a fast pace along the mean street away from them.

Silently Edward took Honor's arm, and the two young people, stunned at the fury that had been unleashed, returned to the children and their little home. Edward's weekend carousing was kept in check for some time to come while Honor, full of admiration for Annie, had a happier time for the following months with Edward and the babies she adored.

Winter was cruel that year. The ground froze solid, and banks of snow lay in the country roads and along the sides of the pavements of the town. All who could afford to buy coal stoked their fires, even through the night, so that smoke hung in the cold misty air for most of the time. Young children and old people suffered most from this vicious weather with chest colds, bronchitis and even pneumonia. Honor had often to hurry out for her shopping, leaving the baby with a neighbour, it being too foul to take the infant out of doors.

Edward's father became very ill towards the end of March. He had succumbed to a heavy chest cold and wheezed around the house for weeks before taking to his bed. The doctor diagnosed severe bronchitis exacerbated by the coal dust in the lining of his lungs. Daily his condition worsened, and Annie was distraught. She tried all the remedies she knew of. Kaolin poultices on his chest, cough mixtures, toddies of whisky, lemon and honey were all administered to no avail. Even William Dryden called a few times bringing his herbal remedies, but John grew paler and thinner.

"The devil is oot tae get me, William, and nane o' your potions and mixtures are going tae do me any good. He's got me by the coat tails, and he'll no' let me go."

"Oh, John! Don't say that. When the better weather comes, you'll be able to sit in the sunshine. That'll soon cure you. Some good fresh air." William was distressed at the condition of his old friend, and returned heartsore to tell Louisa the bad news.

Day and night, Annie attended her sick husband, but still his condition worsened. "Go and fetch Doctor O'Malley, Archie. Your father's worse." Archie rushed to the door. "And call in and tell Ned. He'd better come."

The busy doctor turned up within the hour. He was tired and dishevelled. One after another day of overwork, long hours of administering to chest patients, to children with croup, measles, chicken pox, and babies to be delivered, usually in the middle of the night, that was his lot. He called Annie, Edward and Archie into the kitchen after examining their father. "I'm afraid he's gone downhill since I last saw him. You'd better call the rest of the family. What's his age now, Annie?"

"He's fifty-seven, Doctor." Archie and Edward entered the sickroom and stood beside their faltering mother. Her own health was not strong, and the weeks of tending her ailing husband had taken their toll. The once proud woman with the straight back and elegant posture had developed a stoop, and a sadness was on her face.

"Well, I'm sorry to say," he looked at Edward and Archie, "the years of soakings in the coal seams, and long hours of working in air full of coal dust are to blame for your father's lack of resistance to this chest infection." For once, Edward was lost for words. He and Archie were struck dumb with grief. "You'd best send for the rest of the family. It's only a matter of days." He lifted his bag, and as he got to the door, he said softly to Annie, "And you'd better ask him if he wants to see Father Niven."

The Last Rites were administered to John that evening. He had slipped into a coma, and his last joke had been told, his last song sung. The family gathered the next day, to pay their respects and to comfort their mother. A wake was held in the house two nights before the funeral. Twenty or thirty of close family and friends arrived at the house to pray. They knelt on the floor of the kitchen, the bedroom and the little parlour, along the hallway, and even outside the entrance of the door, chanting the rosary, led by Father Niven. The next day the coffin was taken to the church at a slow pace so that mourners could follow behind. There was a Requiem Mass, the church being packed to capacity, and once again people stood outside. John had been a popular man. One of those people who made life seem lighter and more worthwhile.

After the funeral, there was food and drink provided at Annie's house. After a few whiskies to ward off the cold of the graveyard, folks became a bit cheerier, and old friends and relations who had not seen each other for years shook hands and discussed incidents of hilarity and good times from the past when John used to keep them all amused with his comic songs.

Annie sat through the funeral reception, quietly accepting the condolences of the neighbourhood. Dressed totally in black, her fading red hair almost white now, she felt numb, anaesthetised from all feeling, all sorrow. She saw her children move around serving food, dignified and correct in their manner, and she was proud of them. All she knew was that she must not break down. She must not think of the loneliness of the future without her best companion. She would have to be strong.

That evening when only the family were left, Susan sat down beside her mother. "I'll not take that job in America now, Mother. I'll not go. I can write to them and explain about our bereavement."

"No." Annie was definite. "You'll go. It's a chance. You will take it. It's not everyone who gets the chance, or has the guts to go."

"But, Mother, that will be two of us missing from your life."

"You're going, Susan, and that's that. I'll manage. I've got Archie. I've got to see him get through university. That'll be his chance."

"Oh, Mother! You drive yourself too hard."

"Well, your father wanted you to go and see New York, and he wanted Archie to get on with his studies. He didn't say it much, but he was awful proud of all of you. What date is it that you go?"

"Oh, it's a while yet, sometime in July." Susan looked round at her family. "I'll miss seeing everybody. But I'll only stay two years. By that time I should have saved some money."

Annie knew that Susan would find it hard to leave home and the safe surroundings of her job as a nurse in the infirmary. But especially, the earnest girl would hate having to leave her doting boyfriend, Tommy. They had been walking out together for almost a year. But Annie admired her second daughter for her strength of will. "What's Tommy saying about you going away?"

"He's not too pleased. But he knows I've thought about it and that I want to try my luck."

"Aye, Susan, I think there's a good bit of your mother in you," and Annie's face lit up with a smile for the first time that day.

CHAPTER 4

The great steaming train belched smoke from its engine onto the little knots of people gathered in Glasgow Central station. Outside the station in the busy city streets of Union Street and Buchanan Street, it was a bright July day. Cars and large wheeling black taxis vied with bullying orange and yellow corporation buses for their rights to the roadway while around the great maw of the station entrance scores of travellers came and went, hauling luggage and hurrying and worrying about their timing and travel connections. It was the first day of the Fair Holidays when all the factories, all the steelworks, all the shipbuilding yards of the Clyde closed down, and the large army of men were given a compulsory holiday, some paid, others without any money, and industrial Glasgow shut down for a fortnight. But here in the dimmer light of the station this particular oily train continued to disgorge smoke and steam impatiently. It was not one of the many bound for the Clyde coast and the usual haunts of Glasgow workers at holiday time. This was the London train. And the faces of the people gathered in groups on the platform were serious and concerned. One such group was made up of the family and friends of Susan

Denny, come to say goodbye as she left for the first leg of a journey that would take her across the Atlantic to New York.

"You'll write to us as soon as you arrive, Susan?" Mrs Denny couldn't disguise the quavering in her voice. Already her heart was gripped by anxiety at the thought of her child leaving. Susan flashed back a smile at her tearful mother. Somehow the excitement of her prospective emigration to America had enhanced her looks. Her hair had been cut a bit shorter and waved, and her smile seemed triumphant and heart-stopping to her family surrounding her.

"Yes, Mam, I'll write as soon as I get there," Susan answered. She was slim, but full-bosomed, in her new narrow grey coat and cloche hat to match. "Don't worry about me. I'll go and see the parish priest. I know there's a Catholic church near where the people live. They promised to show me. I'll be all right." Inside herself, Susan longed to laugh out loud at the thought of this great adventure, this wonderful escape. She subsumed all sadness at parting from her family and from Tommy, her faithful beau. Now she was living her dream. In front of her she had an ocean voyage to experience, the first glimpse of the Statue of Liberty, and then the fabled streets of New York, where she could not guess the sights she would see.

Her brother Edward was approaching from the guard's van. "That's your cases on board, Susan. Mind and call a porter at Euston Station when you get there. Don't you be lifting those heavy weights yourself." Susan gave Edward a quick, unexpected hug, tears now appearing in her own eyes.

"Thanks, Ned. Look after wee Louie and the baby, and Honor. I love them and yourself," she said.

To hide his emotion, Edward replied, "Don't let those Yankees push you around, now. You show them what us Scots are made of."

Susan turned to the others one by one, her sisters Mary, Nan and Myra, her brothers, Archie and Joe, and her mother. She held her mother's shoulders.

"Don't cry, Mother. It's just for two years. It will fly by. And you mind and see the doctor about your tiredness. You look pale. I think you're a bit anaemic. You'll have to take more care of yourself.

Do you hear that, Archie? Get Mam to go to the doctor to see about a tonic. She's thinner than she was. She works too hard."

Then Susan took Tommy, her sweetheart, a few steps from the family and embraced him. "Don't worry, Tommy. I'll be all right. They're a good family I'm going to, so I've been told. I'll go to church regularly and I'll write at least once a week."

Tommy screwed up his face to hide his emotion. Looking at Susan with the smoke and steam making a cloud around her slim figure, he felt she was an angel on her way to heaven, and he wasn't going with her. In two weeks he would be back at the coalface, blackened and wet with sweat while she would be on the high seas, a prey to all and sundry. He cursed himself for his poverty.

"Susan, my heart is broken at your going, you know."

"Listen, my love," she replied, her calm now shaken by the force of his anguish. "I'll think of you every day, and remember you at night in my prayers, and I'll be saving up for both of us." She hugged him tightly as she spoke. "You do the same. We'll soon be together again."

"Those Yanks will be after you, and I'll no' be there to fight them off," continued Tommy.

"Och! Silly! Sure I'll be wearing a nanny's uniform and engrossed in a child all day. There's only one day off a week. I'll not have time to meet any other man. And I wouldn't want to. Not when I have my darling Thomas Cairns," she smiled sweetly up at him.

"Oh, sure!" He was resentful at her headstrong decision to go abroad. He loved her dearly and in her guise as well-dressed adventurer, he felt as if he were losing the only thing that mattered in the world to him. "Good luck, Susan! I'll think of you every day." His throat had tightened so that he could hardly speak. "I'll leave now and wait outside for the others." So saying, he turned and left the platform.

Soon she was gone. The family waved and waved even after the train could no longer be seen. It was an empty, sad feeling when Susan had gone, and each of them felt it his own way. They walked slowly back from the platform, through the busy station, not talking, but moving slowly, somehow deadened by the loss of the determined Susan. The most affected by this bitter-sweet parting was the girl's mother. Annie's heart was sore. She was easily moved to tears, and as she turned back to her busy life, wondered if she would ever see her dear daughter again.

At home, Edward had put the parting behind him, and having his brothers join him for a cup of tea, got the conversation going with a joking question. "What do you think of old Ramsay MacDonald now, boys? Dae ye think he'll be eating scones and drinking tea just now?"

"Aye right! More likely drinking champagne and eating caviar," said Archie.

Their mother called, "Take your politics into the front room and leave us in peace. Can't you see wee Louie's not well?"

The child lay asleep in her grandmother's arms, pale skin contrasting with the sweat-laden red curls of her little head. The men lifted their teacups and moved from the kitchen. Archie, the eager young student, continued to speak as they moved.

"We've been studying Hegel at university. To him the essence of history was the dialectic of struggle and conflict." The two older brothers were drawn up short at their younger brother's erudition. They envied him his leisure and the opportunity for education he had been given. "We should be free to fulfil ourselves, to escape from the limitations of self."

"Fulfil ourselves, some chance. Your heid's full o' theoretical rubbish." Edward gave Archie a friendly push. "Try fulfilling yourself working on the railway!"

Archie continued, "No money and no class! That's us."

"Oh, it always comes back to money," Joe was saying. "Mind you, I never had any problems getting the girl I was after." He grinned at both his brothers.

"Aye, those foreign lassies you meet on your sea journeys will do anything for a packet of fags, Joe," Edward jibed.

"Not at all. It was my brute attraction. My personality and good looks that won them over. I had to fight them off in some of those Spanish ports, Archie boy."

Changing the subject, Archie said loudly, "Hegel was a great influence on Karl Marx, you know."

Edward jumped at the name of Marx. "Now there was a man to respect – Karl Marx! What a thinker!" he said.

"You'd better not let Father Niven hear you say that, Ned," Archie warned him.

"Let Father Niven stick to religious matters. He doesn't have to work alongside his mates from seven-thirty in the morning until five-thirty at night for subsistence wages. I go along with my fellow union members. Anyway, look at John Wheatley. He has gone right to the top in this government, and he's a devout Catholic and a socialist. He's a wily bird. He knows how to avoid rubbing the priests the wrong way."

"As long as you don't entertain birth control," Joe warned with a smile and a nod.

"Keep your voice down. The old lady might hear you in the kitchen – talking about contraception. She'll be scandalised at us."

"Well!" Archie answered. "I'm a better Catholic than any of you two heathens. I don't miss Mass on a Sunday like you two. You and your long country walks on Sundays, Ned. You'd please my mother more if she saw you at church."

"Aye, you're young, Archie. Wait until you've seen a bit of the world and got a few grey hairs like Joe and me. See what you're like about the Church then." Edward shook his head as he spoke. "And remember what Marx said, 'religion is the opium of the masses'. Yeah, he meant that we're just like those poor Chinese bastards are – kept down, kept in our places."

"Quiet, Joe. Mother will be in here to sort you out if she hears you," warned Archie.

Edward looked towards the door. "Well, we've all been dunned by the Church long enough, that's certain. I wouldn't upset Mother by saying I've lost the faith, but I just can't thole it any longer. It's against reason." To lighten things, he added, "Anyway, Charles Darwin says we are all descended from monkeys!"

"You still get your children baptised, Ned," said Archie.

"Aye, well, maybe. But just like you and Joe and the rest of us, we're affected by our upbringing and, besides, the women have a lot of say where the bairns are concerned."

"Oh, well, Ned," said Archie. "Mother finds great solace in the Church. She takes her many troubles to church to pray them all away. So do Honor and Susan. I bet that right now Susan's saying a prayer for her safe arrival in America."

"Aye, Ned," added Joe, "that's right. And when she gets to New York she'll have her faith and the Church to sustain her."

"Well, maybe," Ned conceded. "But that doesn't get us poor workers in Scotland very far. You could pray for a week and it won't add a shilling to your pay packet or put a good dinner on the table."

There was a short silence as the three considered the concepts that had been discussed. Then Archie took up the argument, "So you're for revolution, Ned?"

"Aye, and why not?" Edward was quick to answer. "Do you think we'll get improvement of our lot with these Labour politicians?"

"I've got a book at home that tells a bit about the life of Keir Hardie," added Joe. "You know he was born just up the road, in Legbrannock. He went to work at the age of seven as an errand boy to help support his family. He was sacked for being late and had his wages held. The date was the 31st of December, and when he got home that night his mother had given birth to a baby. He wrote himself, 'That night the baby was born and the sun rose on the 1st January 1867 over a home in which there was neither fire nor food'. That's what took him into politics." Joe stopped speaking, and the three fell silent at the picture he had painted.

But these discussions the brothers and their friends had were what made life tolerable for them – the chance to throw ideas about – political, religious or philosophical, to see if they could make sense of their circumstances. Edward, for one, lived for the Saturday evenings of drinking and talking. On this particular Saturday, Honor had finished cleaning the little house and the Sunday dinner was half-prepared. When the children had been bathed and were in their night clothes, Edward appeared in his best jacket and wearing a clean white shirt. As he combed his hair at the mirror above the kitchen sink, Honor looked up from the little picture book she was showing to the children.

"Where are you going?"

"Where do you think? It's Saturday night."

"Well, listen, Edward. I don't think wee Louie's right. She's a bit hot, and seems to have no life about her. Couldn't you stay in tonight? I'm a bit tired and I get lonely, all by myself."

"I've got to meet Archie and Joe. Bairns are always up and down. She'll sleep it off. She'll be right as rain in the morning."

"I hope you're right."

"Of course, I'm right. Just put her to bed and she'll sleep it off. You can send for my mother, or your own mother, if she doesn't settle down." He started to wash his hands and face at the kitchen sink. "I'll be back in a couple of hours. You know the pub closes at half past nine."

As usual on a Saturday night, the place was full to capacity. He spotted his brothers and some other cronies, and soon he had a pint of beer in his hand and was spouting with the best of them opinions about the state of the country and the political system. The smoke from a great number of cigarettes was in the room, and the floor was covered with spilled beer and cigarette ends. But the atmosphere of the bar was one of excitement. Some men were so happy that they embraced those around them while they spoke, in the camaraderie induced by beer and leisure, after a hard week of work on the railway or down the pits. Saturday nights in the Tavern kept them going all week, for at last they relaxed and felt human again. From time to time a group of them would migrate across the road to the rival establishment, the Kirk House. There was little traffic on the road, and they safely ambled across this main thoroughfare without mishap. As was said, 'A drunk man never hurts himself'.

Edward's group each bought two bottles of beer with their last pennies, and exited before the rest. They wanted away from the noise and the crush so that they could continue their discussion of the afternoon.

"It's my house, so I'll be chairman," said Edward. "When you wish to speak, you will address me as 'Mr Chairman'."

"I know you, Ned," said Joe. "You'll be the chairman and you'll no' let anybody else speak."

"Not at all. Not at all," Edward puffed at his cigarette. "We'll open the discussion with a toast." He lifted his glass to the company of half a dozen semi-sozzled men. "To my dear friends. What would life be without our friends?" Then turning to Honor. "And to my beautiful wife who can sew, cook and bake beautiful cakes. To a wonderful woman. She could make a pot of soup out of an old pit boot. I am indeed a fortunate man. To the flower of the Dryden family."

They all solemnly toasted, "The flower of the Dryden family!"

"And now, as your chairman," Edward continued, swaying slightly and with an affable smile on his face, "I invite my brother Archibald to open the discussion by saying something about Ramsay MacDonald's government."

"Hopeless!" someone shouted.

"No better than the Tories!" added another.

Archie stood up. "Lady and gentlemen," he said in mock formality, "for the first time in the history of Great Britain, we have a Labour Government. We must rely on them to fight for the working classes. That, in my view, is the way forward."

"What have they done? Nothing!" one of the men interrupted.

"Mr Chairman! May I have permission to speak?" It was Joe, standing up and swaying slightly.

"Certainly," answered Edward, politeness itself. "As chairman, I introduce to the company my brother Joseph, a sailor and a scholar."

"Go back to sea, Joe! or give us a song," said someone. "Sing 'Barnacle Bill'"

Joe spread out his arms, still holding on to his glass of beer.

"Who's that knocking at my door?"

he sang in a mock female voice.

"Who's that knocking at my door?
Who's that knocking at my door?
said the fair young maiden."

38

Then in a loud, booming voice he sang out:

"It's only me from over the sea.
I'm Barnacle Bill the sailor.
I've just come back from Portaree.
I'm Barnacle Bill the sailor."

Then the female voice again:

"Did you bring me a crocodile?
Did you bring me a crocodile?
Did you bring me a crocodile?
said the fair young maiden."

Joe, politics forgotten, continued the song to the delight of all the company.

"Mr Chairman, may I be allowed to speak?" It was Ernie Gilmour, a student friend of Archie.

"Certainly, Ernie," replied Edward.

"We have been able to vote now since 1918, all of us being over twenty-one." On seeing Honor's face, he said quickly, "Sorry, Honor, except for ladies, of course. Should we not forget all this talk of revolution and of doing away with the system, and have faith in the electoral system?"

"By God, aye, and look what a great MP we've got in John Wheatley," said Joe.

"Yes, I know John Wheatley fine. He's a member of the Independent Labour Party like myself." Edward took a swig at his beer. "He worked down the pits from the age of eleven. Ten of them were brought up in a single apartment, one room for twelve people. No toilet and no running water. He has seen hard times, has John, and that's why he's doing such a great job in the government for working people. He's managed to get some money oot o' the buggers for decent housing. Have you seen the building that's going on in Sandyhills and Carntyne?"

"But he's the best of the bunch in that government. MacDonald kowtows to the bowler-hatted types, and that gets us precisely nowhere. The system is all wrong." It was Joe sounding off again.

Someone started up 'The 'Red Flag', and they all joined in the singing.

The people's flag is deepest red
It shrouded oft our martyred dead, ...

Their rowdiness was interrupted by a small ghostlike figure at the door. Long nightgown trailing, Louie cried, "Mammy, Mammy," holding her throat.

Knocking over the stool beside her, Honor dashed to the door and quickly lifted up the sick child. "She's really sick, Edward. Feel how hot she is," she said.

Suddenly sober, Edward put down his beer. "Come to Daddy," he knelt down and put his arms out to the little gowned figure. She felt limp and weak in his arms, and from her mouth he could smell her sour breath. Her golden curls were wet and clung around her face. Edward looked up and saw the fear in Honor's eyes.

"Somebody will have to go for the doctor."

The men froze with embarrassment at being witness to this scaring domestic situation. Soon they were disposing of their drinks and clearing up as best they could.

Joe said, "I'll call on the doctor and go for my mother on my way home. Try not to worry. It's probably just the croup or something."

The men left quickly, saying, "Good night," as they closed the door behind them. Honor hardly saw them leave, so distraught was she. They filled an enamel bath with lukewarm water, and when Doctor O'Malley arrived with Annie, they were sponging the child down in front of the fire. It was midnight, and the doctor had put his trousers and coat on, on top of his pyjamas. Little Louie was wrapped in a white towel and given to the doctor to examine. The three, Edward, Honor and Annie, held their breaths as they watched. Annie was praying he would not say the word she dreaded. But her prayers were in vain. The doctor looked up at his fearful audience with the words on his lips, "I fear she might have diphtheria. We'll have to get her to hospital right away."

An ambulance was sent for and Louie was quickly removed to Lightburn Hospital. Annie and Edward had to drag Honor home, so loath was she to leave her little girl. That evening mother and father returned to visit the child. She lay wan and motionless in the clinical hospital ward.

"By tomorrow we'll know if she's out of the woods," the doctor said. "Try not to worry. She's a strong-looking little girl."

Honor's face was contorted in anguish. The ward sister approached.

"You're little Louie's parents?" she queried.

"Yes," was the whispered answer. The two clung together for support.

"We're going to set up a steam kettle beside your child today. That should relieve her breathing. We'll sponge her down and swab out her mouth. Come back tomorrow night and we'll see how she has progressed."

The day passed in utter dejection for the parents of the stricken child. Honor could not eat a bite. She sat in a daze in her little silent kitchen, only occasionally taking a sip of hot sweet tea given her by the neighbours. Edward was despairing and wept openly in his mother's arms.

At six o'clock they started the mile-long uphill walk to the hospital. There had been a slight improvement in Louie's condition, and their spirits rose a little. As they bent over her bed she moved her head and opened her eyes. She smiled and tried to lift an arm to Honor's face.

"Mammy," she said.

"Hush now, darling. You'll soon be better," Honor whispered softly.

Edward beamed a broad smile, saying, "Sure, you're a beautiful little darling. You're Daddy's girl and, look, I've brought you a little dolly to play with." He placed the doll beside her.

As they walked home to tell of the change for the better to the neighbours and relations gathered at their home, their hearts had lightened from the pressure of the past twenty-four hours.

"She's a wee bit better," they announced. "They think she'll pull through."

"Oh, thank God! Thank God!" A heartfelt cry arose from Annie Denny. "Tomorrow I'll go with you to see the wee darling. God has spared her. My prayers have been answered," she said, wiping her eyes with her handkerchief.

The smile and relief of all were apparent, and they sat down to discuss past illnesses and former cases of childhood crises.

Honor took her baby on her knee, hiding the bulge of her third pregnancy from the family. Not even Edward knew that she feared there was another baby on the way. By late evening only Mrs Denny remained with the parents, having stayed to help with some ironing and household chores. They had sat down to take a last cup of tea still discussing in hushed tones the hospital and their sick child when a loud, official knock sounded on the front door. Edward folded up the evening paper he had been glancing at, while the two women drew together as fear and tension gripped them. Edward opened the door to two tall policemen.

"Are you Mr Edward Denny?" one of them enquired.

"Yes."

"Would you and Mrs Denny like to come with us? You're wanted at Lightburn Hospital."

Edward felt the blood drain from his face. He turned to see Honor lean on his mother.

"What's wrong?" It was Annie who spoke.

"There's been an accident. You're to come at once."

Somehow they got the fainting Honor into the police car, and Edward, like a dead man, stiff and upright sat beside her. They left Annie to look after the baby.

The ward was in darkness but for one gas lamp above the child's bed, which was partly surrounded by screens. At the bedside sat a white-coated, elderly doctor. The night sister met them before they could see the child.

"You must prepare yourselves. Your child has had an accident. I'm afraid she has pulled the steam kettle over on herself." Edward felt a heavy weight on his arm. Honor had passed completely out. When they roused her she was able to hold wee Louie's hand for the last few minutes of the child's life. Stunned and distraught, the two were taken home by the police to prepare for a funeral.

For many months from that day, when Honor closed her eyes, she saw the forlorn little figure with the bright red curls in the white hospital bed. She saw the tiny coffin in which she was carried away to be buried and the line of dark-clad mourners that walked behind the hearse. She knew she would never recover from that time, and that she would never be the same young woman she had been. At times, Edward and her family feared for her sanity. Often she didn't hear when they spoke to her. She responded to very little in life. Nana, her one-year-old, had to have attention. She had to eat for the sake of her unborn child, but her spirit was almost broken. Grief was ever present.

Edward became morose and cynical. After the first few weeks of mourning he took to going out to the pub whenever he could. If he had no money, he went speechless to bed after his evening meal. Everything Honor did he found fault with. He called her stupid and dull witted. Most of all he resented another child being on the way. Life seemed to him to be meaningless. There was hardly any money and little use of politics or struggle. His mother tried to help where she could, but the manner of the little girl's death was a terrible blow. Although Annie prayed for the family, her faith was quite shaken at this cruel twist of life.

CHAPTER 5

Citizens of New York, Howard and Betty Howlett were very rich – probably, by now, millionaires. At least that was the thought that came into Betty's head within the first ten seconds of waking up.

'Early to bed, early to rise, work like hell and advertise'. Howard Howlett had imbibed these words with his mother's milk. His was the classic 'rags-to-riches' story. Ronald Howlett, his father, had been a hotel porter from the age of sixteen, rising to manager in his forties. By dint of hard work and determination, they had put their promising son Howard through law school. Later, Howard had studied accountancy at evening classes and ended up working for a bank. Now he owned a small firm of accountants and was part-owner of four big hotels. He and Betty had risen steadily up the social scale. This was New York in the early twenties, and the acquisition of wealth was a not uncommon story. It was even expected of those with luck and single-mindedness. The rewards were great. Four times the Howletts had moved house in the space of seven years, and each move had been to a bigger and more impressive establishment. Now they found themselves at 305 Park

Avenue, New York – an unthinkable address for them, just ten years before.

Betty Howlett hid her deep satisfaction at their rise, and outwardly she kept her face composed and inscrutable. She read each afternoon, when she wasn't out with her fashion-conscious girlfriends, shopping and drinking coffee or cocktails. Freddy, the baby, was just three months old, and his first nanny had decided to leave, so they awaited Susan Denny's arrival from Scotland. They had chosen her from the agency list.

Betty couldn't wait to hand over the baby, so that she would have more time for her latest fad. Self-improvement. In an effort at self-education, Betty had become a member of a literary club. She and her friends were keen on the new writing, on the modern art that was appearing, and in the general buzz of inventiveness and self-expression that was in the New York scene in the Twenties.

She was a good-looking woman, tall and slim, and with a wardrobe that was acquired fresh each season. Like her friends, she had to be in the mode. Bobbed hairstyle, the correct jewellery from the jeweller who was fashionable at the time, and dresses, suits and shoes to blend in with the richness of the Park Avenue house and the circle of people she moved among. Betty was not an extrovert, nor had she boundless energy like some of the society people she encountered at the fashion stores and charity events. Quietly she savoured the luxury in which she found herself. She had not forgotten the cold-water flat where she and Howard had started. Of Scottish and Irish descent herself, O'Connell had been Betty's own name, she was kindly to her staff and without the superior air acquired by the moneyed classes of New York. If she could be criticised, it would be in her fondness for cocktails and for her non-stop smoking. Fashionably she favoured long cigarettes held in a long ivory cigarette holder.

And now the day that brought Susan into the house of the Howletts had arrived. This Saturday morning Mrs Howlett led the shy girl, a smaller figure than herself, someone obviously of the servant class, up the grand carpeted staircase. The ruddy-faced girl carried a small leather suitcase. She wore a brownish rough tweed suit, and her whole appearance was of the country. Susan Denny had arrived in New York.

"This will be your room, Susan, next door to Freddy and the nursery. Come and look." Susan walked cautiously over to the window and looked out. She saw purposeful people walking smartly, nannies pushing great deep perambulators, dressed in the modish grey narrow coats and gabardine hats that marked out their profession. The scene was like a monochrome picture of greys and fawns, ever moving. Only the smart limousines, which sallied past importantly, broke up the everlasting movement of humanity. The contrast with her native Glasgow was immense – here there were no ragged children, no shawl-covered women, no smoke-filled air, no factory chimneys, and no grease-covered, overalled men returning from work. It was summer in New York. The trees were in full leaf and it felt as if this warm, fresh weather were eternal here. There was the smell of luxury and money in the air.

"As arranged, you'll be on three months' trial. Was the sea journey from Scotland quite enjoyable?"

"Yes," answered Susan shyly. "I met some quite nice people on board, Mrs Howlett."

"Well, I'm sure Scotland's a beautiful country. New York's very nice, too, but I think, you'll find it quite a bit different. You were born in 1901. That makes you twenty-four, right?" Mrs Howlett's accent was loud and twanging. To Susan it was overpowering, for she was used to the accents of home, to soft Scottish tones, soft like the Scottish wind. And to self-effacing manners, such as she had learned at home and at school.

She took in the tall lady with her narrow pink tube of a dress, which fell into tiny pleats around the knees, the expensive pink leather shoes, and pale pink silk stockings. She glanced at the real diamonds and pearls of the earrings setting off the deep waves of the bobbed fair hair.

The woman was saying, "You'll have Saturday afternoons and Sunday mornings off. Is that all right?"

"Oh, yes. That's fine, Mrs Howlett." Susan felt clumsy in her herringbone tweed suit and clumpy leather shoes. She caught sight of herself in the dressing-table mirror, and saw her brown, straight hair pulled back into a black grosgrain bow, revealing her rosy country face , and wished that she were different.

"I see you're Catholic. So you'll want to go to Mass. St Patrick's is not far. You'll meet other Scottish and Irish girls there, I believe." She smiled kindly. "That should make you feel a bit more at home."

"Thank you. Yes, I'll have to go to Mass on Sundays or my mother would never forgive me, nor would Father Niven either." Susan looked around in amazement at the grandeur of her surroundings. "Your house is lovely, Mrs Howlett."

"Yes, it's OK. Park Avenue's nice and central for shopping. Gets a bit noisy at times. The bathroom you'll use is down the hall. Come, I'll show you." Susan's eyes grew large at the sight of the great, deep white bath and the shining chrome taps, and the enormous, roasting-hot pipes for the bath water. "You'll share with Lotta, our housemaid, and with Bella, our cook. They're both Italians. There's a chauffeur, too, George. He doesn't live in. I think he comes from Poland, originally. Little Freddy, who'll be your charge, is in the nursery. Come, we'll see if he's awake. I know this is your first nannying job, but you have training?"

"Yes, I've done my three years' fever nursing in Belvedere Hospital in Glasgow. I have my certificates with me, and I'm very used to babies," Susan trotted behind Betty Howlett, trying to look into the face of her new employer and hurrying to keep up with her.

"Then, I hope you and Freddy will get on. There's a sink over there, baby's bath, zinc and castor oil cream, dusting powder and diapers. Lotta will help you for the first few days. What do you think, Susan?"

"I'm sure it is all satisfactory. You've thought of everything, I think. Could I see Freddy now?"

"Of course. He must be still asleep in his bassinet." They approached the corner of the room where a chubby little baby boy lay asleep.

"He's lovely," murmured Susan, her maternal instincts aroused, an involuntary smile coming over her face.

Betty Howlett liked the look of her new employee. Scottish nannies were popular in New York, and this one looked intelligent and had nice manners. There was obviously no threat where her husband was concerned. Susan was not the pretty type he usually eyed up. She was a country type of girl, gauche and lacking in confidence, obviously. There was no getting away from that.

"I hope you'll feel at home here, Susan." Betty Howlett sat down for a moment. "My grandmother came from Paisley in Scotland, so we have something in common. New York's a pretty frantic place, but it can be fun. I'm sure you'll soon fit in." She gave a friendly smile.

Nervously, Susan smiled at Betty. "I hope so," she managed to say, "I've been looking forward to this job for such a long time."

"Lotta's going to see to Freddy for today. You'll meet her later. You can start on your duties tomorrow. The kitchen's the last door at the end of the hall, downstairs. That's where you'll eat. Someone will come to your room at one o'clock and bring you down for lunch. You can meet Lotta, Bella and George then. OK?" Susan nodded her agreement. "There's a lock on your door, so you can feel safe. I know you must be missing your mother, and all that big family, but you'll soon get used to us. Why don't you unpack, have a bath and unwind until lunchtime. You stayed at a hotel last night on your arrival? Is that right?" Mrs Howlett's voice was kind.

"Yes, the agency put me up at the Riverdale Court, it's quite near their office."

"Good. Well, feel free to relax and get acquainted with things. See you later!"

Susan sank down into the armchair in her bedroom. It was a plain room but pleasant, with cream curtains and bedspread, a side table with a vase of flowers, some writing paper, pen and ink, and a Bible. She opened the closet and found some empty coat hangers. There was an oak chest of drawers. Opening her suitcase, Susan took out an oval-shaped, framed photograph. She gazed at the picture of her mother, whose auburn hair was pulled back from her serious, saintly face. Homesickness and nerves overcame the young woman, and she broke down and wept. She sobbed for what she knew not. She felt drained of all feeling. Maybe it had all been a big mistake was her main thought, as she sat overpowered by her surroundings. I must do my best. That's all I can do, and pray for help from the Virgin Mary. I cannot let myself and my family down. I must do my best!

Soon, she gained control of herself and dried her eyes. Presently she unpacked and found a photograph frame containing a likeness of Tommy. I must write to him – so much to tell him, she thought. I'll do it tonight. And she put his picture on the cabinet beside her bed.

As she lay back, she day-dreamed of the night of the hospital dance and of the wonderful time she had had with Tommy, just a few months before. It had been a night never to forget – a whole evening in the arms of someone who loved you. It had been at that dance when she had spoken of her thoughts of going to America to Tommy. The nurses' dining hall had been cleared of tables and the walls hung with balloons, for it was Easter Saturday and there was to be a party at the hospital. Not Susan's hospital, Belvedere, but at Meadowfield, where her elder sister, Mary, was Matron. Miss Denny, as she was known to the staff there, had supervised the preparation of sandwiches and cakes, jelly and ice cream. On the long white-covered table, cups and saucers and great tea urns were all laid out in readiness for the Saturday Dance.

Mary, the eldest of the Denny family, was thirty-five. Hard work and ambition had got Mary to the top of this small hospital for patients, many of whom were mentally handicapped in some way or other. Efficient with the nurses and doctors and understanding with the patients, she was a popular and respected figure as she made her rounds each morning. The 'Socials' for the staff and their friends on the last Saturday of each month were of her instigation. The nurses were all away from home, 'living-in' was compulsory, so that these parties gave them a chance to relax and invite their friends. Male partners were often drafted in from the local police force or the unattached local school staff, and relatives, especially brothers, were always welcome. Susan and Tommy, her boyfriend, had been invited.

Now, as she lay on the divan in her bedroom on Park Avenue, New York, the music of the dance that night drifted back to her in her imagination. She saw herself as she had been that evening, in a pale blue chiffon dress trimmed with blue satin. She had taken trouble with her hair for that Easter Saturday, and managed to get it to bunch into curls around her ears.

"Your hair's nice, Susan. What did you do to it?" Tommy asked as they waltzed round to the accordion band.

"You mean it's not usually nice?"

"Everything about you is always nice," said the boy as he held her closer.

"That's better," she laughed.

He, too, had taken trouble with his appearance. His fingers were still tender where he had scrubbed his nails to get all traces of coal dust out of them. His brown hair was luxuriant, newly washed and combed back in waves. His suit was his best Sunday garb, and his shirt had been beautifully laundered by his sister, May, who looked after him and his two coal-mining brothers. He leaned towards Susan, savouring the great treat of this Saturday evening with the girl he was so crazy about. She felt his eyes on her, taking her all in, and she looked straight at him before she dropped the bombshell.

"Tommy, I've heard from the agency in New York."

"And?" he asked stiffly.

"I have to write immediately to say if I can be ready to sail on the 15th of July."

Tommy's face fell. He had lost the struggle to win Susan over to marry him that year, but for her to go so soon was a blow.

Susan's face saddened. "I'm sorry, Tommy. I really am. I feel the same about you. I miss you when I can't see you, and I think about you all the time, but ... I don't want to be trapped."

"Trapped?" He was hurt and angry now. "Is that what you think it would be?"

"You know what I mean. I've seen so much of it. Houses where you couldn't swing a cat. Kids everywhere. No money. Struggling along until pay-day on a Friday. Look at Honor and Edward. Four years of marriage has turned them into different people. Edward's not the happy-go-lucky boy he was. He's serious and weighed down now. He's bored at home with Honor and the children, so what does he do for a bit of stimulation? He takes off to the pub ... it's an outlet from the ... the ... grind," she finished.

"What grind?"

"Well, you're a miner, Tommy. You come home tired out and full of coal dust. Imagine if your wages were to be taken from you by a wife with hungry mouths to feed. And that for the rest of time!" Susan straightened her dress in the silence that greeted her words. "All right, Tommy, you have the church and your faith, but everybody is not like that. It just wouldn't be enough for me. And our Edward seems to have lost his faith, and he ... well, he won't accept his lot. Maybe he is wrong, but I know it's a struggle every day in that household, just to put food on the table. And that's a house where the father is working, not like some where the father is unemployed. I don't want to live from hand to mouth all my days. I don't want that."

"I don't understand you, Susan. Wives and husbands should work together to make a life. I've got a job in the pit. We could be happy," he pleaded. "Please think again. I'll die without you."

"All right," said Susan, "I'll think about it. There's still a few days before I have to decide." She had smiled sweetly at these words and asked him to dance with her again. But she knew she would accept the offer of a job in America. So what if she fell off the world when the boat sailed across the Atlantic! At least she would have made an effort to see what else the world offered.

—.—.—

Now Susan found herself in the place she had dreamed of for so many months. She turned round on her side on the unfamiliar bed and saw her troubled face reflected in the long mirror of the wardrobe. She knew she was not pretty, but she had a face of character and had never been short of admirers. They liked her spirit and sense of fun. She had a quick wit when among friends, and was always reliable and good company. She was not so obviously attractive like her sister-in-law Honor, or any of the Drydens, for that matter. She hated it when any of them came to the dances. Without trying, they stole the show, because of their lovely dresses and gorgeous hair. The prospects for Susan at home in Scotland had been marriage to Tommy and hard work, or no marriage and hard work.

Susan's mind then turned to the morning when the great ocean liner docked at New York harbour, and she tried to keep down the waves of excitement aroused in her by the thought of her great adventure. During the crossing, she had made friends with another girl emigrating to America. Her name was Jenny Hetherington. As they docked, she had chatted to Jenny, who was trying her luck in a job as a nurse in a New York hospital. Both girls stood close together at the rails of the ship, watching the approach of the great city, the royal road so many had followed before them to seek a new life. The Statue of Liberty left them speechless with awe, as did the sight of the tall buildings of the city.

"The letter says I have to take a yellow cab to 27 East Forty-First Street," Susan read, "'There you will see the Blue Star Agency'. Maybe St Vincent's Hospital is near where I've to go, Jenny. We could share a taxi."

"I don't think we should risk it, Susan. I'll get my own cab." They were part of the crush of passengers now descending the gangway. "Look, we might get separated here. I'll contact you through the Blue Star Agency, and you try to find me at St Vincent's." Jenny's eyes looked heavenward, "God help us both," she shouted. A close friendship had developed between them on the ocean voyage, and they embraced with emotion as they parted.

—·—·—

A knock on the bedroom door broke into Susan's reverie. She opened it to find a pretty Italian girl, standing with a smile on her face. She held out her hand. "I'm Lotta. I work here. I'm the maid," she said with a trace of Italian in her accent. "You must be Susan."

"How do you do?" Susan said. "Sorry, I fell asleep."

"Come on. We'll get Freddy, and go down to lunch."

"Can you wait until I tidy my hair?" Susan said, smiling.

"Of course. I'll wait."

"You've been here for a while, Lotta?"

"Three years, almost."

"Do you like it?"

"Sure, it's wonderful."

"Really?"

"Yeah, sure. You'll like it. It takes a little time, but you'll soon get the hang of things. Just watch out for the Casanovas. You know, the ones who tell you're the most beautiful thing they've ever seen. Don't believe them, honey. They'd say that to a monkey." On seeing Susan's amazed face, she laughed heartily. "You'll be all right, kid, don't worry."

"I hope so."

"Sure you will. You'll be fine." Lotta picked up baby Freddy and the three descended the curved stairway to the kitchen.

CHAPTER 6

The gaslight, the bracket jutting out of the mantelpiece above the kitchen range in the tenement house, fell on a bent head of thinning, fair curls. Archie Denny, just twenty years old, was going bald. All the evenings passed in study at the kitchen table did not improve matters, as it was his habit to grasp the curls in an effort to understand and assimilate knowledge for his examinations.

Unless in the company of family or close friends, Archie was plagued by lack of confidence, especially with girls of his own age. In his books he found a refuge. Books of all shapes and sizes, mostly on history, but many books of poetry and literary criticism were there for him to bury his heart and soul in. Also were to be found volumes on political theory, of Marx and of Engels and of Bakunin. On the table lay open *An Introduction to the History of Western Europe*, the set book for his history examination. He read:

To Erasmus, man was capable of progress: cultivate him and extend his knowledge, and he would grow better and better. He was a free agent, with, on the whole, upright tendencies. To Luther, on the other hand, man was utterly corrupt, and incapable of a single righteous wish or deed. His will was enslaved to evil, and his only hope lay in the recognition of his absolute inability to better himself, and in a humble reliance on God's mercy. By faith only, not by conduct could he be saved.

His mother would be horrified at these ideas, he mused. Any criticism of her beloved Catholic Church and the power of charity and good works as taught in her branch of the Christian religion made her very resentful. He laid down the book at her call from the other room. There was his mother resting in an armchair in front of a flickering coal fire. Now there were just the two of them left in the family home. Sadness was on her face as she thought of her husband and his merry bantering ways, now passed on. And little Louie, her first grandchild, too, so cruelly taken from them.

"Archie, dear. I'm real sorry to disturb you from your work, son, but the fire needs a bit of coal."

"Sure, Mother." Archie moved from his books and lifted the coal scuttle. "You're not disturbing me. My head's chock-a-block with facts and figures. I could do with a break."

"Well, while you're on your feet, maybe we could have a cup of tea, son."

"A good idea, Mother. How's the pain in your side, now?"

"Oh, not bad. I just feel so tired. This is lovely, sitting in front of the fire." Then after a pause she said, "But we'll have to stop indulging ourselves with two fires a day. You'll need money for your last six months, and we will have to economise somehow."

"Some day we'll be all right for money. When I get a job as a teacher. Then I'll take you for a holiday. Maybe even buy you a fur coat."

"A fur coat! Archie! Could you see me in a fur coat?"

He looked at the parchment skin of her face and her dulled eyes. "Sure I could, Mother. You'd be the toast of the town. Some day, if I pass that is, we'll paint the town red."

The two dreamed of the future, as Archie made a pot of tea and some buttered toast. Then, they sat together, quietly talking about their day's domestic affairs.

"You've a few pounds left still of your Carnegie grant, I suppose?"

"Yes, I think there's about fifteen pounds left."

"If I feel better with this resting, I'll get some money from the bakery next week. We'll manage somehow. I'll work a few days next week."

"Don't worry, Mother. You work too hard. Some day I'll pay you back." He clumsily adjusted her little woollen shawl as he spoke. "I'll have to start my essay, now. Can I do anything else for you?"

"No, I'll go to bed, now. That tea has helped me. I feel better. You get back to your work."

But in the morning, it was obvious that Annie's condition had worsened. As Archie brought her breakfast to her bedside, he saw that she was really ill, too weak even to sit up in bed. He dressed quickly and packed his books into his briefcase. "I'm going to call in on Honor and Edward on my way to university this morning," he told her. "And Mrs Reid, next door, will look in as soon as she's got the children off to school."

Annie smiled weakly, her eyes following him as he spoke. "Go on. Don't worry. I'll just have a wee sleep, now."

Worry almost engulfed him but he set his face to the door, hurrying to call at his brother's house before catching the bus for his half-hour's journey to Glasgow University.

In the evening on his return, he found Edward at his mother's bedside, staring ahead as he sat, resigned and miserable.

"How is she?" Archie put down his briefcase and removed his scarf and coat.

"The doctor's coming in an hour. I think she's worse. She hasn't eaten a bite today." The two brothers retired to the kitchen where Honor had been busy in her mother-in-law's house that afternoon. Before hurrying back to her children, she had set the table and left a tasty meal keeping warm on the kitchen range. They ate it, hungry in spite of their sorrow.

When Doctor O'Malley arrived, his manner was serious. He knew the two brothers and their mother well, and with head down, medical bag in hand, he was shown into the bedroom. "Well, Annie, you've been at it again. Working too hard in that bakery. And out all hours of the night at confinements. I hear you were there to bring Lizzie O'Reilly's twins into the world. It's too much work for you, Annie. I told you to rest."

"Hard work never killed anyone, Doctor."

"That's just where you're wrong, Annie Denny. I've watched you over the years. Work, work, work. You never stop. Morning, noon and night. Give yourself peace, woman! Archie'll not thank you for killing yourself to get him through university."

"What's wrong with me, Doctor?"

He searched for the correct way to tell her. "You're a nurse, Annie. You must know your general condition is not good. You're anaemic, badly anaemic. I'll prescribe a tonic. And you must drink beef tea, twice a day. Also, ask Archie to cook liver for you as often as he can. And of course, you must rest. No more middle-of-the-night call-outs to confinements. And no more work in the bakehouse. Stay in bed for at least a week."

Annie smiled at him as he left her bedside. She had known him since his first days in the district. She had helped the young and unsure doctor to get patients, at least some of whom could pay the half-crown for calling him out. He was still young, but she was aware that he spoke the truth. She had pushed her body too hard, yet she could not see where she had had any other alternative in her circumstances. You can't teach an old dog new tricks – or an old bitch, she thought.

In the other room the doctor addressed the two anxious brothers, "Well, boys. It doesn't look too good. I've known your mother for years now, and I've watched her overwork all that time." Both their heads seemed to slump into their shoulders, as their thoughts turned to the selfless life their mother had led. These two of all the family owed their mother the greatest debt. Edward had had his life straightened out more than once by his indomitable mother, and Archie knew that without Annie he would never have got to university.

Unable to bear his thoughts, Edward rose. "I'll go and see Honor. She'll want to come and see my mother. Thanks, Doctor! Will you be calling back?"

"Aye, Ned. I'll be back tomorrow about the same time."

Embarrassed and anguished, his cap crumpled between his workman's hands, Edward stumbled from the house. Archie and Doctor O'Malley faced each other in the dimly lit kitchen. "Well, Archie. I think you'd better write to New York and let Susan know about your mother's condition. She'll want to be kept informed. With careful nursing she could survive for a year, maybe. She needs rest and good food. Plenty of liver and red meat." He made for the door. "I know you'll do your best. But you'll have to get the others in the family to help. It's your finals next year, isn't it?"

Archie's face was pained. "Yes. I've got a lot of reading to cover, and a few essays to complete before the exams."

Their eyes met and the doctor's sympathy, unspoken, was felt by the younger man. "Good luck, Archie. I'll call in tomorrow. I'll bring her an iron tonic."

Arrangements were made for the care of his mother, and Archie's mind turned to his extra classes and library studies he had planned for that summer month. And next day found Archie walking through the great, grey sandstone doorways, and past the stone columns of the university. Set on Gilmorehill, above the bustling industrial town, Glasgow's is an ancient university, much loved by students and city people alike, the gateway to a better life for many a lucky hopeful from the tenements of the city and from the humble homes of the surrounding villages and towns. In the cool morning air, all manner of anxious students, lost in their thoughts, solitary and introspective, made their way out of the old high-ceilinged building. Some walked in pairs or threesomes, their spirits already lightening as they left their studies behind for the relaxation to be found in a cigarette and a chat. Archie had missed some lectures that term, but was soon cadging a copy of the notes from a friend. At the end of the day, he joined the students strolling down the hill, their welcome fags being lit in relief at the cessation of work and continual concentration and note taking.

"Are you taking the bus home, Archie?" It was Bobby Russell, a casual acquaintance.

"No, Bobby. I think I'll walk to the Mitchell Library, and do an hour or two studying there." Archie shifted his briefcase into his other hand.

"Aha! Looking for a pick-up," laughed Bobby. "You quiet ones are the worst."

"What would I do with her?" laughed Archie ruefully. "I haven't two pennies to rub together."

"Where there's a will there's a way." Bobby stopped his trudge down the hill and turned to Archie. "I took a wee lassie out on Saturday and the whole night only cost me a couple of bob. We went for a long walk up Mount Vernon, and then had a lemonade in Ferri's Cafe."

"What's the girl's name, Bobby?"

"That's my business. She's a beauty. Curves in all the right places." He used his hands to demonstrate. They walked on and Bobby continued, "I think she likes me – you know, gives me the 'big eyes' technique."

"What big eyes technique?"

"Well, she looks at me and her blue eyes seem to get bigger, and," Bobby stopped to illustrate, "and she smiles straight at me and ..."

Archie burst out in mirth, "You are a nut, Bobby, with a wild imagination."

"Oh, some day, Archie, it will happen to you. There's nothing like it."

As they parted at the bus stop, Bobby called, "Keep your eyes on those books!"

Arriving at the reading room of the library, the quiet, solemn atmosphere and the grim-faced, abstracted expressions on the faces of his fellow students could not hold Archie that day. Not a blue eye in sight! he thought. Restless, after an hour or so he thought of one girl he knew, Sheila Charlton. She would be finishing work in about half an hour. Seven-thirty the hosiery shop closed. He turned the few coins he had in his pocket. If he walked smartly to Sauchiehall Street, he might meet her, and pay her fare home. "But, no! She took the train home. Had a season ticket," he remembered. Anyway, he could see her and talk to her. His heart leapt at the idea.

Weaving through the stream of shopworkers, hurrying for buses and trains in the smoky evening air, Archie arrived at the shop, 'Scottish Wool and Hosiery'. There she was, the junior assistant, putting up the wooden front gate of the shop while her dark-suited boss, the manageress, watched her. Sheila picked up her handbag and said goodnight to the older woman. As her high heels clicked along the pavement, Archie approached her.

"Oh, Archie! What are you doing along here?"

"Well, I was at the Mitchell Library, and I thought I'd stroll past the shops. See how the other half live."

Sheila smiled. "It's hard work, shop work, you know."

"So is mine."

"I stand on my feet all day behind a counter." She shook her eighteen-year-old head of auburn waves and curls. "Miss Webster, that was the lady you saw, she's a hard taskmaster. If there's no customers, she makes you take the stock out and dust the drawers, and refold everything. It's never-ending."

"You look well on it, Sheila." His eyes taking in her beautiful hair and pale skin.

"I've got to hurry, Archie. My train's at ten to eight."

"I'll walk you to the station. Come to think of it, I could take the train home, too."

She laughed, "OK. Let's run!" They arrived, laughing and breathless, on the platform. In the compartment, full of tired people returning home from work, it was impossible to talk much, but the closeness was nice. Soon they joined the others streaming from the branch line station.

"How's your mother? I heard she was ill."

"Aye, she's getting better now. She's to have two weeks' rest and the doctor prescribed a tonic for her, so she should soon pick up."

As she hesitated beneath a slightly sooty tree on the road from the station, Sheila gave him a ravishing smile, and he felt his heart turn over. "Maybe I'll see you at Honor's, some day," she was aware of the effect she had on him.

Tongue-tied and stuttering, Archie met her gaze, "When are you going?"

She caught his look and blushed, "Oh, I'll call in on Sunday after dinner. About three o'clock. I like to see the children, and have a blether with Honor."

"Right! Right, so will I. I'll see you there then, Sheila?"

All that week while helping his mother in the house as best he could, and poring over his books, Archie's mind would switch to Sunday and the possibility of seeing Sheila again. The warm glow she had brought to his being was new to him. He had never been in love. Never felt this ever-present anguish and excitement before. Saturday evening, usually the highlight of the week, when he met some friends and neighbours in the pub and indulged in the smoking and camaraderie, passed less quickly than usual. His mind kept slipping back to her 'Sunday after dinner' promise. It was a secret in his heart. No one could be told.

"You're dreaming again, Archie. Too much book learning's dulled your wits. You haven't said a thing a' night." It was Edward, getting well intoxicated now as closing time approached.

"Will you have one for the road, boys?" A voice called to them.

"Well done, James! I thought you'd never ask," Edward shifted his glass towards the speaker. "Mine's a wee half o' whisky."

"And you, Archibald?" James put his arm on Archie's shoulder.

"No. I'm off home. My mother's still not right. She's fairly frail and needs attention. She looks so old these days. Lost a lot of her gumption. It seems suddenly she's an old woman. Isn't that right, Ned?"

"Aye, that's right." Edward shook his head, quite troubled, "She's had a very hard life, but what woman of her generation hasnae?"

Their friend eyed the two brothers, taking in their troubled expressions. "A fine woman, your mother. Has the doctor said what's wrong with her? I hope it's nothing serious. My wife, Maggie'll be fair upset if she thinks your mother's very ill. She thinks the world of her, for she was there at the birth of our three bairns. Very skilled, and a gentle, kind woman she is, is Annie. A real lady!" James finished his speech, the drink had loosened his tongue and made him maudlin.

"It's anaemia," Edward said bitterly.

"Oh God! Have you written to Susan in New York yet to tell her?"

"No." Archie laid down his pint mug. "I'll have to do it soon, I suppose. But it seems a shame to worry Susan when she seems to be just settling into her job in America."

"Oh, Susan!" James's eyes danced. "An old sweetheart of mine! What a smile! 'Twould break your heart! She'll fit in fine in New York. Aye! Many a sweet smile I've had from your Susan."

"Away with you, James! You're getting drunk. Susan wouldn't look the road you were on." Edward was indignant. "Too smart for that!"

Archie moved towards the pub door. "Aye, and our Mary's coming tomorrow."

"Oh Christ! Your big sister, Mary! The fire-eater, Ned! You'd better watch yourself tomorrow. Be sure she'll be scanning your face for evidence of your ungodly ways. Signs of debauchery, Ned? What do you think?" James was enjoying himself.

"Aye. You're right, James," Archie looked a bit miserable at the thought of Mary's arrival. "It'll be: 'How much do you spend on drink and fags each week?' Criticisms all round, no doubt."

Edward and James were amused. "Oh, I ken fine what Mary'll be like," said Edward. "It'll be 'When are you going to buy Honor a new pair of shoes?' or 'How long were you in the pub last night?' or 'When are you going to wallpaper that parlour?' I'm keeping oot o' her way. She's too used to bossing folk about in that hospital."

The Denny family were a source of discussion and gossip with local folk like James and many of their neighbours. Each member of the well-known family seemed to be filled with drive and a capacity to raise himself or herself above the level of the average. Only Edward did not seem to be climbing any ladder of success. He was stuck in the railway workshops as a joiner and general dogsbody. He ran the union, in his section, but otherwise his energies went into reading books of history or political philosophy or the daily newspapers, which he read avidly throughout the weekday evenings. Regular trips to the public library, a real godsend to him, kept him supplied with reading material for ten days at a time.

As he wearily walked into his home from work at five-thirty each night, he would take his tweed cap off with one hand and lift a book with the other, while Honor put out the evening meal. After years of marriage and the death of his eldest child, his domestic life was little more than a backdrop to the rest of his world outside his home, where life seemed more exciting.

Friday and Saturday evenings were spent mostly in discussion groups in the pub. And Sunday afternoons were given over to long country walks with cronies – Independent Labour Party members or anti-parliamentarians, characters the lot of them, when the political discussions continued through railway lines, over bridges, past spoil heaps from quarries and little coal mines of the past, and on to the woods and lochs just beyond the town.

"Well, we'll have one for the road. What are you boys having?" James called up the drinks from the bar. "They tell me Mary's doing really well, these days," James gossiped on.

"Aye, you heard right. You'd have to be up early to catch our Mary!" There was a mixture of pride and bitterness in Edward's voice. "She's buying a smallholding out by Kilsyth, just a bungalow with a few acres of arable land. But, no doubt she and Norman will make a success of it. And she's going to keep on her job as matron at Meadowfield Hospital in the meantime. So they'll no' be short o' a bob or two."

"You don't say, Ned!" James was impressed.

"Aye, James. She's either working all the hours God sends, or down on her bloody knees praying for forgiveness for some bloody thing or other." The drink was beginning to take over. "Ah hope she prays for us all." Then Edward lifted his glass to his lips, and Archie thought he caught a queer smile on his face.

Archie loved and admired his elder brother – his breadth of character and strong personality, his male sureness, and his popularity in any company. But, sometimes he wondered what really made him tick. "I'll have to be going, Ned. Will I see you at twelve o'clock Mass in the morning? Will you be there?"

"No, but you will, so that will do for both of us."

"How do you know I'll be there?" Archie was annoyed.

"Because that's why you're asking me. You want to keep me on the straight and narrow like yourself."

"You haven't been there for a month or two."

"No, and I'll no' be going for another month or two."

"You've lost the faith?"

"Aye, looks like it."

"Well, don't tell Mother. It would break her heart."

"I won't if you don't!"

"What's wrong, Ned?"

Edward's head drooped and he looked into his pint mug. The crush of people was greater now, and talking was difficult in the noisy bar. "Oh, you know. Since wee Louie died, things have not been the same. Honor's like an animated statue most of the time." He paused. "And I can't seem to get out o' the doldrums – unless I get to the pub."

His mention of the child seemed to bring, for a few seconds, the presence of the fine-featured little girl between the two men – a rare beauty – a golden girl, that first-born child had been. "Ah canna face ma' maker after that horrible time. All happiness is gone, it seems." Edward shook his head sadly and looked at his brother. "But never mind about me, Archie. You get home to my mother, and don't tell her any o' this."

"Aye, right! Goodnight, Ned!" he swallowed hard at the lump in his throat, and turning up his jacket collar, he left the pub.

CHAPTER 7

"I'll call in on Sunday about three," Sheila had said, and the phrase kept returning to the young Archie. She had said it quite pointedly, surely she must mean him to be there at Edward's house, surely she wanted to see him. Excitement made him wake early. From his window he could see the church where his mother spent so much of her time. Rain ran down the slates of the roof of the old building, down the grey sandstone walls and on the oaken doors, soon to open to allow the little chapel to be packed with the hundreds of thirled Catholics to attend their Sunday Mass. For the congregation had grown steadily over the years, as industries thrived in the town and new workers arrived, especially from Ireland.

But not a soul stirred at this early hour, only a clanging tramcar could be heard in the distance, and Archie, lost in thought, waited until the familiar vehicle sped along the iron rails of the main street, resplendent in Corporation colours of orange and pale green and carrying just a few Sunday workers into the city.

When he had given his mother her breakfast, Archie crossed to the little parish church for early Mass.

He followed the usual rituals of genuflexions and prayer, Latin calls from the priest and responses from the altar boys. The practised, loud voice of the priest now broadcast the Banns of Marriage for that week, the meetings of the St Vincent de Paul Society and the Women's Guild. The smell of incense filled the church as the solemn ritual of the raising of the host to the congregation in its starry monstrance was carried out. Queues of people formed at the altar rails to receive communion, and as the priest drained wine from the silver chalice, Archie watched in a semi-dream, his mind back on the station road where Sheila had said goodbye to him. Then a last hymn and the people emerged into the sunny morning, thankful that their religious duty was done for another week.

On his return home, he found Mary, his sister, had arrived with Norman, her husband. She had tied an apron over her Sunday clothes and was cleaning everything in sight. Norman, dressed in a houndstooth-check, plus-four suit, sat smoking a pipe in front of the coal fire burning in the kitchen range. He had a round country face, red-cheeked and with gingery curls around his ears. Opposite Norman sat Annie, hair combed and rolled up in a bun at the back of her head. She, too, wore her Sunday best. Capable Mary had brought a sparkle to their home in the space of just over an hour. A clean, white tablecloth and a carefully set table were the final touch to raise Archie's and Annie's spirits, after the weeks of illness.

The talk was of the proposed farm that Mary and Norman were planning to buy. It was a smallholding really but, both in their late thirties, they were very excited. Annie became animated at this talk of money, and listened to how the two had saved.

"We're going to keep hens and a few pigs." Norman warmed to his subject. "And there's quite a few fruit bushes there already. Mary'll keep on with her work until we see how we get on. Maybe we'll get a wee car eventually."

"You're not serious?" Annie sat back in her chair startled. She was incredulous. Someone in her family owning a car, and she pictured the neighbours' faces as she stepped out to be taken for a drive.

"Aye! You're a lucky pair, right enough. And what if there's any family comes along. You would have to stop your job at the hospital then, Mary." It was Archie, putting his foot in it as usual.

"Archie!" his mother called out, shocked at her son's daring in raising such a delicate matter.

"No, Archie's right. We'll just have to see what the Good Lord sends to us. I'm thirty-five now, but we've only been married for a few months."

"Anyway!" Norman interrupted. "What about yourself, Archie? How are your studies? When's your exams, now?"

"In six months' time I sit the Honours final. I'll have to be ready for the slaughter, God help me!" He pulled a panic-stricken face.

Norman filled his pipe. "Oh, you'll do it fine. You've passed everything up to now. You Dennys are all the same. Not one of you that hasn't been given a lion's share of brains."

Mary chimed in, "Just don't get entangled with girls and jump into marrying too soon, Archie, you've plenty time for that." Archie hid his feelings. Then, in her slightly superior way she said to Annie, "And how are our Edward and Honor getting on? That poor girl! Is she getting over the tragedy of losing wee Louie yet?"

But Annie couldn't bear the discussion. The bitter pain at her heart that talk of the child's death brought she could not tolerate. She had to try to speak of other things. "If you're going to visit Ned today, Archie, you'd better get off now, and take that shortbread with you for Honor. Tell them I'm much better, and Edward's to come and see me this evening."

Saying his goodbyes, Archie moved faster and faster as he left the orbit of his mother and sister, and the Sunday afternoon fireside. When he arrived at his brother's house, Sheila, the light of his life, was there. Helping Honor with the dishes, she had on a blue dress that clung to her young girl's slim figure. Her hair seemed redder, and more springy and curlier than ever. When she talked to Honor, now and then giving Archie a glance and a smile, an enchanting smile, he had difficulty taking his eyes off her. To hide his embarrassment, he concentrated on Honor's toddling child, Nana, who bumbled around, clutching her rag doll.

All the while, Edward's head was buried in a book, but eventually he looked up and followed Archie's gaze, smiling to himself at the new turn of events. Archie in love, what next? he thought.

"You'll have a cup of tea, Archie?" smiled Honor, her third child, a little baby boy, Jamie, was on her knee. "Sit down and tell us how your mother is."

"Oh, much better. Mary and Norman are there with her now, and their visit has cheered her up enormously. She says you've to call in and see her tonight, Edward."

Archie could see that Sheila's visit had been good for Honor. She looked brighter and more herself than he had seen her in months. She was studying a knitting pattern shown to her by Sheila. "Look at this pattern, Archie. It's a little green sweater. Isn't Sheila kind to knit this for Nana, Archie? And so well done, too!"

Sheila said, "Well, I've no brothers or sisters to worry about. Not like Honor or you two. You're all lucky with your big families. There's only me, so I suppose I'm spoiled."

"We should all have small families." Edward's voice was strident and broke into the serene mood. He had been reading some political text, passed on to him by Archie from the university library, and had been thoroughly won over by the argument for birth control. Then the world would be a better place. "That's the way to economic freedom, the only chance the working man has of getting out the bit! Limitation of the size of the family!"

"Oh, come on, Edward! Don't go spoiling Sheila's visit with your soap-box socialism. You're too stuck in your books, now." Honor carried on in a lighter vein talking with Sheila.

"Have you heard about your sister Elsie?" Sheila laughed as she spoke. "She wanted to go to a dance on Friday evening and your mother wouldn't let her. So she put her dance dress in a bag and escaped out the window when your mother thought she was in bed!"

"Never!" said Honor, an amused twinkle appearing in her eyes, "Elsie will come to a sticky end. She's had about four different boyfriends in so many months. Loves them and leaves them, that's her!"

Time passed inconsequentially in gossiping and drinking cups of tea. Sunday was always a time when there was little to do. When Sheila stood up to leave, she smoothed down her skirt, slipped on her coat and picking up her hat, she fixed it on her head with a long hatpin. Archie watched her in fascination – the silver gleam of her bracelet, the sheen of her beautiful, long hair whose softness touched him as he helped her on with her coat. He was enthralled. "I'll walk you home, Sheila."

They left the warmth of the fireside and walked slowly in the twilight of the evening. The darkness of the great stone buildings and the dampness of the pavements went unseen to them. They were absorbed in the nearness of each other and in the attraction that was growing between them.

"Maybe I'll see you on the train home some night next week," Archie ventured.

A glorious smile was his reward. "Yes, OK! That would be nice! Goodnight, Archie. Mum and Dad are looking out of the window, so I'd better go."

He returned home, walking on air. Her smile seemed to stay with him, stuck onto his face, and his fingers still felt the silky waves of her hair. At home, he became more guarded when his mother told him he looked so pleased with himself, and then she asked about Honor and Ned. "Oh, Honor seemed happier, today. Best I've seen her for ages, and by the way, Ned said he'll come to see you tonight."

"Anybody else there?"

"Yes, Sheila Charlton. You know the Charltons, friends of the Drydens."

"Oh, those English folk from Meadowell Street?"

"Yes, that's right."

"So it's the smiling wee slip of a girl Charlton that's put a smile on your face?"

"She's not so wee nowadays."

"Just as long as she doesn't put you off your studies."

"She won't. I've no money to take girls out. You know that."

That evening, after Edward had paid them a visit and left for home, Archie grew tired and unsettled with his work. He hurried after his brother to have a walk and a cigarette before bedtime.

At the corner of the street a woman's figure approached Edward. They spoke together for a minute, and then the two walked on together, so that Archie fell back, unsure how to proceed. The figures drew close together in serious discussion. Archie saw that it was Madge Morrisey from March Buildings, a slummy district in the locality, and he turned and retraced his steps.

A damp drizzle was falling and the evening air was foggy around the street lamp where he paused to finish his cigarette. Saddened and confused to have witnessed the scene of his brother with this well-known 'fast' woman, he thought of poor Honor. Madge Morrisey was not fit to tie her shoelaces, and Edward was disgracing himself to be meeting such a woman. He would speak to him. Maybe there was nothing in it. As he continued home through the dark street, he decided that he would do one more hour before midnight at his studies, and maybe on Tuesday he would come home from university by train.

Unaware that they had been seen, the furtive pair spoke urgently together.

"How long have you got tonight, Edward?"

"Just half an hour. She knows that I won't be later than half past ten. Let's stand in the shadow here, Madge. If we're seen, I'm done for!"

"Can't you get a few days working away from home, Ned, so as we could have some time together. You know how I love you, Ned. I think of you all the time. Put your arms around me, and give me something to dream about."

"You're a light in my darkness, Madge, and I often think about you, but you know how things are with Honor and the children. I can't hurt her now, after all she's been through."

"But you don't love her."

"Ah! Love, the great deceiver!"

"Ned, kiss me. Give me at least that to keep me going."

He took the dark-haired, vibrant Madge in his arms, and animal desire filled them both. As they clung hungrily to each other in the darkness of the archway, the power of the desire engulfed them. "I'll try to get the job on the pier at Mallaig. It would mean spending a week up there ..., it's a long way away, in the Western Highlands. But you can get a train there, and you could visit me there."

"I'll count the days, my love. Oh, Edward, stay just for a few minutes longer."

"No. I have to go now. If Honor or my mother were to hear of our meeting, I'd be a dead duck. And you, too, Madge. Your family would kill you – meeting a married man at a street corner."

"To hell with my family! I don't give a toss for them. I only want you, Ned. You're all I'll ever want. Anyway, I thought all you socialists believed in free love." She straightened her clothes and regained her composure as she spoke.

"Aye, some do. It's easier to put these ideas down on paper as reasoned arguments. It's easy to talk about birth control and free love, but not so easy to carry out these philosophies in real life."

She pulled his curly head down to her broad gypsy-like face, and said, "I love you more than Honor ever could."

"Good-night, Madge. You're a beautiful woman," and he kissed her and turned to hurry homewards. As his steps quickened, he pulled his coat collar up to protect him from the foggy mist that was falling.

CHAPTER 8

July in New York was hot and sticky but yet the evenings were cool with a hint of the ocean drifting in the air. Noise and bustle were everywhere, people moved so fast, with faces so full of purpose, that Susan sometimes had to stop just to look at this new breed of persons who seemed so sure of where they were going. Lotta was chattering on and on, as the two girls proceeded down Fifth Avenue towards the park.

"I'll show you where all the nannies usually go, and you'll easily find your way back to the Howlett's place."

Susan was filled with an inward panic. She envied this carefree Lotta who, after three years working in the Howlett household, was a seasoned New Yorker. She did not tell her how scared and nervous of the city she was, of getting lost, or of finding that the ordinary man in the street might have difficulty understanding her Scottish accent.

"Don't be so nervous. No one's ever got lost in Park Avenue yet. You'll be OK. Look, there's Costa! He's my boyfriend. Come and meet him. Maybe we'll walk with you a little." Costa was slim, light-brown skinned, with straight, very black hair.

His eyes took in Susan's unpolished appearance and her old-fashioned hairstyle.

"This is Susan, honey. She's from Scotland. She's the new nanny for Freddy."

"Hello, sugar. How d'ya like New York?"

"Oh, fine." The Scottish voice sounded like an old mellow bell compared to their confident, high-pitched, nasal voices. "What I've seen of the city is very amazing. What buildings! I can't believe I'm here, really." She finished with a smile.

"Costa, honey, would you walk for a while with me and Susan. She's a bit scared. This is her first day."

The slim Greek boy put an arm round Susan's shoulder and squeezed it. "Scared! Scared! You got Lotta, and you got me. What you scared for? And you got Freddy here." And he made the baby smile with his funny faces.

When they got to the entrance to the park, they left her, and Susan walked along the main avenue pushing the large grey pram. Freddy was propped up and interested in all the passers-by. Now and then, a woman would stop them to have a quick piece of babytalk with him. They called Susan 'honey' and wished her a lovely afternoon in the park. Eventually she sat down beside another uniformed nanny who smiled and asked her about Freddy.

"Freddy. Oh, he's almost four months now. To tell you the truth, this is my first day in this job. I'm a little nervous."

"Oh gee!" the girl said. "I been three months with Willie here. He's six months old." She held out her hand. "I'm Edith, from Amsterdam. You'll love it in New York. The family I work for, the Wotherspoons, they're very rich. They're good to me – except that is for the two boys. They're eight and ten years of age. They are very bad. They make a fool of my accent."

"I'm Susan, from Scotland. What about my accent?" Her eyebrows lifted in amusement. "Sometimes people don't know what I'm saying."

"At least, it's the same language. I have to think what I should say all the time. But it's getting better!" Edith's smile was a wide grin, revealing strong even teeth. Her hair was Scandinavian blonde, done up in pigtails twisted neatly round her ears. She pushed her pram back and forth, even though the baby was fast asleep. "You'll like New York, I'm sure. Already I got a boyfriend."

"Really? What's his name?"

"Bernie. He works in a delicatessen. Just round the corner from my house. He's a lot of fun to be around. A lot of fun!"

Susan searched for something to say. "I've got Lotta, the maid in our house, and Costa, her boyfriend, as friends. Oh! And Jenny, a girl I met on the ship coming over to America. She had a job to go to at St Vincent's Hospital. She's a trained nurse. Do you know where St Vincent's Hospital is?"

"No. I know nothing. But maybe Bernie will know."

"Some day, I'm going to look her up."

"Sure! If you like, I'll come with you on my day off."

"Would you? That would be great!" They both smiled.

Edith stood up. "We nannies must stick together."

Susan stood up also and they started walking. "Will you be here tomorrow, Edith?"

"No. Mondays, Wednesdays and Fridays, I come to this part of the park. Usually, I meet Dinah and some others, but they ain't here today. I'll be here on Friday. Maybe we'll see each other. I'm going shopping with Mrs Wotherspoon and the baby tomorrow. Then we go visiting a friend of hers. Such money they have! You wouldn't believe it!"

They had walked back to the park gates, and shook hands again, promising, for sure, to meet on Friday. Susan found her way home, elated at her success. When she pushed the pram into the kitchen of the Howlett's three-storeyed house, she found Bella standing at the kitchen table, preparing vegetables. Lounging on a kitchen chair was George, the Polish chauffeur. He was smoking a cigarette in a stylish, posing fashion.

Bella helped her to lift Freddy from the pram. "I'm glad you made it back safely, darling. That was good! You haven't met George yet. He's from Poland." She raised her eyes to the ceiling to convey her opinion of her suave-seeming companion. George had stood to attention. He approached Susan, clicked his heels and bowed gravely.

"Enchanted, my dear!" and he took her hand and kissed it.

Bella said, "Susan's from Scotland."

"Ah! Scotland! I love Scotland. Especially Scotch whisky! And Scottish girls are beautiful!" He gave her a soulful look.

"Leave her alone. She's a refined girl and a good Catholic, so you keep your goings-on for those alley cats up the avenue."

He pulled out a chair for Susan, who was holding the child, and poured out a cup of coffee from the pot. "Have some coffee," and he placed in front of her a steaming cup. She sipped the strong brew, but the taste was new to her. She tried not to show her distaste.

"What a nice name 'Susan'!" George was looking directly into her face with his enormous green eyes, and she felt a warm blush on her cheeks.

"Leave her alone, you big palooka!" It was the maid, Lotta, returned from her afternoon off.

"I just being kind and friendly to the little girl. She got no friends yet." His accent seemed to have grown thicker and more risible.

"Well, she'll soon make friends, the right kind of friends!" Lotta had her hands on her hips and leaned towards George to emphasise what she was saying. His face fell in exaggerated disappointment.

"Thanks for the coffee, George," Susan tried to lighten the situation.

"You like it, darleeng?" George immediately cheered up.

"Sure, it sure is good." Then she thought, Goodness, I'm one day here and I'm talking like a Yankee already.

The scene was broken up when the tall figure of the boss of the household, Mr Howlett, hastily entered, calling, "George, I want to go over to Queens for six o'clock. Are you ready?" George jumped up and picked up his cap. Howard Howlett stopped his rushing for a minute to talk to Freddy, who was seated on Susan's knee.

"Hello, son! Are you a good boy?" Freddy's eyes followed his father's face, and he appeared to smile. Howard said to Susan, "And how are you, young lady?"

"I'm fine, Mr Howlett."

"Good! These guys here will help you to settle in. Come on, George! Let's go. Time's awasting." The two men left quickly.

The evening settled down to gossip, and at six-thirty, after Freddy had been fed, Lotta helped Susan to find the nursery things to bathe the child and put him to bed. Dinner that evening was a thick steak, mashed potatoes and gravy. Susan ate with great gusto. She thought it must be the best meal she had ever eaten. That night she was asleep almost before her head hit the pillow.

Susan settled into her new life. Day followed day, with long hours with Freddy and large evening meals with Lotta and Bella. Occasionally Mrs Howlett would appear, and take Freddy for an hour or so, to show him off to her afternoon visitors. Then Susan would take a trip window shopping on Fifth Avenue, or just mix with the teeming masses on the sidewalks. Mostly she was too excited to be homesick. She and Edith looked forward to their meetings in the park, and Dinah and Marie, two other American girls who were nannies, were good friends, too. So far, Edith's boyfriend, Bernie, had not come up with the whereabouts of St Vincent's Hospital, but Susan was too busy to be greatly concerned. If she missed home, Susan found solace in the church, which was always open for prayers.

Susan enjoyed her meetings with the other nannies. They chattered together as they took short walks along the avenues. One day, the uniformed figure of George appeared, tall, slim and smart, his long leather boots polished and shining. He held in his hand two letters.

"These are for you, Susan. I had an errand over on East Seventy-Ninth Street for Mr Howlett, so I brought them in case you wanted to read them in the park this afternoon."

They were from Scotland. Susan's face flushed. Why she should fear to open them, she couldn't tell. But Scotland seemed like a time bomb to her. She felt that so much might go wrong while she was away, and she put the letters in her pocket, hiding her premonitions.

"I'll read them later. Thank you, George. This is Edith from Amsterdam." But he was already gazing into Edith's eyes. "Ah, Amsterdam! A beautiful city." Already he was kissing her hand. "You live near the park, Edith?"

"Don't tell him, Edith."

George looked appalled. "Susan! You don't deserve to have a beautiful friend." His eyes were taking in the plump figure and the well-shaped legs of the Dutch girl. "My dear, I hope we meet again, and we can get to know each other better." Edith laughed heartily.

She said, "You never know, George. You never know." Her eyes were flirty, and Susan thought she saw her give him a wink. The three of them walked, good-naturedly bantering, with the two deep prams out of the park. After dinner, that evening, Susan found herself alone in the kitchen. She sat in Bella's easy chair and opened the first letter which was in Archie's handwriting.

22nd August 1925

Dear Susan,

We received your letter and your address in New York. It sounds very impressive. I'm glad your crossing was enjoyable and that you have arrived safely.

I am sorry not to have written before, but now I have to tell you some bad news from here. Wee Louie took ill with diphtheria and sadly died in a terrible hospital accident. She was taken to Lightburn Hospital on 16th July, just days after you left for the States, and although she seemed to be recovering, there was an accident with a steam kettle, which had been left unattended by her bedside. She died a week after you left.

Needless to say, Honor and Edward are inconsolable. We are not sure if Honor will ever completely recover. She weeps almost all of the time, and it is very hard to have any conversation with her. I know, Susan, that this is a hard blow to you, too, and we are all so sad at the loss of the beautiful child.

On a lighter note, Aunt Nell and Mother are doing well with their little baker's shop, where the old cobbler's shop used to be. We had some worry with Mother's health but she has responded to the tonic the doctor gave her, and thank God, is a bit better.

I am studying hard for my final exams in the spring, so that if God spares me, I may graduate in Master of Arts with Honours soon. I'll have to put my nose to the grindstone for the few months, but you don't need to be told about hard work.

Mary and Norman are buying a smallholding out by Kilsyth. Mary will keep on her matron's job, while Norman works the farm. I don't know if they will ever have children, we'll wait and see.

Elsie Dryden has won the Daily Express bathing beauty competition. A photograph of her appeared on the front cover. She looked beautiful with her lovely hair. It looks like she is very serious with Jim Shields, although she's just as wild as ever, slipping out to dances when her parents are in bed. She's so full of life. No wonder Jim is daft about her.

Well, Susan, I think that's all of the news. Joe is just the same Joe. He's home just now, but he keeps talking of going back to sea. I think it's to get away from the daily grind of keeping a wife and three boys in food and boots. Edward drinks too much and has lost some of his free-and-easy attitude. Since their dreadful loss, who can console them? You must remember them both in your Sunday prayers. I'm afraid they have both stopped going to Mass.

Please write soon, Susan, and don't forget us.

Your loving brother,

Archie

By the time she had reached the end of the letter, Susan was shaking with sobs. Taking a dish-towel from the rail above the fireplace, she gave in to racking cries of sorrow. All her pent-up homesickness for smoky Glasgow and for the close bonds of family were mixed in with the shock of the tragedy of Louie's death. Poor Honor! Poor Edward! How can they stand it! I should have been there! Perhaps if I hadn't come away from home, somehow I could have helped.

It was thus Howard Howlett with the uniformed George found the distraught girl when they returned from the city. She was so incoherent that eventually Howard took the letter from her and read it himself. "Go and get the brandy from the dining room, George." He lifted Susan's head up from the table where she had hidden her face on her arm.

"Susan, my dear, I'm so sorry. What age was the child?"

"Just three-and-a-half years old. She was so beautiful! Poor Edward! Poor Honor. What a cruel God to do this to them!" and the tears flowed afresh down the girl's cheeks.

"Hush now!" Howard gathered her head against his black waistcoat. He felt the tears sting his own eyes at the grief of Susan so far from her family. George returned with the brandy. His face too was deadly serious. After ten minutes, when she had drunk some of the fiery liquid, Susan's hysteria began to subside. The two men sat with her at the scrubbed kitchen table, helping themselves liberally to the brandy.

"That's better, Susan." Howard handed Susan a large, white handkerchief. "You feel worse because you're so far away from your family. But you can't help that." Then looking at George, he said, "See if Bella's in her room, George, and ask her to come down to the kitchen." He pushed her hair back from her face, and smiled at her.

"You're very kind, Mr Howlett. I'm sorry I broke down. It was just such a shock."

"Nonsense! Anybody would have been shattered by such terrible news. But you must know that we are your friends. You are not all alone."

Bella came bursting in next. Straight away she approached the stricken girl and put her arms around her. She hugged Susan close to her ample chest. "Take her up to her room, Bella. I think she should rest. Maybe you could make her a hot drink. "Howard straightened up while still looking solicitously at Susan.

"Of course, Mr Howlett." Susan and Bella left the kitchen.

When Mrs Howlett returned from her evening out, she was told of Susan's sad news. Next morning she spoke kindly to the girl, "Do you want to go home, Susan? You could help your mother and your brother. We would like you to stay. Freddy is thriving and very happy with you, but we will bow to your wishes." Betty Howlett lacked the warmth of her husband, but she was genuinely concerned for Susan.

"No, thank you, Mrs Howlett. It's too late now, anyway. I'll get over it."

"Such a dreadful tragedy for your family. The death of a child is always heartbreaking. If you need anything, just let me know, won't you?" Betty Howlett shook her head as she watched the dejected girl climb the stairway. What a sad life some people had! She could think of nothing more boring and deprived than to be Susan with her dreadful clothes and spending the day with a young baby that wasn't your own child. God forbid that she should ever fall into such a sunless life. However, she soon dismissed all thought of Susan, and her sympathy was quick to evaporate as her mind turned to the events of the day ahead.

She thought she would wear her blue dress and new fox fur, an outfit sure to stun the other members of the Ladies Tennis Committee. With blue hat to match, Betty Howlett's elegant legs were soon taking her to the front door where George waited outside with the limousine.

Looking out of the nursery window, on the floor above the front door, Susan clung to the baby more than usual that morning, as if he could salve the pain she felt for Honor and Edward. Her thoughts switched off, she watched her suave mistress, hair sleeked under a cloche hat, slip effortlessly into the car as George held the door for her. When, later that morning, Freddy had taken a little nap, she pulled out the other letter. It was from Tommy.

26 Forest Road,
Shotts,
Lanarkshire.

29th August 1925

My Dearest Susan,
Your letter telling me of your life at the Howlett's came a few days ago. Thank God you are keeping fine. Just remember if ever you do not fare well with your employers, then you must write to me for the money for your passage home.
I think about you every day and wish you were here. Life has become much duller since I don't have the weekends to see my darling. My sister, May, is keeping the house now since Mother took ill, and she polishes

and shines the place from morning until night. I don't think she'll ever marry. She never takes time to look up from her housework to find a fellow to marry her. If she's not praying in church, she's donning an apron to set to in the house. I am forced to take my pit clothes off at the back door of the kitchen and wash the coal dust off me, before coming into the house. She does the same with my brother, Jim. She has the hot water ready for us every day.

I haven't been to see any of your family since you left. There didn't seem much point, as I don't drink and don't talk politics all the time, like Ned and Archie.

Maybe I'll go and see your mother next weekend. I have started trying to save again and have gathered quite a few pounds now. Maybe some day I'll be able to come and bring you back to Scotland where you belong.

Things at the pit are not good. If anyone is off sick or late for work, they are sacked. The price of coal is falling every week, and there is talk of a reduction in our pay – and an increase in our hours. As if the work is not hellish enough. Somehow I'll have to get out of this job. Maybe, Ned could speak for me at the railway offices. Things really are bad, and the union leaders are talking about calling us out on strike. Then we'll all starve without any pay.

I have joined the church choir and the rehearsals help to fill in the time for me, and stop me thinking about you so much. Please reply quickly to this letter, as I live only to hear from you and long for the day when we can be together again. Remember the marriage proposal still stands.

Your loving,

Tommy. (Ever yours)

Susan stared unseeing at the sleeping Freddy, the letter still in her hand. Poor Tommy! she thought. He sounds so lonely. Have I made a dreadful mistake to leave such a good man who loves me so much? Try as she would that day, Susan could not lift her spirits. Not even George at lunchtime, clowning around trying to raise a smile, could help her.

"Don't go to the park, Susan. Come with me in the limo, you and Freddy. We could go to Coney Island and have some fun. Can't you see, I can make you happy."

The exaggerated pleading and look of undying devotion was comical, but she only said, "You'll get us both the sack, George, you know that."

"I hope I see you at dinner tonight, Susie, and then you can cry on my shoulder."

"You're hopeless, you really are!" But she had to laugh a little at how hard it was to discourage him.

Pushing the pram out of the back door, she was met by the dark, overcoated figure of Howard. Susan found herself liking this tall, powerful man, for he always stopped to speak to her and to his baby son. "And how is Susan this afternoon?"

"Oh, I'm better, Mr Howlett. Freddy takes my mind off things."

"You know if you have any worries, just come to me, Susan. Don't keep them to yourself."

She felt herself blushing at this kind remark, and was at a loss to know how to reply. "Thank you," she stuttered. "Thank you, Mr Howlett," and could think of nothing else to say. Their eyes met briefly, and then they both looked back at the happy child. "Say goodbye to your daddy, Freddy. Bye-bye!" and she waved her hand to the child lying in the pram. "Goodbye, Mr Howlett, we're off for our afternoon walk. I should be back in an hour or so. I think it feels like rain today." She pulled her hat down on to her thick brown hair, and gave a broad smile to her employer.

"Goodbye, Susan. Bye, Freddy!" Howard lifted his hat to them as he spoke, watching them go in the direction of the park.

CHAPTER 9

Betty Howlett was delighted with Susan and the care she was taking of Freddy. Some days, after Susan had returned from their walk, the mother would take the child and play with him for half an hour or so. And she always saw Freddy at breakfast before she left for her daily engagements. But for Susan it was quite hard going. Her charge took up many hours of the day, and it was a welcome relief when he had his afternoon nap. Bathing and dressing him took up a lot of time, but Susan was growing very fond of the child, and she loved brushing up his fair hair. She found she could twist the smooth, silky hair into curls round her fingers, and then she would tell him he was the handsomest boy in America.

Mrs Howlett's day was filled with coffee mornings, fund-raising for charity and gossiping with her cronies. She and Howard had long since ceased to sleep together. They had a friendly relationship and genuinely cared about each other, but all passion had gone. The conception of Freddy had been almost the last occasion when they had made love. Since that time they had given all their energies to business affairs and good works. Howard played golf and cards. They had friends in to dinner and went to parties and public functions together. Their money opened all doors to them in New York. They had both worked hard for this position in the town, and gave their energies to keeping up their standing in their own set.

Often Betty did not feel like dressing-up yet again and going to another function, but the satisfaction of stepping out of a chauffeur-driven car in smart clothes and wearing expensive jewellery and perfume was compensation for the effort. She would sometimes have flashbacks to the unfashionable east side of the city and the half-empty flat where she had started married life with Howard, and thank God that she had made it out of that way of life.

"I'm lunching at Sardi's today, George, but first I have to stop off at Macy's for some shopping, so if you could drop me there, and come back for twelve noon, that would be just fine."

"Certainly, of course, Mrs Howlett," and he held the door open wide for her.

"You sure were having fun in the kitchen, this morning, George."

"Oh, just trying to get Susie to laugh a little, you know, cheer her up."

"I see." Betty took in his broad back, long, straight, thick hair and the pale Mongolian tan of the skin of his hands as he took the wheel. She kept well hidden the attraction she felt for George. She knew the type – Polish, passionate, and needing only the slightest scintilla of encouragement to make a move on her. She spoke to him from the back of the car, "Are you still walking out with Elly from the French restaurant, George? She was nice."

He grimaced. "It turned out she had a boyfriend tucked away in a restaurant down Times Square way, Mrs Howlett. She ditched me, I guess."

He gave her a soulful look through the car mirror, which she returned with her frank, green eyes. Is her smile particularly friendly, this morning? he was puzzled. "I like your hat, Mrs Howlett. You look fine in that colour. Lilac coloured, is it?"

"They call it azure, and thank you, George. Flattery will get you everywhere."

When they reached the busy entrance to Macy's department store, George pulled up, jumped out and opened the door of the impressive car for his mistress. Sheer silk-stockinged legs and two-hundred-dollar shoes appeared before the wide-brimmed hat and narrow pale blue body.

"I hope you have a good morning shopping, Mrs Howlett," he said as she brushed past him like a goddess. Was she just a little closer to him than usual and her smile just a little warmer than normal? George felt a thrill of recognition of the old 'come-on'. Could it be possible? Of course it could! he told himself.

As he returned to the car to find a parking place where he could chat for an hour or so to some of his buddies, he whistled softly to himself. "Can you believe it?" he whispered softly, "I think she gave me the eye." George's emotions were as variable as the weather. His mood could change like a straw in the wind. He was flushed and excited by the small compliment he felt he had been paid, and for the rest of the morning, he was sitting on top of the world. By lunchtime, when he dropped Mrs Howlett at Sardi's, he still felt there was a buzz between them, however, Betty Howlett's manner had changed, and her face was inscrutable.

"I'll take a taxi home, George. Give you time to wash the car. Mr Howlett and I are going to the Twenty-One Club this evening. We'll need you about eight. Thanks, George!" she finished off the instruction with an enigmatic smile, and he was left in limbo.

"Just like a woman! Who could understand them?" In disgust he drove home.

A few days later, when Susan was just emerging with the pram for her daily walk, "Ah, my little sweetheart, Susie! Have a nice walk in the park?" He stood close to her. As she started along the avenue, he followed her. "Can I see you tonight about nine o'clock when you have put him to bed? There's a party over at Mitzi's Bar. It's Mitzi's birthday."

"No, George, I don't think so. I have to write home." She looked at his half-sincere, half-comical face, "I've got to answer my letters."

He put his arm around her. "I'll cheer you up, honey. You are too young and too beautiful to be at home. You need someone to love you. I love you."

She looked at him amazed. It had taken almost two years for Tommy to tell her he loved her. Who could understand these Continentals? she thought.

"George, don't be silly!" She pushed him away. "For goodness sake! People will see you!"

He was pleading now, "Please meet me when you come back from your walk, just for an hour, my darling."

At that moment Howard Howlett appeared. "You heard the lady! She doesn't want to go out with you." As if he had been struck, George straightened up, bowed and clicked his heels. "Good morning, Mr Howlett, sir! You wish me to drive you somewhere?"

"No, I'm gonna walk today. You go off to the garage. I'll see you later."

George was in the car and off like a bat out of hell.

Howard looked at Freddy. "Hello, little boy!" He bent and kissed the child. "I'll walk to the corner with you, Susan." Flustered a little, Susan gave him a nervous smile.

"Sure, Mr Howlett," and she started pushing the pram.

"You're sounding more American every day, Susan."

"Really? At least you can understand me that way, in spite of my Scottish accent."

Howard didn't reply. He felt drawn to this girl, so gauche and raw as she appeared. "Listen, my dear, don't let George away with anything. He's a smooth talker, and well ..."

"I know he's had a few girlfriends."

"Yeah." He looked directly into her eyes. "You're going to the park now? It's a lovely day for it." He looked up at the sky. "I envy you. Bye, Freddy! Bye, Susan!" He lifted his hat to them.

She moved the great pram along the sidewalk, confused and excited by all this early morning attention. She was feeling fragile and lonely and longed to hear the voices of her own folk so far away. Tears started in her eyes as she thought of home and all the trials and tribulations of her family in Scotland. How she missed them and longed to be near them. She stopped to pick up a toy thrown out by the boisterous baby. I'll go to early Mass in the morning. Lotta will cover for me. Maybe this weight I feel on me will lift if I pray for help from God. That night she sat down to write.

c/o Howlett,
305 Park Avenue,

Manhattan, New York.

15th September, 1925

My Dear Tommy,

I received your letter two days ago, and am glad that May is keeping the house and looking after you. I think of you often and wish you were here. Working in the pit, hammering and shovelling that filthy coal is such back-breaking work. I pray that some day you can find a better job where you don't get covered in black coal dust every day. Pray for me, and let us hope that we will see each other again soon.

My work here means long hours but Mr and Mrs Howlett and the staff are very kind to me, although sometimes they have difficulty understanding my accent. Mr Howlett is especially thoughtful, and Freddy, the baby, is very lovable. He and I are great friends.

You don't appear to have heard yet the very bad news from Glasgow. There has been a terrible tragedy happened to Edward and Honor's little girl, Louie. It seems she died in a terrible accident in Lightburn Fever Hospital. They are both inconsolable.

Myself, I feel I should be there to be some help. Perhaps you could go and see them and tell them how sad I am for them.

I send you all my love and hope that conditions improve for you. A strike would be terrible for everyone, especially for the families. I will pray for you every night, Tommy, and please remember me and my family in your prayers.

Yours ever,

With all my love,

Susan

As time passed, Susan became more used to the pace of life in America. Within a few months, she began slowly to transform herself into a slimmer, smarter figure. Discarded were the Scottish clothes, and with lighter and more fashionable American styles, with make-up as advised by Lotta, a new Susan began to appear. She even learned to say 'Hi!' and give a broad smile when she met George, or Howard or Betty Howlett. Freddy was out of the pram now and Susan's task of walking with him, holding his hands, took up much of her day.

"Hi, Susan, sweetheart! You'll stay like that, my dahleeng, if you don't straighten up." Susan looked up at the tall, uniformed figure of George.

"I'm not your sweetheart, George." Susan smiled, but she held her back to show that he was right.

"Look, honey! Would you like to go to a dance next Thursday evening? I hear it's a day off for you." He saw her hesitation. "Please, please, my darling. Every time I see you my heart misses a beat! Please come out with me. I will make you happy." His Polish accent and his grandiose compliments made her laugh, and she picked up Freddy, giggling uncontrollably. George continued to lay it on thick. "You can meet Andre, my friend. You'll love him!" Then he became very serious. "You're a beautiful girl, you know!"

This remark made her eyes dance, and she laughed more heartily than ever. When she sat down to recover and looked at his lugubrious face, it seemed as if a great dam had burst within her soul. The protective wall she had put up against the unknown in this foreign country had cracked, and with the laughter, she felt her heart lighten.

"You'll come?" George asked, his face close to hers, and smilingly she agreed.

Thursday was not long in arriving, and with Lotta's help, a new brassiere and new smart high-heeled shoes, an excited Susan descended the staircase to meet George in the kitchen. This time his compliment was genuine. "Honey, you look a million dollars!"

"Well, thank you, George."

"We'll have a helluva time tonight!" He put his arm around her, entranced by this new, laughing, shiny-haired Susan.

Lotta was scornful. "Laugh if you like, but watch he don't leave you in the soup or whatever. Lucky for me I'm not George's type. Too fiery for our Polish friend."

The dance hall was a riot of noise, colour and fast-moving dancers. The men wore dark suits, with short jackets, while the girls seemed to be dressed mostly in skimpy, short dresses, all fringes and sequins. Legs and arms appeared to be flying in all directions, as they danced to the frenetic jazz music. Everyone was carefree and smiling, and no one looked older than twenty-five. George guided her onto the dance floor as the band played 'The Darktown Strutters' Ball'. She tried to keep time with him, and soon was copying some of the steps of the others.

"This is Andre. Andre meet Susan. Ain't she a peach?"

"Pleased to meet you, I'm sure." He turned to his partner. "Hey, Annette, meet Susan."

"Hi! Susan. Pleased ta meet yah!" said the skinny flapper without stopping her dancing. Her voice was high and nasal, a real New Yorker. "Ain't this fun! Can you do the Black Bottom? It's a hoot!" She looked for all the world as if she lived permanently in this brightly lit palace, and she proceeded to demonstrate the new dance craze to their little group. She stopped, exhausted, saying, "Hey, boys, ain't you brought any booze?"

Andre took a hip flask from his pocket. She took a swig and handed it to Susan. "Here, honey, it's good stuff." The scorching gin took Susan's breath away, and she coughed and spluttered to the amusement of the others.

The band started up in ragtime, and George grabbed hold of Susan. "Come on, honey!" and he pulled her onto the floor, singing in a loud Polish accent, *"Swanee! How I love you, how I love you!"* They laughed and danced through the evening in the packed hall to the raucous music, occasionally switching partners, or stopping for a swig of illegal booze. By eleven o'clock, Susan was exhausted, but very happy at this jazzy baptism.

"It seems like everyone in America is happy," Susan confided to George as they picked up their coats.

"Ain't that the truth!" Annette called wildly, forgetting the long hours she had to spend in the department store all week.

"Yeah, ain't that the truth," echoed George.

The four of them walked home past alleys holding battered garbage cans, past cold-water flats through whose windows could be seen clothes lines and ironing boards or sometimes an open cupboard holding a little electric plate for cooking. Some drugstores and delicatessen shops were still open, their lights falling on the damp pavements. From a window, they could hear the sound of the latest gramophone record:

> *You can bring Pearl, she's a darn nice girl,*
> *but don't bring Lulu!*

"I know the next line," and Susan sang:

> *"You can bring Rose with her turned-up nose,*
> *but don't bring Lulu!"*

Annette added:

> *"Lulu always wants to do,"*

and they all sang:

> *"What the boys don't want to do.*
> *When she struts her stuff around,*
> *London Bridge is falling down."*

The two couples parted at the corner, and George and Susan were soon at the Howlett's house.

"I've had a lot of fun, George. It was great at the dance."

"You sound like an American, already, Susie." He put his arm around her and in his strong accent he murmured urgently, "You are beautiful. I love you."

A great giggle engulfed Susan. "George, don't be silly. You are an idiot."

Exaggeratedly crestfallen, he hung his head. "Why do you laugh when I offer you my heart?"

"Oh, come on!" Susan pulled his jacket. "We've got to work tomorrow. You mustn't say you love someone just like that. Love takes years to happen."

"Not with me, it doesn't," and he held his hands to his heart. "You have hit me here."

Moved and amused at the same time, she put her hands on his shoulders and sang:

"You can bring cake or Porterhouse steak,
but don't bring Lulu,
Lulu gets blue, and she goes cuckoo,"

and they sang together:

"Like a clock upon the shelf."

Still smiling, Susan held her hand out to him. "Goodnight, George." He gave her a mournful, lovesick look, which she ignored, and she hastily disappeared through the back door of the house.

After that night at the dance hall, when Susan got time off and she sat gossiping with Bella and Lotta in the kitchen, George would stand or sit close to her with a proprietorial air. They went out once a week, sometimes to a movie, and often just to walk along the avenues, past the shops, and the towering skyscrapers which were appearing. On Broadway, you could pass the evening just looking at the 'swells' and the shiny limousines which brought them for their evening's entertainment. The flappers in their furs and pearls and their tuxedoed escorts seemed to be in a state of perpetual excitement. Susan and George soaked up the atmosphere as part of their leisure. Coming from poor backgrounds, where money for food was of paramount importance, they were amazed and impressed with the wealth on show.

Walking Susan home one Sunday evening, after a coffee in Mitzi's bar, George asked, "Are you taking Freddy to the park in the morning?"

"I usually do, unless it rains."

"Maybe I could come with you. I don't think they're using the car tomorrow."

"George, you'd better not. I don't think Mrs Howlett would approve."

"Huh, her? Listen, I bet you five dollars, I could persuade her to do anything for me."

"You're romancing again, George."

"Sometimes she looks at me, kinda longingly. You know what I mean."

"George!" Susan was disgusted. "Don't you say such things. She's a very nice woman. And she has a husband."

"Ah, women are all nice until they fall in love. Then their true nature comes out. A tiger comes out of his cage!" he leered at Susan.

"You just stop it, George Lazio. I told you, I'm engaged to a boy in Scotland. Maybe he'll come to America soon."

"Oh, I forgot about Tommy. What a soft guy he must be. I tell you, I would not have let you sail away from me the way he has."

"You know nothing about it. He's a hard-working man and a good person." In her frustration and sudden homesickness, her eyes filled with tears.

"OK! OK! We won't speak of it. But let me walk in the park tomorrow with you."

"No, I'll be working. Freddy takes up all my attention. Besides, I meet other girls there."

"Yeah?" George could not help his eyes lighting up.

"Oh, you're just a wicked man!"

"Let me come to your room tonight, sweetheart. I'll bring a bottle and some cigarettes. We can be alone, and ..."

She pushed him away, "No, George. You know it's wrong."

"Who would know? You're lonely, like me."

"God would know. Leave me alone or I'll tell Father Donahue about you."

"Oh God! You girls are all the same. You're afraid of your own shadow."

"Well, I just know it's only one kind of woman who does that."

"Oh, come on. In New York, free love is becoming very fashionable, you know. You must enjoy life while you can."

"Well, free love is not fashionable with me, George. I'm not that kind of girl."

CHAPTER 10

The winter, bitterly cold in New York, had come and almost gone. Christmas had been a grand affair with glitz and presents all round, something Susan had been little used to as the Scottish mode was to virtually ignore the 'heathen' elements of the festival – at least so the Presbyterian majority would have it – and to go big on the New Year. But as good Catholics, Susan and her family caught the spirit of Christmas with Mass and joy in each other.

One night, Susan was awakened by a howling Freddy. She pulled on her robe and reached his cot to find the child's cheeks were inflamed and he was crying as if in pain. His little fists were clenched, his mouth was a square with his six first teeth showing and dribbles were running down his chin.

"Oh, my poor boy! Come to Susan." She lifted the child and tried to soothe him but he was very upset. "Let's try a warm drink, Freddy. Susan will take you downstairs, and we'll see if there's any of that nice chocolate milk you like."

Just as she got him settled and he was falling back to sleep on her knee at the kitchen table, the door opened and Howard Howlett appeared. He was just coming home from a business dinner, although it was almost two o'clock in the morning. Handsome in his evening suit and long silk scarf, he was just a bit tipsy.

"Having trouble, Susie?" he sat down on the chair opposite her.

"He's just gone back to sleep," she whispered. "I think it's teething troubles. He seemed really to be in pain."

Howard's expression was indulgent, as he took in the youthful figure of Susan and the sleeping baby. "Well, you know you're a big success with Freddy. Mrs Howlett and I are very pleased with your work."

"Thank you," she whispered and smiled. I'd better escape, Susan thought. This is embarrassing, sitting in my dressing-gown in the kitchen with a drunk man.

"What're you doin' for Easter, Susie?"

"I hadn't thought, Mr Howlett," and she moved forward in her chair, still nursing the baby, and looked up at the clock.

"Well, we usually have a staff outing for Easter. I, myself, or Mrs Howlett and me, we take the staff to a restaurant for dinner some evening in the holidays. Would you like that, honey?"

"Yes, I think so, Mr Howlett."

"Well, maybe we'll go to Greenwich Village. Sometimes we go to Dickerman's Pirate's Den. The waiters dress up as buccaneers. It's fun. And they have an orchestra with the musicians dressed in costume, too. Would you like that, Susie?"

"Oh, sure, Mr Howlett. I haven't been to Greenwich Village. I believe there's a hospital there called St Vincent's. A girl I met on the boat coming over to the States works there. I'd sure like to meet her again."

"Well, glory be!" I know that hospital well. Know a couple of the doctors, too. What's the girl's name?"

"Jenny Hetherington."

"She's a nurse?"

"Yes, that's right."

"Then I'll telephone and find out when she is off duty and where you can meet her. How about that, Susie?" He took off his scarf and gave her a slightly cockeyed smile.

"Oh, that's fine. I'd love to see her again."

He was swaying a little as he looked at her. "Listen, Susie. What age are you?"

"I'm twenty-five."

"Well, I'm forty-five. What d'ya think about that?"

"Well, you don't look that old." She hesitated and stood up. "I've got to get Freddy back to bed."

He stood up, too, looking a bit more sober as he said, "And if I was ten years younger, I'd sure be after you, Susie."

"Mr Howlett!"

"Call me Howard."

"I've got to go … eh … Howard."

"You think I'm drunk, don't you?"

"Just a little."

"Well, I am, and I know I shouldn't be saying this, but I really admire you, Susan. You're a friendly and a lovely girl." His handsome face was close to hers, and she felt the blood rushing to her cheeks.

"You'll feel better in the morning, Mr Howlett."

"I never felt better than this, Susie. Good night, my dear. I'm a cad, I know."

It took quite a while for Susan to get to sleep after the incident with Howard in the kitchen. Somehow she felt guilty and a little worried by his drunken outburst. Next morning, she avoided looking directly at him when he appeared in the kitchen just as she was putting Freddy in his high chair to give him his breakfast.

"Did you get him to sleep all right last night, Susan?" Howard said in a low voice.

"Yes, Mr Howlett. He settled down fine."

"I'm sorry if I was out of order last night," he whispered so that the others couldn't hear.

"That's OK! We Scots know about whisky."

"Well, it wasn't just the whisky. Have a good day. I'll find out about your friend at St Vincent's for you."

Howard affected her, not like George, or even Tommy. His air of power, his assurance and his handsome appearance threw her into a state of blood-rushing panic. He seemed like a father and a lover rolled into one. She found he was in her thoughts more every day. She tried to brush aside that night in the kitchen, but as she went about her duties, a new light appeared in her face. She felt happy for no reason, but at the same time, her conscience told her she had no right to feel this way.

Within a few days Howard informed her that he had located Jenny at St Vincent's. On Thursday afternoon Susan was to meet her at the hospital gates at two o'clock. "I'll tell George to keep Thursday afternoon free for you. I can go on to my office, and you can get a taxi home. OK?" He smiled beneficently on Susan and Bella and lifted his son in his arms. "Here, take this little devil." Freddy was struggling to be on his feet, so that he could run off in any direction. Susan took the child.

"What a nice man!" she said to Bella as she dealt with Freddy.

"Nice? Oh, I suppose 'nice' would do, he sure looks happy with himself these days. I think the baby has been the best thing for him. Before, he hardly was at home and didn't speak much to us at all. He just loves this little boy," and she cooed over the child as he lay on his back on Susan's knee.

But when Thursday came, George had to take Betty Howlett to a Literary Society meeting over on Sixteenth Street, and Howard had to take a taxi, planning to drop Susan in Greenwich Village on his way to his business appointment. The baby was left for Lotta to look after that day. Susan was wearing a new suit of greyish-green fine wool, with a thick fur collar against the cold. A little cloche hat of the same green shade held in the brown waves of her hair. She had taken some time with her hair and make-up that day. She felt good, like a million dollars as Howard looked her carefully up and down.

"You look excited about meeting this girl from home, Susie."

"Oh, yes, we met as we were boarding the liner and spent all our time together, so it will be good to see how she's got on."

He leaned over towards her in the back of the taxi. "I wonder if all the men have fallen for her at St Vincent's, just like you've stolen all hearts at 305 Park Avenue."

"Stop kidding, Mr Howlett."

"You think I'm kidding?" His blue eyes were twinkling as he said, "I sure hope you have a good day, honey. You deserve it."

As they approached the hospital, Howard slipped some dollar bills out of his wallet. "This will pay your taxi home, honey. Maybe I'll see you this evening. I should be home around seven, and I'll look in and see Freddy." Unexpectedly he leaned over and kissed her cheek, as she was about to leave the cab.

"Goodbye, Susan."

"Goodbye, Mr Howlett."

She closed the door of the yellow cab, and it sped across town. The modish young woman at the gate waiting for Susan was almost unrecognisable. Where was the shy girl in tweeds and woollens? Where was the Jenny she had got to know on the boat from Scotland? Both girls let out a little scream of pleasure at the meeting.

"Gosh, you look smart, Susan, like a real American."

"And look at you! You've lost weight." Susan took in the stylish low-fronted shoes and the silver-grey dress with short hobble skirt. "Your outfit's terrific!"

"Look over here, Susan. That motor belongs to Brian, my friend from St Vincent's." She teetered towards the car in her tight skirt. "He's going to take us up the Woolworth Building. He has a friend who works the elevator. Can you believe it? It's sixty storeys high."

"Gosh, I hope it's safe!"

"You and me both. Brian'll wait downstairs for us, 'cos he's been before. Then we can go over to his mother's for luncheon."

"Luncheon?"

"Yeah, that's what they call dinner, here."

"He says he'll drive us down to Washington Square. She lives quite near there. Then we can take a walk round the Village, and see the sights. How does that sound?"

The cloth-capped driver of the jalopy was beside them now. "This is Brian, Susan. He's a porter at St Vincent's, but he's studying for his High School Diploma at night school."

"Jump in my chariot, gals! New York awaits youse."

Soon the two girls were being lifted at fast speed to the top of the highest building in New York. Jenny could hardly breathe at the thought. They looked down, arms around each other's waists for reassurance, at the whole panorama of the city. They pointed out buildings to each other, moving to other vantage points to see the unbelievable view.

"There's the Hudson River, Susan!"

"It's just breathtaking! The trip from home to America was worth it for just this sight. I'll never forget it!"

Back in the jalopy with Brian, they were soon speeding down to his mother's apartment. Mina Renton turned out to be a real, born-and-bred New Yorker, of part Russian and part Irish extraction. The table had been laid with about twice as much food as they could possibly eat. Roast beef, cold ham, salad, various kinds of bread, dishes of butter, cheese, salad dressings, horseradish sauce, cream, orange juice, all were set out for her Brian and his friends.

"Don't you think my Brian is a smart boy? Three nights a week he goes to school to study. Some day he will be somebody, don't you think?" Mina beamed on the embarrassed boy. The girls agreed, tucking into the food. "Me, I am just a poor widow woman. What do I know? I was a waitress. I can cook, but I got no chances. But my Brian, he will make it, I know. He is clever like his father was. You two girls? You work at St Vincent's?"

"No, Susan here's a nanny, Ma. She works for the Howletts on Park Avenue. You know the stinkin' rich types."

Mina put a hand on each side of her face to show how impressed she was. "Let me touch you, Susan. Maybe some of the luck will rub off on the Rentons. Oh, to be rich! Some people are so lucky. My Brian, he's all I got. Mamie, his sister, she ran off to Houston, Texas or some place with a guy she met in the restaurant where she was working. We ain't heard from her. It's a year now. Brian and me, we just have each other."

"Yeah!" Brian agreed. "I might go to Houston to look for Mamie some day."

"You! You'll go to no Houston. Then I'll never see you no more, either." She stood up and picked from the side table an ouija board. It was her favourite pastime, to ask the board about the future. "Let's close the curtains and have a go with the ouija board." The two girls looked intrigued.

"Do you think it works, Mrs Renton?" asked Jenny.

"Sure it works. It told me my husband was dead when he got knocked down by a train down at the harbour yard. It told Brian would get a job at St Vincent's. Ain't that right, Brian?"

"Aw, Mother! Don't bring it out right now. The girls want to see Greenwich Village."

"Just fifteen minutes, please."

They sat in a circle around the coffee table in the darkened room. All put their fingers on the glass. "Will I hear from Mamie soon? Please tell her old mother." The glass stuttered and slid one way and another then shot over to the word 'Yes'.

"You see! I knew it! She'll write to us. I know she will." Her face was suffused with happiness.

"Your turn, Jenny," said Brian.

"Will I marry within a year of this date?" asked Jenny. The glass shuddered round in circles and ended up at 'p', then 'e', then 'r' until it spelled out 'perhaps'. Jenny clapped her hands in glee. "Do you think it's true, Brian?"

"Dunno. Ma thinks so."

"Sure it's true. I told you. You've got to have faith. You got a question, Susan?"

"Will I see Tommy next year?" Susan stared at the board as she spoke. A slight hesitation, then 's', 'u', 'r', 'e' was spelled. She couldn't help but be pleased at the message.

"Now you, Brian?"

"Naw. I don't have a question."

"You must have."

"OK. Will I get to the ball game on New Year's Day?"

The glass shot over to the word 'no', then changed its mind and ended up at 'yes', and they all laughed.

After thanking Mrs Renton, they strolled along the cosmopolitan streets of the Village taking in the antique shops and pausing under the impressive grandeur of the Washington Arch. In the Italian section, they stopped at a pushcart to buy apples, and Susan picked up a couple of second-hand books in a bookstore. Here were all nationalities: Indian, African, some Chinese; artists seeming to have all the time in the world to look at paintings, or listen to music which poured from the cafes and restaurants.

"What a wonderful place. I love it here, Brian."

"You should come here at night. It's a magical place. The streets blaze with lights, and the restaurant and nightclubs are just alive with music. Tourists throng the area. Real New Yorkers can't get near the place."

"Oh, I'd love to come here at night. I've never seen so many interesting people and things to look at!"

"We'll have a night out on the town, Susie. We could have an Italian meal." Jenny had caught Susan's excitement. "Do you like spaghetti, Sue?"

"I've never tasted it, but I'd like to try." She was watching a fat Italian man through a cafe window. He had a checked table napkin tucked under his chin and was sucking great forkfuls of tomato-covered spaghetti into his mouth.

"Come on, honey. It's rude to stare." Brian gently took her arm and they walked on. "Yeah. It's fun. It sure is fun in the Village. On Sundays it's great. I come often just to look at the folk."

"Look in there. There's a real fortune-teller, Susie." Jenny had stopped in front of another cafe. They gazed through the window. It was full of Eastern bric-a-brac, batik clothes and smelling of incense. "Go on, Susan, ask her about your future." Jenny gave her a little push. "It's only a dollar or two at the most."

The woman was installed in a booth in the corner of the cafe. She had a crystal ball in front of her and a glass of red wine by her side. Long, greying hair, heavy drop-pearl earrings, and two or three necklaces glittered on her chest. Her dress was of purple and gold. Susan sat down and faced the wrinkled face and the darkest of brown eyes which seemed to bore into her. "Look into the crystal ball, my dear. What is your name?"

"Susan."

The fortune-teller held the palms of her hands a few inches from the crystal.

"I see a large house with many windows. There are two men." She spoke slowly and deliberately. "You are first with one, the older one, and then with the younger one. You can't make up your mind." Susan shifted in her seat. The woman scared her. "I see great riches here." She stopped and looked hard at Susan, then back to the crystal ball. "There is a child. A beautiful child." The fortune-teller looked up at Susan. Her eyes were deep and hypnotic. Susan felt the woman was drawing some of her spirit from her. As she tried to return the powerful gaze, she felt she saw hatred and envy in those eyes. Then the spell was broken, and with an air of resignation the woman looked down again into the depths of the crystal ball. "The child seems to be very important to you."

"Is it a boy or a girl?" Susan felt the voice was not her own.

"I can't say. It's not clear. The picture is fading now, but I can tell you, you will have a very interesting, enviable life. You have a lot of luck and a lot of love in your future. You are indeed a very lucky person."

"No bad luck at all?" smiled Susan.

She was treated to another piercing look. "Don't look for bad luck. Pretend it doesn't exist. It will find you if it wants you." The woman pulled a fringed shawl around her shoulders, and straightened up. "That's all today."

This last remark broke the strong pull that the woman seemed have on Susan. She held the money out to her, feeling drained and shaky. When it was Jenny's turn, her fortune was of children and journeys, and she emerged from the curtained booth quite pleased with what had been forecast. They sat down on the next block, and had ice cream. The women passing along on the sidewalk in their modish clothes had great fascination for Jenny and Susan. One such modern type sat alone at the table opposite. Hair peroxided and eyebrows plucked and pencilled. Her lips and cheeks were rouged, and the dress she wore was so short and narrow that it could have fitted in her little handbag. Her fur cape was thrown across the chair beside her. Jenny and Susan thought this flapper the height of sophistication, as she took out her powder compact and fixed her face. Then from her handbag, she drew out a long cigarette holder and placed a cigarette in it. They were mesmerised. Naturally, Brian ran forward to light her cigarette and received a winning smile for his trouble. The time came to say goodbye, and a yellow cab was very soon dropping Susan back at the corner of Fifty-Fourth and Park.

Lotta was at the door with the baby when she got to the house. "You're to take Freddy to the sitting room at seven-thirty, Susie. Mrs Howlett's having dinner guests. She wants to show Freddy off."

"Oh gosh! I'll have to put my uniform on and ..."

"I'll start his bath for you while you get ready. You got a half-hour, honey." Lotta carried Freddy upstairs while she spoke. "Did you enjoy your day out?"

"Oh, it was wonderful, Lotta. I'll tell you all about it later, OK?"

At precisely seven-thirty, Susan appeared with the baby in the sitting room. He was dressed in pyjamas and robe, ready for bed. The smart guests turned round to take in little Freddy and his nanny. "Oh, my little cutie," cooed Betty Howlett. She kissed the plump cheek while Susan stood leaning against the sofa in her grey uniform. The child was passed from group to group. There were about a dozen people having cocktails, but Howard was not among them. The talk was high-toned stuff about art exhibitions and literature. One couple spoke in loud voices of James Joyce and the publishing of his book. It seemed that Ulysses was all the rage in New York.

"Sure, Harry, I read about the book in the paper. Haven't you read about it? They say Joyce has written a masterpiece. It all takes place on one day in Dublin, and it's supposed to be totally incomprehensible. I can't wait to read it."

Several of the ladies had long cigarette holders, held in elbow-length gloved hands. Almost everyone was smoking and drinking from wide-mouthed wine glasses. Susan felt gauche and ignorant in the short time she was among them. When it was time to take Freddy back upstairs, as she gathered his things, she heard someone say, "Where are we going after dinner, Betty? They say the Purple Pup's fun."

"Yeah!" said another. "There are poetry readings at ten and a jazz band at midnight." The phonograph was playing jazz as Susan got to the door with the baby. Two or three of the guests started to dance wildly to the music, including Betty with a twenty-something young man. His name was Oliver. "OK," Oliver said to Betty. "What do you say to the Purple Pup tonight, hun? The music'll be hot stuff. They say Ellington might drop in."

"We'll see what Howard says, Oliver." Betty said. "He'll be home anytime."

Susan hesitated at hearing Howard's name and heard Betty's partner say, "Oh bother, Betty. I thought it would be fun just you and me. I didn't think Howard would be coming."

"You never stop trying, do you, Oliver?" But she gave him a flirty kiss just the same.

Susan closed the door and carried Freddy slowly up the stairs. This was a new Mrs Howlett Susan was seeing tonight. A Mrs Howlett not a little intoxicated and a lady who was obviously enjoying the favours of this young man. Rescued from the clutches of the elegant guests, Susan decided to give the child half an hour with his toys on the carpet before she put him down to sleep. She knew Lotta would be waiting in the kitchen, anxious to hear about her day. There would be a meal set aside for her and some wine, and just maybe she would have a cigarette with Lotta.

As she sat on the floor with Freddy, only half paying attention to what he was doing, there was a tap on the door and Howard appeared. "I've come to say 'goodnight' to my little boy." Freddy jumped up and toddled over to his father. "All ready for bed, son. What a clever boy!" Howard sat down in a low chair to watch his son play with his building blocks. "Had a good day, Susie?"

"Oh, it was dreamy! I went to the Woolworth Building with Jenny and her boyfriend. We saw the whole of New York from the top floor. I'll never forget it."

"I guess you enjoyed it." He pushed a lock of her hair away from her face.

"Yes, and I had my fortune told in a place called the Mad Hatter."

"You had your fortune told, really? And what great future awaits you, then?"

"Oh!" she was embarrassed. "It's a secret."

"So it's like that. 'You will one day find a really great love', she said." He was putting on a deep, portentous voice, and his eyebrows were screwed together in mock seriousness.

"Don't be silly."

"Oh, well, if you won't tell me I'll go away. I know you want to put junior here to bed and skedaddle down to tell Lotta all your news."

She stood up and smiled. "It was so good of you to find my friend, Jenny, for me. And I met Brian, her friend, and his mother. She gave us luncheon. I can't thank you enough, Howard."

His eyes grew inscrutable as he looked at her. "It was nothing, Susie. I'd do anything for you. Well, almost anything!" He looked around the warm nursery, with its pastel-painted walls, soft lamps, toys and talcum powder smell. "Have you written home yet?"

"Yes, I wrote to Tommy. He's ... he's missing me."

"I don't blame him. I miss you and, oh, I miss Freddy, too, all day long."

She tried to laugh this remark off, but he held her shoulders and looked into her eyes. She raised her hands in an attempt to stop the kiss, but it was too late. The sweetness of desire and longing were revealed in his embrace. "Goodnight, Susan. I – we – I think everyone is going on to a night club after dinner, so – anyway. I'm glad you enjoyed your day." And he was gone.

Confusion filled her. This is not right, but so wonderful! she thought. She put Freddy to bed, just as his eyes were closing. She would keep the new secret to herself. No one would know. She had plenty to speak about to Lotta and Bella. This love she felt was forbidden, but so hard to deny. Where will this all end? Oh my God! She must control herself. She must stop it. She put it out of her mind, and escaped to the kitchen and her friends. She would tell them something of her exciting day.

CHAPTER 11

The lane was narrow and steep with high trees on either side, dark and mysterious in winter. It was known locally as Lovers' Lane, and it led from the suburban houses out to the fields of the country- side. Archie and Sheila stood in the leafy darkness, locked in each other's arms.

"It will soon be Christmas," Archie murmured in Sheila's ear.

"I know. What will you give me?"

"All my love. I've nothing more."

"Will you take me to the pictures on Saturday?"

"I can't think of anything more wonderful than to take you to the pictures." He kissed her and squeezed her young body close to his. "Wear your pink dress, the one you wore that first day, you know, when we came home by train together."

"You liked it?"

"It's a beautiful dress. Just like you are beautiful. You would win anybody's heart, even if you wore a piece of sackcloth." His hands began to explore her warm, curving body.

"Please don't, Archie. You mustn't!" and she drew away from him.

Archie sighed. "Right! We'd better get you home. Anyway, I have an essay to finish."

"Oh! You and your essays!"

"Well, I've got to work to get my degree. When I'm a teacher, I'll be better off and not constantly 'financially embarrassed', as the saying goes."

"You do talk funny."

They walked through the streets of new houses with their cheery lighted windows and tiny front gardens with little patches of lawn. "Does your mother know who you are going out with?" he asked.

"No, I haven't told her."

"Oh, well, she probably won't like her precious only child going out with a poor student, who's also a Catholic and a member of the Independent Labour Party."

"Are you one of those agitators who go to public meetings and shout things at the speaker?"

"Well, that's the only way to improve the lot of the working class, by agitation. They're not going to give us houses and better wages without a fight. There's a meeting on Glasgow Green on Saturday afternoon. Would you like to go with me to hear the speakers?"

"My father would kill me. He hates all this talk of workers' rights and revolution."

"That's because he has a good regular job as an insurance man. He doesn't feel any solidarity with the ordinary workers."

"You'll be a graduate, a teacher soon. That's not ordinary. You'll be important."

"Listen, my little Venus de Milo. Being a teacher doesn't make me stop from thinking about politics and people's rights."

"I think politics is boring. I'd like to move out of the tenements and have a nice new house with a bathroom, and maybe three bedrooms, and well, you know, nice furniture. They're building lovely houses out at Garrowhill."

They had reached her building, and stood together for a few minutes at the close-mouth, delaying their parting. At last Archie held Sheila tightly in his arms, and kissing her forehead, whispered,

"Goodnight, my darling." Then he broke away and stood for a few seconds to see the young girl hurry to her parents' house, before turning to walk the mile or so to his own home.

Lost in thoughts of his sweetheart, he felt happy and fulfilled as never before. As he passed along the quiet road, under the gas lamps, the shadow of two figures emerged from a close-mouth in a building on the other side of the main road. The two clung together very briefly and then parted, the woman going one way and the man slowly making his way in the other direction. Once the woman turned round to look at the retreating man. Archie watched her and following her look he recognised something in the gait of the man. It was Edward. He felt a stab of sorrow as the awfulness of the realisation came over him. Madge Morrisey again! What was his brother doing? They drew near on opposite sides of the roadway and slowed down. Archie crossed over and approached Edward, who took the initiative. "Where have you been, Archie?"

"Out for a walk."

"With that wee lassie?"

"Aye!" Cowardice had overcome Archie, and he couldn't bring himself to challenge his brother. He was sad and disappointed at what he had witnessed.

Edward, hiding his alarm at almost being caught with Madge, said gruffly, "I'll away home to my bed. I'll say goodnight, then."

"Goodnight, Ned." The two men went their opposite ways.

Head down against the cold, Edward hurried homewards, a nervous guilt now niggling at his conscience. Had Archie seen him with Madge? No! Of course not. It was far too dark. He put the idea out of his mind. When he reached the cramped tenement which was his home, he found Honor ironing the children's clothes. The kitchen was silent, and she looked tired, her shoulders slumped, and her hair hanging almost straight and lifeless. He noted her abstracted expression, and knew she was lost in reveries of golden curls and baby smiles of their dead child. Try as she would in the months that had passed, she could not get the child from her thoughts. She realised she had been ironing the same garment for five minutes, and looked up startled as Edward came home.

"You're sober tonight, then?"

"Aye," he sat down and started to unlace his shoes. "Is there a cup of tea going?"

Silently she made tea, conscious of his eyes on her, knowing she did not please him, and too tired to care. For his part, his mind was in a whirl. He must look normal and show no sign of his evening's infidelity. But he could not stop his memory from calling up days that had gone by. Where had his lovely bride gone to? Who was this scullery maid of a woman with the crumpled, sad face? How had he tied himself to this?

"Who did you see tonight at the pub?" she asked as she put the cup and saucer down beside him.

"Oh, some of the railway folk – well, a couple of them. And I met Archie coming home from walking out with that wee Sheila Charlton. She'll lead him a merry dance by the look of her."

"Your mother won't like it if he spends a lot of time with her. It'll keep him off his studies."

"Aye, that's true enough. Mother'll read the riot act. And she won't be pleased that the girl's not a Catholic either."

"You're right. That'll not do for your mother."

"No." He finished his tea. "I'm off to bed. By the way, I've to go to Mallaig with the diver next week."

"Oh." Honor only partly came out of her reverie to receive this news.

"You'll manage the children OK, won't you?"

"I suppose so. I'll just have to."

"Maybe one of your sisters will come and stay with you. Stella or Elsie."

"Oh, they've other fish to fry. We'll see."

Edward hid his excitement at the thought of escaping the domestic deadness that was his life now. And Madge would try and meet him – way out of sight of prying eyes in the remoteness of the West Highlands, and there they could consummate their love. His usual book forgotten, Edward retired to bed to be alone with thoughts of his new love.

Next morning, as he picked up his dinner sandwiches to leave for work, Honor looked up from pulling a sweater over little Jamie's head, "When are you to go to Mallaig?"

"Next Monday. Jimmy Gilmour's going with me. We've to inspect the pier foundations."

"Well listen, you know we haven't been out anywhere for a long time. My sister Veronica has invited us to dinner next Sunday. That's the day before you are to go. Will that be all right?"

"Your well-off sister and her fancy husband." Edward frowned.

"They're not that well off. Veronica is trying to be kind and helpful to get us back to normal."

Edward looked at her and the two children as they sat on the rug. Then he said, "Oh, they're well off, right enough, her and Willie. They've no bairns and plenty of money. I don't know if I can stomach their china plates, and perfect table manners."

"Please, Edward. For my sake. It'll be a change for us – and save me making a Sunday dinner."

He reached the door. "We'll see. I'm late for work." Nana ran to be kissed, lisping her goodbyes. Honor knew from the way he spoke that he would probably agree to go with her to Veronica's, and she walked to the mirror to survey her appearance.

"What on earth will I do with myself? My hair's so untidy, and I seem to have developed bags under my eyes and even some wrinkles around my mouth. At least my neck is still smooth." She made a plan to go to her mother's house later that day to ask for help with shampoos and hairstyles, and to borrow some make-up and a dress from one of her sisters.

As usual, her mother's house was a hive of industry. Lily was knitting herself a jumper. Stella was doing the washing-up. Her mother was bent over the oven, and Jack was polishing his boots for the next day at work. Elsie was curling her auburn hair with curling tongs, trying to copy a hairstyle from a magazine she was studying, and alternately looking in the mirror above the sideboard. "There's my cream print you could have, Honor. It's quite warm and there's a little bolero jacket. Try it on, my pet." They went together into the little bedroom and got rid of their father so that Honor could change in private. The noise of their father's breeding canaries, singing loudly, drowned out the chatter and laughter of the two sisters.

"Do you think you'll marry Jim Shields, Elsie?"

"Maybe. His family's quite well off. They have their own shop, you know."

"But do you love him?"

"Oh, yes, I think so. Look, I've made this dark silhouette photograph of me on West Kilbride beach. I've coloured the sky with pinkish clouds. It's for his Christmas present. I've called it *West Kilbride by Night*. I'm going to copy a few of these for presents. What do you think?"

"Very arty, Elsie! It looks like an advertisement for Evening in Paris. The silhouette makes your figure so slim. You've no breasts or bum for that matter. So romantic."

"That's the fashion, my dear sister. Neither bum, bust nor belly, as our vulgar mother would say." They both giggled at the idea. "Oh, you're lucky, Honor, away from old Louisa, and all her bossing and bullying. She keeps trying to stop me going out with Jim. Doesn't want to lose my wages from the household. Well, I'll give her the slip some day. I think I'll elope. Who wants a wedding with old Sarah Bernhardt presiding over everything?"

"Oh, Elsie. You're awful!"

"She's awful. She made our Jack smoke ten cigarettes one after the other, to try and make him stop smoking. And he's twenty-two. She keeps trying to split him up from that girl Frances Young he's mad about. She interferes in everything."

They returned to the kitchen where their father was teaching Jack how to be a boxer according to the Marquis of Queensberry rules. Dressed only in long johns, they looked a comical pair. Louisa was now scrubbing bread and cake tins, while Stella cleaned the oven. They were preparing for a big bake-up. Mrs Dryden had been asked by the committee of the newly constructed bowling green and clubhouse if she would do the catering, as her scones and cakes were so highly thought of.

"Thanks for the loan of the dress, Elsie."

"That's nothing. You know you're very welcome. Maybe I'll see you next Saturday at the Bowling Green opening. You can use the frock to go to our Veronica's house in, and hold on to it for the Saturday. I think everyone's going to dress up, hoping for a sunny day."

Their day for the visit to her sister and for a slap-up Sunday dinner came round, and the little family set out for the short walk there. The superior apartment was a home where everything gleamed. Here the furniture was heavy and solid, and beautifully kept. The tablecloth of finest silk damask with a lace overlay looked elegant and inviting. From the kitchen came mouth-watering smells of beef roasting and home-made apple tarts. Through the high windows with their rich white lace screens, the sun shone brightly. The whole house had an air of richness and contentment.

Edward and Honor and the children were ushered into a Victorian parlour, furnished with over-stuffed armchairs and couches, and tables and shelves holding many ornaments and photographs. Against the wall was an impressive upright piano left open, with the music on the stand sitting ready to be played. Veronica and her burly husband, Willie, a travelling salesman for a furniture firm, were keen on music, and often had musical evenings when their guests gathered round the piano to join in singing.

Edward managed to drop the gruff manner he had kept up at home in recent months and, to Honor's relief, succeeded in dredging up from his past some of the social manners he had once used. The children were playing on the carpet, and Honor joined her sister in the kitchen to help with the food.

Veronica's husband wore a good suit and had the air of being prosperous and contented. Slightly portly, although not much older than Edward, he made his brother-in-law seem like a dishevelled boy. Secretly Willie was a little envious of this working-class man. He was aware that Edward was renowned in the area for his wide reading and for his knowledge of politics and recent history. Locals called on Edward for advice in a crisis, or just to get his opinion on what the government were saying.

"And how's the railway these days, Ned?" Willie tried not to sound pompous.

"Still hard work and not enough money, Willie."

"They tell me you're the union representative for your department."

"Aye, we've got ninety-five per cent of the men in the union now. I'm voted as their representative, so I do my best."

"You're not planning a strike then?

"No, we're in the middle of trying to get paid for our compulsory holidays. It's hard, you know, for family men, trying to get through the two weeks in the summer without pay."

"Aye. I don't suppose many of the men save up for that holiday."

"No." Edward did not wish to continue this line of conversation, knowing the next point would be the money wasted on beer and cigarettes on a Friday and Saturday.

"We're also trying to get them to give sick pay. Sometimes men are injured and they're lucky to get their jobs back after they've been absent from work. Even though it's the railway's fault half the time."

Willie sighed and looked in the fire. "We're lucky to have employment, I suppose, Ned. You hear some terrible tales of poverty with all the unemployment. I have to travel into town every day, and going through the Gallowgate in the morning you see such ragged, poor people. I don't know how they stand their lives, sometimes." Seeing the danger of a full-scale political debate in Edward's expression, Willie changed the subject. "Did I hear you were going to Mallaig again?"

"Aye. I'm off to the Western Highlands tomorrow. Me and Jimmy Gilmour. We're inspecting the pier at Mallaig."

"Lucky man, Ned! I'd love to take Veronica there in the car." Edward listened as Willie described the virtues of his new Morris motor car, finishing by saying that he and Veronica had never been to the Highlands. Edward devoutly hoped that they wouldn't arrive near Mallaig while he was there with Madge Morrisey.

Edward said, "It's beautiful there, right enough, but lonely, you know. There's not much to do but drink in the pubs and hotels, or go fishing, if you're not there to work."

"Well, maybe we could just go walking and look at the lochs. I've a new camera."

"There's plenty of beautiful scenery. You'll find lots to photograph. The mountains are very impressive. But Jimmy and me, we'll be working eight hours a day, no matter what the weather's like. No photographing for us."

"Aye, it's a hard life, Edward. You should never have joined the army in 1914. You should have been like Archie and got yourself an education."

"Maybe. But when I was fourteen, I had to work on a farm for a pittance. My mother and father needed every penny they could get to feed a big family. My sister, Mary, went into nursing, where she got her keep, but I had to work. The army was a good way out then."

They lit cigarettes and spread their legs out to enjoy the heat from the large coal fire. Willie broke the silence. "Do you think the miners will strike?"

Edward bridled at the question. What did he care about the miners? Willie was well set-up. Part of the old-school-tie circuit, and a Freemason to boot. "Listen, Willie. Those poor buggers who go down the mines every day to earn their bread, they deserve a better deal. They risk their lives every day. It's a filthy job."

"Aye. I know their life is hard." Willie wished he could take back his remark.

"And they want to cut their wages, and increase their hours." Ned's voice was rising at the injustice of it all. "It's international capitalism that's to blame. They're buying foreign coal cheap. Our coal-mining industry is suffering."

The situation was saved by Veronica's appearing to call them into the meal. "Talking politics, you two? That won't do for a Sunday. The soup's on the table, and we've got some beer opened."

Veronica had outdone herself. The food was excellent, and the atmosphere and hospitality was like balm to their jagged spirits. When the afternoon had ended, they had the thrill of being taken home in Willie's little Morris car, a taste of paradise for them – a glimpse of another world for Honor and the children.

That night when the children were asleep, a more mellowed Edward took his wife in his arms. The borrowed dress from Elsie, the newly styled hair, and the perfume and powder Honor had used that day had brought back much of her beauty. She was suddenly herself again, the gentle, soft sweetheart he had married. Tears were in his eyes for the past and its sadness, for the beauty of the afternoon they had just passed and for the sin he would commit in Mallaig with

Madge, his other love. He made passionate love to Honor, an act tinged with desperation and frustration, as well as love.

"You still love me then, Edward?"

"Aye."

"You'll miss me when you're away next week?"

"Aye. You're my wife. Of course, I'll miss you and the bairns."

They fell asleep in each other's arms, happy for the first time in many a long day.

CHAPTER 12

From Mallaig there is a regular service of passenger boats that go
out to the Western Isles, to Mull, to Skye and Lewis and Harris.
A spur line of the West Highland Line meets up with the ferry
service, and the pier is the property of the London & North Eastern
Railway, the company that Edward worked for. His job was to work
the machinery which pumped air down to the diver under the
water. The diving gear was crude and cumbersome. Enormous,
heavy brass boots and a great copper helmet had to be worn. The
men had to have total trust in each other to carry out the dangerous
work, but there was a kind of romance about the whole business.

As Edward got himself ready to leave for Mallaig, he kept his
excitement hidden. A week of daring behaviour – he couldn't believe
he was doing this. He could smell the seaweed of that stony shore
and picture the little hotel bedroom from whose windows he would
gaze out on the crashing grey waves, and who knows what else
would happen there.

"Goodbye, Edward." Honor in her nightgown held Jamie in
her arms. "Be careful, and don't take any chances. What's the name
of the hotel you'll be staying at?"

"It's called the Anchor and Chain. It's a Mrs Brown who owns it."

"Well, I'll look for you to be home on Saturday. What time will you get back?"

"I don't know for sure." He was closing up his case and trying to avoid her eyes. "But don't worry, I'll get back all right. Sometime in the early afternoon."

"We might be at the Bowling Green opening, so if I'm not in, you'll know where I'll be. The whole family will be there. My mother is doing the catering. And Dad's to make a speech. And I think there is going to be a band. Try not to miss it, Ned."

"Aye, right, Honor. I'll see if I can bring home some kippers for you from Mallaig."

"That would be lovely. The last ones you brought were just gorgeous." He embraced her and the baby, and bent to kiss Nana. "Daddy'll be back soon," he said. He opened the door and was gone.

Honor loved Edward. She loved the black, curly waves of his hair, the set of his head on his shoulders, the way he took up a book when he came home from work and awaited his meal. She was in awe of this strong man who was her husband. Picking up the book he had been reading, she leafed through it to try and take in the meaning of the closely written text. It was *The Decline and Fall of the Roman Empire.* She read:

> Money, in a word, is the most universal incitement, iron the most powerful instrument of human industry, and it is very difficult to conceive by what means a people, neither activated by the one nor seconded by the other could emerge from the grossest barbarism.

Honor pondered these words, and a glimmer of the lofty meaning shone through. That her husband could read this heavy prose for hour after hour of an evening and go greedily back to it the following evening astonished her. Lovingly she lifted his 'pepper and salt' jacket, as he called his tweed sports jacket, from the chair and his good bunnet to put them away in the hall cupboard. She turned to answer a knock at the door.

Veronica was dressed in a well-cut blue suit, a white lace collar just showing from her blouse underneath. "Give me an apron, Honor. I'll dress Jamie." Veronica had taken off her jacket, and was lifting the little boy. "Nana's a clever girl. She's trying to dress herself. Look at this." The toddler was attempting to tie the ribbons of her dress. "When will Ned be back?"

"Next Saturday."

"That's the day of the Bowling Green opening. Mam's been asked to do some baking. There's to be a grand tea. And there's a four-piece band. I think Dad's going to sing. Are you going to be able to come?"

"I've said I would go. Told Edward I was looking forward to it, but ..." she sighed as she folded up the washing, "Veronica, you know how unpredictable children are." Already Honor was getting cold feet about going into such a big crowd for fear she would be pointed out as the poor soul who lost her child in a tragic accident. She looked uncertain, and Veronica raised her voice. "Look! There's to be no excuses. I'll lend you my cinnamon crepe dress. It'll hide your tummy." She paused, "You're not pregnant again, are you?" A rush of blood to Honor's face gave the game away.

"Oh, Veronica, don't say anything!" She was shamefaced.

"My God, does Edward know?"

"Well, I'm not totally sure yet. So, I haven't told him."

Veronica put her arms around her sister, "Drink your tea, girl. In some ways, I envy you. Look at me. Thirty-four years old and neither chick nor child, as they say. How I would love a baby, but God has not favoured Willie and me."

"You have everything else, Veronica – a beautiful house, a piano. How I would love a piano. I can still play a little. Remember that teacher, Mrs Grant, and how she used to hit your fingers with a ruler if you played a wrong note?" Honor giggled.

"Look, Honor, I've a friend in the factor's office. I'm going to try and get you and Ned one of those new houses that are going up just past the church."

"We can't afford the rent." Honor was a bit agitated by this proposal.

"Don't worry, you'll manage. I'll see to that." She rose to go, "I'll bring you something back from the butcher for your dinner. Gosh! It's almost eleven, Edward will be almost in Mallaig by now. You'd better get your washing hung out on the line, Honor, it's a nice sunny morning."

Edward, seated on the train with his mate Jimmy Gilmour, was absorbing the mile after mile of spectacular scenery revealed as the little steam train made its way north. Both men were reduced to silent musing as the still snow-topped mountains loomed up before them. The train went where no roads were, and few people had seen the grandeur of the lochs and hills of this part of Scotland. After months of looking at old sheds and huts, of smelly slum tenements and clanging tramcars and street cries, the peace and beauty of the remote mountain area was calming to the two men. It was early spring, and some of the trees were showing touches of green again, after the long winter. Now and again, signs of previous habitation in the form of ruined walls and piles of stone could be seen by the side of a loch, and sometimes, the keen eye would see grazing deer herds, which suddenly took off and came thundering across the mountainsides.

"We're a lucky pair, Ned, to come up to this place for a week. There's just no place like it on earth."

"Aye. You could only be in Scotland. The way the hills rise up from the lochs is just breathtaking. As you say, Jimmy, we're lucky." Edward passed his mate his packet of Capstan cigarettes, and they lit up and settled back for a few more contented hours in this interlude of peace and beauty.

In Mallaig, the Highland air was clean and fresh. The harbour was as busy as ever with fishing boats being cleaned and prepared for the evening's fishing. Around them, the gulls wheeled and cried in a never-ending backdrop to the life of the little town. Installed in the Anchor and Chain with a cheery welcome from Mrs Brown, who provided them with a hearty meal of soup, herring and boiled potatoes, and more scones and cups of tea than they could possibly cope with, the two men ordered themselves each a glass of whisky. They would have to hire a boat and set up their diving machinery on the next day. A path around the herring boats in the crowded harbour would have to be negotiated, and the dark pillars of the pier inspected and tested. Meanwhile, they would rest and talk, taking in the new faces around them, the accent and mores of the Highlanders, so soft and gentle as they seemed to these city men.

Presently Edward stood up. "I'm going to take a walk, Jimmy. I've an old friend to see tonight. I'll be back about ten. Then we can have a dram together, if you like." Jimmy looked startled, but he was a man of the world. Like Ned, he had been in the Great War and he was not easily shocked. Besides he had heard rumours about Edward's peccadilloes.

"Aye, right, Ned. Fine. Fine. We'll just make it one dram when you come back, though, since we'll be working in the morning. I'll have a read at the paper while you're away."

The smell of seaweed was in the cold, salty breeze when Edward walked to the harbour. The gulls were silent now in the evening dusk, as his nervous steps took him towards the sea. She was waiting by the pier. Dressed in a long leather coat with a heavy fur collar, she stood looking at the boats and walking slowly as if out to enjoy the evening air, when Ned appeared. He joined her and they continued to walk, trying not to draw attention to themselves in that remote town, peopled as it was by devout Presbyterians for whom it was nothing for them to attend church three times on the Sabbath.

They were suffused with passion for each other, but it had to be hidden. They must appear like respectable friends meeting in this quiet area. The waves crashed on rhythmically as they conversed.

"It's good you got here, then, Madge? It's good to see you."

"Aye, you, too. I arrived yesterday, but it has been lonely without you." She stepped into the shadows. "Kiss me, Ned." They embraced passionately, all their longing and desire for each other rising to the surface.

"I have to be back at the hotel before ten. You know what they're like in the Highlands, Madge. There's Jimmy Gilmour, too. I have to think what he might be thinking. We don't want to court disaster. And the landlady likes to lock up the place. Late nights are frowned on."

"I know they're very narrow-minded up here in the North. I'll be careful." Madge's face was flushed with excitement. To have her beloved so near, and all to herself, made her feel quite weak. "I've told the landlady that my fiancé was coming up to work on the pier. She won't mind if you are half an hour or so in my room, I'm sure."

Edward kissed her fondly. "I'll call round tomorrow night after we get washed up and have had our meal. I'll call on you about eight-thirty. It's too late tonight."

"Oh, try to make it for eight o'clock, Ned. It'll be such a long day for me."

"I'll try, my love. I'll try."

They wandered around the little town lost in each other and the excitement and happiness that this love had brought them. "This is heaven, Ned, to have you here all to myself. I've longed for this so much."

"Aye, it's lovely to see you and talk to you without fearing that someone will come along and point a finger at us."

"You don't feel guilty about Honor and the children?"

Uncertainly he paused, then said that he did not think his wife had much interest in him any more. His eyes misted over. He felt confused and unhappy suddenly and found himself saying, "All she really cares about are the children. That's the kind of woman she is. When wee Louie died, she just went to pieces. Children are her real reason for living. I'm just on the sidelines for her."

"Well, you're my reason for living, Ned." They stopped walking to embrace each other in the darkness of a doorway. "Yes, Ned, I'm afraid some women only want men so they can have babies. Then their husbands might just as well not exist."

They had reached the edge of the cliffs, and Edward wheeled Madge round, her hair flying in the wind. "I'm glad I exist for you, Madge. You're all woman."

"Stop, Edward! Stop! We're near the edge. We'll fall over!" He stopped swinging her and they collapsed on the grass laughing.

Madge took his rugged face in her hands. "Tomorrow we'll go for a walk down to a little pub I've seen at the other end of the town. It's cosy and private, then I'll take you back for a drink in my room. I've a bottle stashed away. And other surprises!" and she flashed him an enticing smile.

"You're the best thing that's ever happened to me, Madge. You've changed my life."

Next day the work was cold and dangerous. Several times the diver went down into the icy, grey water and several times the great weight of him in his brass boots and helmet had to be hauled up into the little boat. Edward had enlisted a young man from the village to help with the winch. At midday, they retired to the hotel for a meal and a chat with the locals.

"They tell me they have an underground railway in Glasgow. Have you been on it?" a lilting Highland voice enquired.

"Sure. It's very fast. It goes under the River Clyde, you know."

"Do you tell me that?" The questioner was amazed.

Another weather-beaten fisherman spoke up.

"I have a brother in Govan. He's been a year in Glasgow, but he misses his home here. He meets up with other men from the North, at some bridge in the middle of Glasgow."

"Aye. That'll be the Central Station Bridge in Argyle Street. We call it 'the Heilander's Umbrella', because you can't move for them there on a Sunday afternoon."

"Aye, our Donnie misses his home, here in Mallaig, and the family, but the wages are quite good on the docks. He goes to picture shows and sometimes the theatre, and you have all those marvellous shops, things we don't have here."

The two workers rose to return to their work. "You can't have everything in this life, no matter how lucky you are, Hamish."

At nine o'clock that evening, Edward was in Madge's room. The pent-up emotion and desire of the past few months was an ocean sweeping over him, and he pushed his hands under her blouse to reach her full breasts. But the experienced Madge controlled this passionate attack, and bid Edward sit at the foot of the bed while she slowly undressed, and carefully folded her clothes and removed her jewellery. Then she took the pins out of her dark hair and faced him with only a cotton lace petticoat remaining.

"Now you," she said. "I'll turn the gaslight down, if you're shy." She walked towards the fireplace and by the time the light had been lowered, he was naked and aroused, facing her. He made love to her like a starving man at a feast, with little thought for her responses. But she didn't care, for she had lusted after this strong handsome man for so long, that she felt a great happiness at this proof of his passion and the consummation of her desire. Later, when they made love again, he was less in haste, and aroused in her a great ecstasy so that she wished it would last forever. "That woman you married is not getting you back. You were meant for me, Ned."

"She would think differently, I can tell you."

"What can we do? I don't want to live without you. What do you think we should do?"

"What do I think? I think life's a bugger. Here I am, a happy man with a woman I love, but the world sees things different. We feel it couldn't be more right, but the rest of the world thinks it couldn't be more wrong. And Honor and the children, the picture of them in my mind will not go away, and that's it!" He rose from the bed and started to dress.

"What do you mean 'that's it'?"

"Madge, I love you. We are great together. We have another three days, and then I must go back to my family."

"You mean you'd give up our love for that scheming little slut you married?"

"Madge, you can say a lot of things about Honor. She's cold to me, almost sexless. She cares for nothing but the children. She does not look after her appearance. She's not very bright, but ..." his voice was louder now and harsh, "... she's not a slut and she's not scheming."

"Well, a cold, silly bitch, then."

"That's enough, Madge. I'll see you tomorrow if you still want to."

She ran to the door where he stood with his hand on the doorknob. "Of course I do. I'd die for you, Ned." She pulled him close to her pointed breasts and sought his mouth greedily. "Good night, sweetheart."

That evening, Edward made his way back to the Anchor and Chain through the dimly lit street of the fishing port. His heart was full of excitement at the embraces of Madge, but in his head, guilt and frustration fought with each other, and his self-image was dented. Somehow his mother's face kept coming into his mind. Drawing his coat around him against the breeze from the water, he promised himself a double whisky when he reached his friend, Jimmy, at the bar.

CHAPTER 13

The April sunshine rose on the new red-roofed building and the smooth green grass of the new bowling green. Situated next to the Miners' Welfare Hall, and just five minutes walk from William and Louisa Dryden's house, the idea had been thought up by the Glassblowers' Association, and the recreation of bowling was to be a boon to their workers and to many others of the local people. As the opening day had slowly drawn near, an excitement had grown among like-minded people and a club was quickly formed. Louisa had been asked to bake scones and cakes for the opening ceremony. William had to hire a band, and arrange a programme of musical entertainment for the afternoon. Tickets had been on sale for a week and, if the spring rain stayed away, a good turnout was expected.

Honor, flushed with the effort of dressing the two children and herself in their best clothes, managed to get along to the event, the curly hair of the little ones catching the eyes of the leisurely crowd at the entrance gate. "You're looking well today, Honor. It must be that herbal tea your father used to make you take that has given you a nice skin. And what lovely children!" It was Mrs Woods, a neighbour, talking.

"Well, I certainly had to drink plenty of it to please him." Honor laughed and nodded as she walked with her pushchair holding Jamie with little Nana walking alongside. Edward would be home today, sometime, and there was a spring in the step of Honor as she went along. Lights of gold glinted in the brown of her hair, which she had dressed into two long ringlets drawn back with a velvet bow. A softness had returned to her face as the sadness of the recent past faded and when her elder sister, Veronica, appeared Honor gave her a smile.

"You look stunning in that dress, Veronica! What a beautiful print. Trust you to outshine everyone else."

"You don't look so bad yourself, Honor. That frock suits your colouring. It's just a bit loose on you. Have you seen our Elsie? She's had her hair bobbed and set in great waves round her head. A Marcel wave, she calls it. She's helping to set the tea tables." Honor looked anxiously towards the clubhouse where she could see her mother, and other members of the family, scurrying around, getting everything ready for the crowds. "You've enough to do, Honor, looking after these two. Don't you bother trying to help. Is Ned coming?"

"Yes, I expect he'll be home from Mallaig this afternoon, so maybe he'll find his way here. He'll want to see the children. I'll take a walk round the green, and see you later, Veronica." Honor drifted on, nodding to people she knew. The looks of sympathy had gone from people's faces, now that so many months had passed since the tragedy, and other events had crowded in to cover the past.

"And where's the famous Edward today, Honor? He's got no right to leave you alone. Somebody might steal you." It was Billy Bell, her old flame, the boy she had been with on the night she met Edward. He was from Yorkshire like herself, an incomer to Glasgow.

"Hello, Billy! Nice to see you. How are you?" She was a little embarrassed at this meeting.

"Oh, well, you know, not bad. I've got a job in Pettigrew & Stephens' department store. I'm training as a gent's outfitter. It's not bad."

"You're not married then?"

"No. Still pining for you," he grinned.

"What nonsense!" But she blushed just the same.

"Come along and we'll have a cup of tea. This is too good a chance to miss." He took Nana's hand, and they sat down and were served tea and scones while the waltz music of the little band gave their meeting a festive air. When the melody changed, Billy, with his fair, English good looks, leaned towards her, joining in with the band, singing, "*If you were the only girl in the world, and I were the only boy.*"

"Billy! People will see you!"

"So what! I'll never meet another girl like you. You are the sweetest girl in the world, and I don't care who hears me."

Honor lifted Jamie onto her knee. "You mustn't say such things, Billy. Look at me. I'm an old married woman."

"You're twenty-five, the same age as I am. If that Edward Denny ever gives you cause to be unhappy, then come and tell me. You know I'd do anything for you."

She was touched by the sincerity in his voice. "Billy, I ..." A shadow fell over the table. She looked up to see Edward.

"Daddy!" Nana threw herself into her father's arms. Jamie strained towards the dark-haired man with his sunburned face, and Honor gave a broad smile as Edward took little Jamie in his arms.

"So, Billy, how are you?" The two men shook hands, Edward being slightly overshadowed by the taller Billy.

"I'm not bad, Ned. How was your trip to Mallaig? "

"Hard work, you know. Hard work."

"Well, you're a lucky man with such a lovely wife and family to come back to."

"Yes. I know. " Edward looked at the picture the trio made on that sunny afternoon. "I know I'm lucky." He had forgotten how bonny Honor could be.

"Here's your brother Archie coming and with a nice little girl in tow."

Sheila was introduced and the group chatted together. Presently Archie and Edward broke away from the others to arrange to meet on Sunday afternoon. "The meeting's in Glasgow Green. There's going to be good speakers there. It's about the miner's strike. I'll call for you at half past one tomorrow."

"Oh, Archie, he's just home from the Highlands, and you've got him going to meetings already!" Honor was peeved.

"Politics are unavoidable these days. There's going to be a big strike, and we'll all be affected whether we like it or not."

At another table, Honor's brother Jack was sitting with a very pretty local girl and Louisa, busying herself around the tables with a large kettle of tea, had interrupted her tea pouring, to talk to her son and his new girlfriend. Jack was a handsome twenty-two-year-old, and his mother adored him.

"Frances Young, isn't it?" and the older woman eyed up the young girl.

"Yes, that's right, Mrs Dryden."

"I thought so. You're the image of your mother when she was your age. She was Mary Bonnar in those days."

"I wish she had come here today, Mrs Dryden. You've made a lovely job of the tea. The cakes and scones are very nice. My mother would have loved them."

Louisa nodded curtly and returned to her job of supervising the tea serving. Later, when she saw Jack alone, Louisa whispered urgently to him. "Are you seriously going with that girl?"

"Serious? I don't know. I've been taking her out for a few weeks."

"Why didn't you tell me?"

"I never thought to tell you."

"Well, I don't approve."

"Mother, she's a lovely girl."

William Dryden ambled up to them. "What's this? What's this, Jack? Arguing with your mother on this great day?"

"Did you know, William, he's courting Mary Bonnar's daughter?"

Jack caught a fleeting look on his father's face. "What's wrong with that, Dad? Frances is a nice girl."

"Mary Bonnar is a hateful woman, a gossip and a liar. She spends half the day standing in the street spreading rumours with her cronies. I don't like her. Besides, there's tuberculosis in that family.

Jack paled, but he said, "So what?"

"Exactly, Louisa! Leave the boy alone."

"You're as daft as him, William Dryden. The girl will be just like her mother in a few years. It's bred in the bone." Jack started to stutter an answer but thought better of it. He turned his back on them and went in search of his girl.

As Honor and Edward, with their little family, progressed towards the gate to leave the green, the sun was going down. Louisa, to much cheering, had been given the honour of throwing the first bowl. William had pleased the crowd with a rendering of 'Bonnie Scotland I Adore Thee', and everyone was well content with the afternoon. At the gate two figures appeared, the taller of the two women being Madge Morrisey, the other her friend, Rose. With their make-up and jewellery, they stood out from the crowd. Madge was a vision in yellow linen, with white silky high-heeled shoes, her dark wavy hair a massive frame around her rouged face. Rose had a white linen dress with much imitation gold jewellery. Madge spoke first.

"So you got your husband back, Honor."

"Yes," Honor's smile showed how pleased she was. "He's been in Mallaig all week."

"Has he?" Madge looked at Edward and caught his pained expression.

"Did you enjoy it, Edward?" and she added when he looked lost for an answer, "Being away without any responsibilities?"

"I was working, Madge. Earning a living, you know." There was a touch of warning in his expression.

"I see. Well, Mallaig's a lovely place to go to, anyway." She looked at Rose and laughed. "Quite a change from the noisy city. I'll be seeing you." She looked from Edward to Honor, and patted the children's heads. "Goodbye. Be good, now!" They moved off together with much smiling.

"Gosh, she's a bit overpowering in broad daylight, isn't she? Did you smell her perfume? It could have knocked you down."

Edward grunted and lifted Nana. "Let's get home, I'm starving."

"Yes, I've got a nice piece of steak for your supper, and I've got something to tell you."

When the meal was over and the children in bed, Honor told Edward of Veronica's suggestion. "She says she's almost certain to get us a house beside her in York Terrace, Edward. The one she's after for us has a bathroom. And I know you'll say it's too dear for us. It's five shillings a week more than we pay just now, but Veronica says she'll help us for a while and pay the difference until we get on our feet."

In spite of himself, Edward was excited at this news. "There's a view of the hills from that building."

"Yes, the flat is on the first floor. I've seen it, Ned. And I thought we would take it. We'll manage the rent somehow, and maybe we could even buy a wireless."

"A wireless?" Edward was amazed.

"Yes. They're coming down in price. We could pay it up without telling anyone, you know. Oh, Edward, it will be just great!"

—·—·—

Sunday dawned fresh and sunny. From around the city, to the sound of church bells, men walked in groups to Glasgow Green where the dew on the thick grass was drying under a bright sun. Rows and rows of cloth-capped men formed around the wooden stand where the speaker had already introduced himself. He stood above a banner which read, 'THE COMING STRUGGLE'.

"Our brothers in the coalmines must be supported. We must prevent the lowering of working conditions, such as is happening to our fellow trade unionists in the mines. This capitalist attack must be stopped!" Cheers of agreement were heard from all parts of the crowd. The speaker, heartened by this, continued in stentorian tones, "I tell you, brothers, a great strike is coming and we must be ready. We must press the Trade Union Council and the Labour Party to set up a Workers' Defence Corps, to prevent victimisation." More cheers were heard at this, and as the speaker paused for breath, heated discussions broke out among the men.

The speaker continued, "Raise awareness in your own workplaces. The call is coming. A general strike of railwaymen, of all transport workers, of dockers, of steel workers and of newspapermen is coming. We will show these capitalist criminals that we have been kept down at their mercy long enough. We want work!" Cheers rang out. "We want a decent pay for a decent day's work!" More cheers. "Let them try the back-breaking digging for coal, bent double hundreds of feet under the ground! Let those idle rich risk their life and limb to get the coal for the railways and steelworks!" Each time he paused there was another shout of approval from the crowd. By the end of an hour or so, when several other speakers had urged preparation for the coming strike, the gathering of men had greatly enlarged, and all were convinced that a battle with the forces of evil was not far away.

Afterwards, Edward and Archie and their friends started on the few miles' walk home, discussing the meeting, and praising the speakers. "You are all right with your solidarity, but how do I get to university each day if the trains, buses and trams are not running?" Archie threw his remarks into the discussion.

"What about me with four children? That's six mouths to feed. I'd rather be in your position, Archie," one of their number remarked.

"I suppose so," Archie had to agree. "And the hellish thing is that I know quite a few of the students are full of anticipation at volunteering to drive trains and act like policemen in the name of patriotism. I hope the strike doesn't happen, I really do."

As they strolled along the main road, four-storey-high tenement buildings on either side of them, crossing side streets where the sun was trying to shine, they lost themselves in political discussion. Edward chipped in, "A strike of all men and women in trade and industry and in public transport, that's our only weapon against exploitation. I hope it does come off." The rest of the party agreed with Edward and indeed he got his wish.

At midnight on Monday, 3rd May, a general strike was called by the Trades Union Congress in support of the miners. Edward's union, the National Union of Railwaymen, claimed to have one hundred per cent of its members on strike. Similar stories were told by the transport unions and those of many other industries. The streets of Glasgow were strangely quiet on that Monday morning without the clanging tramcars, such a noisy feature of the city. Office and shop workers walked back from the local railway stations in disbelief that their trains to the city were not running, the day that no one really believed would happen had arrived.

CHAPTER 14

The opera cloak was of dove-grey colour, a fine serge with a fur collar and lined with grey silk. Louisa had picked it up in the flea market, 'the Barrows', for six shillings. The prize had been brought home draped over her arm, and for two evenings, under the gaslight in her kitchen, and using a safety razor blade, Louisa sat and painstakingly unpicked the seams of the garment. Next the pieces were carefully washed and hung up to dry on the kitchen pulley, high overhead. A paper pattern was adjusted, so that a spring coat could be fashioned for Stella, Louisa's youngest and favourite daughter.

Soon the pedal of the sewing machine was whirring. Skilfully Louisa placed stiffening in the front and padding in the shoulders, and the fitted coat took shape. The grey fur collar of the cape was used to fashion a new collar, and hours were spent sewing by hand the seven buttonholes down the front of the small-waisted princess-line coat. "Come and try this on, now, Stella, my love. I want to pin the places for the buttons to be sewn on."

Stella, slim and pale, with a haughty, actressy manner, probably picked up from some film star, rose at her mother's bidding, and tried on the beautifully lined coat. It fell round her pretty figure in a perfect fit. She threw back her thick wavy hair, so that it fell down past her shoulders against the back of the coat. She primped in front of the mirror over the dresser in the kitchen, turning this way and that in self-admiration. Already she was imagining the looks of interest of the local people, and especially of one young man she had her eye on.

"I like it, Mam, it's lovely!"

At this the door opened and her brother Jack, good-natured Jack, the apple of his mother's eye, appeared, accompanied by Archie Denny.

"Oh! La-di-da! Aren't we the toffs? You look like a film star."

Stella rewarded his compliment with a winning smile, which included the shy Archie who had come to visit.

"Come here, Stella. I want to mark the places for the buttons." Louisa was holding a bundle of pins, which she transferred to her teeth, and with skill she placed them one by one under the buttonholes.

William who had been seated at the fireside reading one of his treatises on herbal remedies, a prize possession brought from England twenty years previously, laid down his book. "How are you, Archie?" And in his gentlemanly manner he stood and shook the young man's hand. "It's nice of you to come and see us."

"I'm fine, thanks, Mr Dryden."

"You must be nearly finished your studies at university, Archie. You've been a long time there."

"Yes, this summer should see me with my degree, with a bit of luck." Archie sat down as invited in the seat opposite the older man.

"I met Archie in the library, Dad. I found you a book, *Common Plants of the British Isles – Their Medicinal Properties.*

William received the book with a smile and was soon immersed in it. Louisa rose from her knees and removed the coat from Stella. "I'm glad to see you don't get yourself tied up with girls, Archie. Not like some fools I could mention. Fancy free, that's the way for a young man to be."

Archie looked downcast and managed to answer, "The girls don't bother with me, I'm afraid, Mrs Dryden. I'm not a lady-killer like Jack here."

Stella glanced in surprise at Archie, "Aren't you still going out with Sheila Charlton?"

"No." Archie's face was a picture of misery. "She's thrown me over."

The three young people moved to the parlour where Stella questioned him sympathetically. "What happened to you two, then?" She and Jack sat close to him to catch what he had to say, his voice being muted with unhappiness.

"Well, I turned up at the Scottish Wool and Hosiery on Wednesday evening to go home with Sheila on the train."

"Don't tell us she stood you up?" Stella's sixteen-year-old eyes were wide with curiosity.

"Not exactly. I arrived just in time to see her step into a smart Riley sports car."

"Whose was it?"

"A smart-looking guy – I don't know who he was – sounded like Derek somebody-or-other. She's so pretty, I'm sure lots of men would ask her out."

Jack put his arm on Archie's hunched shoulders. "Did she see you, there?" he asked.

"Oh, yes, quite brazen she was. Gave me a heart-melting smile and told me she wasn't going home on the train that night. She was going out to dinner."

Stella was riveted by the story. "Did she introduce you to him?"

"Oh, yes. Casually she said, 'Archie, I'd like you to meet my friend, Derek Preston', or something like that. And then, 'Derek, this is Archie Denny. He's an old friend. We travel on the train together sometimes. He's a student'. Then they were off."

Jack stood up and started pacing the parlour. "Maybe it was just a one-off thing for her," he suggested.

"No. I saw her yesterday. I kind of hung around to see her come home. She told me it's over."

Stella looked sad for him. "I'm sorry," she said.

"Trouble is I can't settle to my books, and my mother is nagging me all the time to study."

Hugging him, Stella said soothingly, "Oh, you can't study night and day, Archie. I'm really disappointed in Sheila Charlton. Mind you, she always was a bit shallow."

Archie stood up and changed the subject to control his rising emotions. "I think I'll go over and see Ned. He wants help with a speech he has to make to the Railwaymen's Union."

"Oh God, this bloody strike, Archie! I'm sick of the talk of it," Jack said. "I've just started this job in the railway offices. My pay will be down. Do you think the railway clerks will join the others in the strike?"

Archie looked serious, "I've heard talk of it, Jack."

"Yes, so have I. They've voted in favour,, I know, but no one believes they will strike. If they do, Frances will be really upset." Troubled, he told them of his plans to marry in secret to bypass his mother's disapproval of his sweetheart and her family.

"Congratulations, Jack. You're a lucky man!" Archie slapped his friend on the back. "Well done! I hope you'll be very happy!"

"Thanks, Archie. I hope you find somebody else soon. Listen! You wouldn't think of being my best man on June the 3rd? I'd be really pleased if you could, Archie."

"Why is Mother so against the wedding?"

Jack was troubled by the question and looked down at his feet. "She doesn't like Frances's mother, or any of her family from way back. Some family feud. You know what she's like. Nobody's good enough for her family."

Archie was impatient at this. "Listen, Jack, if you and Frances are happy and sure of each other, that's all that matters. Let the future take care of itself. I know what loneliness is. I know I have my mother, but to have a girl close to your heart, it's wonderful, and you're very lucky."

Stella broke in, "When are you going to tell Mother, Jack?"

His handsome face wrinkled in worry. "A few days beforehand. That will give her less time to make trouble. I should tell Father, to be fair, but it will be easier if I don't. He'll understand."

"Maybe," smiled Archie, "we could have a secret party when the storm dies down. Yeah, I'll speak to Ned about it. He's good at throwing parties."

"There's going to be a shortage of money with the strike," grumbled Jack, "but what's new?"

"Cheer up, Jack. Our Joe will be home from the sea. He makes any party go with a swing. He's great on the banjo. OK?"

"Thanks, Archie. You're a pal. Roll on June!"

Within a few days the strike was a reality for everyone. All other subjects of discussion paled into insignificance as Britain divided into two camps, the striking workers and those against the strike. Edward, as a union representative, was a member of the Area Strike Committee. One of his tasks was to distribute official bulletins issued by the Scottish Trades Union Congress in Glasgow. Also he gave out the strike paper, the *Scottish Worker*, to union members. Lines of communication were kept open by couriers who regularly cycled from one district to another. There was heightened excitement everywhere among the strikers at the great show of solidarity.

On the second day of the strike, Edward was reading a strike bulletin when Archie called. "I see a lot of the engineers on the Clyde have come out on strike, even though they've no' been called out."

"Aye, Ned!" Archie's young face was full of smiles. "We've got them on the run, this time. But you know it was bad tactics not to call out the engineers. They should have called out the whole Clyde."

"Maybe they were thinking about food supplies."

"Aye. But I still think they're wrong. They should have called out the engineers."

Edward continued, "I hear some of your fellow students from the university volunteered for emergency work to break the strike. I'm disappointed that educated boys could do that. Bastards! – taking the bread out of the mouths of the workers."

"Mind you," Archie took a seat opposite his brother, "it's only a few hundred blacklegs out of over four thousand at Glasgow University. At Edinburgh University, over half the students have volunteered for strike-breaking work. And, I've heard that at St

Andrews every student at the university has signed up for the Government's Emergency Organisation. They've been promised a lot of money, and they have had their examinations postponed. Lucky sods!"

"Well, I'm glad the students in Glasgow have got more morals than those privileged parasites in Edinburgh and St Andrews. At least they're not working against their fellow men, the most of them, anyway." Edward sounded tired and bitter.

"They say Edinburgh Corporation has promised to pay the Edinburgh students double time for working on the trams and buses. No wonder they're tempted. I could be doing with such money," Archie looked ruefully at the fireplace.

Honor joined from her position at the kitchen sink. "Mrs Thomson, upstairs, told me that there were women in the Gallowgate throwing stones at any trams that were still running. Where will it all end?"

Archie reached in his pocket and produced three pound notes. "Honor, I forgot, my mother sent this money. She thought you might need it." Honor blushed with embarrassment at this gift, but she took it, secretly relieved that the next week's food would be secure.

"Your brother Jack's got a secret, but I think he won't mind me telling you and Ned." Both gave him their undivided attention. "He's going to marry Frances Young on the 3rd of June. It's to be a very quiet ceremony. At the Registry Office." Then he added with a grin, "He wants me to be the best man."

"Oh goodness!" Honor wiped her hands on her apron to hear more of this news. "What will my mother say?"

"Aye," Edward agreed, "auld Louisa'll be livid. Goin' against her wishes. And Jack her favourite son, too."

"You'll say nothing, though. Jack told Stella and me, but he doesn't want your mother to know yet. He's at his wit's end with worry and planning. This strike won't help. Jack's managed to rent a small flat, but it's a bad way to start – with your parents' disapproval."

"Oh, my Dad will be all right about it." Honor stopped her dish drying to muse about the situation. "Poor Jack! He's my favourite out of all the family, too. If he wants to marry Frances, then I for one am happy for him."

"Aye, let him live his own life. Louisa's had her turn." Edward agreed.

Archie continued, "I thought we could have a party for the happy couple, just something quiet, you know."

"Sure we will!" Edward loved talk of social gatherings. "But we can't plan anything while the strike's on."

Archie put down his cup and saucer, "Well, I'd better be getting back to my books."

"I hear you've broken up with Sheila Charlton," Honor said softly.

"News travels fast." Archie hung his head, looking miserable.

Roughly Edward put his arm on Archie's shoulder. "It's for the best, Baldy," his pet name for his brother. "She just wasn't good enough for you, you know."

Archie fought with his emotions. "I was very fond of her ..."

For once it was Edward and Honor's turn to stand back and watch another's grief. Their hearts went out to the disappointed boy. "You'll meet someone else, Archie, you'll see." Honor gave him a hug. He nodded, and unable to discuss the matter any longer, he left hurriedly without saying goodbye.

The strike continued. There was talk of accidents on the railways where students and volunteers were manning trains, for they had little understanding of what they were doing. A bad crash occurred in St Margaret's Tunnel where a train driven by an assistant works manager smashed into another train. This was a refuse train manned by a medical student, and the assistant signalman in the nearest signal box was also a blackleg. Three people were killed and eight were injured. Two women, mothers of large families, were arrested and jailed without bail for throwing stones at buses and tramcars driven by strike-breakers. Hard news was scarce, and so rumours abounded of trenches being dug in the streets by strikers to fight the army which the government had standing by in readiness, and of policemen being killed in riots.

It was Archie who had the idea of producing a local strike bulletin. Unable to travel to university and sick of hours of studying under his mother's watchful eye, he joined with some other ILP members in duplicating on foolscap paper, news of the progress of the strike. It sold for one penny per copy. Happily they crowded into the little local offices at seven each morning to put out the latest news from the couriers, and printed anything gleaned from other sources, such as the radio. By late morning, Edward and Archie and some others were selling their news sheet at street corners and at gatherings all over the area, to the people hungry for news.

The world of the exhausted strike workers fell apart when without warning the strike was called off. They were stunned. It was Wednesday, 12th May. Many were sure that great concessions for the workers had been won, others were angry and booed and hissed their fury at the announcement. Some were reduced to tears at the pointlessness of the whole effort. They felt they had been sold down the river. They cursed the Trades Union Congress and the government, shaking with frustration and despair.

"Well, Ned. You'll have heard that they're no' takin back the shop stewards on the LNER." Danny Devlin, a railwayman, was speaking.

Edward's face paled. They were in a pub on the evening after the call-off of the strike, drinking half pints of beer slowly as there was no money about. "Who says they're no' takin' back the shop stewards, Danny?"

"My brother-in-law frae Cowlairs. He's a union representative, and they've told him he won't get his job back. That's what they're saying. He's dumbfounded by the whole thing."

Edward's voice rose in anger. "Nine days without pay and the bastard union bosses betray us. They just cave in, and the men sent back with no guarantees about their jobs or conditions – and now not to give the shop stewards their jobs back?"

"Well," Danny continued, "that's what they're saying, Ned. The ringleaders won't get their jobs back. It's a disgrace."

Edward thought of the baby that was on the way. He thought of the few shillings left in Honor's purse. She had unwillingly given him a shilling for the pub, but he would get no pay now for two weeks and maybe none at all if he didn't get his job back. All through the strike he had kept men's spirits up with the promise of victory and better conditions in the future. He felt sick and sad at this uphill battle. "By Christ! It's a soul-destroying bloody business! Those parasites should be roasted in hell."

Joe Garritty, a railway colleague, set him up a glass of whisky. "Here, drink this in good health, boy. I tell you, Ned, if they don't take you back, the boys are going to go on strike again, the whole of the railway in this district is of the same opinion."

When Edward turned up next day, twenty out of the eighty in his workshop were sent home. The reason given by the railway company was that they could not put on a full train service as there wasn't enough coal for the engines, due to the miners' strike, and they had no need to take back all the workers. After three days, ten more men were taken back. The remaining ten turned up each morning and eventually only Edward and Andrew Johnston, the two best workers in the shop and also the union shop stewards, were left without being given their jobs back.

At the end of that week, a deputation of ten men was chosen to approach the management. Their message was clear. Edward and Andrew would be reinstated, or two thousand workers would be called out again on strike. The railwaymen were angry and the bosses caved in. On the following Monday, Edward was allowed to start back at work, and the following day, Andrew Johnston also got his job back. The two had lost a week's pay more than the other railway workers because they were union representatives. They could do nothing about it, but the injustice lived on in their memories. Soon the excitement of the strike faded and people were left to pick up the pieces as best they could. The government had won and the whole episode became a period of wonderment in the country's history, truly, a nine-day's wonder.

— ·— ·—

In Glasgow, the graduation ceremony was delayed until the beginning of July, due to the disruption in studies caused by the General Strike. For Archie this was a long-wished-for day. The Denny clan, breasts secretly bursting with pride, gathered at the family home to see Archie and their mother setting out for Glasgow University. A car had been hired for nine-thirty in the morning. Annie looked frail in a grey suit and hat, her hair, too, now grey, drawn back into a bun on the nape of her neck.

Words could not express the happiness that Annie felt that morning. Satisfaction at the realisation of her years of ambition for her son was disguised behind the brightness of her eyes. The appointment of her son to the teaching staff of St Mungo's Academy in the City of Glasgow was to her a great achievement, and she found herself looking at her youngest child and shaking her head in pride and disbelief, Master of Arts with Honours! Who could believe it?

"I'm only sad that auld Jock, your faither, is no' here to see you." Annie's eyes shone as she looked at the shy boy who was now a rare wonder to all of the neighbourhood. "Your faither would have been so proud!" But true to her nature, she put the thought of her dead husband out of her mind, and she turned, old and stooped, to face the assembled family.

"The car's coming in fifteen minutes, and I want to say to you all, that one of you here, Mary, Edward or Joe, could come with us. The ticket I've got is for two people." They looked at each other. "By rights, I suppose, Mary being the eldest, it should be her, but ..."

"I know I'm the eldest, Mother," Mary dropped her eyes, embarrassed at her own voice on this occasion, "but I'd like Ned to go in my place. I feel he deserves to go more than me."

"Is that all right with you, Joe?" Annie was judge and jury today.

"Yes. That's fine with me, Mother. It's Edward's place to go with you, but maybe I could come in the car just for the ride. I'm his brother, too. I'd just like to walk around the old, old buildings of the place. I could wait for you all to come out." Annie looked at her three sons, dressed in their best, dark Sunday suits and white shirts with shoes polished and white handkerchiefs showing in their top pockets.

"It's settled, then," Annie stood up, "the four of us will go."

And so the Dennys arrived in grand style at the stately old college buildings of Glasgow University on Gilmorehill in the West End of the city. Throngs of students and their families moved around outside the great hall where the ceremony was to take place. Those about to graduate, togged out in black gowns and mortar boards, milled around, nervous but happy, each one the pride of his or her family. Cars kept arriving at the great gates depositing little parties of happy people.

Annie soaked in the atmosphere of the occasion. It was her first time in such a place, and she was overawed by the grandeur of the stone columns and the great arches and doors. The people, too, who stood around had bearing and good manners, and, she had to admit, were just different from the people she had met with throughout most of her life. But she had always known that this world existed. In her own midwifery studies, she had had glimpses of the academic world, and now through her son, she felt justified and fulfilled. Her lifetime goal had been achieved. She looked at Archie and caught his eye. He was highly nervous, rubbing his hands, flicking back his gown, and moving from foot to foot as if cold under the summer sun. She gave him a beatific smile, and he smiled back shyly. He was glad she was pleased because it was for her he had worked all these years.

Edward stood stiffly beside his mother, taking in the scene. He watched his brother Joe, who looked mesmerised by the grace and beauty of the columns and spaces, the doors and windows carved in stone, the hallowed atmosphere of the old university – five centuries of learning. Joe's artistic soul was struck dumb and an unidentifiable longing to be part of all this filled him with regret. Lost in thought, he left the family group and wandered around in wonderment, his normally extrovert personality muffled by the impressiveness of this place of privilege.

Annie leaned on Edward now, the grey suit hanging on her rounded shoulders. In her heart she knew that each of her three sons would have been able enough to take on studies to degree level, some of her daughters also. She held her head up – a glint of fire in her eyes and a determination to see this day through.

Surveying the scene, as everyone awaited the sign to enter the great hall, Edward was struck by the assurance of the people. How clean and smooth their faces! How refined their voices! How rich and smart their clothes! These young men had that precious thing in life – a little advantage over their fellows, a boot up the social ladder, by dint of what? He wondered what had made Archie different. Himself, he would don his cloth cap and overalls on Monday morning and be back to his manual labour, while his young brother was marked out for a life of privilege and respect. Annie glanced at him and read his thoughts.

"It could have been you, Ned, with a bit more luck. If only there had been enough siller aboot then, when you were younger." She had dropped into the vernacular. "If only ye hadnae had tae leave school at thirteen. For ye had the brains just as much as Archie, if not more. And so had Joe, but he was too wild. But you could ha' done it."

"I'm quite happy, Mother. I've seen a bit of the world. I've got a wife and family, a job ..." He paused and patted her hand. "We all did our best. This is Archie's day and your day." As he spoke, the university porter appeared and everyone was ushered into the high-ceilinged hall and seated on the rows of chairs set out. To the dramatic strains of 'Gaudeamus Igitur', the students entered to take their seats.

They came forward one by one as their names were called out to be capped by the Principal, to applause from the admiring spectators. When the name of Archibald Denny was called out, Annie held her breath, but there he was, her youngest son, with all eyes in the hall upon him, a sweet moment indeed for her. In what seemed like no time, the list had been gone through, and then with the ceremonial music playing again, it was over, and happy, smiling bunches of people emerged into the bright sunshine. A photograph was taken, and Archie's party returned by car to the family tea that had been planned.

CHAPTER 15

Honor's fourth baby was born, another boy, over twelve pounds in weight. It was a dreadful, painful and bloody birth. The poor girl screamed in agony as, using the most primitive equipment, the doctor and midwife fought to bring out the baby, in the set-in bed of the little tenement house. Even the walls surrounding the bed were bloodstained on that awful day. They called him Billy, after Honor's father, a great, pink bundle of a baby he was. His chubby arms and broad chest were too fat for the baby clothes she had prepared for him. Lusty and active with wispy red curls, he was very heavy to lift out of his cot. But Honor was never happier than with a baby at her breast. For four months they lived in their tiny flat in a sea of drying nappies and baby clothes, and then came the happening that Honor had been praying for. Veronica called to tell about the apartment that was vacant in the same superior block of flats as she lived in herself. York Terrace! Honor could not believe it to be possible.

"It's a dream come true, Edward. Hot and cold water, and a real bathroom and a bedroom for the children. I can't believe it." They hurried as soon as it was possible to look at what was to be their new home. Honor went rushing from room to room, taking in the sizes of the rooms, stroking the fireplaces, and looking out of the windows of the empty house unable to comprehend that this could possibly be hers.

"Aye, lass, maybe our luck has turned at last."

"I'm sure it has, Ned. And that wee bit extra money you're getting now since they gave you extra responsibility makes all the difference."

"I'll get Sandy McDougall to paint the front room and the bathroom, if you like. We can do the rest next year, maybe."

They returned to Veronica's to pick up the three children, and prepare to move house. The floors of their new place were already covered with linoleum, and a present of two lovely rugs was given by Honor's family. They bought a mahogany chest of drawers and two new beds. Mrs Denny gave them a gate-legged table of inlaid walnut and some chairs she had no more use for. Honor scrubbed and polished the little flat until it shone. The day after they moved, they went to buy a radio. It was delivered on the Monday morning, a big polished ebony box with three knobs. Entranced with this new acquisition, Edward sat it on top of the chest of drawers. Avidly they listened to the news and to dance band music. From then on, Edward's chair was always the one beside the wireless, where he listened to programmes of discussions and current affairs. In the evenings, there might be comedy programmes on, and occasionally they would tune to Honor's favourite, light opera. The difference to their lives was astonishing.

Edward hated all forms of snobbery, tending to play down any of his accomplishments, unless that is, he had had too much to drink, when he could boast and brag as well as the next man, and would praise to the skies his beautiful wife and family. But even he was proud of his new home and the small rise in their standard of living. He took more to going to the library in his spare time, saving his social evenings in the pub until Saturday nights.

Louisa Dryden was impressed with Honor's sudden change of lifestyle, surprised that such luck had come to her slow-witted daughter. Outspoken as always when she made her first visit, she scolded Honor for letting the children eat so much, and then gave her opinion of the place. "It's very nice, your house. You've made it comfortable, I'll give you that, but you've a long way to go to equal the beautiful place our Veronica has. Her house is like a palace."

Honor was cut to the quick, but she wasn't letting Louisa get away with it. "Veronica has no children to look after. And she's got plenty of money, Mam."

"Well, you shouldn't have had these bairns so quick. You've totally lost your figure. Look at you. You're like a rake. When I was your age, I still had a beautiful figure."

Years of such insults had put a shell around Honor where her mother was concerned. She could even see the funny side of the situation, and had to hide a smile from the old tyrant. "Have you heard anything of our Elsie?" she asked of her mother to change the subject.

"No, she's gone to Bearsden to live with the Shields family, and I understand she's going to marry Jim Shields as soon as it can be arranged. I don't care. She hardly put a penny into the house, and she never let me speak to that boy to find out about his family. And as for that going out the window at eleven o'clock at night and creeping back in the small hours of the morning. That was the last straw. She thought I didn't know what she was up to. Immoral! Giving the family a bad name! Well, she can stay away. His people, the Shieldses, they could be paupers or pickpockets, for all I know."

"Oh, Mother, come on now. You know Elsie said they had their own business and were well off."

"Then why was I not allowed to meet them?"

"You will one day, Mam."

"Between Elsie eloping and Jack marrying that Frances Young, Mary Bonnar's daughter, I'm just plagued with misfortune. I've lost two of my family within a few months."

Jack Dryden had been married the month before, the only cloud on the horizon being his mother's attitude. Jack had moved into the Young's house in the same street as his own family, having told his mother of his intention to marry, a few days beforehand. Louisa had been speechless with fury that her favourite son could do this to her. As the happy couple left for the Registry Office to the cheers of the neighbours, Louisa pulled down all the blinds at the front of her house, this usually being the sign of a death in the family. The neighbourhood was appalled at this cruelty. But for years she refused to recognise her son or daughter-in-law, although they lived close beside her and she might see them every day.

Honor had a softer, sweeter nature than her mother. On this day of Louisa's visit to Honor's new house, she let her prattle on while she thought of her brother Jack and his new wife, and wished she could see them. When Louisa did finally leave, Honor took out the packet of cigarettes she had hidden from her mother in a drawer, and looking out the kitchen window to the hills, lost in thought, she enjoyed a smoke to calm her nerves. When she moved on to prepare the vegetables for the evening meal, there was a ring at the doorbell. Weaving her way through the toys and children on the carpet, Honor opened her door to see a girl of about nine or ten holding an envelope. "My dad, Brian Burns, says I've to give this to Mr Denny."

"Well, thank you!" And she gave the child a penny.

'E. Denny' was written on the envelope with flowing twirls and curlicues. The gum was only partly stuck on it, and it looked so unusual that Honor could not stop herself; the curving ornamental writing continued on the page inside.

> *Dearest Edward,*
>
> *I don't know how I have lived for the last few months without seeing you. I know you said it was over, but I just can't believe you don't miss me and want to see me as much as I want to see you. Those few days in Mallaig still live in my memory. I have tried to meet you sometimes, but you always seem to be with someone else. On Saturday, I will be in Coia's Cafe for a snack about seven o'clock. See if you can get away, my love. I long to talk to you.*
>
> Forever yours,
Macushla

Honor collapsed onto a chair, still holding the note. She was dazed at what the letter revealed, and in ten minutes that was how Edward found her, on his return from work. She heard him come in and pause in the hall to remove his overalls. A smile on his face, he entered the kitchen, and the children toddled over to him excitedly. At the same time, he noticed his wife's position as she sat, pale and stunned on a chair at the table. He took the letter from her hand and read it. Shocked by its contents, he approached his wife. "Where did this come from?"

"Who did it come from, more like? Tell me that!" Her tone was bitter.

"Oh! someone's playing a joke." He threw down the note.

"Do you think I'm that stupid, Edward? I know a woman's handwriting when I see it. And it stinks of cheap perfume." Edward sat down and put his head in hands. "And she met you at Mallaig. It's disgusting. You, a married man with three children. Who is she?"

"Look! I don't know. It's not true!" Their voices were rising and the children were clinging to Honor's skirts. Edward thought to change the subject by demanding his evening meal.

"Food? How can I cook food in a state like this?" Then the tears came bursting out. She stared at him, her face contorted. "I've a pain, a searing pain at my heart!" Now the children were screaming and crying at seeing their mother's distress. "How could you? How could you do this to me ... to us?" and she looked down at the little ones.

"Oh, for Christ's sake! I've had enough o' this." He rose and bolted to the door, banging it behind him. For perhaps an hour, Edward walked the streets, miserable and shaken by this turn of events. After his third cigarette, he thought of going to the pub, but he had no money, so he turned into his mother's house. He found Annie busy with some darning of socks, seated at the kitchen table, while Archie sat by the kitchen range smoking a cigarette and reading a novel.

"What's brought you here at this time, Ned?" Annie sensed a crisis.

"No, I just ... We've had an argument, Honor and me. I just came out to cool down."

"I'll make you a sandwich." She rose and took some bread and butter and a piece of cheese from the cupboard. "Put the kettle on, Archie." Their calm, polite manners soothed the hurt in him.

Annie's experienced eye saw that he was very troubled, and she left him to lick his wounds.

"Soon be time for the flat racing, Ned. I'm gonna try and get a party up for the Lanark Races, a week on Saturday. Dae ye fancy it?"

The thought of Lanark Races cracked the dour scowl on Edward's face, and he gave a rueful smile. "Aye, there's nothin' like Lanark Races, just nothin' at all. I can hear the thumpin' o' the horses on the turf in my head just thinkin' aboot it. But where's the money to come from? That's a different story." He put his hand in his pockets and turned out the lining to show they were empty. "Look, two shirt buttons and a collar stud, that's the total of my wealth." They laughed at this buffoonery. He continued, looking down at his old, torn work trousers, "And look at me! The rags are lashing me to death here."

Annie burst out laughing. "Oh, you're your father's son all right, Ned. You can always make me laugh." However, a bit later in the evening Edward's face had changed at the thought of returning to his own house. "Mind and tell Honor I'm asking for her. And by the way, I've a wee nest egg put by." She had their attention now and she eyed them both directly. "Maybe I'll crack it open. I sold my share o' the baker's shop to my cousin, Meg McDonald, and I hav'na used the money yet. So, I'll maybe treat my two good boys to a day out at the races."

Edward shook his head in disbelief and he squeezed her frail figure as she smiled up at him.

When he got back, Honor was just coming out of the children's bedroom. She ignored him as she lifted the children's clothes, folding some and putting others aside to be washed.

"Are you not goin' to look at me?" he ventured.

"Why should I look at you?" Her eyes were red with weeping. "Where have you been? Out looking for your true love?"

"Don't be daft! I went for a walk and then called in at my mother's."

"Did you tell your mother why you were walking the streets – what we were fighting about?"

"No."

He tried to put his arms around her, but she pulled away. She poured hot water and soap onto the children's clothes and began to wash them furiously, scrubbing them on her washing board in the kitchen sink. "Please, Honor, just listen to me. I can't stand it!" But her tears dripped into the soapy water, and she sobbed uncontrollably. "Look!" he said gently. "It was a long time ago. I told her it was finished. It was just an aberration."

"That's a new word for it! Your drinking and gambling are bad enough. My mother's full of disgust for you already without this! You know the kind of men that do what you've done, and the kind of women."

"More men than you think, Honor."

"Well, I'm sick ..." But this time he managed to hold her, and she sobbed on his shoulder.

"It was after wee Louie died," he said softly. "I was miserable as sin. You were cold as ice, going about like an automaton."

"I suppose she was warm and desirable!"

"I've never stopped loving you, Honor. I've not seen her for months, and I don't intend to either."

Honor sat down and dried her eyes with the kitchen towel. He knelt in front of her. "You promise?" she said weakly.

"Sure, I promise."

"I'll get your tea."

Relief flooded him. "Aye! Get my tea, wife, and I'll have a read at the paper."

"Do I know her?"

"No, you don't know her, so just forget it. It's in the past. I'll check the bairns are all right." He cuddled her from behind and kissed her hair. In his heart, he thanked God that she loved him so dearly.

He was a lucky man, he knew. Ten days later, a sunny Saturday morning, there was a great buzz of excitement in York Terrace. Archie and Edward awaited the arrival of their gang of friends for the trip by train to Lanark and the famous ancient racecourse in that market town. Cecil McLuskey, Jimmy Gilmour, Wee McGreegor, Martin McEwan, Johnny McNab, all friends through drink and politics, gathered together and set off for the local station to catch the train for Lanark. In high spirits, at twelve-thirty, they alighted at Lanark Racecourse station. The racecourse was a sea of mainly men, dressed in sports jackets, flannel trousers and checked caps. There were red-faced farmers with their shooting sticks and plus-four trousers, and even trench-coated confidence tricksters looking for the main chance. There were folk from all walks of life, saints and sinners, beggars and even a few aristocrats, jostling each other in crowds around the course. Joy and excitement was what they had in common. They talked loudly to each other of past form of the horses, good jockeys and bad jockeys, and above all they told each other which horse was their fancy from the parading horseflesh on display in the paddock.

Edward and his party now mixed in with the crowd. In such a kaleidoscope of colour, among the horseboxes, cars, ponies and traps, gypsies and rogues, bookies and punters, high-class ladies and harlots, the rough, weathered skin, and thickened workmen's hands of Edward and his party went unnoticed. Tipsters called out their prices, and bookies standing on their wooden stands signalled the odds to each other with skill and urgency. Ned's party were soon pressed close by the rails, cheering on their chosen nags with all their hearts.

At the fifth race, Edward had a strong fancy for His Lordship. He had seen the horse in the paddock, and he knew the form of both horse and jockey.

"I'm putting five pounds on His Lordship," Edward told his brother.

Archie was aghast, "Five pounds, Ned! You must be mad."

"Well, that's half of the money I've got. I'm on a winning streak."

None of the others could match the daring of Edward. Two of them had almost empty pockets, so they all agreed to let him bet alone for that race, and everyone cheered for the sleek, brown His Lordship as he galloped away at the starting pistol. With hoarse throats and the unbelievable roaring of the crowd in their ears, with disbelief in their eyes, they watched Ned's horse round the bend and romp home at twenty to one.

"I knew it! I knew it! I knew I was on a winning streak!" They patted Ned's back, and smiled with delight as they joined him at the windows to pick up his winnings. He felt like a king, as they crowded around him with his wad of one hundred pounds – an unheard of amount. Archie shook his head in disbelief. How could one man be so lucky? he thought.

Flushed with excitement, Edward called out, "What do you fancy in the next race, boys?"

"I'm for French Farce," said Martin McEwan.

Wee McGreegor shouted, "I'm putting my last two pounds on Polly Wolly Doodle."

Edward looked at the runners listed above the bookie's head. He clutched his money. "I think I'll go for Malone's Rose."

Archie cut in, "Listen, Ned. You watch what you're doing. That's more money than any of us has ever had."

Edward was drunk with success, "Faint heart ... Archie boy. I tell you, it's my day, today. The bookies are all afeared of me."

Archie lost his temper. "You're a fool, Edward. Just as I've always thought. There's Honor sitting at home with three kids, a good saintly girl and you're holding the means to transform her life, ready to throw it away." A look of anger crossed Edward's face at this attempt to prick his bubble of triumph, but he knew there was truth in what Archie was saying. "Give me the bulk of it. Go on, have a flutter but for God's sake, Ned, let me hold the rest."

Edward peeled off a fiver. "Right, I'll have five pounds on Malone's Rose," and he gave the balance to his brother to hold.

With much cheering the last race was run, and Malone's Rose came in fourth. Archie sighed with relief. Elated and flushed with success, they trooped off to find a table in the pub for a drink before taking the train home. It was, of course, Edward's treat and Archie, in charge of the money, was sent to the bar for seven whiskies and seven half pints of beer. He decided to miss out the whisky for himself. After three such trips to the bar, the party got merrier and merrier. The laughter was loud and jolly as the winners from the track cheered up the losers with free drinks. Edward was just breaking into the strains of 'I Belong to Glasgow' when Archie interjected, "Come on, Edward. The train's at seven o'clock. We've only got quarter of an hour."

"Oh! What do you make of my brother, boys? Bloody Jeremiad! His brother's keeper. Sit doon, Archie, and be at peace! It's Saturday night."

"Aye, and we're far from home. If you don't catch the train, I will."

"Come here. Give me my money."

"I'll keep it here."

"No!" Edward's voice rose, and he scowled but Archie stared him down. "Give me some of it, anyway." Edward lowered his voice, a bit taken aback at his young brother's determination. For a second, Edward thought he saw his mother's eyes in Archie's.

"Take this, that's twenty pounds there." Archie was not pleased. The cronies sat round the table, fascinated by Edward's antics. They watched as he peeled off three single pound notes.

"Toys for your children," he lisped drunkenly, and handed the man beside him the notes. "Toys for your children." He passed three pounds to the next man, and so on round the group, until he had dispensed fifteen pounds. "And now, since we've all got our return tickets, we'll have one for the road, and go home to our spouses. We must remember the ladies, boys." Having the limelight, he threw an arm out in front of himself dramatically, and paraphrasing Robert Burns he recited:

> *There they sit in the gathering storm,*
> *Nursing their wrath to keep it warm.*

Laughing, the friends quaffed down their drinks and ambled off, arms around each other's shoulders in deepest friendship and brimming with joie de vivre, a group that was the envy of the whole pub.

And so, Edward, Archie and Cecil McLuskey arrived at Honor's door, slightly the worse for wear, but carrying the pleasure of the day with them in their manner. "We bring tidings of great joy, Honor." Archie was waxing lyrical at his success at getting his rumbustious brother home in one piece. Smiling a bit stupidly, Edward waved to his wife as she stood by the kitchen range and her copper kettle, trying to take in the situation.

"What a day! What a day I've had with my friends! Honor, my darling!" The intoxicated Edward sank into the armchair by the fire, and within two minutes was fast asleep.

With Cecil looking on, Archie ceremoniously handed over the wad of notes to Honor, "Your husband's winnings, my dear."

Honor almost dropped the teapot she was carrying at the sight of so many notes.

"There's seventy-five pounds here. Ned doesn't know how much is left, so keep the amount secret. You'd best hide the most of it."

She was speechless. In her mind's eye, she saw new curtains, dishes, clothes for the children, and perhaps a bank book, money for a holiday, a little security for a rainy day. "Oh, Archie! Thank God for you!" She hugged and kissed him, and left the room to hide the money.

The three of them drank tea and ate sandwiches around the sleeping Edward. Cecil was first to stand up to leave. "What a day! A day at the races with Edward! I'll never forget it."

"Neither will I," agreed Archie, rising and joining Cecil at the door.

"Thank you for bringing him home." They tiptoed out through the door she held open for them, so as not to awaken the slumbering hero.

CHAPTER 16

Six o' clock in New York was the time when the city took a breath between the working day and the evening that was still to come. The traffic thinned out, and the noise became less frenetic in the streets as people escaped from the offices and department stores of the centre. For some it was the cocktail hour. Betty Howlett looked forward to that straight line on the clock, which on some days seemed to take longer to come round than on others.

"Look, Betty, I've got to take off for Chicago on some business. I'm going at seven in the morning. I'll be gone about two weeks. Joe Riston is trying to buy a vacant lot there to put up a hotel. He wants me to go in with him, finance-wise. I want to check it out. Do you want to come along?"

Betty's fingers with their long, painted nails clutched harder round her dry martini, "I can't, honey. I've promised to help Caroline with the fund-raising concert for St Mary's Free Hospital for Children. They're way behind in the planning. You know the Wallaces, my friends in the theatre – they know everybody on Broadway, and Caroline wants me to approach them to help, you know. I can't get out of it."

"Oh, yeah! I forgot about that!"

"Also I'm directing a one-act play that's part of the programme. I can't walk out on that, Howard, honey." Her voice was pleading and sexy, and he saw that she was slightly drunk. He sat down opposite her and watched as she raised her legs in their silk lounging pants and placed her exquisite, high-heeled evening shoes on the cream satin cushions of the couch. Like a blue and silver snake she curled sensuously along the cushions. "Get me another drink, hun." She held up her empty glass to him. "Dinner's not for half an hour yet. You're not going out, are you?"

"No, I'll have to pack for my trip."

"Oh, well. Get yourself another one, too, and come and sit by me." Howard wondered what had happened to make Betty more aware of him – nicer to him lately. She was just as self-obsessed, spending hours in front of her dressing table, making up her face, and choosing clothes for lunch dates and dinner dates, but there was a subtle difference. As he brought her drink to her and sat down, her exciting perfume hit him, and her green eyes twinkled at him in an unusually seductive manner.

"We haven't both been at home together for dinner for a week or so," he said.

"No, honey. We don't do it often enough." There it was again, the seductive tone. It was quite unsettling.

Howard carried on talking, resisting her flirty behaviour. "Yes, Joe's got the bug for expansion. This will be his sixth hotel project. He's a good businessman. You must remember Joe, he's a lot of fun to be around. We might get in a game of golf in the windy city."

She put her hand on his shoulder, and looked deep into his eyes, "I sure wish I could come."

He moved uncomfortably at this unusual familiarity. There was a knock at the door, and Susan and little Freddy were in the room. He was aware of Susan's embarrassment at seeing Betty and him in such an intimate position.

"Hi, Freddy boy! Hello, Susan." He stood up quickly.

"We've come to say goodnight." She took the baby over to his parents. Betty kissed him with a great, noisy show of affection.

"My precious boy. Goodnight, sweetheart. Kiss Mummy."

The child, clean and rosy from his bath, his fair curls hanging round his ears, was enjoying being the centre of attention. A lively two-year-old now, he ran around the room, delighting in the space and the many places to hide in the elegant sitting room, until Susan caught him and started out for his bedroom with the promise of a story.

"Goodnight, Susan."

"Goodnight, Mr Howlett, Mrs Howlett." She did not let her eyes meet either of theirs. Howard followed them into the hallway, leaving the door half open.

"Daddy's going away for a couple of weeks, Freddy. Will you miss me?" Freddy nodded seriously. "I'll miss you, too." Howard was suddenly quite emotional. He stood up and looked straight at Susan. "It will soon fly by." He stood for a moment at the foot of the steps. "Goodnight, goodnight, my dear!"

"Goodnight." Susan climbed the stairs with her charge, chatting nonsensically to him about Wee Willie Winkie. But her heart was heavy. She felt as if life would be empty for a while without the possibility of a smile or word from Howard. Their chance meetings kept her going, and she thought of him every night after she said her prayers, before she fell asleep.

Howard felt that night that Betty must be aware of his attraction to Susan. All through dinner, she was animated and kittenish in her behaviour, flirting with him as if she were seventeen and they had just met. For the first time in two years, they shared the same bed. She made passionate love to him, as if there had been no rift between them. He was overwhelmed by her embraces and submitted to the unexpected show of love and affection with a mixture of pleasure and surprise. Next morning, he left very early, still puzzled by this new turn of events. He knew she had had a few lovers throughout their marriage, just as he had, but why had she come back to his bed? Had her latest paramour thrown her over? Did she think she was in danger of losing him? He had planned to steal a clandestine meeting with Susan, sometime in the evening before his trip, but this was now not to be.

Meanwhile, Susan had been invited to the St Vincent's Hospital staff dance. She was to stay overnight in the nurses' quarters, and great was her excitement when Saturday evening arrived. More sedate than the dance hall evening with George had been in her first few months in New York, at least at the beginning, the orchestra played waltzes and foxtrots, and Jenny's friends all danced with her. When it came to the ragtime sequence, she found herself partnered by a young medical student, Paul Ballantyne. He was ruggedly handsome with dark, curly hair. He reminded her of her brother Ned, with some of the same smiling Irish charm, and like Ned he danced with feet as light as a feather.

"Can you Charleston?"

"Well, I've done it once," she replied, as he swung her into his version of the dance. She was a swirl of pink crepe, her golden slippers flying in front and behind, her arms swinging wildly, as they laughed their way through the dance to the jazz band music.

At the next dance, he skilfully guided her in a foxtrot, "I know where I've seen you before. St Patrick's Cathedral at eleven o'clock Mass. It was you, wasn't it?"

"That's right. That would be me, half asleep probably. But I haven't seen you."

"Well, you stand out. You always sit in the same pew, wearing a little red hat. I've been watching you. Every Sunday. I've noticed your crinkly, smiling blue eyes. And sometimes, when I've seen you light a candle after the service, you look so serious and devout!"

"For the folks back home," she said. "They're in my thoughts on Sunday mornings, but I must look out for you, Paul."

"Better still. I'll meet you tomorrow morning. We can go for a cup of coffee afterwards. OK, Susan?"

"It's a date!" They left the dance floor, their arms around each other.

Next morning, as the faithful streamed out of the cathedral, Susan spotted Paul among the crowd. "A fine morning now, Susan! Is it not?"

She blushed at the tall, virile man, whose arm had quietly slipped behind her, guiding her down the steps. "Yes, but it's been raining overnight. How's your head this morning, Paul? Are you suffering for all that hooch you drank last night? You sure have an Irishman's head for drink, Paul."

"Clear as a bell, my darling! Wasn't that a swell dance? You were the belle of the ball. Let's go to Harbour Lights. The coffee's always fresh there." Confidently he guided her along the street. They quickened their pace along the damp sidewalks, past couples taking taxis home from night-before parties, past night-workers making their ways home, and past newcomers to New York whose pace was so halted as they paused to take in the great skyscrapers around them. Soon they were seated in a booth opposite each other, drinking steaming cups of coffee, and eating soft, sugary doughnuts.

"Tell me about yourself, Susan. How long have you been in New York?"

"I came here in July '25 to work as a nanny."

"Do you like it?"

"Oh, yes. Most of the time. I miss my folks in Scotland, though."

"Yeah! Me, too. I miss the folks in Nova Scotia. I'm Canadian, but way back, I've got Scots and Irish blood. Do you get much time off from your nannying?"

"Saturday afternoons and Sunday mornings, usually."

"Can you play tennis?"

"I've never tried."

"Well, next Saturday, I'll book us in at the courts near where I live. I'll give you a lesson. How would you like that?" He took her hand and smiled, looking into her surprised eyes.

"Well, you work fast, don't you?" She looked at the door to hide her feelings.

"Can you make it for two in the afternoon? I'll pick you up. My friend Jack'll lend me his Ford."

"What shall I wear?" she sounded panicky.

"Oh, yeah! Well, a tennis skirt and a white blouse, I suppose, and you know, tennis shoes."

"I'll see what I can do."

They were joined by a pair from the dance of the previous evening, a girl with long, straight, gingery-coloured hair, pretty, plump and smiling, and then along came Jenny, Susan's friend from the crossing. The other two girls were giggling.

"Why, Paul Ballantyne, you devil! I thought it was me you were going to take out. You double-crosser!" The ginger-haired girl swung her head to smile at the Italian waiter who was eyeing her, so showing the glints of gold in her beautiful mane. Her eyes were laughing.

Paul said, "You know me, Millicent. I'm the world's greatest lover. Come and sit beside Susan, Jenny. How did you know we were here?"

Jenny was a bit disgruntled. "Oh, old Sherlock Holmes, that's me. You stole my lovely girlfriend Susan from me. I see little enough of her, you know. And Millie and me are back on duty in the maternity ward at six o'clock this evening."

"Well, well, well! Did you know that Susie here lives with a millionaire on Park Avenue?" he smiled disarmingly at them.

Millicent was jealous of Susan's success with Paul and was anxious to get in on the act. "Aren't you the lucky one, Susan. Do you often steal other girl's boyfriends?"

Susan was wrong-footed by this remark, but managed, "No, just on Sundays!"

"Good for you, Susie kid. Anyway, who said I was your boyfriend, Millie?"

"You're hateful, Paul Ballantyne, you know that?" Millicent was sulking now.

"Listen, Susan," it was Jenny speaking. "We're having a little party in the nurses' home next Saturday evening. Do you think you can come? Around eight-thirty? Say until eleven. You can stay over and go to Mass next day before going home."

Susan was flustered, "Eh, I've got a date for the afternoon, next Saturday."

"Oh, I see." Both girls eyed Paul. "Fast work, Paul!"

"I'm giving Susie a tennis lesson."

"You're invited, too. You can both come after the tennis. That'll be about ten of us in the Common Room. Just a nice number. Brian Renton's bringing some hooch. It'll be all right if we use cups and disguise it with coffee."

"Sounds like fun." Paul rolled his eyes to show his enthusiasm.

Millicent pressed closer to the good-looking boy, "And we've got a phonograph. How do you like that, lover boy?"

"OK! I'll bring Susan after the tennis. Can you get the evening off, honey?"

"I'll ask Lotta. She'll stand in for me, I know. But right now, I'd better get back. They'll be expecting me back from church."

He walked her to the corner. "Bye, honey, I'll pick you up at two on Saturday."

The next week passed quickly. The usual round of feeding, dressing and amusing Freddy, of fending off the advances of the irrepressible George, and of gossiping in the kitchen with Bella and Lotta. She managed to borrow a white tennis shirt from a friend of Lotta, and she bought a shortish tennis skirt and rubber-soled shoes.

"I know who you look like." Paul had appeared at the front door of the Howlett's house. "Greta Garbo. Innocent and yet daring! Get in the car!"

She threw her bag onto the back seat, and joined him in the front. He leaned over to her, "Shy and yet provocative!" He winked at her.

"Oh, shut up, Paul."

"Is she a nun or a harlot?"

"I'll jump out next time you stop the car if you don't stop fooling around!"

"Just kidding. You look terrific!"

She felt as if she were setting off around the world instead of just to a little tennis court. The sun was shining, and New York seemed the only place to be that Saturday afternoon. On the tennis court, Susan often missed the ball or hit it so hard that it went sailing out of court, but by the end of an hour, she was showing definite signs of improvement.

"Three cheers for effort, honey. Let's have a lemonade." Paul put his arm around her and led off to the clubhouse. "You take the prize for good looks, anyway, my little bobby-dazzler!"

Her cheeks glowed with the exercise, and her brown curls clung round her damp forehead. When they sat down with their drinks, he leaned over and rubbed his nose against hers. "Don't you look a peach, today?"

She smiled a dazzling smile of pure happiness. "Thank you for bringing me here today, Paul. I've never had so much fun."

"Are you looking forward to the party tonight?"

"You bet! Oh, do I sound like a Yankee?"

"A Scottish Yankee."

"When you finish your studies and are qualified as a doctor, are you going to look for a job in New York?"

"I think so. I like it. There's a great buzz about the city. Every day is exciting."

"Oh, yes, and lots of pretty girls to choose from."

"And I've chosen the prettiest, right now."

At the piano in the corner of the clubroom, one of Paul's friends was leering over at them as they spoke.

"By yon bonnie banks, and by yon bonnie braes,
Where the sun shines bright on Loch Lomond,
Where me and my true love will never meet again
On the bonnie, bonnie banks of Loch Lomond,"

he sang in mock sincerity.

"Very funny, Jerry!" Paul shouted to the pianist, who reacted by whisking Susan out of her seat and waltzing her around the room.

"Oh you'll tak' the high road, and I'll tak' the low road,
And I'll be in Scotland before you."

Susan pushed him away, laughing and returning to her seat.

"You sure picked a peach this time, Paul. All the way from Scotland, too. Are there any more at home like you, honey?"

"Look, this is my date." Paul pushed the culprit away. "We've got places to go, Jerry, you find your own girl." He turned to Susan. "Time to change, pussycat. We've got the town to paint red. You can shower in the ladies' locker room."

"You got a party to go to, Paul?"

"Nope. Don't know of any party."

Showered and dressed and pretty as a picture in her new red dress with red sandals to match, Susan appeared, drawing a few whistles from some males still hanging around. Paul claimed her and drove off at speed. They went to a speakeasy bar where the noise was deafening. The place was packed. The band was playing, and the singer was singing, but all round the bar, the thirsty Saturday evening crowd were calling for drinks and regaling each other with shouted remarks. The result was chaotic, and those struggling back from the bar held their glasses aloft like trophies won in a war.

"What is it?" she asked him as he handed her a glass.

"Treble gin and it."

They moved nearer to the band, and soon found a space to sit down to enjoy the atmosphere of frenetic fun while they drank their booze. Two-thirds of the way down the glass, Susan had to give up. For the first time in her life, she thought she must be drunk. "I think I'd better leave this, Paul. My head is spinning."

"OK, sweetheart, let's go."

They arrived at the nurses' party to find it in full swing. Fast and furious dancing was going on. They were trying to do the Black Bottom. Suddenly Lawrie, a young doctor, jumped up on a table and started doing a mock striptease while the others clapped and cheered as he wiggled his way around. When he got to his underwear, he took cold feet, and laughing he jumped down. By eleven o'clock the party had sorted itself into couples. They smooched around to dreamy music from the phonograph.

Presently, Millicent dragged Paul away from Susan. "Come and dance with me, big boy. Please, you promised."

"I promised? Oh, OK." He made a face at Susan. Millicent clung to him with her curvaceous body pressed against him quite brazenly. When the music stopped, he had difficulty pulling himself away. He sat the tipsy girl in an armchair where she sulked with her head leaning on her hand in disgust at this rejection.

"Let's get some air," he said, and placed Susan's jacket on her shoulders. The night air in the hospital grounds was heavy and damp with dew. They could see patterns of street lights, in long parallel lines and crescents from the little rise on which they were standing. A new moon lit up the forest of tall buildings, and neon lights changed colours ceaselessly in the distance. Traffic honked and an occasional ambulance or police siren could be heard, as they walked hand in hand along the driveway.

"This is the best day I've had in a long time, Paul. It's been fun."

"You're a nice girl, Susan. If you weren't ..."

"What?" She turned to face him.

"I would have had you in bed right now. That's what." He drew her close.

"You know we can't do that."

She felt his hands exploring her body, and thrilled as he softly fondled her breasts. Desire mounted and she clung to him as he kissed her parted lips. "You want me, too, don't you?" his voice was hoarse. "Don't you?"

"Yes, but I can't ... I've promised ... There's someone in Scotland who ..."

"Scotland is a long way off, and I want you, I think I love you."

She pushed him away, "We've Mass in the morning. How could we go if we gave in to our feelings like this? We both know better."

Reluctantly he straightened his clothes, and pulled her jacket around her to protect her from the cold. "Let's go back and get another drink," he said.

CHAPTER 17

Howard returned from Chicago, having invested eighty thousand dollars in the projected building of a hotel. His friend, Joe Riston, already owned five hotels, two in Texas, one in Niagara Falls, one in Chicago, and one in Baltimore. They had had a fine time, wheeling and dealing with bank managers, and socialising with hotel men and speculators around town. Howard was in his element in this risk-taking business. He loved the excitement of big business, the deals absorbing every fibre of his being in the last few days before a new acquisition was made.

But now that the papers had been signed and the banks had been satisfied with the soundness of the project, Howard, leaving the nitty-gritty to Joe, his partner, stuffed the papers in his briefcase and turned for home. Glad to be back in New York, he took a taxi from Grand Central Station, and was opening his front door by ten o'clock that night. He dropped his bags in the hallway, and as he reached the top of the stairs, he was just in time to see his chauffeur, George, emerging from Betty's bedroom.

"Good evening, George," Howard left the unspoken question in the air.

"Mrs Howlett was feeling unwell, Mr Howlett. She sent me out to try and get some brandy. You know I've got connections – I got her a bottle across town. Just back." George was flustered, but quickly put on a show of bravado. He smiled broadly and saluting politely, he said, "I'll just put the car in the garage, Mr Howlett. Goodnight."

Howard opened the bedroom door to find Betty lying languidly on top of the bed, smoking a cigarette in a long holder. She was dressed in a pale yellow silk negligee, her beautiful legs showing where the gown fell open. On the bedside cabinet were two empty glasses and a bottle of brandy little more than half full.

"Why, darling, I thought you weren't coming back until tomorrow." He watched her struggle to appear sober, but the battle was difficult. She put the cigarette in the ash tray and stood up to greet him. Approaching him, swaying a little, and putting her perfumed arms on his shoulders, she kissed him on the cheek. "Glad you're back, dahleeng. I've been so lonesome."

"Where did you get the booze?"

"Oh, George got it for me. It's good stuff. Would you like a little snifter?" She put on a babyish voice.

"No, thank you." He was angry. "Do you think it's right that you should have George deliver hooch to you – while you're in bed – and I'm away from home?"

"Why not, sweetie? Old George is harmless." She giggled drunkenly and patted the bed beside her where she was posing. "Come and sit by me, darling."

"Oh, for God's sake!" He turned for the door muttering, "What a bloody homecoming!" Angrily he closed the door and quickly reached the door of the nursery. There he found Freddy fast asleep. He kissed the pretty child, and went straight to the kitchen where he found Bella.

"Why, hello, Mr Howlett. Did you have a good trip? Are you hungry?"

"Yes, Bella. I had a very successful trip, thank you, and I sure am hungry." He slumped into a chair.

She put a cup of coffee in front of him. "You look bushed, Mr Howlett, sir, if you don't mind my saying so. Could you eat a roast beef sandwich?"

"Sure could, Bella." While she made the sandwich he said, "Where's Lotta?"

"Oh, she's gone to a movie with Costa."

"And Susan?"

"Oh, Susan's got a new beau. A fellow called Paul Ballantyne. A nice guy. Seems very fond of Susan. They went to the Cafe Davide, I think they called it. Over in the Village. They were celebrating. Yeah, I think it's Paul's birthday."

"Oh, yeah?" Howard felt cheated, disgruntled, unsettled. The burning question was how long had George been in Betty's bedroom. What was going on?

He ate his sandwich, thoughtfully, and drank a cup of coffee. "Has George gone home for the night, Bella?"

She put down her knitting. "Why, yes, Mr Howlett. It's ten-thirty. He'll be home by now. Did you want him?"

"No. I'll call a cab." He freshened up, and within ten minutes, he was telling the driver, "Cafe Davide."

For an eternity the cab progressed along Broadway, past police cars with their winking beams, through jets of steam rising from the road from the city's heating systems. People were streaming out of the theatres around Times Square where the lights were going out, but the movie houses were still lit up and thronged with people coming and going. Neon signs, greens, reds, yellows and blues flashed overhead, and people homeward bound scuttled along the canyons between the great buildings of Manhattan.

The Cafe Davide was a high-class speakeasy, and there was usually a delay at the door before entry was allowed. A dollar bill slipped to the doorman usually did the trick. The place had a Continental air about it. Many of the waiters were French, and the waitresses and cigarette girls were dressed in skimpy black satin dresses with tiny white lace aprons and lace headdresses, each girl prettier than the next. They shimmied around provocatively, flirting with the customers, and securing tips way above what the waiters were earning.

At one end of the room, a jazz band was warming up. In front of them was a tiny dance floor, but no one had yet taken the floor. When Howard entered, he went straight to the bar and ordered a double Scotch. A girl singer joined the band and started to sing, "Yes, sir, that's my baby." Howard's eyes scanned the room until he saw what he was looking for, a noisy table of young people having a raucous party. He saw Susan, her dress cut low enough to reveal the pale luminous skin of her throat and bosom. Her hair was in deep waves, and a diamante clasp glistened on one side of her head. She wore earrings to match the clasp. Her dress was of navy blue silk, and Howard thought she had never looked more attractive. She had a young man sitting on either side of her, and they were all singing along with the band.

He ordered another double, and surveyed the table while he drank. There were six of them there. One of the girls was Jenny. He remembered her from the day he had seen her standing outside the hospital. The other girl had long red hair. She had tried to curl it, but it hung heavy and straight around her pretty little face. They were all having a great time. He tried to pick out which of the three men was Susan's partner, and guessed it must be the broad-faced, broad-shouldered, rugged guy, whose arm was now stealing around her. Howard felt a stab of anger at this. What did this upstart think he was doing? He took a swallow of whisky. Who is this creep? he asked himself, and he ordered a third drink. Without thinking he picked up the glass and walked over to their table.

"Hello, Susan." She jumped with surprise. "What's a nice girl like you doing in a dump like this?"

She laughed and held out her hand. "Well. Hi, Mr Howlett," she said.

He bent and kissed her hand.

"Oh, wow!" they all called out.

"This is my employer, Mr Howlett, folks."

Paul stood up, "Paul Ballantyne. Won't you sit down, Mr Howlett? Can I buy you another drink?"

"Not right now, thank you, Paul. You kids celebratin'?"

Millicent moved closer, giving her shiny, gold hair a shake. "Why, sure, Mr Howlett. It's Paul's birthday. He's twenty-five today."

"Congratulations, Paul!" Howard tried to smile.

"When did you get back from Chicago, Mr Howlett?" Susan felt slightly ill at ease at this new turn of events.

"Two hours ago," he said.

"Was Freddy all right?"

"Asleep." He gave her a hurt look. She knew he had expected to find her at home.

The band was getting more frenetic. Several new musicians had appeared, refugees from bands in other clubs who felt like sitting in on this one. The pace was hotting up.

"Would you care to dance, Mr Howlett?" Millicent's flirty eyes searched his face.

"Call me Howard."

"Well, Howie. Will you dance with me?" She spoke in an affected, high-pitched, dumb-blonde voice that she thought was sexy. Howard thought it was sexy, too. On the dance floor, she pushed her curves close to him. "You can call me Millie."

Her disturbing perfume combined with the three whiskies he had just downed were working on him, dulling his jealousy and the blues he had arrived with. Susan watched them on the dance floor. Every time it was possible, Millicent pressed close to the older man. She's got nothing to learn, that Millicent, she thought.

"Hey, honey. I'm here," Paul said. "Never mind old Bluebeard."

She laughed, "Let's dance, Paul," and she threw herself into a wild attempt at the Black Bottom.

At last the party broke up. "I'll take Susan home, Paul." Howard lifted Susan's wrap and placed it on her shoulders, and smiled at everyone. The combination of age, charm and money were too much for Paul to argue against.

"I'll see you at church, Susan. Tomorrow morning." Paul had come part of the way to the door of the speakeasy.

Howard was gently pushing Susan to the door. He called a cab. Susan pulled her little white fur cape around her shoulders, and then drawing away from Howard, she walked towards Paul and kissed him.

"Good night, Paul. Thanks for a wonderful evening and Happy Birthday!" Susan flashed him a smile as she was gently pulled away.

The little crowd of young revellers stood under the neon sign of Cafe Davide, unsure of their next move. They watched the yellow cab move swiftly along the street.

"That's the way to do it," said Brian.

"Sure. What a fast worker!" said Joe.

"Well. Howard was going her way, anyway. To the same house. And he is her boss. She couldn't refuse." It was Jenny, trying to pour oil on troubled waters.

"Let's go to Rudi's place and have one for the road," Paul said. "I'll see Susan tomorrow. Let's go, folks!"

In the back of the cab, Howard gave Susan a soulful look. The lights from the passing traffic were lighting up Susan's face intermittently. She felt disturbed by his silence. Eventually he said, "So that's Paul?"

"Yes, he's a student doctor at St Vincent's."

"I see."

They both eyed the back of the head of the driver. Then Howard leaned over and was kissing her hotly. She responded to the kiss like a thirsty plant to water. His hand caressed her slight body, and she thrilled to his touch. Then, she pushed him gently back, and looked at him, not knowing what to say. "Howard ..."

"I love you! I love you, Susan. I can't bear to see you with anyone else. Young men! I can't stand them near you. I hate Paul. I hate all your friends." Her cheeks burned. She looked straight ahead so as not to carry on talking.

Howard leaned forward, "Stop here!" he called to the taxi driver.

"But, we're not at the house, yet," Susan was puzzled.

"I thought we could stroll from here. It's not cold. I just had to have you alone for ten minutes."

Hand in hand they walked, their passion held in check. People passed, going home from their evening on the town, and the avenue was quite busy with cabs and private cars. At a little basement cafe, they stopped for coffee. They found a booth where they were quite private.

"You look so pretty, Susan. I can't see the old Susan you used to be at all. She's gone! And who is this new, streamlined, modern girl, this flapper I'm seeing here?"

"I can take plenty of that kind of talk, Howard. But, you know, tomorrow's Sunday, and I've got church to go to, and then Freddy to take care of over lunch."

"But, it's still Saturday night, Susan."

"You're a wicked man."

"No, just mad about you."

"This is not fair, Howard."

"It's true. I love you. I think about you all the time. But ... I know ..." he stumbled, lost for words, "I know you have your future in front of you, and I'm just an old has-been."

"You're not. You're a handsome, charming man. I ... love you, too, but you belong to someone else."

He drank his coffee. She saw his change of mood. "Do you know when I came home at ten this evening, George was coming out of Betty's room. And she was nearly naked on the bed, and drunk."

Susan was shocked. "George! You don't think ..."

"I don't know what to think ... but ... Oh, let's forget about it. He wouldn't be the first. She's had others. It's modern life in New York, I'm afraid. People's morals are elastic to suit the situation."

"It's just as well my mother doesn't live in New York. She would see me as a scarlet woman, talking in this way with a married man. She would have me saying the rosary until it was coming out of my ears." Susan smiled ruefully.

"Look, Susan." As he spoke his eyes burned with feeling. He seemed to be looking into her soul. "You got away today. I'd like to take you out. Show you a bit of the countryside. My house at Oyster Bay on Long Island. Nothing wrong. I wouldn't harm you. Just some time together. To ourselves. What do you say?"

Susan's eyes widened, "I couldn't, Howard."

"Sure, you could, Susan. These things don't happen too often in life – these strong attractions. It's now or never, my love. Take a chance! I can't get you out of my mind. Even in Chicago, doing business. Those soft, misty blue eyes of yours were always with me."

She caught the urgency of his voice. She picked up her wrap. "All right, Howard, so long as we take Freddie with us." Her mother's saintly face was fading from her mind. She put a scarf around her hair.

"Say it's very special. A special date!" he urged.

"A once-in-a-lifetime occurrence," she smiled sadly.

"If you like," he answered.

They left quietly to walk home. She was aware of the soft pleasure of his closeness, and knew that this head-spinning feeling could only be love.

CHAPTER 18

In Scotland, after the upheavals of the General Strike and the excitement of Archie's graduation, normal life soon resumed for everyone. It was in the following year, towards the end of July, Edward and Honor and the three children were able to afford a week's holiday. They chose to go to Rothesay on the island of Bute. As Edward was a railway employee, they had free passes on the train and on the steamer, and this sunny Saturday morning found them hurrying as fast as they could, Edward with a large suitcase and little Jamie, Honor with the plump, months-old Billy, bursting out of a white lace shawl, and little Nana, trooping by her side. For some reason, the passengers were always in a great hurry to cover the few hundred yards between train and boat, perhaps it was to be among the first to board the Clyde steamer, or just to find a good seat on the deck, or maybe they were a little scared that the boat would go without them.

Children carrying spades and pails for the beach, most dressed in new summer clothes, fathers puffing and panting under holiday luggage, and mothers anxiously scanning their broods making sure that none of their little ones fell off the side of the pier.

All kept in their own small enclave, sometimes with a grandpa or grandma in tow and maybe even a family dog.

From the first whiff of sea air and the first ray of bright sunshine, the children seemed to blossom. On board for the sixty-minute sail on the *Lucy Ashton*, they happily ate their sandwiches and listened to the band that played on deck. The holiday mood was instant. A visit to the engine room was a must for the children, where they watched thunderstruck the workings of the steamer, the great paddles being pushed round by enormous steel shafts. When the boat had safely docked at Rothesay pier and cheers had gone up for the accurate throwing of the ropes to tie her to the bollards, the holidaymakers trooped happily down the gangplank. Edward and his family set off up the hill to the little house with the two rooms and toilet that they had rented for the week. There was an old saying among women like Honor in those days, 'What holiday? I'm sure you're just exchanging one kitchen sink for another', but Honor didn't mind. She doted on Ned and the children, and would have worked until she dropped to see them enjoy themselves on this brief holiday.

On the third day, her better-off sister Veronica and her husband, Willie, had promised to visit them on a day trip and Honor, Ned and the children made their way to the pier to greet the arrival of the steamer. Majestically the *Lucy Ashton* sailed into the bay, seagulls screaming in the wake of her mighty paddles as they mashed the water. As the ship docked, the passengers moved to the portside so that the vessel sat lopsided in the water. Those on the pier all watched anxiously to try to distinguish their own friends among the arrivals. Honor made out her brother-in-law and her sister, and to her great delight, she saw that Veronica was holding on to a shiny pram on the deck.

"Oh, Edward! Look! How wonderful! Veronica said she would try to find a second-hand pram for me." She moved the fat Billy to her other arm, relief and simple joy flooding her at her sister's kindness. Honor felt a real toff as she installed her baby in it. And what a great relief to her aching arms! They walked past Rothesay Castle to the little house. There they had a great meal of steak pie and mashed potatoes.

In the afternoon, they promenaded along the front, taking turns to push the pram. At Port Bannatyne, Willie treated them all to a fish-and-chip tea, and by six-thirty, Veronica and Willie, their day-trip ended, were saying goodbye on the pier. Just before she stepped on the gangplank, Veronica, taller than her sister and much more elegant in her dress, bent down to whisper to Honor.

"I think I'm expecting. I think I'm three months gone."

The warm-hearted Honor threw her arms around her sister. "Oh, Veronica, I'm so happy for you. I know you have always wanted to have a child. This is great news." Neither of them mentioned the still-born baby Veronica had had three years earlier, nor how most people considered that Veronica and Willie would be a childless couple. They waved one another goodbye until the steamer was almost out of sight, then Edward and Honor walked along the front with the pram, now accommodating two of the children.

Next day they were to have a picnic and Edward took charge as he remembered from his youth a little-known, almost secret place at the other side of the woods. After picking their way along a narrow path through the trees, carrying their bags of pop and sandwiches, they came eventually to a hidden loch. It was called Loch Fad. A supernatural quality hung about the place. A body of dark water about half a mile all round, surrounded by silent hills, and all in the middle of nowhere. It was a stunningly beautiful place, but eerie at the same time. Gladly they sat down to rest, and the children seemed unperturbed by the atmosphere. But Edward, especially, felt uneasy. What was it that hung over the place? What past history of druids or savages, of deer or rabbits, of foxes or hares, one could not tell, for the place was silent as the grave, and not a blade of grass stirred. They stayed only half an hour and left the cold beauty behind. The Celtic blood in Edward's veins was disturbed by the place, and he secretly scanned the ferns and shrubs for spirits or unknown forces.

Within not much more than half an hour, they found themselves back in the sunshine and sand of the beach just round from the pier. There they had the pleasure of the company of other families, and they sat and watched, without ever being bored, the tanned limbs of their children, as full of joy they raced backwards and forwards into the sea.

On the day before their holiday was finished, they decided to take the children for a sail and laid out the last of their money on a boat trip up the narrow arms of the waters of the Clyde, the Kyles of Bute. A midday dinner was included in the cost of the ticket, and small children travelled for free. Here again the scene was tranquil, as the little craft slowly inched up the waters between the silent, remote hills of the Firth of Clyde. Such was the air of secrecy and beauty about the trip that the passengers fell into a hush. The combination of quiet mountains, so green and lush with rhododendrons and bracken, of deep still water, and of bright sunshine was awe-inspiring. But it was the silence, the stillness, the feeling of being the only ones ever to have seen this little spot on earth that affected the passengers on the quiet ship. Even the children, in imitation of their elders, sat down in the unusual atmosphere to look in puzzlement at the scene.

On the return trip, Honor sat downstairs in the passengers' lounge, feeding the fat mushroom of a baby that was Billy. An older lady joined her, feeling sympathy for her pale face and her air of being drained dry. Indeed, she was dry, for her breasts hung limp and empty where the infant had been feeding. Still the baby was restless and unsatisfied. He whimpered as she wrapped him in his shawl and placed him against her chest.

"You'll never feed a big lump like that yourself, lassie. You'll have to get a feeding bottle and some baby milk for him. You'll kill yourself, and you with another two bairns to look after."

Honor smiled. "Do you think so? He is very big for six months old."

"Think so? I know so! I've reared five boys, and that bruiser there'll kill you. Don't you be so silly! You can still give him the breast at times, but he needs a supplementary feed. You ask your doctor."

It was good advice. Next day they purchased a baby's bottle and a tin of dried milk. For the first time since his birth, the child, after downing three-quarters of a bottle of the mixture, slept until the morning. Edward, returning early from his evening pint in the local hostelry, was pleased to find his wife smiling and relaxed, reading a magazine. The house was tidy, and the three children were asleep. That night, also for the first time since the birth of the child, they were lovers again. Honor was the happiest woman in Scotland as she cradled her dark-haired darling in her arms. Edward lay awake, thoughts of love and life, of the strangeness of experience, of his workmates and the strike, all crowded into his brain at the release from tension brought on by his wife's caresses. And, when just for a minute, the voluptuous sensual body and the demanding lips and arms of Madge Morrisey invaded his mind to efface the gentleness of Honor, he pushed the image aside, and even prayed to God for forgiveness for his past wickedness.

CHAPTER 19

"If it's to be on Saturday, I'm going to stay with your Auntie Maggie. I can't abide noise and carryin' on." Annie Denny was not in favour of this projected party for Archie.

"We'll make it a double celebration. Elsie and Jim are coming back from their honeymoon. They've promised to come next Saturday to see my mother."

Edward laughed, "The return of the runaway bride! I'd like to be a fly on the wall at that meeting."

Honor was annoyed at Edward. "It's a serious matter, Ned. They want to make it up with Dad and Mam. Mam was broken-hearted at missing seeing Elsie getting married. Oh, it'll be great to see her again. I have missed her!"

Archie sat Honor down at the table with paper and pencil to make a list of guests to be invited to the party. They came up with fourteen names. Archie became chief organiser, as it was to be in his house.

"You can do the food, Honor. Maybe your Stella and Lily will help you. I'll give you some money. Joe can bring his banjo."

An idea brightened Honor's face. "Maybe my mother will let us borrow the gramophone."

"Oh, great!" Archie strolled around the parlour thinking. "We'll invite Euan McEwan. He can bring his dance-band records."

Like most quickly arranged parties it was a great success. By half past eight on the following Saturday things were in full swing. The third round of drinks had been supplied and people were loosening up. Archie put on some dance music and soon half a dozen people were trying to foxtrot to the dance music.

Honor had managed to find a neighbour to look after the children for a few hours, and she was enjoying the fun of the occasion. She was excited about her sister's imminent arrival with her new husband, and hoped Elsie had not become too grand to socialise with them now that she had moved into a bungalow in Bearsden.

At last the newly-weds arrived, young and happy. Classically good-looking, with auburn hair, and a skin like alabaster, Elsie was the reigning star of the family. She had won a bathing beauty competition, and had appeared, posing sedately with a beach ball in a bathing suit, on the front of the *Daily Express* newspaper. She was artistic and full of personality, always up to some practical joke or other. The girls in the family were sorry when she left, for she could always be relied on to start up some fun.

They stopped the music to congratulate the bride and bridegroom. Elsie, dressed in a powder blue coat with a fox fur collar, had the arm of her husband, a smartly dressed young man-about-town, who was as proud as punch of his new wife. To see three of her sisters at once was a great joy to Elsie, and she turned to Honor, "How are all the little ones, Honor?"

"They're thriving, Elsie. You must come and see them tomorrow before you go back. How did Mam and Dad take you two turning up, married and independent?"

Elsie took off her coat. "Oh, you know old Louisa. She was tearful at losing her 'dearest girl'. You know the martyr bit. About how her heart was broken at me running away. But she changed her tune when she saw how happy we are, and especially when she saw the ring, she was all right then eventually, and of course, you know Dad. He was delighted to see us."

Later, as things warmed up, there was dancing, and at ten o'clock, a cake was brought in. Edward announced in his usual tipsy fashion that the cake was to celebrate Elsie and Jim's wedding and also the graduation of Archie as MA with Honours. Archie took a bow to everyone's amusement. Next he was presented with a woollen scarf and gloves, and forty Capstan cigarettes, and taken aback at this, he stopped fooling around to accept the gift.

When the music stopped, Edward asked for someone to give the company a song. "Oh, be quiet, Ned, you're always taking charge!" It was Elsie, and she gave him a little push. Swaying slightly at this tomfoolery, he landed heavily on the armchair, and a loud, rude noise was heard to the screeches of hilarity of everyone watching. For, of course, Elsie had placed a 'whoopee cushion' under the chair cushion, and Edward had to take the joke with as good a grace as he could muster.

"Give us a song, Edward. Come on, one of your favourites!" It was Archie making the request and hushing the noisy company.

Suitably flattered, Edward stood up. "I will sing a song – my father's favourite song – to my wife and her lovely sisters:

"Believe me if all those endearing young charms
Which I gaze on so fondly today,
Were to change by tomorrow and fleet in my arms,
Like fairy gifts fading away,
Thou would still be adored as this moment thou art
Let thy loveliness fade as it will
And around the dear ruin each wish of my heart,
Would entwine itself verdantly still."

The song was very moving, and Edward had a tuneful voice. The listeners were rapt when there was a knocking on the door. Joe Denny answered the knocking and entered the room, "I'm afraid we have some gatecrashers, folks." So entered Madge Morrisey and Rose.

Joe, well intoxicated, started to sing, "Macushla, Macushla, my sad heart is calling ...," not noticing the consternation of Edward and Honor.

The realisation of who was the author of the secret note to Edward dawned on Honor, and the pieces of the puzzle began to fall into place. She felt giddy, and her sister Lily, feeling her sway and about to faint, held her up and asked for a glass of water for the shocked girl.

The two newcomers were dressed in party wear and wore a lot of make-up. They looked out of place as they stood at the door smiling. "We heard there was a party and thought you wouldn't mind another two joining you. I wanted to see the star from the Daily Express." The attention of the room was on them. "Hello, Elsie, I hear you're married now, and gone up in the world."

Archie sized up the situation. "Come into the other room, Madge and Rose. Just a minute. Follow me."

Edward stood frozen in the centre of the room. His romantic song had died on his lips, and he stared dumbly at his pale-faced wife. After much patting with eau de cologne and rubbing of the wrists and temples, Honor came round. She could not speak, so agitated was she. And she could not tell anyone what was wrong with her, for she had not divulged Edward's indiscretions to a soul. But Archie had read between the lines and knew that Honor had had a great shock. "Edward," he called, "could you come here a minute?" Out of the hearing of the revellers, he said sternly, "Will you ask these two women to leave? You see how upset Honor is."

Edward, sober as a judge with the shock of the arrival of the ghost from his past, entreated the two intruders to leave his mother's house. But they were quite drunk, having spent a few hours in the pub, working up the courage to barge into the party. Eventually, after much argument and raised voices, Rose flounced out of the door, and Archie gave Edward a few seconds to speak to Madge.

She stood very close to him, her perfume overpowering. "I had to see you, Ned. You've been avoiding me, and you know how I feel. It's torture knowing you're so near and with someone else. I love you. I can't live without you," she pleaded, and tears ran down her face.

"That someone else is my wife, Madge. I have three children. You shouldn't have come here. That was stupid." His voice was just a hiss. He was scared of what the knowledge of the woman he had been unfaithful with would do to Honor.

"Well, I'll go, but only if you promise to meet me tomorrow."

"Anything, Madge. Just go! You've caused enough trouble." He looked behind him stealthily to make sure no one could overhear them.

"One o'clock on the Gartocher Road, under the bridge, or I'll tell Honor all about us, and I'll tell her you're crazy about me."

"Just go! I'll be there. Don't worry, I'll see you tomorrow."

For Edward and Honor, the party was over. They left quite quickly, and Archie sat bemused in the corner, while the party went on around him. He gazed unseeing at the gift of scarf and gloves and the two packets of Capstan cigarettes in their pale blue wrapping. He was joined by the newly-wed Elsie as she sat laughing and exhausted after dancing. "Well, Archibald, you're a success in life at last, I hear, earning a fine salary at the Academy of St Mungo – patron saint of the great city of Glasgow."

"Success in life?" he smiled wryly. "Well, Elsie May, I'll call you by your full name, since we're giving each other titles tonight, I might be a little intoxicated, Mrs Shields, but I think you're a bigger success than I am."

"Me? Not me! It's just life that makes me bubble," and she laughed happily to prove it. He thought her the most stunning woman he had seen in his life. Such perfect teeth! Such luminous eyes and perfect features! "You could have been a film star, Elsie. Do you know that? By Christ, that Jim Shields is a lucky man."

"You're sweet, Archie," and with a tipsy smile she kissed his cheek.

"How much money did you get for winning the beauty competition?"

"Fifty pounds. We've put a deposit down on a bungalow. So that will give us a good start."

"Are you still working in Elsmore's, the photographer's?"

"Yes, I'm chief colourist now. Oh, hang on! I'll show you a sample of my work." She opened her handbag and took out a photo of herself on a pebbly beach. It had been taken in the early evening so that her flat, shapeless flapper's figure was almost in silhouette.

Her hair and dress were blown slightly by the breeze, while her face and limbs had been delicately coloured. The sunset background, too, and the sea had received masterly treatment of reds, browns, purples and blues. It was indeed a work of art. And she gave the picture to him as a present.

"Give us one of your ciggies, Archie." She was back to her kidding, emancipated woman manner. They each lit up one of the fat, luxury cigarettes.

"Well, these are precious." Archie looked at the packet. "I should keep them for show, to draw out when I wish to impress the staff members in the academy. I'll keep my cheap packets of Woodbines well hidden."

"Come on, Archie, you're not as poor as that."

"Well, I haven't earned much yet, and I owe such a lot to Mother and others who treated me when I had nothing. Even some of the older boys, the sixth-year pupils smoke expensive cigarettes, while I stand around the school, hoping they won't notice my poverty."

She laughed at the picture he painted. "You're a caution! How's your love life? No girlfriend on the horizon?"

"Elsie, you know you were always the only one for me. But you passed me by. And Honor's married. Lily is sweet on Johnnie McNab. There's only Stella left." They both glanced at the sixteen-year-old, pretty as a picture, flirtatious and conceited, she would definitely be the downfall of any man she set her cap at. "She's gorgeous, but too rich meat for me, I'm afraid."

Elsie smiled sympathetically, "You'll meet the right one some day."

"I'm like the maiden aunt – stuck on the shelf, but living in hope of being noticed and taken down and dusted one day."

A loud voice interrupted their tête-à-tête. It was the eccentric local character, Guy Aldred. He had drifted into the party from a political meeting, looking for some discussion with his old friend Edward. He was dressed, as always, in plus fours and knee-length woollen stockings, his plump good-natured face beamed at Archie and Elsie, and he greeted them in his southern English accent, his voice loud and projected due to a lifetime of speaking on public platforms.

"Well, Archie, and how are you this evening?"

Archie stood up and shook hands with him. "Still banging the drum for anti-parliamentarianism, Guy?"

"Banging the drum for the right to Free Speech, my dear fellow. And who is this enchanting creature?" Guy took Elsie's hand and held on to it.

"This is an old flame of mine, Elsie Dryden, now Mrs Shields, I'm afraid."

"Enchanted, my dear," he said in an old-world manner. "I was told that your learned brother Edward would be here. I wanted to have a word with him."

"Ned and Honor have had to go home, sorry. A bit of crisis, I believe. Anything I can do?"

"No, dear boy. I'll see Edward some other time. There's a meeting on the Glasgow Green. I wanted to talk about my speech with him. He's always well informed and level-headed, that brother of yours."

"And you're still the rebel, Guy?"

"Still trying to avoid the dark dungeons, where the authorities would like to throw me. But my heart is sometimes heavy. The great General Strike failed because of those traitors in the trade unions. They let us all down. You call me a rebel, but the rebel of today is the orthodox of tomorrow. I don't give up."

Elsie was listening, fascinated, to this larger-than-life character. "Are you the famous anarchist?"

"Anarchist? Atheist? What does it matter what you call me? I am an enlightened man. I was a preacher when I was a young boy. I know the Bible backwards. My task is to inform people. We must look to the future when the ordinary worker will take power. Already men have revolted in Russia. Soon the real deserving people of the earth will take power. That day is what my friends and I are working for. But right now I want to speak to Edward, my friend and fellow worker."

Archie handed Guy a cup of tea, as he knew he wouldn't take any alcohol. "Ned is tickled with the name of your new office in Shettleston Road, Guy."

"Ah. 'The Olde Redde Booke Shoppe', also known as the 'Red Spot in the East'. Have you read our paper, *The Commune*?"

"Yes. I've seen it, Guy. You run down everybody in every party but your own."

"Charlatans, double-dealers, the lot of them, and especially Ramsay MacDonald – the worst of the lot. My philosophy, Archie, is that all men are self-perfecting beings, and I believe that some day, some great day in the future, we will live in a perfect world – a Utopia. But sometimes it is hard to go on when you see the rats who get into power. Still we fight on!" He raised his fist in mock salute. "I'll say goodnight," and he shook both their hands and made for the door.

"What a strange fellow, Archie! I don't think I've ever met anyone quite like him."

"There isn't anyone quite like him, Elsie. He has been jailed quite a lot for his stand against authority. He's one of those divine discontents that history throws up now and again. And thank God for them! They make life more interesting and, to faint hearts like me, more bearable."

Honor and Edward had walked home from the party in silence. The evening which had started in such good spirits had ended in disaster. Shocked by the appearance of the loud-mouthed Madge and realising that she was the woman who had been Edward's lover had made her feel sick with hurt and heartache. Soon, the neighbour who had been looking after the children had gone home, and she found herself breast-feeding her baby in the silent kitchen, while Edward had gone to bed. He lay totally concealed by the bedclothes, trying to hide from the scene that kept re-enacting itself in his mind. The half-drunk Madge swayed in front of his eyes, mouthing over and over, "I can't live without you, I can't live without you ..." until he fell asleep, disgusted with life.

Next morning the church bells from the three or four churches nearby seemed louder and more invasive than usual. Edward and Honor, silent and ignoring each other, went about their morning business. He helped to feed the children. Then announcing to an unresponsive room that he was going for a walk, Edward left for his assignation with Madge Morrisey.

There under the low, sooty railway bridge that straddled the side road, she stood. Edward approached. "We'd best go up the hill to the country road where we'll not be seen so much," he said as they started to walk. When they had passed the mansion houses at the edge of the town and reached the fields, Edward looked at her. "You had no right to do that last night, Madge. It was a private party. You and Rose barging in, half drunk! What did you think you were doing?"

"Oh, that's right. You think you and your family are the crème de la crème. You think you can just pick me up and drop me whenever it suits. The smart Dennys and the fancy-mannered Drydens! You've no time for the likes of me from Hareshill – too slummy for the likes of you!"

In the harshness of the morning light, her rouge and mascara looked overdone. Her anguish detracted from her dark good looks, and she seemed jaded, like a party that had gone on too long. Edward struggled to deal with the situation.

"Look! My wife heard our Joe call you 'Macushla'. So she knows about Mallaig, and all the rest." His face was drawn and lined with worry.

"You should have thought of this when you were swearing undying love for me. You remember that hotel. You remember how we loved each other, because I can't forget so soon!" She cried quietly for a minute, and then she looked at his dejected face. "I'm sorry, Ned. I don't want to mess things up for you, but ..." she was afraid to meet his eyes "you know there'll never be anyone else for me ..."

"Look, Madge. I don't know if Honor will ever come out of the shock she got last night. She was just getting over wee Louie's death, and now this." They walked on, both of them troubled and sad.

"Well, Ned. It takes two, you know," she had found her voice again.

"I know I'm partly to blame." He stopped to look at her, and over her shoulder he saw a tall, heavily set figure coming up the hill towards them, walking quite rapidly. A little in front of him was a large black and white collie dog.

"My God!" Madge stuttered. "It's my father."

Red-faced and puffy-nosed, eyebrows bushy, Lachlan Morrisey was the epitome of the rural bully. He wore an old-fashioned waistcoat, and trousers of brown and fawn check. In his hand he carried a stout walking stick. "Well! You'll be Edward Denny. I've heard about you. What are you doing out walking with my daughter?"

Edward opened his mouth to speak, but nothing came out.

"You're a married man."

"We met ..." Edward tried to find the right words.

"Oh, you met? By chance, are you trying to say? Dae ye think we're a' that gullible? Dae you think I don't ken whit ye are up tae? Ah kent your faither. If he was alive today he would have something to say to ye! And as for that smart-as-paint mother of yours, I think Annie would be very interested in what I have to tell her."

"What have you to tell her, Mr Morrisey?"

"Dad, Dad! Let's go home. Leave Ned alone."

But Lachlan had got hold of Edward by the shirt-front, and was brandishing his stick above his head. He was taller and much more powerful than the younger man. The dog barked and barked, cavorting around them.

"Bloody Catholic bastard! What does your parish priest have to say about this? You lying, thieving bastard!"

Edward managed to pull away from the hot whisky breath that was coming from the massive jowl of his adversary. "I'm not a criminal! And I'm not a liar or a thief."

"So it's not a crime to make a lassie pregnant, and you married already?"

Edward paled at this unexpected jibe, and Madge took his arm to pull him away from her father. "It's nothing to do with Edward."

"I'm supposed to believe that?" He spat in disgust. "I know you're daft about him. You have been for years. You'd jump in the river if he told you to."

"Father, look. Give me a wee while with Ned by himself. You go on home. I'll be home in half an hour." Edward faced him, white and stony faced with shock. Lachlan's eyes burned back at Edward, then he turned to Madge and took a step back.

"See that you're home within the hour." With a threatening scowl he turned to Edward, "You haven't heard the last of this, so don't think it!" and he waved his stick in a threatening gesture before making his way downhill, the dog running ahead of him. Edward looked into Madge's eyes, fear and sadness on his face.

"What's this now, Madge?"

"Let's sit down on that tree stump." He offered her a cigarette and they both lit up while she organised her thoughts. "I was lonely, crazed with jealousy when I got back from Mallaig. That day I saw you at the Bowling Green, you looked so happy with your little wife and family, I couldn't stand it. The next time Cadie Weir asked me to walk out with him, I decided to go with him."

"Cadie Weir?"

"Aye, that wild man. Anyway, it wasn't long before he ... I found I was pregnant." Her eyes were full of tears as she drew on the cigarette.

Edward was shocked and saddened at this story, for Cadie Weir was a well-known philanderer. "What will you do, Madge? Will you marry him?"

"He'll not marry me here. He says he's going to Australia. Only if I can get the fare to go, he says he'll take me with him. We could get married over there."

"How much do you need?"

"Oh, I've got some money saved, but Cadie says I need another thirty pounds before I can go."

"And then he'll marry you?"

"Aye, in Australia."

"Does he know about me?"

"He doesn't know the whole story, but he knows I was mad keen on you."

"Oh, Madge! Madge! What a situation!"

She broke down then, "I know. It's terrible. I've made a real mess of things."

Edward gave her his handkerchief to wipe her eyes, unbelievably relieved that the child wasn't his, but he had to smother a tear or two of his own, for poor senseless Madge. "You've always been headstrong and passionate, Madge. What can we do with you?" This softness made her tears of sadness flow freely. She felt as if her heart would break.

They sat for a while in the bright, warm afternoon, oblivious of the fields of corn, the wild flowers and the insects all around them. Eventually, Edward said, "You don't have to go to Australia with him, Madge. You don't have to marry him."

"I know, Edward. But it's a chance. He's settled down a lot, and I think, if we got away, he would be kind to me. There's work and a chance for the future in Australia."

"Well, I'll try and get you some money if that's what you want. But what will you tell Cadie? Where will you say you got it?"

"Oh, I'll invent a generous aunt or something. I'll throw him off the scent."

They started to walk back now, soon to separate at the crossroads. "I'll meet you at the same place under the bridge. Let's say Tuesday. That'll give me time to get a hold of the thirty pounds. Seven o'clock in the evening. All right?"

"I don't know when I'll ever pay it back, Ned."

"Well, you never know. I might look you up in Australia, someday."

"Now, you're talking. I'll remember these words. They'll give me something to dream about."

They parted quickly, and Edward, instead of going home, went to his mother's house. She and Archie had just finished their Sunday dinner, and sensing there was something afoot, Archie excused himself and left his mother alone with Ned.

"Sit down, Ned. Will you have a bowl of soup?"

"No thanks, Mother." He thought how old and frail she was becoming, but her eyes were still quick and perceptive.

"What's wrong, son?"

He told her the whole story. She paused before she spoke, shocked and bitter at his fall from grace and at their family name being involved in such a matter, but she was wise enough not to be surprised by what he was unfolding. "I know the lassie. She's common and looks wild. Her mother should have been more in charge of her. But I think the mother was of the same ilk. There's no point in telling you that you've been a fool, Ned, I think you know that yourself. I feel sorry for the girl."

"So do I, Mother." Edward's head was bowed, and he was near to breaking point.

"What about Honor. Poor lassie! She'll be in a state, too."

"Aye. She will."

"Get me that Gladstone bag. You know the brown leather one that belonged to your grandmother. It's under the dressing table, beside my bed." He gave her the bag, and she counted out thirty pounds onto the kitchen table. "There," she said. "Take it. Let's hope it brings luck to the poor creature." He stood up and lifted the money. "Tell Honor to bring the children to see me for a cup of tea this afternoon."

"Aye, Mother." He left her gazing into the kitchen fire, her face inscrutable and her shoulders thin and bent.

Monday evening passed with hardly a word being spoken by Edward or Honor. Her face showed her suffering and disappointment. So bad was the atmosphere that Edward, tired as he was from his hard day at work, changed and went out walking, the envelope with the thirty pounds still in his pocket. He passed the pub, but with a great effort of will he resisted the urge to go in and drown his sorrows.

On the Tuesday evening, when he had the arranged meeting with Madge, Edward silently changed out of his overalls and put on his sports jacket and flannels. He felt the pocket and found the money to be still where he had left it. After his meal, he stood up to make for the door.

"Where are you going?" Her voice sounded strange.

"I have an appointment."

"It's with her, isn't it? That tart?" Honor lifted the baby on her knee and started to feed him.

"Yes. It is. But not for the reason you think."

Tears started up in her eyes. "Oh, Edward! What have you done to us? A wife and three lovely children, and you have to drag our name in the mud like that. How could you?" Her words were like a blow to him, but he found himself lost for an answer.

"It's not the way you think." His voice was low and dispirited.

"There is only one way to think about that. You know it. What's more, they say she's pregnant."

"Not to me. The child is Cadie Weir's." He saw Honor's face change from bitterness to bewilderment.

"Cadie Weir! Never!"

"Yes, he's going to take her to Australia. They're going to get married there."

"Then what are you doing with thirty pounds in your pocket?"

"It's for Madge. She needs it to get to Australia. To get set up there."

"Where did you get it?"

"From my mother."

She put little Billy down in his pram. "Dear God, Edward, what are you bringing us all to. Is it the gutter you would like to see your family in?"

"That's enough, Honor. I did wrong and I'm sorry. You didn't deserve to be treated that way. It's over now. Just thank God she's going away and that my mother stood by us with the money."

Honor stood up and they looked each other straight in the eye. "And it's really all over with you and her?"

"Yes."

Honor covered her face with her hands and sobbed. The two older children, agitated by this, ran to her and clung on to her skirts. He pulled her hands away. "It will be all right, Honor. You'll see. It'll be all right." He folded his arms around the sobbing woman, and smoothed her hair. "Please forgive me," he pleaded. She looked and smiled. Words would not come. He turned swiftly and made for the door.

When he approached the raincoated figure under the bridge, he steeled himself for another emotional scene, but Madge was made of sterner stuff. "Thank you, Ned." she said as she took the money. "I'll never forget you – maybe I'll send you a postcard to let you know how I'm getting on, and where to find me. And if Honor ever gets tired of you, you'll find me in Sydney, Australia. You'll always be a friend close to my heart."

"You leave quite soon?"

"Yes, in a week or two. We're all packed, not much to take."

"Goodbye, Madge, and good luck!"

"Goodbye, Ned. I'll be seeing you." She managed a bright smile, but there were tears in her eyes, as she turned quickly and walked away.

CHAPTER 20

"He wants me to go to Oyster Bay, Long Island to see his house there." Lotta was mopping the floor of the large bare kitchen of the Park Avenue house while Susan followed her about, knowing that the girl would soon be off to meet her boyfriend, it being Friday afternoon.

"When? This Saturday?"

"Yes, and stay over. I think there might be other guests."

"Let's hope so!" Lotta gave Susan a knowing look. "There's Jethro, the housekeeper, and I think there's a maid. Are you taking Freddy?"

"Of course!"

"Why 'of course'? It's you Mr Howard's sweet on. He wants to get you alone. You have to admit it." Susan's eyes glazed over, and, highly embarrassed, she looked at the pattern on the kitchen wall. "Look at you. You're gone on him. I don't blame you, though you've got that crazy Polack mad about you and Paul running after you like a puppy dog. You sure have got something, honey. Maybe it's your ample bustline."

"Oh, it's just because I'm unattached and different from the usual, something new on the scene."

"Yeah, maybe. I ain't seen Mr Howlett look twice at any other woman around the place, before. He's usually too high and mighty for that. Does she – her ladyship – know you and Freddy are going with him to Long Island?"

"I suppose Mr Howlett will have told her, but she's going to Chicago to see her mother, so she wouldn't be here, anyway."

"Well, take plenty of warm clothes. I sure hope it doesn't snow before the weekend."

"Is there a Catholic church in that area, Lotta?"

"Yeah, I'm sure there is. There's lots of churches in Oyster Bay. You're goin' to stay overnight with Mr Howlett. You won't need no church in the morning."

"Oh, Lotta, don't be silly. I'm Freddy's nanny. I'm going as part of my job."

"Hm!" Lotta looked in the mirror in the kitchen, admiring her thick, dark hair and the arch of her newly plucked eyebrows. She started when she heard the cook's voice.

"Get that table set in the dining room, Lotta. There's dinner for six tonight."

"Who's coming?"

"Oh, some fancy folk from Queens, you know, cocktails and jazz records, and lots of strong cigarettes and cigars. Lots of crumbs and cigarette butts everywhere."

"Oh God! Up till one o'clock in the morning again! I hope if it's that Norris Newton and his wife that she keeps him under control. He tried to get up my skirts the last time they were here!" Lotta was now repairing her lipstick in a little compact mirror.

"Lotta, you're not serious? He really? Norris Newton was really up your skirt?" Susan was aghast.

"Sure he was! Mrs Newton, she didn't even notice. She's mad keen on Mr Howlett. I've seen her sly flirting with him behind Mrs Howlett's back." Lotta sounded disgusted "Right there in the same room. You wouldn't believe it!"

"Never mind about that now, Lotta. There's work to be done. Get your ass over to this table." Bella busied herself about the kitchen, working up a steam and cursing under her breath. "Mrs Howlett's going to Chicago at the end of this week on the train. George is taking her to the station on Friday. Her mother's not very well. She's going to visit with her family."

"And to the clinic, don't forget!" Lotta added.

"What clinic?" Susan looked surprised. "Is she sick, Lotta?"

"She's seeing a psychoanalyst. Trying to stop drinking."

Susan was shocked. "Oh, what a shame! Poor Mrs Howlett."

"Ain't much poor about her, if you know what I mean." Lotta gathered the cutlery from the box to set the dining room table.

"Yeah," Bella stopped her cooking. "Mrs Howlett, she sure is one unhappy lady. Just shows you, honey, money isn't everything. Where you goin', Susan, honey?"

"Oh, I've got the afternoon off, from two until seven o'clock. Mrs Howlett said I could have it. She's going to look after Freddy. I'm going to take the bus up Madison Avenue to St John's Cathedral. It's said to have beautiful stained-glass windows. It's on One Hundred and Twelfth Street."

George entered from the back door. "Off at two o'clock. Who? You, Susan? So am I! Mr Howlett's gone in his car to his office. I think he'll be takin' some cutie to lunch." Susan walked Freddy out to the courtyard at the back of the house. "Need a friend this afternoon, Susie?"

"I'm going to visit a cathedral, George. There's a guided tour at four o'clock. I want to see the stained-glass windows. There's mosaics and sculptures. I've been reading all about it. It's the second largest cathedral in the world, after St Peter's in Rome."

"You don't say?" George's Slavonic green eyes almost popped out of his head at the picture Susan had painted. "I ain't never been inside a church in New York. In Poland, when I was a boy, I used to have to go every Sunday. You'll let me come with you?"

His long, pleading face made her smile. "If you like," she said. He was as delighted as a child, and rushed to change out of his uniform and make himself ready. They took the bus up town and were soon entering the massive building, and joining the little crowd of sightseers being shown around the beautiful cathedral. They listened to the guide of this Episcopal cathedral of Gothic design, and stared at the lofty piers and arches repeating themselves along the length of the nave. George's face was a study in amazement and awe as he gazed down the church to the altar at the far end.

"Look at those lights, Susan. They're enormous! They're a knockout! I can count at least twenty." George took Susan's hand as they listened to the guide's exposition of the glories of the building. They touched the massive pillars and gazed at the stained-glass windows. Their spirits were filled with the beauty of the place. Absorbed in the atmosphere of the building, the time passed quickly and it seemed like no time until they emerged into the cold December air and pulled their collars up against the bitter wind. "I'm glad you brought me here, Susan. I would never have come myself. I sure am amazed that I could spend so much time in a church."

"It was a lovely afternoon, George. New York is just full of interesting and beautiful places. I've been reading about them. I intend to visit some of the churches and museums, whenever I get the chance. And I'd love to visit the Bronx Zoo."

"OK! We'll go there some day. You English! Always searching after something – knowledge or culture!"

"Scottish, George!"

"It beats me, Susan. It really does. Where did you get your love of book learning and hankering after cathedrals and such like?"

"Who knows, George. My family are all like me. Born that way, I guess. My mother spent all her spare time studying for nursing qualifications. It's a way of life. Maybe it's self-improvement. I don't know."

"Well, all I know is that I'm starving after all this education. I hope Bella's making soup for dinner tonight."

"So do I, George, it will heat us up."

"We sure need something. I think it will snow soon."

"Oh, yes. You might know. Just my luck! Rotten weather in time for my trip to Long Island. I'll probably be stuck in all day with Freddy."

"Mr Howlett's not much company, anyway. He's always busy with his business papers. Never lifts his head for hours at a time.

That's how he makes his money, worrying over company reports and stocks and shares. Unless he gets a bit, you know, lovey-dovey." George leered at her and put his arm around her waist as they hurried along the avenue.

"Oh, stop it, George! He wouldn't do that! Anyway, I'll have Freddy every minute of the day."

"What about the nights?" She hit him with her handbag.

"Cut it out, George. You're becoming a pain in the neck. Really, I would like some nice weather that I can go out in and see the place. They say Oyster Bay is beautiful."

"I shall miss you, and I'll miss little Freddy."

"It's just for two nights. We'll be back on Monday."

"Mrs Howlett will be away, too."

"You'll miss her, George. You like her, don't you?"

"She's good to me." His face was doleful.

They sat down in a little cafe to have some coffee before going for the bus. "How is she good to you, George?" Susan unwound her scarf.

"Well, she listens to me. Asks me about my life, and what I do in my spare time."

"And what else?"

"Nothing else. What are you saying, Susie?"

"Oh, nothing. I know she drinks a lot. I just thought she might get a bit amorous at times."

"Amorous – yes! She does. I get a bit scared sometimes. I could lose my job. But she's lonely and unhappy."

"How is she lonely? She's got a husband, a child, servants and loads of friends."

George took off his gloves and drank some coffee, holding his cup so as to warm his hands. "I think Mr Howlett and she don't find much to talk about anymore – and her friends, they're not much good. Social climbers, if you ask me. And that charity work. That's just showing off. Who can get the most attention of the papers, who can make a hit – give away the most money – pick the right charity to support? They're all so full of themselves."

"It's sad. Isn't it, George? An outsider would so envy her. No need to work or kow-tow to anyone. All those clothes and that wonderful jewellery she has, and a chauffeur. So many smart friends and beautiful cars."

"And a nanny. No boring bringing up children for her!"

Susan laughed, "Yeah, and a nanny."

"Freddy will end up more attached to you than to her. Some day I'm going to tell her that. Some day, when I get another job, I'll tell that silly woman a few home truths." George was talking himself into a bad mood.

"You're really thinking about looking for another job? Gosh, George! You wouldn't give up your place with the Howletts. It's so safe and secure. New York's a bit of a jungle, you know." She looked out the window at the people hurrying, heads down against the biting cold. It was already almost dark.

"I've been looking at the papers. Good chauffeurs can always find work."

"Oh, George! It won't be the same if you go."

He smiled a wide ingenuous smile of pleasure at her remark, and took her hand in his. "Susie, look! I can't have you, I know that. You're interested in your man back in Scotland. For sure, you're not falling for yours truly!" He gave her a sad-eyed look. "Mrs Howlett's making a play for me, and one of these days, Mr Howlett's going to catch us. It's hard to escape her clutches, and she's drinking like a fish. I mean it's a worrying situation, Susie."

"Don't you have any family, George?"

"I have parents, sure! They live in Yonkers. They're happy – retired people. They worked hard all their lives. Long days for little money in the restaurant business. I help them when I can but ..."

"Do you visit them, sometimes? Tell them your worries?"

"Huh? They think I live in the lap of luxury. They think I've landed in a bed of roses. They don't know nothin'. I see them about every two weeks. Sure, I see them. Maybe I give them a few dollars. They would like me to get married and give them grandchildren. I got a brother who went to Canada. I could look him up, I suppose. But I like New York. I like the buzz of never knowing what's going to happen next. Like, someone like you comes along." He took her hand across the little marble table. "I wish it was Monday and your weekend away was over, so I could see you back, safe and sound."

Embarrassed at the affection in his eyes, she said, "Why won't I be safe in Long Island, George?"

"Well, you know. I know Howard Howlett likes you, and you wouldn't be the first."

"What do you mean?"

"Well, I think he has, you know, affairs – girlfriends."

She searched for a reply. "That's what he says about you."

His big green eyes widened, and his eyebrows shot up, "I? I have girlfriends?"

She had to laugh at his expression. "Yes, you know. You're a flirt!"

"Well, maybe, there's been one or two little girlies along the way."

She became serious. "Look, George. I like Howard and I know he's fond of me. But I'm not a stupid wee lassie. Like you, I don't want to end up with no job in a big city far from home."

"I've seen him look at you, Susie. I think he – anyway, be careful you don't, you know – get carried away with all that stuff he's got around him."

"I'll be careful," she said.

"And what about poor Paul Ballantyne? I've seen him with his arms around you. My God! Some 'wee lassie'! You collect men like a honeypot collects bees!"

"What an exaggeration! You're nuts, George! Paul's nice, but well, I've still got Tommy writing to me from home. So I must keep Paul at arm's length. He knows that. One day Tommy might come over to America."

"Well, he'd better hurry, or his wee lassie Susie will be gone."

They stood up to leave, and he suddenly embarrassed her by burying his lips in her hair. "I'll always love you, Susie, even when I'm old and grey." As her cheeks grew pink at this sudden declaration, he gave her a serious look, "Remember, be careful in Long Island."

"Of course. I'll have Freddy to run after. Besides, if those fancy New Yorkers are there, whose goin' to notice me? Nobody, that's who!"

"Wanna bet?" He kept his arm around her as he paid for the coffee. They left the cafe to catch the bus.

—·—·—

On Friday, Betty Howlett made an emotional farewell to the staff in the kitchen. She hugged Freddy who smiled up at her, waving his little hand and saying, "Bye-bye!"

"Goodbye, my darling. Do what Susan tells you. And eat up all your cereal." He hugged his toy horse and stared at her. When she briefly kissed Susan on the cheek, Susan thought she detected the smell of liquor on her breath. "Take good care of my baby, Susan. And both of you have a nice time at Oyster Bay."

"Thank you, Mrs Howlett. I'm sure we will."

"I won't be gone much more than a week." Her face was very well made up, her beautiful arched eyebrows and mascara-laden eyelashes standing out on her face. Her manner was very gay and light-hearted for that time in the morning, as if she were going to a ball, instead of on a train trip to Chicago.

In the back of the limousine, Betty placed a cigarette in her long holder and lit it carefully with her gold lighter. Sitting back against the leather interior, pulling her deep-piled fur coat around her, she puffed quietly, staring unseeingly at the traffic. At the next corner, a very drunk man was holding on to the granite corner of the building to try to steady himself. He was fairly well dressed, and his scarf blew in the wind, an idiot's smile on his face. The passing crowds on Fifth Avenue hurried on, ignoring him, and his irrelevance to their daily preoccupations. Betty shivered and withdrew her eyes quickly. Her mind floundering to find the solution to her feeling of loss of control of her life in this battle with alcohol.

George was drawing up. "Here we are, Mrs Howlett, Pennsylvania Station." They stood amid the noise and bustle of the busy station, trying to concentrate on what to say amid all the distractions.

"I'll telephone you, George, and let you know which train to meet, next week."

"Sure, Mrs Howlett."

"I'll visit with my folks, and while I'm home I'll see my doctor."

"I hope you have a pleasant trip, Mrs Howlett." Around them, the noise of the engine, the steam and smoke were suffocating. She slipped a twenty-dollar bill into his hand.

"Take care of yourself, Georgie. I'll miss you and ... but, you know I have this problem. My nerves have been bad lately ..."

"I know, Mrs Howlett. A few days with your folks and you'll be a new woman. I'm gonna miss you, too."

"I'll bet you've got a nice little girl waiting for you somewhere, George."

"I wish, Mrs Howlett. I wish. Maybe I'll try and find her." His eyes were quite tearful as she held out her hand from the carriage window.

"Call me Betty, just today, George."

"OK, Betty." The train started slowly to chug along out of the station. They waved goodbye like lovers, then, when the train was out of sight, George turned for home. Tonight, he thought, I'm getting out on the town, somewhere. I've seen some nice girls down in Quinn's pub in Washington Square. Yeah, that's where I'll go. As he drove home, he planned which of his suits he would wear, and pictured in his mind the handsome fellow he would be. He had a friend who worked in the kitchen at Quinn's, another Pole, Joseph Plotowski. Maybe they could paint the town together. Joseph always had a couple of phone numbers. His thoughts turned to Susan and her sweet body. Right now she'll be at confession in the church, or some such holy occupation. He parked the limo and went in to tell Bella and Lotta that he was off work for the day.

But, he had been wrong about Susan. She was there in the kitchen working hard, ironing clothes for Freddy and herself for the next day's trip. "Not going to visit the Holy Father this evening, Susan?" George leaned over her, teasing.

"No, George. Unfortunately, I can't manage. I've too much to do. We leave on the ten-thirty train, in the morning, you know. You've to drop us off at the station."

"OK. Yeah, maybe confession would be a better idea when you come back from Long Island, honey." He laughed as he made for the door. She threw a dish-towel at him, but he escaped just in time.

When Freddy was in bed and the cases were packed, she washed her hair, and in her dressing gown sat chatting in the kitchen to Lotta. Earlier, George had appeared dressed to kill, hair slicked down and a fiery gleam in his eye. "Well, look out, New York, here he comes," Susan teased. "Just call him Rudolph Valentino."

"Don't you drink too much, George." Bella's ample figure had appeared as they were teasing George. She brushed his shoulders with her soft hands. "And don't go with any loose women."

"I might as well not go out then, Bella."

Susan had piped up, "Listen, George. I'll tell you a joke about an Irishman who was a secret drinker. He disguised his breath with peppermints. Then one night, for the first time in his life, he came home sober, and do you know what?"

"What?"

"The dog bit him!" Susan laughed heartily at her own joke.

"We haven't got a dog!"

"Oh, forget it, George!"

George retaliated. "The Irish are all stupid! I know an Irish joke. There were these two Irishmen in a strange part of town, watching a funeral come down the street one day. 'Who died?' asked Murphy. 'I think it's the one in the hearse,' said his friend, Riley."

"Goodbye!" Susan shouted at him as she pushed him out the door.

"Let's have a little glass of port," Lotta suggested. "Bella won't mind." She had washed her hair, too, and Susan was rolling it up in curlers for her. Lotta got up quickly, and locating Bella's secret stash in the cupboard, took out a bottle of port and two glasses. They sat enjoying the dance-band music on the radio and drank their port.

"Do you think you'll marry Costa, Lotta?"

"Costa? No, no fear. He's my boyfriend, and, boy, can he make love, but he's never grown up. He's too scatterbrained. I have to pay our way most of the time when we go out."

"Why is that? Doesn't he earn much money?"

"Sure, he earns money, but like all Greeks, he gambles, and he likes to buy nice clothes for himself. I love him. I'm crazy about the guy. But marry him? That'd be a life sentence the way he is now. He's too young to settle down to a wife and kids. Maybe someday.

Meanwhile, I have to be very careful when we are together. I don't want to get myself into trouble and land in a mess." She took another sip of the wine. "Not this Lotta! My mother taught me well. You got to control these guys in the city. Otherwise you'll pay the price." The corners of her mouth drooped and she nodded her head at Susan to show she was very serious.

"You mean, you let him … you know?"

"Kid, I'm an Italian, I'm twenty-two years old. I'm only human after all."

Susan was silent, and they decided to have a second glass of port. They were joined by Bella who poured herself a good-sized glass. She started to talk to them, seeming to be a little embarrassed. "The house is going to be empty from tomorrow morning, when you lot go away, Susan. My fella over at the Jones's, you know the butler, Rupert, from two blocks down, who sometimes takes me to the movies? He's coming over to stay the weekend while everyone is away. Don't say nothin' to Mr Howlett. You hear me?" Her Italian accent was thicker as she let them in on her secret.

"Wowee! Bella, you old devil." Susan's eyes popped out of her head. Bella was sixty-five if she was a day.

"Now, Susan, don't you go saying anything about this to Mr or Mrs Howlett!"

"Of course not, Bella. Gee whizz, Bella, I won't say a thing! Oh gee!" She swayed around. "That wine's gone to my head." She steadied herself for a minute, and laughed at the two others. "Well, who'd have thought it? And I thought I was the lucky one, going to Long Island. You two take the biscuit with your secret love lives. I'd best be off to bed." She had reached the door. "I'll sleep well tonight, I think. Thank you for the port wine, Bella."

"Goodnight, Susan, honey. I'll call you at seven-thirty, in case you oversleep."

In the station next morning everything was in a state of flux. An undercurrent of anticipation was felt everywhere. Susan, in her grey uniform, walked beside Howard as he carried little Freddy to their reserved seats. George followed behind along with a porter, both carrying luggage.

Then they were off. The train reminded her of home, and she fell into a reverie as she sat there with Freddy on her knee. As the train slowly gathered speed, the little boy watched with fascination the moving picture from the carriage window. Faces began to disappear from sight, and they were on their way out of the city. It was a very long train with added locomotives to help the engine. A great cowcatcher in front was the beginning of this magnificent apparition as it made its way triumphantly across the country, with coaches that snaked along behind, into the distance. Out of New York it went, making a regular, quickening rhythm on the rails, its whistle hooting loudly now and again, as if to show its joy in its power and movement.

The corridor was alive with restless travellers, and porters and officials. Every moment aboard the train seemed filled with movement. From the window, the countryside soon appeared, quiet and still, with farmhouses dotted here and there. Susan sat facing Howard who had spent most of the last twenty minutes reading his morning paper. "Will there be someone there to meet us?" she asked when she got his attention.

"Yes. Jethro will bring the Oldsmobile down to the station, that is if the old jalopy is still functioning."

"Who's Jethro?"

"He looks after the house. Stays there all the time. He'll bring in his daughter, Maria, to cook for us, and she'll hire a girl to help her serve at table. They just work there when Jethro needs help. He's alone now since Mabel died a couple of years ago. She used to be there, too. She helped to keep the house."

"And you said your mother will be there?"

"Yes. Oh, don't worry, Susan. You'll like her. She's OK. She's remarried now, since Dad died, and she lives, most of the time, in the San Francisco area. She hasn't seen Freddy since he was a few weeks old. Her husband's a man called Harry Banyon. He was in banking before he retired. They're staying with Uncle Robert who lives in the village. He's a bachelor. She never comes to New York to visit because she and Betty don't get on."

Susan nodded, trying to take all this in, and he continued. "They're just different types, Mother and Betty. Mother thinks Betty is too full of art and poetry, and doesn't look after me. She doesn't care for the set Betty and I mix with. You know what mothers are like."

"Oh, I know. My mother's a bit like that about my brothers. No woman has been born who's really good enough for their sons. I think that mothers must be the same the world over." Howard nodded in agreement, and she asked, "Will there be anyone else there?"

"Yes, there will be seven of us altogether. Mum, her husband Harry, Uncle Robert, and Baxter and Tania. They're old friends of the family. They'll want to see Freddy, too. But you don't need to worry, Susie. Things are informal in Long Island. We don't dress up or anything. You'll eat with us. They'll want to meet you." She felt butterflies in her stomach at the thought.

"But, don't you think ...?"

He interrupted her, "No 'buts' now, Susie. You'll love them. It'll be fun." His fond look across the carriage stemmed the rising panic she felt. "We'll keep Freddy up late. He can have dinner with us for a change, and that will take the spotlight off you."

At last, the clickety-clack of the wheels started to slow, and the train had arrived, bathed in a steady stream of smoke and steam. It was a pretty station with scalloped white woodwork edging the roofs. Standing prominently in the centre of the platform, among a dozen or so people to meet the train, was a tall, grey-haired man, Jethro Paxton, Howard's housekeeper and chauffeur on Long Island.

CHAPTER 21

The house was an enchanting brick-built mansion, the wood of the windows and eaves in need of some painting and with a large garden also showing signs of neglect. Above the front door, you could just make out the name through the creepers, Havencrest. There were about ten rooms and a cottage at the back for the hired help. The front door opened to reveal a gracious hall with an elegant, carpeted staircase, which wended its way to the six bedrooms and four bathrooms on the floor above. Built around the turn of the century, the furniture was a bit old-fashioned and lacklustre, but the whole place had a rustic kind of charm. Jethro had laid a log fire in the living room, and the table was set for luncheon.

"I just got cold cuts and salad, Mr Howlett. Hope that's OK?"

"Fine, Jethro. Looks great."

"Maria will be here at six to make dinner. She'll probably bring a girl with her. You're staying until Monday mornin', is that right?"

"Yeah, got to get back to work on Monday. Business is business, you know, Jethro."

"It sure is great to see you, Howard, and that little fellow looks just like you when you were a boy."

"It's swell to see you, too, Jethro." Howard put his arm around the old man. "You don't change. You're like Old Man River, you just keep rollin' along."

"God's been good to me, Howie. That's the truth."

"This is Susan, Freddy's nanny, and a good friend of the family."

"How do you do, Susan? It's a pleasure to meet you." The two shook hands. "You know, it's been almost two years since you've been here, Howie. And that's a shame. House needs people, you know."

"I know, Jethro. Too busy, I'm afraid."

"I hope you'll bring Master Freddy here more often. There's the beach in the summer and the funfair. And they got new ponies over at the stable. Just right for a little boy."

"You're right, Jethro. Freddy deserves to come and enjoy himself like I did with Georgette in the old days."

"I sure wish, Howard, your sister Georgette would visit."

"Yeah. She's still down there in New Mexico. Never comes north. Haven't seen her for years. Let's see, she'll be forty-two now. She's a grandmother three times over. Beats me! Maybe I'll take Freddy to visit with her some day."

"Your mother arrived yesterday. Came to see me. She looks happy, anyway. She's over at your Uncle Robert's place."

"Yes, they're coming for dinner tonight, along with Baxter and Tania."

"I'll show you to your room, Susan," Jethro smiled at her. "I've put a cot in the adjoining room for the little man. I hope I did right."

"I'm sure it'll be fine, Jethro." She followed him up the stairs.

In the afternoon, Howard, Susan and Freddy went out to explore. After they had been round the garden and walked down to look at the ocean, they came back for a cup of tea in front of the fire. Susan had never felt so much at home in America as she did that afternoon. Perhaps it was the nearness of the sea, or the moist air of the coast, or even the coal and wood fire flickering in the fireplace that made her sentimental. She sat on the rug in front of the fire with Freddy, playing with his toys, and talking intermittently to Howard. The pressures of the New York house and the traffic and the pace of things seemed a world away.

From the kitchen came the aroma of roasting beef and other enticing smells. Maria proved to be capable and friendly. She and the hired maid, Wilma, were delighted with little Freddy, so that Susan found she had little to do. Howard had changed into a different outfit, plus fours and a sporty shirt and pullover.

"Tonight, for dinner, you must get out of that nanny's outfit. Put on something flattering."

"Will your mother and friends be dressed up?"

"Well, maybe, just a bit."

"I have a nice pale blue dress I brought with me, and my good pearls. But they know I'm just the nanny."

"So what? You're my nanny. You're my lovely Susan, and you're a little piece of Scotland in America. We all love you, you know." He kissed her forehead. "I relax around you. You're good for me, sweetheart."

"Well, Howard, I don't feel relaxed. I'm a bag of nerves."

"You'll walk it, honey. You'll see."

Seven-thirty found little Freddy changed into a navy blue sailor suit with white socks and new white kid boots. He was the centre of attraction and Susan followed him around, the soft folds of her dress falling around her slim, pretty figure. Jethro opened the door to usher in Howard's mother and stepfather, Harry Banyon, Howard's uncle Robert, and some friends. There was a rushed greeting for Howard, then the older people's eyes lighted on Freddy as he climbed around the armchairs and footstools in the old shabby room.

Roseanne Banyon let out a scream. "Well, look at this little man, Harry! Isn't he darling! Are you Freddy?" The child stopped his climbing in amazement at the clucks of admiration. "Come and see me. I'm your grandmother! And this is your new grandfather. Oh! He's gorgeous, Howard!"

Harry Banyon bent down to talk to the fair-haired toddler. "Well, I hope I'm gonna see a lot of this little chap. I sure would love you for a grandson, Freddy."

Howard put his arm around Susan's shoulder. "Listen, folks, this is Susan. She looks after Freddy for us. She has done for more than two years, now."

Roseanne, Howard's mother, was a handsome woman, white haired, cultured and with a kind, friendly attitude. Susan liked her immediately. "How do you do, Susan? I've heard about you from Howie's letters. You've done a fine job with Freddy. He's delightful."

"Yes, he's a good little boy, and very easy to manage. Very lovable. He's getting a bit adventurous and determined now he's past two years old. I have to watch him all the time."

"Well, that's natural for a little boy, Susan."

Jethro entered, "Mr Baxter McManus and Tania are here, sir."

More squeals of delight and greetings ensued. "Baxter, you old rogue! Tania!" Howard was pleased to see his old friends.

"Why, Tania, you are slimmer and younger looking than ever!" The couple were aged around their mid-forties, and were neighbours and playmates from Howard's and Georgette's childhood. Baxter was tall with a touch of a middle-age spread, while Tania was petite, slim and pretty.

When they were seated at dinner, Baxter waded in with questions about New York and the state of business there. Talk of stocks and shares was above Susan's head, and she was glad to concentrate on her table manners. "How's Betty? Sorry she didn't get down this time. She hasn't been here since '24, I think. Is she still mixing with that lot, spouting poetry and all that arty stuff?"

Howard smiled inscrutably, "She took up painting for a while, and gave that up. She does work for charity – keeps her busy."

Baxter said, "She's an impressive woman, your wife, Howie, beautiful and intelligent."

"Yes, she's very well up on the writers who are all the rage with that bohemian set, you know, James Joyce, D. H. Lawrence, and all that lot. She always was a prolific reader, and, I suppose, a sensitive soul, Betty."

Tania leaned over slightly towards Howard as she spoke, revealing her perfect teeth. "We must come and see her in New York, sometime. We're not that far away from your place in Manhattan. We just never seem to make it over there somehow."

"Well, Betty's in Chicago right now. Her mother's been ill, and she also was due to see her doctor there." Harry and Tania exchanged glances.

Roseanne's face was serious. "Oh, what's wrong with her, Howard? You should have told me. Why is Betty seeing a doctor?"

"Well, Mother. She's had a bit of nervous trouble lately. I think it could be her age, you know." Howard smiled. "You know what women are like. She's coming up to middle age, you know."

There was an embarrassed silence around the table, then Harry Banyon spoke to Susan, "You know, my dear, my forefathers came from Scotland. My grandmother was a MacDonald. Do you know what the MacDonald tartan is like? I wouldn't mind getting a kilt, someday."

"I don't know, Mr Banyon. You'll have to go to Scotland and find out. But," she teased, "we don't all run around in kilts with swords drawn, you know."

"You don't say? You mean it's not all heather and highland glens and bagpipes? You don't say?" He winked at her. "Tell me, then. How do you like living in the United States, Susan? Very different from your country, eh?"

She put down her knife and fork. "Well, I think it's great here. New York is a fabulous city. You could spend years there and not see it all."

"Yeah!" he agreed proudly, "no place like New York!"

"The people are so friendly, and Howard and Mrs Howlett have been so good to me." Freddy was moving around somewhere under the table, having abandoned his meal, and finding great interest in the shoes of the guests. Susan bent down to pick him up. "I'll think I'll take Freddy off now, Mr Howlett."

"No, Susan. Take him to the kitchen until we've finished our meal. They'll look after him, and you come back here. After coffee's time enough to take Freddy up to bed. You're here for a holiday." The guests chatted on about mutual acquaintances, and how good things had been in the old days. By the time coffee was brought in they had arranged a grand family reunion for Easter. They all decided that they must lean heavily on Howard's sister and get her to bring her two children and three grandchildren to join them from New Mexico. Roseanne and Harry would come from San Francisco. Baxter and Tania would try and bring some of their family from Connecticut.

"It will be just like the old days! Loads of family and friends to have fun with!" Baxter declared. Pouring himself a large brandy, he felt on top of the world. "Can I interest anyone else in a drink?"

When Freddy had to be taken to bed, Susan tried to say goodnight, but Howard would have none of it. "You come back down. It's only nine o'clock. We might have a sing-song. Uncle Robert will give us a tune on the piano."

"Well, I'm sure it's out of tune by now," Uncle Robert protested.

"No, Siree," piped up Jethro, "I had it tuned last week when I heard you was comin'. Spring-cleaned the home and aired the beds."

"What a great friend to the Howlett family you are, Jethro," Uncle Robert said and he rose and approached the old upright piano. He lit the two candles in their candle holders with his cigarette lighter and sat down to play. Up and down the keys a few times his fingers went, and then he broke into 'Toot, Toot, Tootsie, Goodbye!' and soon they were all round him singing their hearts out, their voices lubricated by some good French brandy. They moved on to slower airs, and when they got to the 'Bonnie, Bonnie Banks of Loch Lomond', Susan's voice began to falter with emotion.

The servants, drawn by the music, came out of the kitchen, and were asked to join in. When they had tired themselves out, they finished up singing 'Yankee Doodle Dandy' to much laughter.

Howard's mother and Harry were beaming. "What a grand evening! Thank you, Howard, and Jethro, Maria and Wilma. I don't know when we had such a good time!"

"I sure agree with that!" Uncle Robert added as he took his coat from Jethro.

Susan and Howard stood at the door as they were leaving, saying goodnight like a happily married couple. Roseanne disguised her curiosity as to the relationship between the two. She had concluded that there was something there. The light in Howard's eyes had not been there for many years. "That serenity and calmness of spirit must come from her deep Catholic faith, Harry," she said to her husband that night when they were getting ready for bed. "What else could explain her quiet, happy character. To be so calm and contented is a God-sent gift." But Harry was only half listening, the wine and brandy having clouded his brain. Roseanne soliloquised on, "Perhaps she's a reflection of her homeland, that place of hills and lochs, and yet she loves America and feels at home here." Harry only grunted. "I've invited her and Freddy with Howard tomorrow evening for dinner. What a sweet child Freddy is! I could keep him myself." But soon Roseanne found she had really been talking to herself, and she lay down to a familiar chorus of snores, her nightly lullaby.

When Susan and Howard closed the door, he looked silently at her for a few seconds. "I'll check with Jethro, then we can have a drink together by the fire." When he reached the kitchen, Jethro was already cleared up and on his way to say goodnight to them. He had a large pipe of tobacco in his hand ready to light. He waved goodnight to Susan and shook hands with Howard who was saying, "Thank you, Jethro. That was a wonderful evening you made for us."

"It was nothin', Howie. Just like old times." His eyes were sleepy in his seventy-year-old face, and his grizzled hair gleamed white above the shiny darkness of his skin. "I'll lock the kitchen door behind me. See you in the morning. Goodnight."

From the refrigerator, Howard picked up a bottle of the best champagne and returned to the lounge. Susan was sitting on a footstool by the fire, the folds of her blue dress around her. "To celebrate your true arrival in America, Susie! What else – champagne!" The cork flew off with a loud pop, and he poured out two flutes of the sparkling wine. "To Susie!" They drank, and she was soon showing the instant effect of the wine with giggles and eyes widening. They chatted by the dying embers of the fire over another glass, and then he reached over to kiss her on the lips. Susan seemed slight and willowy in his arms. She relaxed for a few minutes against his muscled shoulders. Shoulders built up in his college football days. "Are you sleepy, baby? I'll put you to bed." He took her hand, and they climbed the old staircase, stopping to peep in at Freddy. Her nightgown and robe were lying white and lacy on the deep rose-coloured quilt. He picked it up. "I'd like to see my honey in this! I'll go and get ready in my room. I'll be back to say goodnight."

She was brushing out her brown hair, when Howard returned in his robe. Now his embraces were fiery and full of desire. He did not speak but she felt the passion within him and she lay back on the bed in ecstasy, until she mumbled, "Howard, I ... you ..."

"It's the first time for you, Susan, isn't it?" She nodded and he kissed her tenderly. "You sure you want to?" She nodded again and he took her with great care and passion, so that the awakening was heaven to her. They lay in a dream for some time.

"I'm crazy about you! Have been almost since the day you walked into my life."

Tongue-tied, she said, "You make me so happy, and I have dreamed about you and me together. But I'm a little scared, you know, if anyone finds out."

They were awakened in the morning by a toddling Freddy and his toy horse. He pulled at the bedclothes and Susan jumped out of bed, lifting him and his toy horse and taking him to the bathroom, as if to hide her guilt from the baby.

They took Freddy to the stables nearby that day, and Howard rode around the place on one of the fine horses there, while Susan held Freddy on a little Shetland pony.

"You've never ridden a horse, Susan?"

"No, never."

"Then some day, I'm going to teach you. We'll come back here together some day." She was still in a daze from the shock and pleasure of their lovemaking of the night. Standing in Oyster Bay, in the winter sunshine, breathing the ocean air, and smelling the brown, fecund earth turned over by the horses enhanced her love-struck mood. Her whole being glowed with contentment.

In the afternoon they went visiting Howard's mother and stepfather, and Uncle Robert. Really it was Freddy's day. He was cuddled and kissed and cooed at by Roseanne's friends, who envied her this cute little boy. His blonde hair and baby smile were like a magnet to the local matrons.

At dinner at Uncle Robert's that evening, Roseanne, dressed in expensive cashmere, her hair, newly coiffeured, sat Susan next to her. "Tell me about your family, Susan." As best she could, Susan described the members of her family. She tried to convey her admiration for her mother, telling how hard she had worked and how she had persisted with her midwifery studies for her diploma. She told of her pride in her young brother, Archie, and his place at the university in Glasgow. "What a wonderful family to come from! And you'll go back to Scotland one day, Susan?"

"Oh, I think so, Mrs Banyon." Roseanne caught the quick exchange of glances between Susan and Howard. "Yes, I love Scotland. I miss my family, a lot of the time." She had to stop talking to prevent the tears forming in her eyes.

"Well, I'm glad you came to my son's house to look after Freddy. I know my son loves you, and we love you, too."

Startled by this direct declaration, Susan blushed and looked away before she managed to blurt out, "Oh, how nice of you to say that, Mrs Banyon."

"I hope you'll be staying for some time? Freddy needs you." The child was standing, leaning against Susan's knee.

Susan put her hand on his fair curls. "Oh, I'll stay for some time yet, won't I, Freddy?" He pulled her skirt so as to try and climb onto her knee, and she lifted him up for him to see around him.

"I believe you have a sweetheart in Scotland." Roseanne was a direct type of woman, and wanted to know what she wanted to know.

"Yes. Tommy." Susan tried to picture him, but in these surroundings, the candlelight, the perfume and jewellery, the servants and beautiful food, she could hardly bring his face to mind. "Tommy Cairns is his name. He comes from a little town in Lanarkshire called Shotts." She thought she must sound inane to this grand lady, but she felt she had to keep talking.

"He writes to you?"

"Yes, yes, we keep in touch."

"What does he do?"

"He's a miner. A coal miner."

Roseanne, if she was surprised, did not show it. She knew her own past was pretty lowly. She was descended from poor immigrants from Yugoslavia, and she knew there was Irish and English blood in her somewhere.

After the meal, they sat around, the men drinking brandy and talking politics mainly, while the two women played with Freddy. At last, Howard extricated himself from the discussion and suggested it was Freddy's bedtime. Howard and Susan said goodnight and drove back to Havencrest, where the sleeping Freddy was put to bed without awakening him.

The house was deserted, and Susan and Howard were soon in each other's arms. Their passion rising to new heights, he was more urgent and more demanding than he had been the previous night. Susan was more easily aroused and clung to him in moaning desire. Sated at last, they fell asleep in the great oak bed, sinking down into the feathery luxury of swansdown quilt, and lavender-scented bed linen.

Susan, awake first, spent a few minutes in the delight of gazing at her lover. He lay snoring slightly, dark stubble showing on his chin, his eyes closed in misleading, boyish innocence. Then, she sat up, her thoughts straying back to New York, to Betty Howard, to Father Donahue in St Patrick's, and at last to her saintly mother. She looked back at Howard. He's got a wife, who has been good to you. What are you doing here? Was it her conscience or her mother talking to her? She is the mother of his child, and she pictured Father Donahue standing over her in shocked disbelief at her sinful behaviour. "No!" she cried aloud, and she shook her head so that her brown hair fell round and covered her face.

Howard's eyes opened, and a silly smile crossed his face when he saw her still there beside him. He reached up and touched her shoulder, caressed her arms and then her breasts, until she slid down beside the warm Adonis so full of love for her. A few hours left! A few stolen hours. Let tomorrow take care of itself. These last few hours, out of life, will be ours. Her desire had won the battle with her conscience, and Susan kissed him sweetly and passionately, giving herself willingly to his love.

— · — —

George met them at the station at four o'clock and by then they had managed to hide their new feelings for each other. Susan knew she had the hardest task in the weeks ahead, to keep their love hidden, and worried about her new, difficult position in the household.

"Hello, George. Glad you could make it to the station. Can you take this luggage?" Howard was dealing with the bags.

"Good to see you folks again, Mr Howlett, Susan, and here comes little Fred!"

"Hello, George. We had a wonderful time, didn't we, Freddy?" and Susan lifted him up for George to kiss. Freddy smiled and nodded his head.

"Thanks for being here, George. Good to be back in New York. How's the weather been?"

"Well, we've had another fall of snow, and it's been so cold! Coldest days this year in New York, they say." George drove through the city, which seemed so full of people and traffic after the peace of the countryside. "Bella was making a pot of broth when I left, so that's something to look forward to."

Lotta and Bella greeted them at the kitchen door with hugs and cries of welcome. Howard left them in the kitchen, and went off to make some phone calls.

Bella reached to the shelf above the kitchen range saying, "Oh, Susan, this cablegram came for you," and she handed it to her. Nervously, Susan read:

ARRIVING NEW YORK 20th DECEMBER, AFTERNOON. WHITE STAR LINE. SHIP, 'ORDUNA'. PLEASE FIND ACCOMMODATION. LOVE TOMMY.

Stunned, the poor girl looked up at the others in the kitchen. They had stopped what they were doing and seemed to Susan to be in suspended animation, as their questioning eyes searched her face. Only the toddling, chattering Freddy moved in the still kitchen for those few seconds. Susan sank down into a wooden chair at the table, unable, for the moment, to say anything. Lotta took the cable out of her hand and read it out.

The two women sensed her perturbation. They somehow saw she was a different girl from the carefree person they had waved goodbye to, two days before. They could see that the news was not welcome and felt her panic and unease when they looked at her young face. George was disturbed at the thought of an intrusion by an outsider into their circle and could not know that the startling news had put Susan in a deep dilemma. Tommy arriving! Someone from home. It was unbelievable, but how could she face him in just a few hours from now, after her time in Long Island with Howard?

CHAPTER 22

Thinner than she remembered, dressed in a belted, gabardine raincoat and a soft hat, he was carrying a small bag and a slightly battered leather suitcase. Straining among the crowds, Susan caught sight of Tommy as he arrived on the pier at New York. She rushed to greet him, her heart racing, a broad smile lighting her face. At first, he did not see her. Then the delight of recognition almost overcame him, so that his smile outshone hers. How many hours, days, weeks and months he had dreamed of this moment. But who was this Yankee beauty that rushed to greet him? In high-heeled shoes and dark suit, she was slimmer and taller. Had her eyes always been so large, were her teeth always so white?

Susan, too, saw her old friend in a new light. To her he looked like what he was, a boy from the old country, his eyes full of wonder as he arrived in this different world. Then she remembered the things about him from their first days as sweethearts. She saw the familiar joking expression and read there again his obvious good nature. These things had made her love him. She recalled the way he put up with her ambition to make money and to get on in the world. Perhaps most of all, she admired him for his readiness to enjoy his time away from work, away from the hard labour in the dust and darkness of the coalmine. The words tumbled out of her as they met, and she found herself telling him he looked thin and pale, the first thing she could think to say as he beamed at her.

"That's with pining away for you, my girl." He hugged her tightly amid the thronging crowd.

"Let me take this bag, Tommy. You are to come home with me, and then we'll show you the digs we found for you." It was difficult to move because of the crowd, and for a few minutes they stood still, trying to take in their momentous reunion.

"I'll take that." It was Howard, tall, tanned and assured, who stepped in and took the bag from Susan. He held out his hand to Tommy. "I'm Howard Howlett. Welcome to the States." He smiled and put an arm around the young man's shoulders. "Follow me. We're parked over here."

George was standing by the car in his smart uniform, bursting with curiosity about the new arrival. Smiling stupidly, his prominent eyes shining, the chauffeur shook hands with Tommy and said, "Welcome to the United States of America," and he bowed and clicked his heels, and then, embarrassed, he shot into the driving seat of the big white car.

"Did you have a good crossing, Tom?" Howard asked.

In a broad Scottish accent and with a shy smile, Tommy said, "Well, I wasn't sick. And the food was very good. Otherwise it was a long time to wait on that ship before we saw this wonderful New York Harbour."

"Yeah? What do you think of it?"

"It's terrific, Mr Howard." His deep voice contrasted with nasal New York voices calling out to each other all around him, but Tommy was unaware of this. "We've all seen pictures of New York, but the real thing just takes your breath away. It is some city to arrive in after the long time at sea. I won't soon forget my first sight of it."

Pleased with this response, Howard seated himself beside George in the front of the Cadillac. He would not resent this newcomer. He would focus on the smart shops and buildings, the large shiny automobiles and taxis as they travelled uptown. He would try to see the city from Tommy's eyes, and make an effort not to turn around to see Susan and her young man together. George, too, felt childishly jealous of Susan's beau from Scotland. Only the fact that he knew Howard was upset at the situation made things bearable.

And on that wonderful first journey through the canyons of stone and steel, Tommy spent the time, one minute beaming stupidly at Susan and the next in ducking down to try to see the tops of the buildings.

At the Howletts, a kind of party of welcome was set out in the kitchen with Lotta, her boyfriend, Costa, Bella, George and the Howletts, including Freddy, joining in. There was enough for twice as many people – roast beef, roast chicken, mashed potatoes, beans, peas, and cauliflower. For dessert, there was apple pie and cream, followed by coffee and brownies. Tommy was overwhelmed by this lavish food and by all the new faces and the sheer friendliness of the people.

"What kind of work are you planning on doing while you're here, Tommy?" Howard spoke from the head of the table.

"Well, Mr Howlett, I'm a miner, but I don't think there's much coal mining in this city. I'll just have to try my hand at whatever I can get."

Costa said, "Oh, you'll find something. They're looking for waiters in the Delaney's restaurant across the road from my place. It's mainly European or French food. They serve a lot of steak. The only trouble with working there is – their waiters are singing waiters."

Bella said loudly, "Yeah! You'll have to sing 'You're the cream in my coffee. You're the salt in my stew'," as she poured out coffee.

Howard and Betty Howlett stood around the kitchen in this party atmosphere. The excitement was building, and Howard said, "Listen, Bella, you're not getting any more money in your salary for dancing and singing, if that's what you think." But Bella just smiled and went on with her singing.

Then George spoke up, "Listen, Tommy. Costa and I, we can help you to be a waiter. He is a waiter, and I used to be one. There's nothing to it." He stood up, taking up the stance of a high-minded maître d'hôtel, putting a table-napkin over his arm. "It's easy!"

He flashed around the kitchen giving the air of efficiency, lifting plates and straightening cutlery.

"I forgot about that, George," Costa laughed at the memory. "You were more a cabaret act, the way you used to forget half the orders, drink whisky with a spoon out of soup plates and ogle all the women." Everyone laughed while George put on a threatening face.

"Just you shut your trap, you Greek ... ballet dancer!"

"Shut up, you Polack palooka."

Howard pulled them apart, telling them not to scare the guest.

George was as high as a kite. "I'll show you how to be a waiter. We'll practise at my place, down at Mrs Walters'. We got you a room beside Costa and me."

Costa joined them, saying, "We'll show you the ropes, that is if you can tear yourself away from sweet Sue here."

And Susan was happy with the way things had worked and relieved that they were taking care of him. "I'll see you in the morning, Tommy. We can go to Mass at St Patrick's." He managed a quick kiss before he left the Howletts as she said, "Happy Christmas, Tommy! It's great to see you again. I still can't believe you're here. It's a miracle!"

The Howletts had decided to go for a few days to the country. Before they left, Howard managed to speak to Susan. But there wasn't much that either of them could say, and confusion and hurt were kept hidden from the rest of their world.

Susan's voice lifted. "Yes. I'd almost forgotten what he looked like. He's different from his photograph, but still he's a very good person, I know that. I can't thank you and Mrs Howlett enough for helping me at the boat and for the party and everything."

"It will be a few days before I see you again, Susan." He reached in his pocket and handed her a little package. "Have a good Christmas. This is for you. It wasn't expensive so don't feel guilty."

She took the parcel. "Thank you. I've got nothing yet for you, for Christmas."

"You'll think about me while I'm away. Don't get totally wrapped up in Tommy. You won't forget me or Long Island, will you?"

She blushed, looking round to make sure they were alone and then, remembering the past, she whispered, "I can tell you, I won't ever forget that weekend. It was wonderful but crazy, you know ... I must go. And you have to pack for your trip." With a quick and furtive embrace they parted.

Back in Mrs Walters' rooming house, a pantomime was taking place. In the dining-room, George and Tommy were seated at the table, while Costa, arrayed in a long white apron and with a towel over his arm, was being the waiter. He handed the menu to Tommy. "I can recommend the roast duckling. It's fresh from the country this morning." He kissed his closed fingers in an expansive gesture to show the quality of the duck. "It is served in an exquisite orange sauce." Tommy tried not to laugh at all this play-acting, then Costa said, "Now you, Tommy. You be the waiter."

Tommy tied on the apron and took the towel and attempted to copy Costa's style in serving at table. "No, no!" Costa was not pleased. "You must walk in a hurry. You can't stroll around in a restaurant in New York."

"Yeah, that's right." It was George talking now. "You must look sharp. I used to always look sharp when I was a waiter." He took the cloth and rushed about the room to illustrate his point. "Even if you are cursing them, you must smile and look ready to jump when they speak. The customer is king in New York."

They made him set the table with the proper cutlery and then acted out the scene as two customers.

"Remember to talk loud and smile all the time." George threw out advice as they went to wait in the hall. "Try to remember every customer's name."

When Costa and George entered, Tommy, in loud voice and Scottish brogue, called, "Good morning, sirs. Walk this way." With great style, the trainee waiter swerved round and smiling servilely showed the two diners to their table.

"You got the job! You got the job!" George had to sit down to rest from laughing at Tommy's efforts to be a smooth New York waiter.

"Just tell the bosses you used to work in a restaurant in London. They don't know London from a hole in the head. Make up a name for a restaurant in London."

"The Top Hat?" Tommy ventured.

"OK! The Top Hat, near Buckingham Palace. It's a cinch!"

George stood up to go upstairs to his room. He stretched his arms above his head. "What a day! And it's Christmas Day tomorrow, Tommy! We're all going to Clancy's in Forty-Second Street for our Christmas Dinner. Susan has booked the two of youse in, but you'll have to endure church first, if I know Susie."

"Christmas Day in New York." Tommy's voice was full of wonder. "I feel as if I've died and gone to heaven!" and he followed his two new friends upstairs.

The twin Gothic towers of St Patrick's Cathedral that Christmas morning were a revelation to Tommy. Almost medieval in appearance amongst the skyscrapers of Fifth Avenue, it was drawing people to its great doors. Although half an hour early, the faithful were swarming in to find seats near the front for the twelve o'clock Mass. Susan and Tommy had a brief walk around before they sat down. Tommy stood amazed at the beauty of the side altars, but it was the windows that drew his eyes. Enormously tall great sources of light, they ranged down both sides of the nave of the building. The carved white marble traceries were illuminated as were the stained glass windows, where stories from the Old and New Testaments were depicted. They sat down near the back, Tommy in silent awe. Then, devout Catholic as he was, he fell on his knees and prayed his own prayer.

Quite at home with the Latin of the Mass, they emerged with the rest of the congregation, spirits uplifted on that cold, crisp morning. "Merry Christmas!" and "Happy Christmas!" were heard and smiles and handshakes were seen all around the door, as people greeted each other. Tommy felt as happy as a sand-boy to be here on the steps of St Patrick's Cathedral in America with his beloved Susan. Years of longing and planning had gone into this moment for him. And she was prettier and more desirable than ever. He told himself, "Well, they can't take this moment away from me."

The staff dinner at Clancy's was noisy and fun. Half the chauffeurs and domestic staff in New York seemed to be there. Soon many of them would be back in their kitchens, but right now people were taking pleasure in table-hopping, giving Christmas greetings to their friends and downing glasses in celebration of the day.

Tommy managed to slip his gift for Christmas to Susan. It was a beautiful heart-shaped gold locket, and though she was moved by his thoughtfulness, she could not help thinking of the gift from Howard, at home, unopened. She closed her mind to it.

"There's nothing inside yet, Susan. I thought you could choose a photograph to put there on your own."

She leaned over and kissed him. "You are too good to me, Tommy. This must have cost a fortune."

"Nothing's too good for you." He stood up and fastened the locket around her neck. She told him that she hoped he would be happy in New York.

"I'd be happy anywhere with you, sweetheart. If I can earn some money, then who knows?" His eyes said all the rest.

"We'll all be rooting for you at Delaney's tomorrow, Tommy. I'll keep my fingers crossed that your luck will be in."

And the morning came. "So you've worked in London as a waiter?" Delaney sat behind a desk in a tiny office in the restaurant. He was rotund of figure, wearing a flashy satin waistcoat and smoking a big cigar. "Our waiters here, you know, are first class. They've got to be good, and have good backgrounds. Be reliant! Did you bring references?"

"Well, I have a letter here from the parish priest from where I lived in Scotland." He handed the letter to Delaney.

"What did you call the place you worked at in London?"

"The Top Hat," Tommy gulped.

"A classy place?"

"Very classy, Mr Delaney."

"Well, when Frank and Jerry come in, we'll see if you can sing. If you can harmonise with them, you can start in the morning. You see Frank about wages, but I can tell you, it's mainly tips you'll earn here." He told him to wait in the corner of the restaurant.

The restaurant was a large room, almost Victorian in decor. A long, polished wooden bar, tall gantries with concertina-type wooden shutters, behind which could be glimpsed innumerable bottles of whiskies, brandies and other liquors. Frank told him that if the cops raided, the shutters would descend and all that could be on show would be soft drinks.

The tables had red check cloths on them, and the lights suffused the place with a pink glow. Frank sat down at the piano and played a few quick chords. "OK, Tommy. Let's hear. What are you going to sing? Do you know 'Me and My Shadow'?"

Frank sang the introduction while he played. He sang with gusto:

> *"Shades of night are falling and I'm lonely,*
> *Standing on the corner feelin' blue.*
> *Sweethearts out for fun,*
> *Pass me one by one.*
> *Guess I'll wind up like I always do,*
> *With only ..."*

And Tommy croaked out the first line, "Me and my shadow, strolling down the avenue ..." He started again and his singing got better. Dan Delaney came out of his office.

"Guess he's in, Frank, eh?"

"OK. Start tonight. You'll have to buy a waiter's apron. Be here at six-thirty."

Tommy passed his first week in Delaney's in a blur, but he had made thirty dollars in tips to add to his fifteen dollars pay.

A few days after Christmas, Betty and Howard with little Freddy arrived home from their trip. It had been a disaster. They had spent most of the time with other people, and Betty's drinking was getting worse. That first evening back in New York, sloshed as usual before dinner, slouched at the table, she said coquettishly, "I think, Howard, we should get a dog. A dog would be fun. I'd like a spaniel."

"You're drunk, Betty. But you're right. Maybe you could look after a dog. You sure can't look after Freddy."

"What do you mean?" She glided carefully over to the mantelpiece, trying to hide her tipsiness, and she lit a cigarette. "I love little Freddy."

"You hardly looked at him all the time we were away. You were too busy with your endless gossip and your cocktails. You'll have to stop drinking!" he was shouting in frustration.

"And you'll have to take more interest in me. Why do you think I drink? Because you ignore me half the time."

"You drink because you like to drink, because you think it's smart and also because you haven't anything to do in your life."

"I've loads to do, thank you."

"If you don't watch, you'll be an alcoholic. If you're not one already."

Betty stormed out of the room, and Howard heard her phoning. She was speaking to her new arty friend, Justin Roots. "Yes, darling. I just got back from a trip and I'm missing everyone. The Cafe Continental? Will you call for me? Right, I'll be ready in half an hour. Bye, darling." Howard stood beside her as she put down the phone.

"At this time of night, you're going out?"

"That's right. I'm going where people like me for what I am."

"What are you, Betty?"

"I'm a fun person. That's what I am. People like my company."

"You wouldn't be so much fun without your fancy clothes, your money, your chauffeur ...," he was lost for words in his temper, "your accoutrements!" he shouted.

Betty rushed upstairs. She shouted out, "Arrogant bastard!" in Howard's direction before banging the bedroom door. She pulled out her most outrageous outfits, chose a bright red number and piled on some more make-up. Howard stood at the foot of the stairs, and Bella answered the door to Justin.

"Hi there, Howie. How you doin' there? Had a good trip?"

"Good trip, Justin," Howard said woodenly.

"Hurry up, Betty. The others are waiting. Time's slipping by. Good night, Howie."

Bella turned to return to the kitchen. "Where's Susan, Bella?"

"Oh, she asked me to keep an eye on Freddy. She said she would be an hour or two. She wanted to see Tommy singing down at Delaney's, Mr Howard."

At Delaney's the atmosphere was smoky and noisy. Most folks had almost finished their meals, and some, knowing the entertainment would start soon, were casting glances towards the piano. Howard entered in time to see the three waiters begin their act. Tommy wore a drooping false moustache. The harmony was good, and their actions and expressions added a comical slant to the performance. The diners applauded noisily, and they went into:

"Ramona, I hear the mission bells above ..."

But Howard wasn't watching the singers, just Susan, as she sat at a side table, her eyes following Tommy in his new job. She clapped louder than anyone when they had finished, and Howard felt a stab of jealousy for Tommy and his uncomplicated life.

"Is this a private party or can anyone join in?"

Astonished, she said, "Howard! What brought you here?"

"You. Who do you think?"

"What's wrong?"

"Oh, the trip to the country was a disaster. And the misery continues. Betty's gone out nightclubbing with bloody Justin Roots, and she's half-drunk already." He looked at her sadly, "Did you like my Christmas present?"

"It's lovely." She looked down at the ring. It held a single pearl.

She looked up to see Tommy about to join them. He had taken off his apron, and Howard invited him to come home with Susan and have a drink with him.

"Sounds good, Mr Howlett."

"Call me Howard."

When they got back to Park Avenue, Bella joined them for a drink and soon left for her bedroom. The three sat on, talking of the sensational crossing of the Atlantic by Lindbergh, the previous summer. "Three thousand miles in thirty-three and a half hours," Howard said with amazement. "Can you imagine! An average speed of one hundred miles an hour!" Tommy nodded in agreement, saying he had read it in the papers and they talked of the terrific ticker tape welcome for Lindbergh in New York.

Howard warmed to his subject. "Sure was terrific. You couldn't move in New York that day. Over four million people cheering Lindbergh. You remember that day, Susan?"

"Yes, I went up to see him with George, Lotta and Bella. It was amazing!"

"And nowadays," Howard was saying, "you can go from coast to coast in less than twenty-four hours. Yes, siree! I plan to buy aviation securities. Soon, there'll be passenger airlines all over the USA. Aviation! That's the thing to get into." They talked, until Howard saw that Tommy was trying to outsit him, and he was forced to leave Susan with Tommy as the conversation ran out.

Two weeks passed, and somehow Howard could not manage to be alone with Susan. So frustrated did he become that he went looking for her on the day she had taken the child to the zoo in Central Park. He sat with her on a bench while Freddy ran around in front of the monkeys' cage.

"What's happening, Susie? I never see you. I can't take this nothingness."

"I can't live in that house with you, Howard, and carry on a love affair under the nose of Mrs Howlett. I can't do it. You must mend your marriage. You must patch things up with your wife. That's what Father Donahue says."

"You told him about us?" He was incredulous.

"You know I'm a Catholic. I have to go to confession."

"My God, Susan! Does he know me?"

"No, not your name. I suppose he could find out, but he won't. Don't worry! Anyway, he's right." She bent her head now, quite upset. "What we did was wrong."

"But you love me?"

"Please."

"Look at me. I love you, Susan."

"And what do you propose that we do? Run off and take Freddy, and leave Betty to her own devices."

"Her own vices, more like. She would leave me if it suited her."

"You are wrong, Howard. She watches me all the time now. I'm sure she suspects and she's jealous."

"What about her boyfriends?"

"They're not real boyfriends. They're just to make you jealous. Anyway, Tommy wants to talk to you. He has experience of alcoholics."

"Alcoholic? My God, I suppose she is. You've told him about Betty?"

"Not everything."

"About you and me?"

"No, not that. He couldn't stand that."

"Do you think I can stand to think of you in bed with him?" She was silent. "Do you hear me? Have you forgotten that wonderful weekend in Oyster Bay?"

She took a while to answer. "I'll never forget, Howard, you know that. But I can't throw Tommy over. I just can't. And I can't take another woman's husband. You must have loved her once. She needs you, and Tommy needs me."

He was too sad to continue. "I'll see you at the house. Don't stay here too long." He strode out along the path without looking back.

CHAPTER 23

"Y ou must get rid of all the drink in the house, Howard, and you must not drink in front of her."

Howard looked at Tommy keenly, "You think that would work?"

"You must spend time with her, all day and every day for a week or two, until she gets over the initial withdrawal. It's the old story. It can only be done one day at a time." Susan looked on, feeling sorry for Howard as he received the advice from Tommy "Use your imagination to think up places to take her out to, places she would like. Don't go where there may be drinking going on."

"You're very worldly-wise for a coal miner." Howard could not help sounding a bit bitter.

"I did a lot of work for the Church to fill my time when Susan left home for America. I was in the church society, the St Vincent de Paul, and they train you to help people in trouble."

Howard rose, "I suppose it's worth a try. There's not too much booze in the house, anyway." He looked in the cocktail cabinet.

"First she must agree she has a problem, and she must want to conquer it as much as you do."

"OK. I'll try this evening."

Howard took his chance with the subject at dinner. He and Betty sat with their customary rare beef steaks, Betty slopping red wine after each mouthful. Howard looked across the table at her and said, "I want to speak to you, Betty."

"Why do you always need to look so miserable?"

"Maybe, because I am miserable. I want to speak about us. You and me, you and your drinking, and the rest."

"What are you talking about?"

"I mean you drink too much, and you don't seem to know it. I want to help you to stop."

"Why?"

"For your own good, and because I want us to try and make a go of our marriage for Freddy's sake. He's about all we've got left." He saw her shocked expression. "You must admit, there's not much going for us the way things are."

"So we're playing Happy Families tonight?" Her voice was bitter, and she sloshed down some more wine.

"For God's sake, Betty!"

"Jesus, Howard! You're a bloody, stuck-up, self-satisfied idiot. You're never here, are you? Hardly ever in this bloody house! And if you are, it's in body only. You've lost interest in me ..." she paused to locate her handkerchief, the tears smarting in her eyes, "... but I'm supposed to soldier on, in this vacuum that I live in. Everything's always my fault. My God, if the sky falls, it will be Betty's fault!"

"Well, at least, I'm trying now. You could try, too."

Laughing mirthlessly, she said, "You know what the poet says:

'My candle burns at both ends;
It will not last the night;
But ah, my foes, and oh, my friends –
It gives a lovely light!'"

She stared at the empty fireplace, and a tear started to roll down her face. "I'm so tired, Howard, so tired of everything, of trying all the time, of running after a great dream!" She looked bitter and then dejected. "And then what have you got at the end of all that effort? Tell me that."

"Then, we'll stand still, honey." He knelt down and embraced her where she sat.

"So, Susan's thrown you over? That's the reason for this charade tonight, isn't it?"

He was stunned by this remark. "What are you saying?"

"It wasn't too hard to work out. You're a transparent kind of guy. And I knew something was making you happy, and it wasn't me." She broke down at this, and they clung together, their tears flowing freely as the twilight outside deepened. After a while, Betty stood up and switched on some of the table lamps, and, withdrawing a cigarette from a box on a side table, she placed it in her cigarette holder, and said, "Well, at least I can only give up one vice at a time." She laughed ruefully. "What do you say, Howard?"

"You're doing fine." He, too, lit a cigarette. "I'll try to stop drinking, too. They say if you stay off it for a few months, you can have some wine and the odd drink. Just so long as you watch what you're doing. Didn't they tell you that at the clinic?"

"Oh, something like that. Who remembers?" Betty looked out of the window at the passing traffic. "I had a letter from my sister Minnie in Philadelphia, this morning. She and Dick are coming to New York on Tuesday. They want to see some of the town and take us out to dinner on their last night, that is next Saturday. They're staying at the Lexington."

"Well, that's just fine, honey. I'd like to talk to Dick about my stockholding. He always was sharp about what to buy."

"OK! I haven't seen the old girl for ages. If it's all right with you, I'll telephone Minnie and Dick in the morning and invite them to dinner on Thursday."

Dick Jackson was a doctor in a suburb of Philadelphia, an amiable fifty-year-old. Both he and Minnie were pillars of the community, he being a member of the Rotary Club and Minnie involving herself with the local charities. They approved of Prohibition and never drank anything stronger than tea.

Betty and Minnie, although sisters, were a complete contrast. Where Betty was intense and artistic, avidly studying the writings of Freud and, with her friends in Greenwich Village, easily espousing the ideas of freedom of expression, Minnie had no time for this intellectualism. Somewhere along the way, the paths of the two girls had diverged. Minnie's path led her to regular churchgoing and set middle-class values, whereas Betty had chosen agnosticism, pleasure seeking and, like all her set, had developed a taste for daring and recklessness, easily fuelled by the fact that she was married to a millionaire.

Minnie's husband had lately got himself interested in the stock market. Like millions of Americans, the pages of stocks and shares in the daily newspapers were the first ones he turned to at breakfast each day. Minnie, too, was becoming caught up in this speculation, and both of them had increased their money several times over, on paper at least, from the great stock market gambling years of 1928 and 1929 in America.

In a fashionable restaurant in mid-town New York, where they had invited Howard and Betty to dinner, the talk had naturally turned to money. "What do you think of the New York Times Industrials. Do you think they're going to keep going up, Dick?" Howard was one of the few sceptics around who felt uneasy about the rise and rise of stocks. "I bought them at two hundred and they're standing at over three hundred now."

"Industrials are a sure-fire certainty, Howard. Mine were bought at one hundred and twenty, so I have trebled my money in five years. General Electric, too. Why, Betty made hundreds with her shares in GEC. Listen, anyone can be a millionaire in this country if he's got his head screwed on, fella!"

The talk of speculation excited Minnie, as this was her latest passion. "I invested three thousand dollars in Radio Corporation of America, and it's worth over ten thousand now." She looked around the table for approval. "Do you play the market, Betty?"

Betty twiddled with her club soda, "No, Minnie, I haven't so far. Howard's the whiz-kid with finance in our family."

"Oh, you should try it, Betty. It's fun. But I suppose you don't need to. You have plenty of money. And enough of everything anyone could ever want."

Howard saw the panic spread over Betty's face as she got stuck for an answer to her sister's probing remark. "Let's have this dance, honey," he said to her, offering his hand, "you know you love a foxtrot." On the dance floor, he said, "Just keep calm, sweetheart. Minnie's just trying to rile you. I think she knows that you've got a problem."

"I wouldn't tell her about it, anyway. Self-righteous wolf in sheep's clothing."

"All the same, they're both worth a fortune, and they don't seem to have done much for it."

"Oh, come on, Howard, they're not as rich as you, and you know it. My God, you part-own three hotels and you've been investing for years. You're the manager's best friend at the Chase Manhattan."

"I wish it was as straightforward as that. Business is a tricky thing. A lot of confidence is required to keep on top. Nobody will like me for saying it, but I worry the way people buy shares, hold them for a few days and sell them on for a profit. It doesn't seem healthy to me."

She shrugged, "Well, the government don't seem worried, and everybody's doing it. I just never found the time for it."

Her midnight-blue, sequinned evening dress shimmered under the chandelier above the dance floor. She looked young, vulnerable and unattainable all at the same time. Who would believe, Howard thought, that this classy woman had worked as a salesgirl in Woolworth's, for a time? Money has given her the appearance of good breeding and class, he thought.

"Why don't you come out on the terrace for a minute, honey? It's cooler and quieter out here." On the balcony, Howard put his arms around her, "You're doing very well, honey. This is just like old times, you and me out dancing together."

"You mean it, Howard?" she searched his face, testing his sincerity. She knew how he had been bowled over by Susan, and inside she was hurting.

He nodded, "You look very lovely tonight, Betty."

"Do you think we'll ever be happy, like we were in the old days?"

Howard laughed, and lit a cigarette. "You mean in that place in Yonkers? We were in love then, all right, and we had no money."

"So you haven't forgotten those heady days when we both worked our butts off and passed each other on the stairs as we rushed out every day."

Howard smiled at the picture, "Have you?"

"I'd have to think about it. It was a long time ago." Her voice sounded cynical, but she put her long, slim arms around his neck, saying, "I wish we could get those years back, Howard."

"We'll work at it, honey. We'll just have to work at it. We've still got something, if we try hard, and above all we've got Freddy, don't forget. He must come first. But let's get back to the table. I want to pick Dick's brains a bit more."

There was an orchestra playing, and the noise of chattering and laughter was everywhere. On all sides the waiters rushed around carrying trays of food. This was an expensive place, but the price was the least of the worries of that well-heeled, evening-dressed crowd. Almost every table in the restaurant seemed to be in a mad party mood that night and, although there was no alcohol on sale, there was an air of frenzy around. It was clear that some of the customers had been imbibing some illegal liquor before they came, or else they had bottles hidden under the table. The two sisters and their husbands finished the evening on a happy note, Dick saying he would be sure to phone Howard with some hot market tips on the following Monday, and Betty and Minnie promising to keep more in touch with each other.

For months to come their luck held. But that fateful Thursday in October was just around the corner. When the Crash came, within a few hours, as stock prices began to fall, billions of dollars in value were lost. Howard came home, ashen faced with shock, to find Betty waiting for him, worried and concerned. She stood over his chair in silent sympathy. The very air of New York that day was electric. "I heard all about it on the news, honey, will we survive?" She, too, was pale with worry.

"God knows, Betty. You should have seen it downtown today. The Stock Exchange was a sea of paper, the brokers were dumping stock all the time. Millions of shares have changed hands. Radio Corporation has fallen to forty-five. Forty-five, can you believe it? By eleven-thirty, it was obvious it was curtains for everybody. The crowds outside the stock market were hysterical. They had to call in the police. At one point Morgan's bank was thought to be going to intervene, and prices started to go up, but it's obvious that the party is over. It's all gone. No more easy-money spree!"

"How much do you think you've lost?"

"Well, it looks like, at least two million dollars." He looked at her where she stood frozen with horror and shook his head, "But some poor suckers have lost more. They've lost everything. It's a sad, sad day for New York and the whole country."

"The President should have stopped it. He should have been able to do something," Betty said.

"It was too far gone. Everybody wanted to gamble. Anybody who suggested that anything could be wrong was denounced out of hand and considered to be unpatriotic. It was just crazy. Just crazy! Nobody could do anything. Everybody wanted a fast buck. Christ, I was just as bad!" Howard strode to the window trying to contain his agitation.

"It's just so hard to take in. Who would have thought such a thing possible. What are we going to do, Howard?"

"I'm going to see Joe Riston. He owns at least twenty hotels, and he has a lot of friends in banking. There's nobody he doesn't know. He might lend me some money if he's all right himself." Howard thought for a moment, then decided, "He was too rich to go under. Old Joe will survive all right. I still have a part share in the hotels, but there'll be nobody in them now."

Over the next few days as the Crash continued, the newspapers were full of stock market news, and the evidence of the nightmare drop in shares was everywhere to be seen. Banks closed. Some businessmen jumped from windows, unable to face financial ruin. Some shops closed, and gradually many factories ground to a standstill. To buck the trend, Henry Ford gave his workers a rise in wages, but among the population, in general, nobody seemed to have any money, and despairing, destitute people were everywhere. Men, who had previously been prosperous, were to be seen guarding a few possessions and sleeping on the streets, while proud owners of automobiles put them up for sale. Queues for dole money or for a hot meal were commonplace. The whole nation was shaken, as the numbers of unemployed people mushroomed into millions. The mood of the city was bleak, and subdued.

Within a few weeks, Betty and Howard called a meeting of the staff in the house in Park Avenue. There was no surprise. They knew there was no one who had escaped the calamity of Wall Street. The meeting was in the dining room, and Bella, Lotta, George and Susan were seated there to hear of their fate. "Mrs Howlett and I are sorry to tell you that, due to our losses in the market, we are going to have to close up the house." They looked at each other, but nobody could think of anything to say. "I am giving you three weeks' notice, but you may leave any time with one month's pay."

"You're moving out of the city, Mr Howard?" It was Bella who found her voice.

"Yes, Bella. We thought we'd try Long Island for a few months. Lie low and wait for the dust to settle. Meanwhile, we just don't have the money to live here any longer. We will have to try to sell the two automobiles also. Sad but true." He shook his head and looked down at the floor.

Betty Howlett took up the helm of the meeting now, "Mr Howlett and I are very sorry it had to come to this." She turned to Lotta, "What will you do, Lotta? Go home to your family?" she asked.

"I suppose so, Mrs Howlett. For the time being, anyway. Safety in numbers, you know."

"And you, Bella?"

"I might just retire and settle down with Rupert, Mrs Howlett. He's the butler over at the Jones' place. He's my beau. Has been for years. We might just both put our feet up and live on our immoral earnings," she laughed.

"Well, good for you, Bella. That's the spirit." Betty Howlett turned to George. "Do you think you'll find something, George?"

George's large sad eyes became even larger. "Oh, sure thing, Mrs Howlett. Tommy, Susan's fiancé, has promised to get me a job in the kitchen at Delaney's. I'll be all right. I got lots of friends and I'm a good worker."

All eyes turned to Susan where she sat with Freddy by her side. "What about you, Susan? Will you stay in New York or go home to Scotland?"

Susan's face flushed and she managed to look straight ahead in her embarrassment, "Tommy wants us to get married right away. He has asked Father Donohue to call the banns this Sunday."

The room erupted in congratulations. "Good news at last, Susan! Why, I hope we're all invited to the wedding." Bella was hugging her and patting her back.

"Yes, everyone's invited. It's to be in St Patrick's on the 30th of November, that is, St Andrew's day, and afterwards in Delaney's restaurant."

Susan glanced at Howard. He stood quietly, his face inscrutable while the hubbub was going on, then he approached her side. "Nice going, kid," he whispered. "I wish you all the luck in the world." Howard turned swiftly to the gathering. "Well, it's just too bad Mrs Howlett and I are on the wagon for the next few weeks, or else we would have broken out a bottle. But we ain't got none in the house, I'm afraid."

"Just you all come down to the kitchen and I'll have some fresh coffee ready for you in no time." Bella was off her mark to brew up the coffee. Somehow she had turned a bitter-sweet occasion into a reason for cheerfulness.

Later that day, Howard and Betty called Susan and Freddy into the living room. "You know, you'll be welcome at any time to come out to Long Island to see us and Freddy, Susan."

"I'm going to miss him." Then her voice dried up and she shook her head. She felt a panicky, sinking feeling in the pit of her stomach at the thought of not seeing the little boy who was so close to her. Only the thought of her wedding and a new life in prospect kept her from being too sad. "It's going to be a wrench," she said as she fought to control the tears.

"For him, too. We'll just have to tell him you've gone on holiday," Howard laughed. "Seriously, we may have to call on you for advice. Betty and I are no experts at child rearing."

"Oh, Freddy's no bother. Just as long as you don't try to railroad him into things too quickly. He likes to take his time to make changes from one situation to another."

Knowing he was the centre of attention, Freddy climbed on Susan's knee, "Susan, come upstairs. Upstairs." He was pulling her arm now.

"He's got his train set out in his room, and he wants to play."

"Go on, Freddy, you go on up. Susan will be upstairs in a little while."

"Daddy come upstairs?" Freddy was not giving up.

Betty stood up, taking a drag at her cigarette through her holder. "Listen, Susan, Howard and I have been discussing a wedding present for you. We thought of giving you either a present of money, or else a real, swish wedding outfit from Macy's. Which would you like?"

Susan was taken aback. "Goodness! I don't know. I would have to ask Tommy."

"No!" Howard intervened. "This has to be your decision."

"Then, I'll take the wedding outfit."

"Right, that's settled, Susan." Betty was pleased. "We'll go shopping next week. You shall have nothing but the best."

"Now you're both happy. Spending money! A sure-fire way to please a woman!" Howard was secretly delighted at seeing the smile on Susan's face. She looked like a child at her own birthday party. He came over and put his arm around her. "I just can't wait to see this vision of a bride that you're going to be. It will be the event of the year, I'm sure."

———

Around St Patrick's Cathedral surged the great city, noisy, ceaseless, restless, yet one step inside and all is peace. There on the table a beautifully penned quotation from Cardinal Spellman lay:

The grandeur of this holy place has lifted up
the lowly and taught humility to the mighty.

And the faithful feel that every step inside the building, taking them past the heavy oak pews, under the great, tall windows, past the marble and bronze carvings on every side, to the magnificent communion rail in front of the altar, takes them nearer to union with God.

Proud as a peacock, Tommy stood at the altar of the Lady Chapel in St Patrick's Cathedral that Saturday morning in November. Beside him stood George, his lugubrious face white with nerves at his part in the drama, yet still with his height and bearing, he made an elegant best man. The congregation was small for the ten o'clock Nuptial Mass, but the organ filled the whole church with the triumphal bridal music.

The entry of Howard, with the bride on his arm to lead her to the altar, was dramatic. Susan walked in serious dignity, drawing the eyes of the congregation as she passed. On her head was a bejewelled, stiffened-satin, cloche headdress decorated mainly with seed pearls. The depth of the cloche threw into relief the regular features of the girl, and the steadiness and honesty of her eyes, now lit with excitement. Gone was the mousy little girl who had come, a rough diamond, to the New World. On that morning of her wedding, her face serene, her lips slightly parted, Susan was breathtakingly pure and lovely. From the cloche headdress sprang a voluminous silk net veil, and close to her face she carried a bouquet of seven arum lilies, straight and pure white, surrounded with greenery. Her dress was of a classical empire line with a slight train at the back. Had you been told that a duke's daughter was being married that morning, you would have not been surprised.

In new suit of dark pinstripe material, Tommy was the perfect groom. Smiling with happiness, he stood in front of the priest to make his vows of fidelity in a strong, deep voice, his eyes constantly straying to the saintly expression on the face of his bride. A deeply religious man, Tommy thanked God for the beauty of the moment when the priest announced, "Go with God. I now pronounce you man and wife."

They left the church to the smiles of the congregation and the blaring of the great organ, whose triumphal chords seemed to be trying to tell the whole of New York about this wedding ceremony. Outside, on the steps of the church, the hurrying citizens paused to admire the bride, as she stood smiling broadly, while behind her, also in white, were her two bridesmaids, Jenny, her friend from the Atlantic crossing, and Lotta, her other best friend in America. Confetti and rose petals were thrown with much gaiety and hilarity, and then the party took off in taxis and cars to Delaney's restaurant for the wedding lunch.

The place had been quickly decorated with white satin bows and balloons, and on one side of the room a table had been set for the guests. Delaney was guest of honour and had produced a few bottles of champagne from under the counter. For the occasion, Betty and Howard allowed themselves a couple of glasses to toast the couple, and soon, with the help of a lively band, a wonderful celebration was underway.

For a honeymoon, Tommy had chosen the Hotel Bossert in Brooklyn. One of the customers in the restaurant had suggested it, because of the view of the city from the roof. At midnight, Susan and Tommy stood there watching the lights of the tall buildings of Wall Street sparkle in the darkness.

"It's just brilliant and beautiful, Tommy. It's like being on top of the world."

"I know, sweetheart. So much energy and so much sheer imagination to build a city like this. It's almost beyond belief, Susan." He took her in his arms, and his kiss told her that he was hers, "I love you, my beautiful bride."

"I love you, dearest. I don't quite know how I climbed this high. Maybe I should pinch myself to see if I'm dreaming."

He smiled and held her close. "I think it's time for you and me to go to bed, but it's not time for dreaming yet."

The hour that Tommy had waited for, during many a long, lonely night had arrived. The newlyweds were lost in a world of love and emotion, clinging to each other unable to believe the happiness that had come to them.

"Do you think we'll stay here in America, Tommy? I mean make our home here?"

"Sure, we'll stay. The restaurant is doing a roaring trade. Admittedly it's a bit quieter since the Crash, but the Singing Waiters are a wow with the public, and the booze is quite cheap and reliable. People know you can always be sure of a good time in Delaney's. We'll get by all right, Susan, my little bobby-dazzler. You'll see. We'll be Yankees yet. At any rate, nothing could be worse than being a miner at home."

"I know, Tommy. That's a blessing, anyway." As she thought of her home and family, she found it hard to picture the road where she had lived, or the house where she had been born. "You know, Tommy, I often think of home, but it's gradually becoming harder to picture it. My thoughts usually turn to the mornings in June when we used to walk the two miles to the sandy hills where we played all day. We could slide down into the deep and climb back up the sand hills to our hearts' content. Those were happy, endless, sunny days in Scotland."

"Yes," he said. "And the Hogganfield Loch where we used to take out rowing boats and fish for baggy minnows. And the long walk up to the loch past the Sugarally Mountains."

Susan's eyes were troubled, "I just can't picture Mother or Archie or Honor and Edward or any of them any more. It's quite sad. We must send a telegram tomorrow to tell them about our wedding."

"Yes, sure we will," he said. "And when the photograph of us is developed and your mother sees what a beautiful bride you were, she'll be happy."

"Poor Mother, I wish she could have been here."

Tommy kissed her on the forehead. "Don't worry. Some day we'll go back for a visit. You'll see. Things will pick up again in this town. I know there's a lot of misery around on the streets now. A lot of destitute people. But it's not much better at home."

"I could maybe get a job in nursing beside Jenny."

"We'll make out. And we'll save up. This bad situation here, with people down on their luck, it can't last. Why, I've had more good times here in New York in the past few months than I had in years at home. It will take a helluva lot to make me leave this place. As long as you are here, that is."

She cuddled into her warm, young husband. "I'll always be where you are, sweetheart. You won't escape from Susan, don't worry."

"Aha, you've seen my bank book. Over a thousand dollars already, honey!"

"You're a magician, do you know that?" and she smothered him with kisses before he had time to answer.

CHAPTER 24

I n Scotland, things trundled on much as usual with the Drydens and the Dennys. Some excitement was generated at Number 10 Ardgay Street when they got news of a visit from the eldest of Louisa's children, Willie, long abandoned to relatives when the rest of the family moved to Scotland.

"How you gan on then?" It was an unmistakable Sunderland accent calling from the door. The voice filled the air of Honor's mother's house. Louisa and William had just cleared up from their midday meal, and she had taken out some sewing. The cloth fell from her hand as she recognised the voice of Willie, her first-born child. When they had left their home in England and come north, he had been working in a grocer's shop in Seaham Harbour, and, because he had found work, he was left there to lodge with his aunt Liza.

William wept openly when he saw his son. It had been ten years since they had seen each other. The boy had married Josephine, a girl six years older than himself, when he was only eighteen, but how he had missed his family. His father dried his eyes and wiped his long Victorian moustache. It had caused him pain and heart-searching to leave Willie behind. Louisa, preoccupied with making a home for the rest of the family, had quickly put the decision behind her. "My, but you're looking prosperous, lad. I like your suit!" William felt the material of the lapel.

"Not bad, eh, Dad? Came up in my own car, too."

"For Gawd's sake, we've a toff for a son, William." She placed a plate of sandwiches in front of Willie.

They hurried outside to admire the car and found it surrounded by children and a few curious neighbours. "Come on, come on. Don't touch. This is our Willie's car."

"I'll wash it for you, Mr Dryden," one of the ragamuffin children said. "I'll wash it for sixpence."

After lighting up a cigarette, Willie swaggered off to see his sister Honor. He was a tall, debonair figure, handsome and personable like all the Drydens. Once again he opened the door and called in a loud voice, "Anybody at home?" She had almost forgotten that she had an elder brother, but she flew to the door to embrace him. They smiled and hugged each other tearfully. "It's been ten years, my flower, since I've seen you. You were seventeen. Do you remember? I was twenty-three."

"Yes, you brought Josephine and your two little girls."

"We've got five kids, now."

"Really, Willie? So many? I can't believe it."

"You look well, Honor. And your children are lovely." The children sat on their best behaviour, weighing up their strange uncle. Willie showed photographs of his own family, and he played with the children while Honor peeled the potatoes for the evening meal. When Edward came home from work, they had a great discussion about work and politics and the state of the country, although each had to strain to follow the accents of the other. Honor gradually dropped into the English accent of her childhood, as she listened and talked to her brother.

"I remember putting you and Nelly on the train at Newcastle, with a little travelling case. You must have been about nine years old, and Nelly was about six."

"That's right, Willie. I remember."

"Aunt Liza and I, it was. Took you to the station. I still see your long fair ringlets, and Nelly's ginger curls. You wore little pinafores and long woollen stockings. The two of you sat in the train compartment like orphans of the storm. Fancy our mother leaving you two behind! Aunt Liza said to a lady passenger, 'These children are going to Glasgow. Will you keep your eye on them?' You had a piece of paper with the address of the rest of the family, here in Ardgay Street. Do you remember?"

Honor's face was almost bitter. "I remember all right. How my mother could have let us travel on a train, two little girls by themselves, I'll never know. When we got to Glasgow, there was a mix-up and Mother didn't meet the train. I think she got the station wrong or something." Edward and Willie shook their heads in disbelief at the picture. "There I was, showing the address to strangers. We were quite overwhelmed by the buses, taxis, cars and tramcars of the strange city. They had all kinds of destinations on their fronts. It was a miracle how we got to Number 10, Ardgay Street."

Edward seated himself at the kitchen table, washed and with hair combed back, and obviously anxiously awaiting his evening meal, after his hard day at work.

"I'll hope to see you two on Sunday. Mam's having a little party for me. Can you get someone to look after the children?"

"I'll ask our Archie," Edward said. "He doesn't do anything on Sunday nights. He might do it to please me, but he might not, we'll see. He might want to come to a party. And especially if Elsie's going to be there."

—·—·—

The gramophone played Strauss waltzes and, later, foxtrots and quicksteps by a more up-to-date orchestra. Louisa had baked and the girls had made piles of sandwiches, which were quickly disappearing. As the evening wore on, and the beer started to flow, and the laughter got louder and louder, and the cigarette smoke got thicker, Elsie decided to go outside for a little air. Knowing that her old flame Archie would be alone, except for the children, in Honor's house, she told someone that she was going to the Italian Ice Cream shop for cigarettes and hurried on for a chat with Archie. She found him reading by the fire, the three children asleep. Amazed to see her, he offered her a cup of tea. She watched him as he moved around with teapot and tea caddie. His shyness and quiet charm intrigued her. She felt sorry he had not found the right girl. Slightly tight from the drinks at Willie's party, she crossed the room and put her arms around his waist.

Archie hid the shock and thrill of this move and he said coolly, "Is Jim treating you well, Elsie? Are you happy?"

There was a slight hesitation. "I love him, but he's very domineering. His mother is a real pain in the neck, too. They think they have done me such a favour, allowing me to marry into their family."

"Snobs, I suppose. You must miss the fun of the old days."

"Well, I do a bit. I'm always on guard in case my manners don't measure up. They're very Scottish Presbyterian, you know. I have to go to church, and follow their ways. They'd rather be found dead than shown to be sinful or loose-living, or worse still, lower class."

"Sounds a funny sort of life. Living to impress your neighbours."

"I know." She sat down as he poured out the tea, and they lit up cigarettes. She smoked in a sophisticated, ladylike fashion, displaying her long, painted fingernails. Smiling, she studied his youthful, serious face. "A confirmed bachelor!" she mused.

"You'd better be getting back, soon, Elsie. They'll wonder where you are."

"You're so controlled, Archie. Are you happy? Teaching those snotty-nosed kids?"

"Never mind about me."

"Don't you want to break out now and again, really?"

He stood up agitated. "Elsie, you're disturbing my equilibrium. Sure, I'm controlled. I practically chain-smoke, and tonight, when I get home and Mother's asleep, I'll have two or three very large whiskies. That's how controlled I am!" His voice had risen as he spoke, so that the last words hung bitterly on the air until she spoke.

"Well, I'm not much better off than you," she said tears springing to her eyes, "he won't even let me have children. It would spoil our easy life, according to him. And it would spoil my figure, or so he thinks!"

"What a cold bastard!. Couldn't you take up your painting or photography again? You were so talented, Elsie."

"His mother hates me. She's jealous of me and discourages anything except sitting around entertaining her friends."

"Come on, Elsie. Where's your old spirit? God! You used to be the life and soul of the family. Now you're rich – and bloody miserable." He pulled her to her feet and kissed her full on the mouth. Soon their hands were searching out each other's bodies.

"Do you want to make love to me, Archie? I know I'd like to." She saw his face pale.

"You mean it?"

"For old time's sake." She kissed him passionately. "You know I've always been fond of you, and I know you haven't … ever, have you?"

"No." His voice was hoarse. She turned the key in the lock. She took off his jacket and embraced him warmly, then she stepped out of her long, narrow skirt, and there on the rug in front of the fire, she seduced him. It was a coupling partly out of frustration and unhappiness in her own life, and partly out of pity for his loneliness.

For Archie it was like thunder and lightning, Christmas and New Year rolled into one. He was scared and elated, frightened and flattered. The climax was a moment he would never forget as he clung to her firm white body. "I love you, Elsie. I wish you'd married me."

"I wish I had, Archie. I wish I had. But that's not what happened." She spoke matter-of-factly with just a hint of regret. Then she pulled on her long skirt, and they held each other silently for some minutes. Both of them were sad, their paths had diverged, and to question fate was almost unthinkable. She told him that she would try to see him again quite soon, and throwing back her beautiful waved hair from her pale-skinned face, she turned to unlock the door. He stood there alone, his book abandoned on the fireside chair, his cheeks red with emotion. She said, "You'll find a girl, Baldy," his nick-name. "But I'll always keep a bit of you in here," and she pointed to the velvet of her blouse, to the place where her heart should be.

"I love you. Couldn't you stay a little while with me? They won't miss you at the party."

"If I stay too long, then they might get suspicious."

"They won't be suspicious of me. Harmless old Archie. Oh, Elsie, I will miss you! But at least now, I have something to dream about."

"It was lovely, Archie. Jim's coming for me tomorrow morning, so I'll be back to reality then. But I'll think of you, too, Archie."

"You promise? I love you, Elsie. I always will."

"You've really helped me, Archie. Your suggestion about taking up painting again is a good one. I'm going to stand on my own two feet."

"You're right! Don't let those Holy Willies, holier-than-thou, narrow-minded snobs ruin your life."

"They won't even let me have my parents or family or anybody to visit, you know."

"Why not?"

"Oh," a wry smile crossed her face. "Mother and Father arrived one afternoon, not long after we were married, and Mrs Shields had some guests for tea. Dad was, of course, his usual gentlemanly self, a bit shabby, but all right. Mother had a flowered hat and looked so ... well, outrageous compared to that tight-lipped lot. She monopolised the conversation, you know, talking about her family, and drank three glasses of sherry. Then she entertained them with singing – you know that one she does when she's a bit tight at parties – 'There was an old man, he had an old sow', and making rude animal noises. It was comical, but so lower class to Mrs Shields' friends. She's never been asked back."

"Poor Elsie. You will just have to make some friends of your own. Get out of the house, away from that old bossy woman."

He took her in his arms again. "I'll come over to Bearsden and defend you from them. Just let them look sideways at my gorgeous Elsie."

She snuggled into his broad chest. "I'll have to go. Can I just peep at Honor's children before I go?" They tiptoed into the bedroom and both gazed down at the three sleeping children. "They're so lovely, Edward and Honor are so lucky, and they don't even know it." She squeezed his hand, "Goodnight, Archie. Let's hope God will forgive us," she said.

"I'll try and call into your mother's around eight to catch a glimpse of you before I take off for St Mungo's. Leave your cigarette case here, and I'll bring it round saying you forgot it." She pulled her coat around her, and slipped out quickly into the night air, her cheeks flushed with the excitement of the past hour.

Next morning the lovers managed a few precious seconds together when Archie called to return the cigarette case. Gone was the festive air of the previous evening, and all was busy and bustling, as people left for work and Willie packed his car for the journey south. Archie made his way to school, his thoughts far away from the classroom, his nostrils full of the perfume of the auburn hair of the previous evening.

The next event awaited in the Dryden family was the birth of a baby to Honor's sister Veronica and her husband Willie. In January a little boy was born to them and they called him Duncan. He was christened in the Parish Church of Scotland when he was six months old. No expense was spared on the christening party. It was a lavish affair. Veronica was considered at a late age to start a family and, as their first child had been stillborn, they treated this new baby like a gift from Heaven.

Veronica's cooking and baking were legendary, and it was a packed apartment that Sunday morning in June with friends and relations who gathered to bring gifts, to feast and to share in the joy of the parents. Jim Shields deigned to accompany his wife to this function, dressed in a dark business suit, very much the up-and-coming young man. Elsie looked radiant in a grey pleated suit, she, too, quite obviously expecting a baby.

When the gathering was in full swing, Elsie sat chatting with Honor. They spoke of the baby and of baby clothes, then Elsie dropped her voice. "I'm very happy," she said, and looked around to make sure they were not heard, "but I want to share a secret with you." Honor sat riveted as Elsie confessed. "This child I'm expecting, it could be Archie Denny's."

Honor eyes widened, "You're not serious, Elsie?"

Elsie shook her head sadly. "It's a secret. If it ever gets out, I'm done for, but I have to tell somebody. So only you and I will know. Don't even tell Edward. I'm not going to tell Archie."

"Oh, Elsie! How could you?" Elsie told her a bit about the evening of the party, when she had slipped out and gone to visit Archie. "In my house, too!"

"Don't tell Ned, whatever you do. And especially don't tell Archie."

Honor wished she had not been burdened with this knowledge. Her face was still and calm as she looked into the troubled eyes of her sister. "I'm sure it will be a beautiful baby, just like its mother, Elsie."

"Oh, Honor! You're so good! You're a wonderful sister to have!" and she put her arm around her.

Edward was restless and wanted home from the christening party. The whole scene of limitless food and drink, of gold watch chains, and Freemason handshakes and camaraderie were too much for his socialist soul. "Honor, we'd best be away. It's after seven o'clock. Time the bairns were in bed." In truth, he wanted home to work on some union papers, and he had to be in bed before eleven, in order to be fit for his work on the Monday morning. Times were getting harder for the ordinary man, and work was becoming more difficult to find, as the world-wide depression which had started in America began to be felt.

There followed a terrible time for a great section of the population of Britain. In Scotland, one in five men could not find work. Often they had difficulty surviving, for obtaining even subsistence level payments from the authorities was made difficult. They had to prove that they were genuinely seeking work before these very small payments were conceded. Men walked miles from factory gate to factory gate but it was a hopeless exercise, day after day. They had no money for bus or tram fares and were often treated as nuisances by those in charge of the gates.

Hardship, poverty and malnutrition were everywhere. The hated Means Test had been established so that every penny coming into a household was taken into account before any money was given to those without work. If your brother was earning money, then he was expected to keep you and unemployment payment was cut off. The result of this legislation was that families broke up so as not to be a burden on those lucky enough to have work. Members of households took lodgings with strangers so that they could obtain benefit.

Apprentices were paid off as soon as their years of training were finished. There were protest marches on a regular basis in all the big towns to try to draw attention to the plight of people for whom there was no work.

Edward had become much more active in politics. He was involved in trying to help those who came to him for advice, as union representative. When people were being evicted from their houses, warrant sales they were called, their goods and chattels were dumped on the street for non-payment of rent, and their houses taken over and locked against them. Edward, with others, would go and occupy the house to stop the action of the sheriffs and police. Often they would be able to arrange that the arrears be paid off over some time, as the victims were usually too distressed to speak for themselves. Being a good speaker, Edward also became the spokesman for youths who had fallen into crime through lack of money and would plead for them with the powers that be, so that the young men would be given a second chance.

Chalking the streets with thick pieces of pipe clay to announce public meetings about the unemployment situation, or chalking slogans on street corners, slogans against the government, were favourite occupations of the politically active of those days. Edward was often absent from the family home, speaking with fire and passion as only the politically convinced can. He became a well known and respected figure in the area. In the November of 1931, Honor had given birth to a baby girl, making the family up to four. The child was christened Greta, and although life was a struggle for them with six mouths to feed, at least Edward was not out of work.

Joe, Edward's brother, had been two years out of the merchant navy, and had yet to find work. He had joined the Unemployed

Workers' Movement, and was a popular figure on marches as he could play the flute and had taught others, so that the men could march to Highland tunes and to rousing songs like 'The Red Flag' and 'The International'. Joe also was expert on the banjo, and with his devil-may-care smile and his humorous outlook on life, he was a much sought-after figure.

One evening, Joe arrived on a visit to Honor and Edward. He had brought with him a friend, by the name of Barnie Dunn, an unemployed worker like himself. They were going on a hunger march from Glasgow to Edinburgh in two weeks' time and had been asked by the leaders to try and obtain a hall for the marchers to sleep in, on an overnight stop.

"How about Kilsyth, Ned, out near our Mary's farm? They have a hall in the village there. It's a good walk from George Square in Glasgow to Kilsyth. The men could bed down there."

"Aye, that's a possible place, Joe," Edward was pouring out cups of tea for the two visitors, as Honor bathed the children and prepared them for bed.

"You know, Ned, you should come on this march with Barnie and me. You wouldn't be the only employed person on the march. There's a few coming from Parkhead and Cambuslang that feel they should show solidarity with us. They wish to protest about the Means Test and all the injustices they see around them. What do you say, Ned? You are a well-known figure in the locality. You could walk with Barnie and me. It would give more weight to the boys."

"Joe, I've got four kids. I've got to go to work on Monday morning." He saw their faces falling and realised that they had children, too, and had no work to go to on Monday morning.

"You could take the train back on Sunday, Edward, from Waverley Station. You wouldn't have to stay on with us in Edinburgh." Joe was unusually serious, almost pleading.

Edward paused for a few minutes, to think things over, while the other two drank their tea. At last, he said, "OK! I'll go over to Kilsyth with you next Sunday and see if we can get the use of the hall. And maybe I'll march part of the way with you on the following Saturday."

Honor came in and heard the end of this conversation, and an idea for a trip with the children was occurring to her. "Edward, your Mary has often asked us to visit her at the farm. Could we go on the Friday evening and stay over until Sunday? She said she could put us up, and we could see her baby. We've never seen it."

"That's a big undertaking, Honor. Six of us to arrive at Mary's?"

"She's at home all the time, now that she has the baby, and she would appreciate the company. I'd love to see her little girl. Honestly, she wants us to come over. She said so in her last letter. The children could see the animals. They've got a litter of piglets. Oh, Edward, the kids would love it!"

Great was the excitement of the little family as they boarded the bus for their trip. Soon they were chugging along on the ancient country bus, past fields and farmhouses, on a beautiful, warm June morning. The trees and hedges were fresh and green, and blackbirds and thrushes could be spotted and even the occasional hawk, hovering above the ploughed fields; sheep and fat lambs, and cows with great hanging udders delighted the children.

Within an hour of arrival, they had inspected the hen houses, chased the cockerel and been round the fruit garden. Jamie had been butted by the billy goat, and they had drunk goat's milk with faces screwed up at the unaccustomed flavour. Edward's sister, retired from her hospital job, was now thirty-nine and her first child, a baby girl, had brought her great joy. She loved Edward and his family and was delighted to have them there to visit and admire their new cousin.

Lunch was farmhouse bread and enormous omelettes made from new-laid eggs. In the afternoon, they visited the pigsty, which housed a boar and a sow with her piglets. Mary and her husband had named the pigs 'Honor' and 'Edward', causing much protest and hilarity. Squeals of delight came from the children as they watched the great pink, fat, bristly animals wallow around in the muck of their pens, with what seemed to be smiles of contentment on their big-snouted faces.

Next day, about ninety unemployed men, four abreast, soon came marching into the village which was to be an overnight stop for them on their way to protest in the capital. They were dressed in trousers, pullovers and jackets, some with cape-like raincoats, and all with haversacks on their backs carrying toiletries and a change of socks and maybe underwear if they could afford it. Most had heavy boots and carried walking sticks. The flute band started up at the outskirts of the village, and the men, to put a cheery face on it, started singing to the music:

> *"Oh where, tell me where has my highland laddie gone?*
> *He's gone far away where doughty deeds are done,*
> *And it's deep in my heart I miss him so today."*

The villagers clapped and cheered as the men reached the village hall and threw down their packs. Edward spotted Joe and Barnie with their flutes, and they all greeted each other. Mary passed out some packets of cigarettes to Joe's and Edward's friends. "Good luck, Joe. I hope it doesn't rain for you. We'll be thinking about you," she called.

The next morning was Saturday, another lovely bright June day. Edward joined the men as they walked eastwards towards the city of Edinburgh. Many of the men knew Edward as a fighter for justice in the east end of Glasgow, and a little cheer of appreciation went up as he fell in beside them on their long march. By evening, they had walked almost twenty-five miles and had reached the town of Bathgate. It was obvious that they were not going to get to Edinburgh early enough to make a good entrance, so they passed another night at a hall in that town. There was a reception for them in a local drill hall. Minced beef and potatoes were provided and each marcher was given a packet of cigarettes.

On Sunday morning, the 11th of June 1933, their numbers swollen to several hundreds, they arrived marching and singing, flute bands playing, down the centre of Princes Street, to the surprise of the local well-heeled shoppers. The cry went up:

> *"We're going to fight the Means Test,*
> *We're going to fight the Means Test,*
> *We're going to fight the Means Test,*
> *Or die, die, die."*

Now and again a private car would stop and the driver would put something in their collection boxes. Sometimes a parcel of sandwiches would be thrust into one of the marchers' hands, or even a packet of cigarettes.

Proudly and with great dignity, the cloth-capped army marched to Holyrood Palace to the rebel tunes of the flute bands. The Assistant Chief Constable had been instructed to give the marchers Waverley Market to spend the night.

"Too cold for my men. It's freezing on that stone floor. The men would never sleep in that cold place." The speaker was one of the leaders of the march, Harry McShane. The police group of constables and officials consulted each other.

Then the Assistant Chief Constable spoke to the march leaders again, "There's Leith Links. Your men could march down there. You'll find plenty of grass to lie on there."

Harry raised himself to his full five feet six inches, "If we're to sleep in the streets, we'll choose our own street." Then, he called to the men who had been appointed as stewards of the march.

"Princes Street, boys, and when you get there line your men up against the railings. Blow your whistles as a signal to sit down." And so it was that the hundreds of marchers lined up against the railings of the gardens of Princes Street below the brooding castle. Passers-by watched in amazement the discipline of the men. The whistles blew and the men stopped walking. They blew again and they sat down on the warm pavement.

"You can't sit there, you're causing an obstruction." The police chief was beside himself with rage.

"Blankets out, boys!" Harry McShane shouted. As far as the eye could see along the most fashionable street of the capital, men sat or lay, removing their shoes and stretching out their limbs. Next the chuck wagon drove up, belching smoke into the warm June air. Soon the men were tucking into rolls and fried sausages, and mugs of strong tea. They ate their evening meal under the windows of the Conservative Club and the Liberal Club and in full view of all the biggest and most expensive hotels in the city, with the ancient craggy castle as a backdrop. Edinburgh citizens, on their way to evening services in the churches or just strolling in the gardens in their Sunday finery, were open mouthed with astonishment at the sight of these underdogs of society. They were disciplined and well behaved, and intent on making a statement.

Most slept well. A few had blistered feet, or had worn holes in their shoes. There was a cobbler on the march, and he worked hard at each stop, to try and resole the worn footwear. Joe, Ned and Barnie kept together. Ned had become so carried away with the emotion and camaraderie of the march, that he had decided to leave not that evening, but early in the morning. Soon they were smoking and talking politics in deadly earnest. Then Joe, always the light-hearted one, produced his banjo from under his cape. He strummed a tune soon recognisable as:

"When you wore a tulip, a sweet yellow tulip,
And I wore a big, red rose ..."

Joe was good on the banjo and soon he had the men around joining in with his cheery songs. He finished up with a sad, nostalgic rendering of 'My Little Grey Home in the West', and the voices rose all along the street:

"It's a corner of heaven itself,
Though it's only a tumble-down nest.
But with love brooding there, why no place can compare
With my little grey home in the west."

The morning dawned bright and fine, and Edward left quickly to catch the train back to his home in Glasgow and his work that Monday morning. Edinburgh citizens, who filled the buses and trains on their ways to work, were very surprised to see dozens of men washing in the fountains in Princes Street Gardens and even men shaving, using the large, plate-glass windows of the big shops as mirrors to see their reflections.

The next night was spent under cover, and the strike leaders were given an interview with officials of the Scottish Office. There were twenty-three items on their list of requests to the Government. These included abolition of the Means Test, a hot meal for children of unemployed fathers, and shoes for schoolchildren. They did not obtain even half of the things they asked for, but the men felt better for having done something in protest at their hopeless condition.

The camaraderie of the event cheered the men, knowing they were not alone in their situation of poverty. While their leaders held consultations with the politicians, the men danced reels and sang songs to the tunes of the flute bands. The police gave the marchers a hot meal on the second day, and buses were found to take them back to their own towns, many from as far away as Aberdeen.

Next day, the newspapers had many good stories and photographs of the marchers, under the headline 'TWO DAYS THAT SHOOK THE WORLD'.

CHAPTER 25

The years since Elsie's seduction of Archie had not settled her discontent. She continued to feel troubled by her in-laws, their lifestyle and expectancies, and their snobbery. Jim and she got along all right for she had inherited her mother's skills at housekeeping. But he was not the pleasant, loving man she had fallen for. As he grew older, a greater arrogance and self-centredness grew in him. He domineered her and, if things got too heated, he would tell her how lucky she was to be married to a successful shop owner. He would remind her that she was much better off than any of her family, thanks to him. They envied her lifestyle, little aware of its tensions or of Elsie's unhappiness, for he had discouraged her from inviting them to their house. Jim, in the meantime, had had to overcome his reluctance to have children with the unexpected arrival of Robbie and later a little girl.

The house that Jim Shields had bought was built of brick in 1922 with an arched entrance and small-paned windows. It was well designed and had a prosperous aura about it. Like all the houses in Lime Crescent there was a good-sized garden with a pleasant front lawn. Outside the house sat a little Austin car in which Jim left for work at the bakery each morning. He employed ten workers, and now that the place had expanded he spent most of his time in the office when he was not visiting his three baker's shops.

"Are you remembering that it's tonight that the minister has asked to call and see me, Elsie? We'd better clear away the tea table before he comes." Elsie looked resigned, even bored, at the thought of the evening ahead, but Jim was all bustle and urgency, "Gosh, it's almost seven. Come on, Robbie. Up to bed!" The little brown-haired boy playing on the carpet with his trains was disappointed. Now five years old, he was a quiet, intelligent, sensitive boy. His sister Felicity, just three, was plump with the auburn, waving hair of her mother and the face and stocky build of her father.

When Robbie protested, Jim's voice became stern. "Go upstairs with your mother, boy. It's seven o'clock. You have school in the morning." Knowing it was hopeless, both children started upstairs. Elsie followed them, reciting nursery rhymes to keep them amused through the evening bathing ritual. She heard the minister arrive as she dried the children's hair, and then the dining-room door shut. The meeting was to be in private. When the two men emerged from their discussion, some time later, the children were asleep, and Elsie was reading by the living-room fire. As she stood up to meet the minister, she could see that Jim was very pleased, the reason being he had been invited to become a church elder.

Elsie was nonplussed. "You'll be out in the evenings, then, Jim?"

The visitor stepped in to explain, "Oh, perhaps once a week or once a fortnight. That's all. And, of course, helping on Sundays with church business and so on." He smiled directly at Elsie. "Maybe you'd like to join the Women's Guild, Mrs Shields."

Panic started behind Elsie's pleasant expression. "Well, Mr Moore, Felicity and Robbie take up all my time, I'm afraid." Underneath she was hissing to herself, Make me old before my time, sitting there yakking about cakes and cushions and choirs singing in hospitals. God, I'll go mad!

When their dignified visitor had left, Jim let out a whoop of delight. "Isn't it great? An elder, who could believe it? It will be the Rotary Club next. You wait and see, Elsie. Your husband's going places."

Her eyes glazed over. There was never anything at all about what she wanted. It was always Jim and his ambition. Her words of protest died inside her. But Jim was in full flood. "I think we should have a new car now. Ours is the oldest in the road," he was looking out of the window. "I think I could afford to buy something a bit bigger." He turned to see if his wife was as impressed with him as he was with himself, and in so doing he tripped over Robbie's locomotives. "For God's sake! You must make that child put his toys away. You are too indulgent with him." Elsie rushed to pick up the train set before there was any further complaint. "He's growing into a softie, and it's your fault! You spoil him! Felicity's got a lot more strength and determination of character than he has. He sits there dreaming away with those toys. Have you watched him?"

"He's sensitive, Jim. He has a different nature from Felicity. He's not rumbustious like her." Elsie was hurt. Always she seemed to be defending the boy.

Bending to pick up more toys, Jim said, "Maybe we could get your daily help to stay on a bit later in the evening to help with the clearing up. She could start a bit later in the day. Babs is much firmer with the children than you are."

"I don't want anyone to be firmer with my children. I'll manage the way things are."

He grabbed her. "But I want my wife beside me at nights. Not washing dishes and reading to children."

She pulled away, "Jim, I ..." There were tears in her eyes.

"You're not pleased about the church and me being an elder, are you?"

"Of course I am, if that's what you want, but what about what I want?"

"What do you want? Look around you. You live in a beautiful house, in a lovely street. You have two children, as you wanted. We have a car. You are miles above that lot in the East End where you came from. My God! Your family slept four to a room, and there wasn't even a bathroom." When she didn't reply he carried on. "They'd give their eye teeth to have what you've got."

She nodded, trying to hold back the emotion that was choking her. "I just miss them and the fun we used to have, and I wish I could have Mother and Father over some time."

"After that last showing-up?"

"Listen, my mother is a clever, well-bred woman. She's just different from your mother. She hasn't got such nice clothes. She doesn't get her hair coiffured every week, and she's not ..."

"Not what?"

"Uptight, narrow-minded and ... snobbish!"

He rose and took the whisky decanter from the sideboard. He poured himself a double and squirted soda from the siphon into it. "Look," he said through his teeth. "My mother is coming here for coffee in the morning. She asked me to tell you to expect her about eleven."

"Why is she coming?"

"Why do you think? She wants to see you and Felicity. She has a wonderful set of friends. They visit and have coffee and discuss things. You should try to join them. You'd enjoy it."

"I don't think so, Jim. But I'll try and please your mother and you. Mind you, I'd rather settle down with a good book, or visit a museum or something. I miss my painting and the photography work. It was very absorbing."

He poured himself another drink. "You should be happy you don't have to work. You're a married woman now, and that should be your interest. You should be happy for me, not lost in your own little world."

"May I have one of those drinks and one of your cigarettes?"

She placed the cigarette in a long cigarette holder, and he lit it for her. She took the glass from him and stretched out on the couch, his eyes noting her figure still as lovely as a young girl's. They sat with their drinks, talking of domestic matters until, mellowed by the alcohol, Jim said, "Maybe we'll celebrate later in bed." She felt his breath in her ear. "Right now, I could eat you. You look more like your old self. The tantalising Elsie of days of yore." He knelt down and caressed her. He kissed her throat. "Do you love me?"

Taking a gulp of the whisky, she smiled one of her old smiles, "Of course I love you. You're my husband. Why should I not love you?"

That night Jim made love to her, his caresses firing her body, and he spoke her name in a low whisper. He wished that the night would never end, so that he could live on this cloud of happiness forever. She wore a lace nightdress so that her slim ankles peeped out at the hem, and she looked up at him teasingly. She kissed him and turned over lazily. "I'm so sleepy. Goodnight, my darling. I think we'll have bacon and eggs for breakfast, Jim. I really fancy that. What do you think?"

"Whatever you say, my darling. Whatever you say," Jim said, as he fell into a blissful sleep.

Next day, when she heard the garden gate close, Elsie looked out to see her mother-in-law, Frances Shields, approaching. "Good morning, my dear. Another sunny day! This is turning out to be a lovely, warm month for June." She took the three-year-old on her knee while Elsie made the coffee. They talked of Jim and his father, Lionel, and of the bakery business, now known as 'Lionel Shields and Son, Master Bakers'.

Eventually the talk turned to the dinner party to be held the following Saturday. Elsie voiced her most pressing concern to the older woman, "What on earth shall I wear?"

"Well, I hope you won't mind me saying so, but I'd like it if you didn't wear that silver and white dress you wore to the Masonic Dance at Easter. It's too low cut."

"It's my best dress!"

"Well, the minister will be there and that new young Doctor Russell, and young Gregor Fletcher and his father. We don't want all the men looking down your cleavage, do we?" Her expression changed from disapproval to sweetness. "How is my little Robbie?"

Elsie sat down, reeling from the lecture. "He was a bit off-colour this morning. Let's hope he's not sickening for something." Her mother-in-law, oblivious to the dashed spirits she had brought on in Elsie, continued to prattle on about the Women's Guild and how great the church was.

"I haven't made up my mind about the church, yet, Mrs Shields. I'm still thinking about it."

Frances Shields put down her cup. "Well, there's no rush. Take your time, my dear. And thanks for the snack. It will keep me going

until I get down to Wilma's for lunch. I did enjoy our little chat."
She stood up to leave. Looking in the hall mirror, she pulled on her
little felt hat. "You're not half-keen on colour, Elsie. I don't think I've
ever seen lilac used in hall wallpaper before. Don't people have
different tastes!"

"I think it makes the hall seem light and airy. This is the most
attractive room in the house, I think. I decorated it myself."

"Goodbye, dear, and remember seven-thirty on Saturday."

Let down and drained of energy was how Elsie felt. Always
Mrs Shields had this effect on her. She's like a bloody vampire! Elsie
thought. A wave of homesickness came over her. My own mother
may be argumentative and bossy, but at least I could talk to her, and
I always felt she loved me and was on my side, but deep down I
don't think Frances Shields really likes me. Thinks I'm not good
enough for her precious only son!

On the Saturday, Elsie, dreading the whole affair at the
affluent Victorian mansion that was Jim's parents' house, wore a
pale beige dress that emphasised the slimness of her figure and
toned in with her auburn hair and the ivory of her skin.

There were several cars in the drive, and the house was lit
up and festive looking. A uniformed maid answered the door,
and her mother-in-law, in long black velvet evening dress,
descended on Elsie and Jim, almost the second they stepped into
the house. "This is my daughter-in law, Elsie. Elsie meet Sam and
Lily Fletcher." From the black velvet sleeve of her dress, Frances
Shields held out a plump white arm to introduce her guests to
each other. She wore diamonds on her fingers and in her ears,
and the silvery white of her hair gleamed under the light in
her hallway.

"Call me Sam!" the prosperous-looking man presented to
Elsie was saying. As he spoke he accepted a glass of whisky from the
maid. Elsie thought from his florid face that this would not be the
first drink of the night for him. Mrs Fletcher smiled a faltering smile,
and seemed as if she had heard about a better party some other
place at which she would rather be.

In soft tones she said, "Nice to meet you, Elsie. We'd heard
you were good-looking, and I can see it's quite true."

Short of stature and rotund, like a modern-day Mr Pickwick, Sam stood close to Elsie and said conspiratorially, "They tell me you're from the East End of Glasgow. I've got a sister in Sandyhills – Ellie Fletcher. Do you know her?"

"Afraid not, Sam. There's a lot of new people moved into Sandyhills with all the new houses there now."

"Yes, they're lovely houses. I remember it was all green fields and sandpits up that way when I was a boy." He took a sip at his whisky. "Just hope those people who moved into those council houses appreciate what's been done for them. All that government money that's been spent."

There was no answer to that, and Elsie was glad when they were asked to sit down to dinner. When the roast beef appeared, served by the maid and another woman hired for the occasion, some good French wine was poured out. Jim's father addressed the company as he moved around the table. "What do you think of our Jim? He's opened a third shop now. A new one down at Partick Cross, and we have three vans on the road. Yes, 'Lionel Shields and Son' are doing well!"

Sam Fletcher spoke. "Well done, Jim!" his deep voice carried authority, "you keep your nose to the grindstone and the money will roll in. Just keep your eyes open and watch all sides of the business. That's how I got started. Father had just one tiny stationer's shop when I joined him in the business. Now we have a large warehouse and are stockholders of all kinds of paper and the like. Just watch out for slackers that stop work as soon as your back's turned and chancers of all kinds – petty pilfering, you know. Got to keep your eyes open. They'll take the milk out of your tea, some of those workers in Glasgow. My boy, Gregor, here, he's in the motor business. Can't steal your cars, Gregor, eh? Have to be up early!" His laugh was loud and theatrical.

A chill went down Elsie's spine; how often had she heard conversations like this from these people – so self-righteous. Her mind went back to an earlier dinner party, indelible in her memory because she had first disgraced herself in the eyes of her husband for voicing contrary views. That was soon after the hunger march of the unemployed and their supporters from Glasgow to Edinburgh.

She remembered her heart pounding that evening when she had found the courage to disagree with them. Now here it was again. Down with the workers! Jim's father, Lionel, was now bringing it up.

"I do agree with you, Sam," he was saying, laying down his knife and fork. "Those wasters who marched to Edinburgh a few years back. Do you remember them? Caused no end of trouble for the police. Demanding more dole money, free meals for the unemployed's children, free footwear, who do they think they are? Frances and I were shocked by the reports in the papers. Sleeping in Princes Street, indeed!"

"Well, we shouldn't be talking politics at a party, but I'll just say," Frances Shields paused for breath before putting her point, "I think it's disgraceful what they allow these folks to get away with. Why do they let them march like that? Wearing out shoe leather, and trampling over other people's property!"

"Well, Mrs Shields," it was Mr Moore, the minister, speaking, "the march, if I remember, was quite well disciplined. They carried their own food, and their leaders had things well under control. And Glasgow to Edinburgh is a long way. The object of the whole thing was to ask for the government to start projects that would give them work, so that they could support their families. They certainly drew attention to their plight."

"But, Mr Moore," the hostess was indignant now, "they were dancing reels in Drumsheugh Gardens. My aunt lives near there. I'm sure she was horrified by that rabble."

The high, piping voice of young Maria Fletcher sounded off next. "You know there's a man always coming into our garage looking for a job. He's so repulsive! Unemployed he may be, but he's always got cigarettes, and he needs a good wash!"

Gregor was annoyed with his simpering wife. "Come now, Maria, the fellow wants work. He may be a bit unsavoury looking, but I knew him when he finished his apprenticeship, he was a first-class man with car engines. His name's Willie Barr. He's just down on his luck. If business picked up I'd give him a start, but we haven't sold a car for weeks."

Lionel Shields leaned over towards Gregor, "How on earth does your business keep going, Gregor?"

"Just with repairs and sales of petrol. It's not always easy to balance the books. We hope for better times. America's in a worse state than Britain with this Depression. At least we haven't had financially ruined people jumping out of windows."

Sam Fletcher had lit up a cigar, and he puffed furiously during the discussion. "Our main trouble in this country is the unrest among the poor. They're constantly talking of revolution. 'Change the system! Change the system!' They don't understand venture capitalism and the dangers faced by businessmen. You know," Sam looked around the table, his cigar in his hand, "I work eighteen hours a day, sometimes. They're work-shy scroungers, the lot of them!"

The minister spoke up at this. "That's a bit of a generalisation, Mr Fletcher. I know one or two fellows in this area who would be very glad to have a job, any job – no matter what the hours."

Elsie had found her voice at this point. "I agree with Mr Moore. My brother-in-law was in that march from Glasgow to Edinburgh that you're talking about." A silence followed her remarks.

Her father-in-law asked quietly, "Was he unemployed?"

"No, he just was so much in sympathy with the action of the men, he wanted to join them. It wasn't illegal. They didn't do any damage." Elsie finished on a descending note, her face flushed with embarrassment. She caught the eye of her mother-in-law, whose face was like fizz, having had her worst fears realised that her dinner party would be spoiled by this non-conformist girl.

The hostess addressed everyone at the table. "Edward Denny's one of Elsie's colourful in-laws, he's always been an idealist. You know the type. He's a handsome man. I can see why your sister Honor married him, Elsie," she smiled indulgently on her daughter-in-law, "but he's too political for his own good. Going on a hunger march when you've got a job. It's ridiculous!"

Again there was a silence until Sam Fletcher asked, "What do you think of the new playing fields they're making for the High School? They're fairly getting on with the work."

"First class, Mr Fletcher. Saw them the other day," Jim was relieved at the change of subject. "I hear there's to be tennis courts and a rugby pitch."

"Sounds wonderful," the minister added.

"Yes. We're going to put Robbie's name down for the school soon." Jim nodded across the table to the other guests. "Can't be too early nowadays in choosing a good school." Elsie looked surprised, but said nothing. They talked of golf and cars, until the happy release for Elsie came at ten o'clock. She knew she had displeased Mrs Shields, but she didn't care. Better than sitting like a dressed-up dummy, listening to their condescensions and downright distortions of the truth, she thought.

Jenny Moore, the minister's mousy wife, laid a hand on her arm in the hallway as Elsie put on her wrap. "I admire you, Elsie, for speaking out for your brother-in-law. It made me feel better."

The handsome young doctor, Mike Russell, and his wife, Rosie, too, seemed to go out of their way to smile and wish her goodnight. They hadn't joined in the discussion but seemed to be sending out sympathy to her. This cheered her up, but Jim was silent and moody in the car going home. Only when they were undressed for bed did he say, "I wish you'd keep your family out of dinner-table discussions. It doesn't go down well."

"I can never please you. You want an automaton for a wife."

"It gives us a showing-up with people who matter, that's all."

Back home and in bed, Elsie lifted her bedside book. She would lose herself in the story and forget the hurts of the dinner party. Under her breath she muttered, "These people may matter to you but not to me."

On the Sunday morning they arose, still sleepy after their late night and a little hung-over from the wine. Robbie was really off-colour. All day he clung round Elsie's skirts, and next morning, he was feverish and tearful, and obviously not fit for school. "I'm going to call Doctor Russell, Jim. Robbie's not well at all, this morning."

"Oh, all right, but I don't think the boy is that bad. Just a cold probably," and he rushed from the room, his mind already on the golf course.

When Mike Russell arrived Elsie was relieved. "He's very hot, Doctor."

"Please, Elsie, could you close the curtains a little?" He moved quickly to the child's bedside. When he had examined Robbie's tongue and behind his ears, and taken his temperature, the doctor straightened up, "Yes, I'm afraid it's measles. You'll have to keep the light down in here, so that his eyes are not affected. Keep him in bed for as long as possible. He'll have to stay off school for fourteen days."

"Do you think little Felicity will get it, Mike?"

"Maybe. It would probably be better if she did. Get it over with." He looked again at the sick child. "Keep him on a simple diet, mostly liquids, and keep the room warm. I'll call in on Friday to see him."

By the end of two weeks, Elsie was worn out with nursing the fractious child. When Doctor Russell arrived she sat pale and dowdy-looking, too listless to pick up the toys and biscuits dropped by the children. "Well, he's on the mend, but you look like the Wreck of the Hesperus. What's wrong?"

"Oh, I'm so tired! I suppose I'll feel better soon, but I've no energy at all."

"Hasn't Jim helped you through Robbie's illness?"

"Well, no. He's been working overtime. They've had big orders come in for rolls and cakes for functions in Glasgow, and he didn't want to lose the extra business."

"You need a day out. Look, Rosie and I are going up to Luss tomorrow to see Fiona."

"Fiona?"

"You remember her. She was my receptionist. She married an art teacher and they now live near Luss on Loch Lomond. They've a big garden and a little boy who'll be three years old now. She remembers you, anyway."

"How could I forget about her? She wears her hair in a big plait down her back. She was very friendly when I came here at first and Robbie was just weeks old. She's a nice girl."

"I'm sure Robbie and Felicity would enjoy a trip out, and it might put some colour in those pale cheeks of yours. What do you say? I know Jim works all day on a Saturday, so he won't mind. I'll pick you up around ten, and home about five in the afternoon. I'll phone Fiona and Ralston this evening."

"Oh, Mike, a day out at Loch Lomond. It sounds wonderful. I feel better already."

"That's what we doctors are for." He smiled as he picked up his bag and left the house. For the first time in weeks Elsie felt her spirits lift.

CHAPTER 26

There was no question that Elsie had made it from the crowded tenement flat, where she had been born, into a life much more luxurious. Of all the ten children of Louisa and William Dryden, she was the best off, at least financially. From a house where four or five children shared the same room, Elsie now had a bedroom for each of her two children and a spare room for guests. In the eyes of the rest of the family, struggling with long hours of work and little money, Elsie was well on her way to being a toff and probably a snob.

On this particular Saturday morning, the sun shone brightly for Mrs Dryden's most successful daughter. It shone on the last of the May blossom in the lane beside her house and on the smart, black car that arrived to pick her up. The children were speechless with excitement and Doctor Russell and his wife helped them aboard. Elsie was pink in the face with the rushing around from early morning, getting the children ready for their trip, and she sank back in relief as the car was starting.

"All set? Off we go!" Mike Russell was in high spirits. He and Rosie had been married for only a few months, and were young and fancy-free. "This little beauty of a car will soon eat up the miles!"

And it wasn't too long before they had left the built-up areas behind and were nearing Loch Lomond. They drove along the winding road that skirts the shores of the loch, with magnificent trees overhanging. Every twist in the road brought a new perspective of the hills and the islands in the loch, rising sheer out of the water. They stopped for five minutes for Mike to take a picture of Ben Lomond, its magnificent slopes brown and green in the sunlight. Leaning against an ancient hawthorn, taking in the scene, Elsie smiled at Rosie, "Isn't this wonderful, Rosie?"

"Yes, this is a good time of year to come, in June. Before the road gets too busy with tourists."

They each took a child by the hand to stop them diving into the water. "It makes me want to start painting again," Elsie said as she looked around.

"Oh, well, if it's painting that interests you, you'll fit in just fine in Luss today with the Hunts. Ralston and Fiona both paint. They're very arty-crafty. He teaches art."

And just as Elsie had imagined Fiona would look, she wore a long romantic dress with a floppy hat when she came to the door of the rambling old house at the lochside. Freckled and pretty, her brown hair was done up in one long plait.

Ralston, middle-aged, grey haired and romantic of appearance had joined them. "Come away in. There's food in the kitchen. Come on, kids. Sandwiches!" He shook hands with Elsie, his smiling dark-lashed eyes looking at her, and noting Elsie's famous Dryden classical features. Telling them that they had brought good weather, he welcomed them in to the kitchen. In the afternoon, it was enchanting in the old garden, with the children playing around them under the trees. Elsie relaxed in a hammock, almost falling asleep in the balmy air.

Mike pushed the hammock gently.

"Yes, Doctor, this truly is the best prescription you could have thought up for me."

"Then, my dear," said Ralston, the host, "you and the children must come out to see us more often. We lack good friends and company so far out of town. Perhaps, next time you could bring your husband, if you like. You could do some drawing. I hear you're a bit of an artist."

"I haven't drawn or painted for a long time, Ralston. With the children, there hasn't been much time." Elsie faltered.

Fiona looked puzzled. "But you were always painting when Robbie was a baby, when I first met you."

"Ah! In my palmy days. I thought I was quite the Bohemian then, but lately ... I don't know. I've lost my touch, I think."

"You've got tired housewife syndrome!" Rosie declared. "My mother warned me, when I got married, not to let myself become part of the house furniture, to try and keep interests outside the house."

"That's not always easy, Rosie." Elsie's smile had vanished.

Mike sat down on a garden bench, saying "I've told you, Elsie, as your doctor, my advice to you is to take up your creative activities again. Break out! Get your personality back!"

"You're all making the artistic way of life sound very attractive." She looked at them through the dappled light, embarrassed by their confidence.

Ralston stood up. His tall, broad-shouldered frame and artistic persona, set off by his broad- brimmed summer hat, made him the centre of attention in the garden.

"Right!" he said loudly. "It's settled then. Next weekend. If you can manage. Entrance fee – a couple of bottles of wine. Arrive Saturday lunchtime. Leave Sunday teatime, or whenever you wish."

By the end of the next week, Jim's resistance to the weekend visit had been broken down. "You realise that Saturday is our busiest day, Elsie. There's the cash to be picked up and put in the safe. And lots of other clearing-up work to be done."

"Then I'll go myself with the children. I really want to go, Jim."

"Oh, I suppose I can get Dad to stand in for me, since you're so dead set on the idea. You certainly have been a lot brighter since your trip last Saturday."

Already, when they arrived, the others were working, with great absorption on their easels and sketch-pads. Ralston was down at the lochside, trying to capture the colours of the hills on his canvas. Fiona was in the little wood at the back, drawing a clump of bluebells. Rosie and Mike were discussing where would be the best place for her to place her easel, when Elsie broke in with her family.

Later, Mike asked Jim to walk to the village where they passed a happy hour in the hotel bar, while the children played all afternoon in the woods. The evening meal, with so many exuberant people, was a noisy affair. The women, their faces sunburnt from their day outdoors, had all helped to prepare a simple meal of roast lamb washed down with some good red wine. When the children were finally in bed and they could have some peace, they sat around the lovely old wood-panelled dining room talking of art, of jazz and of the changing times.

Ralston was in his element, with the wine and the company. "If it's a nice morning, you can continue with your sketching, ladies, or we can take a sail on the loch. Arthur Butterworth has a little boat with an outboard motor. He would lend it to me. What do you say?"

Rosie spoke up, "We could sail up to Arrochar."

"That's a beautiful sail," Fiona said. "I'll make sandwiches, and we can take flasks of coffee."

When the talk turned again to art and to Ralston's experiences in the Glasgow School of Art, Elsie spoke of how she used to love to paint and Ralston said, "Your tulips sketch, you did today in the garden was beautiful. You could try stylising them, along with some of your other sketches from nature, into designs. We have a fabric design department at the school."

"It sounds great, Ralston," Elsie said. "I've always wanted to go into that building. It is such an arresting design."

"Yes. I'm afraid our Mackintosh was not appreciated. The building was ahead of its time. We get visitors from the Continent to see round the school, all the time. But the citizens of Glasgow don't know what a gem it is. I could show you around sometime, if you like. But you think about our Saturday morning class."

"What do you think, Jim?"

"Where would the children go while you were being an artist? I have to work on Saturdays."

"Maybe Babs will take on Saturday morning work."

Jim did not look pleased and soon changed the subject.

—.—.—

The steps to the door of the art school in Glasgow, for Elsie, were a passageway to a gentler, more sympathetic world. Her class had only eight students, herself, two young men, and five other girls. The first part of the morning was given over to the learning of drawing skills, especially still life. In the second half, after the break for coffee, each person was free to develop their personal preference. Elsie was helped to turn her flower drawings into designs, engrossing and rewarding work. After several classes, she began building up a portfolio of floral designs.

"Your work shows a great delight in colour, Mrs Shields." Alan Baird, the class tutor, was encouraging as he looked at her work.

"I agree!" They had been joined by Ralston. "I can see a good deal of development here, Elsie. Well done!" Elsie blossomed under their praise but had an attack of nerves when told there was to be a public show of work soon.

"Come on, Elsie. You know your work is good. No false modesty." He told her to bring her work to the library at noon so they could discuss what to put in the show.

There among the stylish ladder-backed chairs, she saw his great leonine head bent over a book, he was every inch the artist in his smock and spotted cravat. He was startled by her suddenly appearing, and a pause ensued while he tried to find the right words, "I wanted to ask if you would be a model for me. For my class, that is, next Tuesday evening."

"You don't mean nude?"

"No, but I must tell you," he was circling her as she stood in the light from the high window. "Your skin is just remarkable – truly ivory. And these shoulders, the set of them is quite beautiful, they are so broad for a girl – and your profile is perfect. Could you possibly model for us?"

"I don't know. It's been enough to be allowed to come to the class on Saturdays, Ralston. I'm not too sure if I could wangle it. To get out in the evening, I mean. It would be difficult for me."

"Tuesday, at six o'clock, is my class. You would do me a great service, my dear, and an honour. Tell him it's for art."

She giggled, "For the sake of art!" She mocked him, her hand on her chest, her eyes rolling to the ceiling.

"That's right, Elsie. I know you can bring it off."

So Tuesday evening found her perched on a stool, on a dais, clothed only in a piece of green satin. Her shapely, long arms were extended, her hands together in a pose. She had been made to gaze straight ahead, so that a semi-profile drawing of her could be made. There were ten students in the third-year class. Ralston had joined them, working absorbedly, trying to capture her beauty. She had agreed to three sittings, having told Jim it was a special class she had to take for the development of her fabric design.

In the twilight of a September evening, after class, Ralston was driving her home. "Can you come out to Luss, at the weekend? You and Jim and the children, I mean."

"Really, Ralston, it's time that Jim and I entertained you and Fiona." He had stopped the car.

"Let's have a cigarette before I drop you," he said. He threw the spent match out of the window, and turned to face her. "You know it, don't you?"

"What?"

"I'm falling for you."

She felt a thrill of fear and excitement go through her. "No, Ralston."

"Don't be alarmed. I won't touch you. I just had to tell you." He looked morosely through the window.

"You shouldn't have said this. Fiona is my friend. She trusts me, and you for that matter."

"You're right, of course. But I can't seem to stop myself. You're so cool and unattainable. And I don't think you've ever been really loved. Not the way I love you."

In the closeness of the car, she was shaken by the force of this declaration. He kissed her full on the lips and she pushed him away. "She trusts you to drive me home without this."

"I know you feel it, too, my dear. You're just afraid of your feelings." They fell silent for a few seconds. "Are you and Jim and the children coming out to Luss next weekend?"

"I don't know."

Saturday found Elsie dressing carefully in grey country tweeds and brown walking shoes for her weekend of healthy country pursuits. Babs, her housekeeper, had agreed to come, too, so that she could keep the children busy while Elsie did some sketching. Jim was too busy.

The packed car arrived, driven by Mike, and the children spilled out, making straight for the tree house at the back of the garden. During lunch, Fiona was describing the puppies that had been born on a friend's farm, near Tarbet. "A beautiful gingery colour. Ginger and white. Absolute beauties. They run around. I think there are nine of them altogether. I'm trying to talk Ralston into letting me have one for a pet. They're so active and comical. You could watch their antics all day."

Rosie got fired up with the talk of the puppies. "How I would love to see them. Oh! Please, Mike, couldn't we go and see them? It's not far. Is it, Fiona?"

It was arranged that Fiona should take Mike and Rosie to see the puppies while Ralston took Elsie out on the loch to look for sketching sites.

"I've borrowed Arthur's boat for this afternoon," Ralston said. "I want to go sailing, and Elsie said she wanted to see Inchmurrin. She wanted to sketch on the island, and it's a fine afternoon." Elsie had no recall of saying anything about Inchmurrin, but for some reason felt unable to contradict her host. And so her afternoon was arranged for her.

"Right!" said Fiona. "We'll go off and take the children and Babs along with us to see the puppies and the other animals, and leave you two artists alone. We'll take two cars. I know the road quite well now, so I'll drive our car. Don't stay out in the boat too long, Ralston. Everyone has to help with the dinner."

The loch was calm and made little lapping noises around them as they stepped aboard. Ralston steered her out towards the islands and around the grassy banks of Inchmurrin. The sun shone, and the quiet atmosphere out on the water, as they sailed past the lonely banks of fading heather, made Elsie relax on the deck of the boat, as if they had escaped from the world.

"Would you rather have gone to see the puppies?"

"No. It's beautiful here."

"Well, not many people sail round here. These little bays are quite unknown. If you are lucky you may see deer on Inchmurrin. Over there is Glen Fruin, where the Colquhouns were massacred by the MacGregors. You can read about it in Rob Roy. There's Ross Priory, an old haunt of Walter Scott, and over there is Buchanan Castle. That island there is Inchcailloch, the 'Women's Island'. It's called that because there used to be a nunnery there. We'll tie up for a little while at Inch Fad. There's a little beach where you can do some sketching. The views are really good."

As they stood together admiring the sheer rise of the hills from the water, his arm went round her and he drew her face to his and kissed her softly on the lips. "You are like a flower. Your husband is a lucky man. It is wonderful for me just to stand beside you."

"I shouldn't have come here today, Ralston. I should have stopped it."

He kissed her again, while she protested, and she resisted him. "You are being unfair on me."

"Beautiful women should be loved. They are born to be loved." She saw the passion in his face, and suddenly she saw herself from the outside – a married woman, with her friend's husband.

"Let's go back, Ralston. I don't feel like sketching this afternoon."

"You want to go back already?"

She was agitated. "Well, at least, let's get back in the boat."

He let out a great roar of laughter that echoed round the loch and startled the blackbirds. "You can be ravaged in a boat, you know. There is no problem, there, my sweetheart."

"Ralston Hunt. You are a rogue!"

"A rogue who goes crazy when he is near you, who loves you."

"You have a wife to love."

He held her to him roughly. "One kiss before we go." This kiss was fiery and demanding, his hands starting to caress her. She pushed him away.

"No. I am not a gypsy or a peasant farmhand to be made love to in the heather." What her lips were saying, her body was denying, and Ralston knew, as she knew in her own heart, it was just a matter of time until their desire for each other was consummated.

When she returned to Bearsden after that weekend, she had become so afraid of herself and her feelings for Ralston that she suggested to Jim that she give up her art classes. "But the course runs for a year, and you're doing so well. Why should you give it up? Don't be silly. You've been happier lately than I've seen you for ages."

"I have been toying with the idea of opening a shop. You know the kind of thing – gifts, artists' materials like paints, pastels and paper. It might be an outlet for my work. You know, my flower paintings. Also, Rosie and Fiona have some nice pictures that might sell."

Jim considered this. "Yes. Sounds a good idea in the right place."

"Maybe in Byres Road. There's lots of passing trade there, near the University."

"Oh, Elsie. You know students never have any money."

"It's not just students."

"Well, we'll see. I'll think about it and see how the land lies. Meanwhile, you finish your course. We must always see things through. Finish what we start."

Echoing his mother, Elsie thought. What an idiot!

—·—

Family duty started nagging at Elsie.

It had been seven months since she had taken the children to visit their grandparents, and a letter from Lily pricked her conscience so that she felt obliged to make the trip by bus and tramcar across the city. She would stay overnight, sleeping with Lily and Stella, three in a bed, and the children could sleep in the little bedroom.

And so Elsie landed back in Ardgay Street, in her old home. She saw that her mother had not changed. She still baked her own bread, and her cakes were still light and delicious. When the cooking and other household chores were over, the dress patterns came out and then the ironing board. Everything she made was finished perfectly. And she found her ageing father still fond of his gardening and herbal remedies, and although he had only two cages of canaries now, their song still filled the house, like bottled sunshine.

"Oh, it's our Elsie, Louisa. Come in, girl. And these two beauties," he said, lifting one in each arm. "Well, this is a treat. You're a sight for sore eyes."

Louisa came through to greet them. "I wondered when you were going to favour your mother with a visit. Come and tell us all your news. Let's hear how the other half lives." As she spoke, she gave each of the children one of her little Madeleine cakes and a cup each of lemonade.

Relaxed at home, Elsie gradually, after a few hours, reverted to the camaraderie and bantering that was the normal day-to-day life in her parents' home. The newspapers were discussed, and neighbours and family dropped in to carry news or spend ten minutes before settling at home for the night. These were simple pleasures of the community that she had forgotten about.

On the Sunday, Elsie visited Honor and Edward, taking Robbie and Felicity to meet their cousins. There they exchanged news, drinking down endless cups of tea, and again there were the comings and goings of family and neighbours. They talked of old times, people they hadn't seen for a while and of how they might be getting on.

"We used to get out to the pictures, Ned and me, Elsie. We saw Charlie Chaplin and a Shirley Temple film, but Mrs Denny is getting too old to walk there now, so we don't get out as much. She used to be so good at looking after the children. But she has anaemia, pernicious anaemia. Poor Archie. He hasn't much of a life. School all day, and then a sick mother at night. No wonder he escapes to the public library, or the public house, when he can."

Elsie looked at her little boy and hid her thoughts quickly. "How is Archie?" But it was not long before, as was usual, Archie appeared for his daily visit to the household. She was as delighted to see him, as he obviously was to see her. His eyes never left her face. "By God, you look well. More stunning than ever!" Archie turned to Edward and Honor. "Our rich relation!"

"Don't be stupid, Archie," said Elsie, "it's you who are the star. You're my brilliant, clever, professional relation. How's St Mungo's?"

"Hellish! Anybody who goes into teaching should be boiled in oil to cure them of their stupidity." Elsie laughed at this outburst. "Oh, sure. It pays the rent and buys me my beer, but ..., never mind me. What about you? We've heard you're an artist now."

"Yes, well, I've been taking lessons. I'm thinking of opening a shop. A kind of art and craft suppliers, where maybe I can display my pictures. I might even have a little tea-room attached."

"I knew you'd be a raging success one day, Elsie."

Lily and Stella, the two younger sisters, their curiosity having got the better of them, joined the little gathering in Honor's. The small kitchen was overcrowded with people downing cups of tea and bread and jam, and scoffing the last of the cakes from the morning's baking. Children playing hide-and-seek, or trailing toys, wove in and out of the adults almost unseen.

Elsie's two little ones came rushing through to where she sat, calling for pennies to buy ice cream from the van at the corner of the street. "So these are your two?" Archie looked at the children. To Robbie he said, "And, what's your name?"

"Robbie."

"And what age are you?"

"I'm six." The fine blue eyes looked back quizzically at Archie.

To Elsie, he said, "He looks a bright boy. A bit like yourself in looks. The same expression in the eyes."

"You think so. You don't think he looks like my husband, then?"

"No. Can't say I do."

"Neither do I." She looked at him directly, and a flush of colour suffused his face. But it was more than the introverted Archie could take. Only Elsie and he were riveted on the thought that he could have fathered this little boy. He would have to withdraw from this tension. He couldn't take this knowledge. He stood up in agitation. Edward and Honor looked on, unaware of his feeling.

"I must get back to Mother, Ned. I've been away long enough. She will need her tea. Are you coming to visit her tonight?"

"I'll be up later, Archie."

"She's not good, Ned! She'll be glad to see you." He turned his attention to his old flame who, in her fashionable tweeds, sat there looking cool and exotic in the modest little kitchen.

"When will you be back to see us, Elsie?"

"Oh, I'll let you know, Archie. I'll write to Lily or Honor."

"Your visits are so few I don't want to miss your next one." He shook her hand, and she kissed him quickly on the cheek, giving him a hug, which brought the emotions of both of them to the surface. Swiftly he was out the door without looking round.

She called out, "Goodbye, Archie. Take care of yourself, now."

CHAPTER 27

The Dryden's flat was on the ground floor of a grey sandstone tenement building. Playing on the gramophone was Al Bowley singing 'Love Is the Sweetest Thing' and, lost in thought, Elsie stood looking out of her mother's parlour window for Jim who was due to collect her with the children at four o'clock. Beyond were more buildings and, to the south of the main street, miles and miles of poorer tenements, all built to house workers who had flocked to what had once been a quiet country village. Industry took over and everywhere there were weaving mills and metal foundry works and glassworks – all manner of business which in the nineteenth century had spewed outwards to the countryside from the great city of Glasgow. Elsie silently counted her blessings at having escaped from this concentration of humanity and poverty to her garden suburb on the other side of the city.

Now her two younger sisters, Lily and Stella arrived home. Stella entered her mother's kitchen, saying, "I wish you could stay longer, Elsie. It used to be a lot more fun when you were at home." She hugged her older sister affectionately, her pretty face pouting.

"Listen!" said Lily. "Isn't it your birthday next Sunday, Elsie? It's the 29th of November. Do you think Jim would let you invite us to your house? We could have a party." They went on to discuss that they had never seen their sister's new house, and she had now been living there for some time.

"But how would you get there?"

"Well, you got here by bus and tramcar," Lily was determined. "Anyway, Stella's boyfriend has his own car. Gilbert would drive us there, I'm sure, wouldn't he, Stella?" Stella nodded her agreement.

Elsie looked at the two of them. She couldn't think of a reason for not inviting them, except that Jim had never been keen on her family. "And you have a boyfriend, too, Lily ?"

"Yes, the same one, Johnny McBride."

"Edward's friend?"

"That's right. A left-wing activist, as you know."

Elsie looked at the two of them. Stella, her pretty young sister. She's like a ten-year-younger version of myself, she thought. Dressed quite expensively in a pale blue, moygashel linen skirt with a soft, woollen sweater to match, she was very carefully made up. Even her long eyelashes had been curled before the mascara had been put on, and with her curls bouncing on her shoulders, there was no doubt that Stella was the town beauty. Lily, in her own way, was attractive, too. The only dark-haired one in the family – always smiling, she had a sharp sense of humour and a merry, infectious laugh.

"All right. If I can borrow your Al Bowley record you can come. Come next Saturday about six o'clock, and bring your boyfriends. Are you sure I'll like them?"

Lily said, "Oh, Elsie, you'll love them. They're both perfect. Right, Stella?"

"Well, my Gilbert's perfect."

Elsie smiled at this hyperbole. "And what does Gilbert do for a living?"

"He works for his father. Wilson, Hutchison and Begg, they're big house factors and property agents."

"And what does Johnny do, Lily?"

"He's a tailor. A cutter, really, with Burton's, the gent's outfitter's in Glasgow. It's a very skilled trade, you know."

"Well, I'm glad you two are so happy. Mother's a lot softer with you two than she ever was with me. I used to be terrified to tell her I had a boyfriend. She interfered with every romance I had. Nobody was good enough for me. You two are lucky being the youngest. You get away with murder. We had to work outside the house and inside. And she was never satisfied. That's why I eloped. I couldn't stand it."

"Oh, she's a lot better now. They're both getting old. I don't think she can be bothered to dominate us. She's a bit worn out with the years of effort. And Dad just goes his merry way as usual, with the vegetable plot, and his herbs." Lily looked out of the window, "Here comes your Jim, Elsie. Will he come in for tea?"

"He'll come in, but I don't think he'll stay for tea. He's always in a hurry. Come along, kids. Here's Daddy." Within five minutes, he and Elsie and the children were off. "Until Sunday," Stella called after them.

— · — · —

One of the most sociable and fun-loving people in the world, Elsie had never felt able to have a party in her Bearsden home, due to the damper put on things by Jim and his family. They preferred to invite influential people to a dinner or lunch, and thought of parties as a frivolous waste of time and money. But Elsie was trying her wings after all these years. In more than seven years of marriage, and she had never been able to break out to be herself and do what she wanted to do. Now, at last, she was gradually becoming a force to be reckoned with. No longer could she be fobbed off with refusals of her suggestions, as if being a woman and from a so-called lower-class family, she was inferior to the members of the Shields family and their friends, and had to abide by their decisions and listen to their criticisms of her ideas.

"What's the party supposed to be for, Elsie?"

"It's my birthday on Sunday, remember?"

"Oh, of course." Jim was lost for an obstacle to put up.

"And who is coming?"

"Well, I've asked Lily and her young man, Johnny McBride. And there's our Stella and Gilbert Hutchison. And I thought I'd ask Ralston and Fiona, and Mike and Rosie Russell. Also, I thought of Arthur Butterworth and Wendy. You know, the people who own the boat on the loch. They're a lot of fun."

"Can we accommodate ten people?"

"Oh, they would all go home afterwards. It will just be a buffet. You know, 'help-yourself', with a few glasses of wine and some chat. And you could provide a birthday cake out of the shop, if you want to be kind. You'll see. It can serve as our delayed house-warming party."

And so it happened. Eyes glazed with excitement, Elsie greeted her guests. It was a noisy, cheerful party. The conversation flowed, and Stella and Lily were impressed with the fineness of the house and the beauty of the china and silver. When the guests were finished eating, Elsie put a record on the gramophone. "It's Al Bowley, folks, listen! It's the latest!" The record sang out:

Love is the sweetest thing,
What else on earth could ever bring,
Such happiness to everything,
As love's old story?

Jim pulled Elsie to her feet to dance a foxtrot to the music, and pretty soon there were several couples dancing alongside them. Elsie could feel Ralston's eyes boring into her as she passed him. Fiona was watching her husband and the way he followed the swaying of Elsie's body, as she moved around the room.

"Let's dance, darling." Fiona stood up and took her husband's hands to pull him out of his chair. "Come on, you used to be a good dancer, Ralston, if you remember." She put her arm on his shoulder and pressed her body close to his. "Come on, Fred Astaire. Let's show them how it was done back in Victorian times."

"You're mad, Fiona. I've forgotten how to dance to this kind of music."

"Put on a Highland fling, for 'Scots wha hae' here, Elsie. He can't do this modern stuff."

"Oh, I'm sure you'll teach him, Fiona. There's nothing to it." Elsie was highly embarrassed. She knew that Fiona had caught her husband's eyes straying towards her.

At midnight, Elsie blew out the candles on the cake, the party ended and folks started to leave. As he said goodnight in the hallway, Ralston managed a few minutes with Elsie. "Your sisters really are terrific. Almost as pretty as you, and they're such fun!"

"Stella is more better-looking than I ever was."

"No, she might be prettier, but she doesn't have your classical features, and personality. Stella is a pretty doll." He put on his overcoat. "Listen, can you manage to come on Tuesday evening to the art school? There's a first-class guy coming to give a demonstration on fabric printing. He might be useful to you in the future. You can show him your portfolio. He's Mr Sabatini from Flaxton's, big fabric people. He's talking to my class from six until eight in the evening. He comes every year as part of the fabric design course."

"Don't know. I'll do my best," she whispered as she closed the door.

Elsie and Jim sank exhausted into armchairs when the last guests had gone. Surveying the empty glasses and the usual ashtrays brimming over with cigarette ends, they decided to leave the lot until the morning. As they went upstairs, Elsie said, "That was the best evening I've had since we met, Jim."

"You enjoyed it?" At the top of the stairs, he stopped her and kissed her forehead. "You did well, darling. What a hostess!"

"Gosh, I'm almost asleep." Elsie drifted into the bathroom and washed her face. Then as if in a coma, she kicked off her shoes, unzipped her dress, dropped her underwear and stockings, and threw on her nightgown. The whole operation took but a few seconds. "Goodnight, Jim." Within ten seconds, she was sound asleep. Jim looked ruefully at the beautiful body. He slipped in close beside her, and put out the light.

In the morning he said, "Listen, you minx, I have to go to the office today, but I have a surprise for you." He took out a gold bracelet and put it on her arm. "Happy birthday, darling!"

"Well, this is more like how a girl should be treated. God, Jim! It must have cost a fortune." She was very touched. "It's the best present you've ever given me. You improve with age, you know."

"I haven't told you my second surprise, yet."

"What's that?" Elsie smiled sleepily at him.

"I've rented a double-windowed shop in Byres Road where you can sell your work, and I've got a girl lined up to look after it for you."

Elsie jumped with surprise, her voice was a squeak. "How fantastic, Jim. I can't wait to see it."

"I don't get the keys until Friday, and it will need to be painted and titivated up. But that's up to you. There's a catalogue in the hall cupboard of artist's supplies. You can look through it while I'm away."

"You're too good to me, Jim."

"You could make one side a studio and artists' supplies part, and the other side could be a tearoom. But you'll need another member of staff. I don't want you spending all day there, do you hear? You have the children, after all. Are you still going to that thing in the art school on Tuesday evening?"

"Yes. It's quite important that I meet with this Mr Sabatini. He has good contacts in the world of fabrics and can give me an opinion on my work."

She waved him goodbye, thinking that at last things were going her way. And I won't let his old mother throw cold water on it either, she thought. I'll pretend it's not all that important to me, this studio and shop. That will put her off her guard, if she thinks I'm not getting any pleasure out of it. She'll have to be up early to spoil my life! Unconsciously she had clenched her fists as if ready for a fight.

On the Tuesday evening, Elsie managed to arrive at the art school halfway through the talk on fabric printing. Mr Sabatini had brought samples of the prints made by his firm that were fashionable for house furnishing and for curtains. There was a workshop in the last half-hour, while his assistant demonstrated something of the method of screen-printing used by their designers. Afterwards, when the class was finished and the other students had gone, Ralston took them to his office in the school, so that Elsie could show her patterns to Mr Sabatini.

"You know, Ralston," Sabatini remarked, "this building never ceases to amaze me. These great unadorned windows and the little offset towers. Such inspiration! Such a fantastic architect! Such a building! Glasgow is lucky to have such a place for its art school."

Ralston looked around him, "Yes, it's the interplay of light and shade that always fascinates me. The whole place is just a succession of surprises."

They walked up the stairs to the studios. "The casual arrangements of these rooms is like no other building I have ever seen. Artistically it's inspiring. Such an innovative man! How lucky you are to work here, my friend!"

They had entered Ralston's room. "I know I'm lucky. Every day is a pleasure working here." He pulled out two chairs for Elsie and Sabatini. Slowly the bearded artist turned over her work. Eventually, he said. "Your work is excellent. I love your tulips. The geometric shapes you have included in the pattern, and your colours are terrific."

"You're very kind, Mr Sabatini."

"Yes, your roses and these tortured flowers are very original. And once again, your sense of colour is first class. Yes, Mrs Shields, I am impressed. This daisy pattern could be done in several different colour combinations. But my favourite is this one, the blue, stylised tulips! Magnificent! How long have you been at the art school?"

"Just three months."

"She's a very gifted pupil with a natural ability. Only in the stylising of her flower and plant sketches, have we helped her. Her colour sense is her own, and really quite startling at times."

"Remarkable! I've seen designs by experienced design artists less good than these. There is a freshness and originality about them. Very modern. Sort of jazz age-like."

"I told you, Elsie. Your work has commercial possibilities. Congratulations!"

"They haven't bought them yet," Elsie laughed.

"Would it be a possibility for me to take these with me? I think my firm might be interested in them?" Amadeo Sabatini looked at his watch. "I have an appointment at nine o'clock this evening, so I haven't much time. I'd return them to you next Tuesday."

Elsie looked at Ralston, who said, "Could she bring them to Flaxton's office herself?"

"You mean to our office in Edinburgh?"

"Sure. I think if she meets your bosses she'll make a good impression. They can talk to her about them. Perhaps make suggestions."

"If that is your wish, Mrs Shields, I'll try and arrange an appointment for you."

When he had gone, Ralston opened his filing cabinet and took out a bottle of gin. "A little snifter before I take you home." He handed her a glass of gin and soda water, and they lit up cigarettes.

"Gosh, what if they buy my designs, Ralston. I might make some money in my own right!"

He smiled at her. "I hope you make a lot of money, my dear. And why not? You have a lot of talent."

A broad smile from her was his reward, and she told him, "You've brought me luck. You've changed my life. I'm not the same person you met just six months ago."

He took the glass from her and pulled her to her feet. "I'm not the same person, either. I'm crazy about you!" He was unbuttoning her little woollen jacket, and his hands were caressing her.

"Ralston!" She felt weak and giddy. His breathing was heavy and he kissed her ears, her hair and then her neck. He lifted her hands to his lips. She touched his chest to push him away, tried to resist his advances, but desire engulfed her as his hands grew more daring.

He locked the door and advanced towards her, and she knew resistance was hopeless. When it was over, she whispered, "Oh God! Ralston. What have we done?"

He kissed her protesting lips. "You're like a flame that never goes out." Her passion rose to his and soon they fell back exhausted from their lovemaking.

When she had recovered herself, and scrabbled in her handbag to repair her make-up, Elsie said, "Tonight was wonderful, Ralston." His arms went around her. "But, I don't want to start an affair with you. It mustn't happen again."

"But you love me. I know you do. You would not have fallen into my hands like a ripe plum if you hadn't loved me."

She sounded logical. "I love your lovemaking. You're very good-looking. You're a wonderful lover, but ... well, you know why ..."

"Do you think I make love to Fiona like this?"

"No. And I don't make love to Jim like this. But don't you see? It's because Jim and Fiona are familiar to us. Too familiar. We've got used to them. That's all."

"I don't believe that's the whole story. I can't think about anything else but you. For days at a time I am possessed by you. And tonight, my darling, for me that was the best lovemaking of my life." He pulled her close to him.

"Sure, but you are married to Fiona. She loves you, too. And she has your son. So you can't talk your way out of that."

He was crestfallen. "Well, promise me that, at least, you won't say, 'never again'. Promise you won't say we can never love each other again as we did tonight. Promise me that you won't say that?"

She smiled and kissed him gently and sweetly on the lips. She caressed his grizzled curly hair, "I won't say 'never again', Ralston, because never is a very long time."

CHAPTER 28

Edward stood outside the railway office, looking at the large oak door. The sign said 'Works Manager'. He smoothed down his dungarees and looked at his work-worn hands, before knocking on the door.

The door opened, "Come in. Ah, come in, Ned. Have a seat. You'll be wondering why I sent for you."

Edward eyed the dark-suited man with whom he had had many a confrontation on union matters in the past. Ross Turnbull was nobody's fool, but pragmatic enough to avoid trouble brewing up, if it could be avoided.

"Well, Ned, as you know, our yard supervisor, John Reid, is retiring this month. We intend to make the job a bigger one, with more responsibility. As you know, there has been a good deal of expansion in the goods yard lately and, of course, our workforce is now up to thirty-five, including apprentices. John has been struggling lately and his retirement has come at the right time."

Edward knew there was something afoot, but he could not quite put his finger on what it was. "To cut a long story short, Edward, we're offering the job to you. You have a good head on your shoulders and are a reliable worker." The older man saw the surprise and disbelief on Edward's face. "I know we've crossed swords in the past. We know your left-wing tendencies, but we hope that these won't interfere with the running of the station and the yard." Still, Edward could not think of a response. "You will be given a substantial rise in wages, and of course, your base will be here in the railway offices, in the station. What do you say?"

"I've never worked inside before." Edward's mind was racing. Suddenly he saw himself, young, free and unattached, a red-faced soldier, just one week back from the war in France, standing in those same railway offices asking for a job. A lifetime ago – almost twenty years.

"We know that, but we think you can do it. Do you think so?"

"Yes."

"Good man. That's it, then. On Monday, you can start alongside Reid and learn the ropes from him. You'll be directly responsible to me." Turnbull shook Edward's hand. "Congratulations, Ned. I must say you deserve it."

His was a quicker step than usual at five o'clock that day as he hurried home to tell Honor the good news. He saw her at the corner of the street with Nana, Jamie and Billy, but no Greta. Holding the hands of the children, Honor was wearing her apron in the street, which was unusual, and she looked up and down, obviously quite distraught.

"Oh, Edward, we've lost little Greta!" Greta was his favourite. The youngest of the brood, just three years old, she had dark curls like himself and was quick and intelligent. "We've looked up and down the street. We've searched the back green, even over the walls of the farmer's field. She must have wandered off."

Fear gripped his heart. My God! he thought, she could have been stolen. His pretty child! But he said, "Don't get into a state, Honor. Don't cry." He put his arm around her. "How long has she been gone?"

Honor looked at Nana, "When did you last see her?"

"She was playing with us when the fever van came. It took away Jim McDonald. He's got scarlet fever."

The neighbours who had gathered looked at Honor and Edward. "The fever van?"

"Oh, my God!" Honor screamed. "She's not gone away in the fever van?"

Their next-door neighbour said, "There's a phone box round in Gateside Street. I'll phone Belvedere Hospital and see if the child's there." She returned in a few minutes, waving her arms and smiling. "Don't worry, folks, the ambulance is on its way back with her. The little devil must have crawled into the van while the men were collecting wee Jim upstairs." The child was returned, none the worse for her adventure, and Honor clutched her to her bosom, and sat pale and exhausted in the apartment while Edward tried to tell her the story of his promotion.

"That's wonderful, Ned. I'm so happy for you. But I can't quite take it all in just now. I'm just not worth a button after that scare today."

He was the one who served the meal that night, and after an hour or two Honor had recovered. She looked fondly at him, "Oh, Edward, do you realise, you'll have no more soakings in the cold and rain, and no filthy dungarees. No dirty, cold hands in the winter."

Edward looked at his workman's hands, swollen and callused with a lifetime of manual labour. "That's right! No more," he said, as if mesmerised.

Later, when the children were in bed, he said, "I'll just get changed and go and tell Archie and my mother about the job."

Annie was seated close to the fire in the kitchen range, so changed and so failed that Edward was shocked to see her. She looked up saying, "Oh, it's you, son. Come away in!"

"And where's the bold Archie, Mother?"

"Oh, he's staying with a friend. Somebody from the school, I think. In the town. There's some party on. I told him I'd be all right."

"Well, Mother, you don't look too well."

"I'm fine. You make me a cup of tea, son, and I'll put on my nightdress." When she returned she said, "Lizzie McFarlane's been in and told me aboot Greta being away in the fever van. You must have got an awful fright."

"Aye, Honor's a shivering wreck tonight. You take this tea, and bread and butter, Mother. I'll go and put a hot-water bottle in your bed."

When she had got into bed, he sat by her bedside, "I got some good news today."

Her eyes opened quickly, "What was that?"

"I'm to be made the yard manager, foreman, if you like. There's more money in it."

"And you'll wear a suit to work?"

"That's right, Mother. How did you know?"

"Oh, son. You've made me a happy woman!" She put out her hand to his, and he held it. "Two of my sons now gentlemen. I can hardly believe it. And poor Honor, good news for her at last. She must be awful happy."

"Aye, when she realises there will be more money about as well she'll be twice as happy." He sat by her side for an hour or two as she sunk into sleep, but somehow he wasn't happy with the way she looked or with her breathing. He called in the neighbour to wait with her while he went for the doctor.

"You'll have to stay all night with her, Ned, or find someone who will. She's pretty low." No one knew how to contact Archie, but presently Joe arrived and sat the night out at his mother's bedside.

"I was going to come and see her tomorrow, anyway, Ned," Joe said. "Come out here to the kitchen where I can have a fag." The two lit up and Joe continued, "I was coming to see Mother and you tomorrow, because I've applied to go and fight in Spain. The Unemployed Workers' Movement is sending me. I'll be off to London, soon. That's the first stop."

"My God, Joe, don't be a fool. The Germans have been dropping bombs on Spain. It's carnage over there. Besides, the Republicans have practically lost the war."

"If every country in Europe sends men to stop the fascists we can still beat that bastard, Franco."

"You stay with your wife and children. I know what war is like. It might seem like an adventure to you, but it's bloody mud and bullets, Joe. It's a mug's game."

"I'm committed to go, and I'm going, Ned. The Workers' Movement will give Bessie and the kids enough to live on. Better to get rid of this bloody hatred of the system and of the capitalist bastards over there than to rot in squalor here. There's just no work around, I've tried."

"Could you no' go back to sea?"

"There's nobody being taken on just now. There's just no trade, the Merchant Navy is dead because there's a world depression. They say it's spread here from America, and it's affected everything. I've tried to sign on with a few shipping lines, but it's just impossible."

"Well, it looks like we'll all be at war, anyway, the way the bloody Fuehrer Herr Hitler is going on. Maybe, Joe, if I was ten years younger and, like you, I didn't have a job, then I'd be off to Spain as well. Anyway, you surely can't leave while our mother's like this."

They stood looking at the dying woman. "Poor old Annie," Joe was moved by the pallor of his old mother's face. "She's had a hard life, it's true enough, but you know, she always cared more for Archie and you, than she ever did for me. I was the wild man in her eyes."

"She loved you, too, Joe. You're the one most like my father."

"Oh, sure. Everybody loves a clown!"

The doctor came at nine in the morning. He looked severe, "I'm afraid she'll not last the day. You'd better inform the rest of the family." Sadly, in deep thought, Edward washed and shaved, and taking the tramcar into the city, he arrived at St Mungo's Academy, where the Headmaster led him to Archie's classroom. There, in the stuffy, chalk-laden corridors, Edward had an unaccustomed picture of his brother, begowned and with a severe expression on his face, an open book in his hand, in front of a sea of black-blazered boys who listened intently to him.

When they entered, the boys rose as one. "Good morning, Brother O'Malley. Good morning, sir," they chorused, and with a clatter they sat down.

Archie had paled at their appearance. "It's Mother, isn't it?" Edward nodded. Brother O'Malley was very kind and solicitous, telling Archie not to worry about the class, he would take care of it, and they were soon out of the school and into a taxi, speeding homewards.

Of the three brothers, Archie was least able to cope with the crisis, and he had to force himself to look at his dying mother's face. She opened her eyes and smiled at him, and then she turned to look fondly at her other two sons. The three of them stood together as she drew her last breath, tears of grief blinding them. The priest came and gave her the last rites, while outside the house a little crowd had gathered in silent respect. It was as if royalty were passing away.

— · — · —

The funeral was large, one of the largest ever seen in the area, with a crowd of hundreds following the hearse to the church. For Annie had been loved, not just for her skill as a midwife, but for her unspoken humanity and her sympathy for the oppressed. Many a half-crown had she slipped to penniless mothers at the birth of another hungry baby, and many a prayer had she said for stricken households in their loss and sorrow. A very moving requiem mass was said, and there was much grief in the packed church, as the town said its goodbyes to a well-loved friend.

Nevertheless, life had to go on, and for Honor it was still hard work, for her brood was growing fast. There was not a minute of the day when she was not shopping, and then carrying home bags of groceries and heavy bottles of milk. Her time was spent cooking, or washing and ironing, or trying to keep their house clean and tidy. "The back's made for the burden," was her mother's response when Honor sat down exhausted after the evening meal. The one recreation she loved, as did most of her contemporaries, was going to 'the pictures'. With the advent of Charlie Chaplin films and stars like Al Jolson and Fred Astaire, she could lose herself in the lives of her screen idols. And children became caught up in their cowboy heroes and in Saturday morning cliffhangers, so that they waited anxiously to see what had happened to the star they had left in trouble, the previous Saturday.

"But, Mum, the matinee is only threepence. It's *The Three Stooges* that's on. I love them, Mum." Little, red-haired Billy, eyes popping out of his head with excitement at the prospect of the pictures, melted Honor's heart. Past eight years old now, a chunky little boy, he was already a favourite with his mother.

"You can take Greta with you. The two of you wait down at the close-mouth until five minutes to two, before you go over to the cinema. I don't want you mixing with all those rough children from down the road." Billy was rushing to the door, clutching the money, and Honor called after him, "And ask to be put across the main road. Wait downstairs just now. Don't move away from the bus stop." The two children scampered down while Honor turned to her usual place by the sink, and then her sister Stella called with the news that Lily was getting married.

"Never!" This news warranted sitting down. The two sisters, one plain and dowdy in her apron and straggling hair, the other who could have stepped out of a fashion magazine, groomed from her beautifully curled hair to her long, painted fingernails, got their heads together over a cup of tea to discuss this turn of events. "Gosh, next June, Stella? I'll need to save up for an outfit for that."

"But that's not all, Honor. I'll probably not be far behind them. Gilbert and I are to be engaged at Christmas, and married probably in August. But I want to have a big white wedding."

"Oh, you always were the lucky one of the family, Stella. Mam will make a big fuss of your wedding. And Gilbert's family are the type she will want to impress."

"Well, you know, Honor. All this talk of war, who knows how long we'll have our men? We thought we ought to grab our chance while we could. We've being going with the boys for years now."

"I know, Stella. Every day they talk on the news of the serious situation in Europe. Ned is riveted to the radio nowadays ..." She was interrupted by little Greta who burst into the kitchen, so agitated and out of breath, she could hardly speak, "Billy, Billy!..." and she pointed to the door. The two of them jumped up and flew down the stairs to the street.

A small crowd had gathered around Billy who stood, red faced and choking.

"Hit him on the back," someone was saying.

"Turn him upside down ..."

While Honor and Stella looked on, a passer-by, a big man, turned the child upside down and shook him. But nothing came out. Honor grabbed her son, hysterical with panic, "Where's your picture money. Where's the money?" The choking child opened his hand. There lay two big, brown pennies, the two half-pennies were missing. "Spit them out! Spit them out!" she cried. Billy made a hawking, gurgling noise. Honor thumped him on the back, and then the child stopped his noise making, looking at his mother, wide-eyed. He had swallowed the two coins.

In her state of anxiety, Honor shouted at the boy, "How did you do such a stupid thing? You stupid boy, giving us all such a fright." By now, the crowds of children, mainly little boys, were gathering for the queue at the picture house opposite, and Billy was the centre of attention.

He looked at the bus stop pole. "I climbed up to the top of the pole with the money in my mouth. And when I came down, I had only two pennies left." The boy seemed amazed at the whole thing himself.

And so the intrepid Billy was dragged to the doctor's surgery, a familiar stamping ground for Honor these days. The doctor examined the boy. "I'm afraid there's nothing to be done, Honor. You must examine whatever he passes each day to see if the coins come out. Otherwise, I wouldn't worry." The amused doctor looked from the worried mother to the sanguine little boy. "Billy Denny – worth one penny!" he said, laughing.

That evening, while she and Edward were sitting having a quiet cup of tea by the fireside, Edward put down his newspaper, saying, "The government are going to issue gas masks to all school children in the near future. That's what it says in the paper."

"Oh goodness, what kind of world is it that we've brought them into, Ned? They haven't been told anything about gas masks at school yet, or we would have heard. The only thing they've been told is that they are being taken to the Empire Exhibition. That's to be at Bellahouston Park."

"Huh, exhibitions while the Germans are marching into countries all over Europe. Just typical of the bloody establishment in this country!"

The news got gloomier and gloomier, and Edward, like most men of his generation, feared that the coming war would be even worse than the horrors of his experiences of the trenches of the First World War. He kept his head down and absorbed himself in his work and in his regular trips to the Public Library. Honor had her own special worries. She practised putting on the gas masks with the children, but she knew there was something not right with her health.

"I'm thirty-eight, Doctor, and I haven't had any periods for a while, maybe four months. Do you think it could be the change of life?"

He examined her, and then sat down opposite her. "It's my opinion that you are pregnant, my girl."

Honor was truly shocked. "Expecting? Oh, no!" She had thought she was finished with babies. The mixed feelings of elation and shock, so common to women in such circumstances, filled her.

"I'd say you were about four months now, Honor. Don't worry. It's not the end of the world. Just eat well, and try and rest when you can."

She picked her moment that evening to tell Edward. Just when he had relaxed with a cup of tea and a nice piece of fruit cake by the fire. She watched his face as she told him, "I was at the doctor's today, Ned."

"What on earth for?"

"Well, I thought I wasn't quite right, and he says that ..."

"What?"

"He thinks I'm expecting. Four months gone." She saw the mixture of reactions he was experiencing, as she kept her eyes on his face. "I know it's a surprise. I don't know what to think."

"Oh, my God! All those nights of being wakened up with a crying baby, and nappies all over the place." He closed his eyes, and shook his head. When he looked at her he saw that she was crying into her handkerchief. "I'm sorry, love. It's just such a shock. I can't believe it."

"You're as much to blame as I am. More, in fact."

"You're right. Well, if it wasn't so late, I'd go out for a pint."

"A pint? You mean to celebrate?"

"And why not? Plenty people would be pleased to have such a family as ours, as your father is always telling you."

"I know. I love new-born babies. And it will be in May. That's a lovely time to have a baby, just when the good weather is starting. It's just with all this talk of war, I thought it was foolhardy to be bringing more children into the world."

"Oh, there'll be a war. Make no mistake about that. But people will still have children, war or no war."

On the 15th of May 1939, a baby girl was born to Honor in her home. They called her Sally. It was a beautiful spring and summer, and the baby was always out in her pram in the sun, healthy and thriving.

The only damper on things was when the baby was a few weeks old, a baby's gas mask was delivered to their house, and Honor was reduced to weeping as she practised putting her little baby inside the rubber contraption.

The news from Europe was very bad, and Edward followed the newspapers and the radio avidly, cursing Chamberlain and the government. At last the tension was over, and on the 3rd of September war between Great Britain and Germany was officially declared. There was relief and grim satisfaction in the country that at last a stand was to be made. By the time Sally was one year old, in the following spring, there was a new coalition government of all the parties, with Winston Churchill at its head. "An old warmonger!" Edward called him. "Still, at least he knows something about the conduct of war and what should be done."

As Honor prepared the children for bed, she had some visitors. Her sister Lily, with her new husband Johnny, called, and then, not long behind them, who should appear, but Stella with Gilbert, in his Naval Officer's uniform. Both the men were on embarkation leave. "All we need is our Archie to appear in his uniform now, and we'll have all the family servicemen." Ned laughed as he poured out little glasses of precious whisky to wish the boys luck. "To absent friends," he said. Just then the door opened, and in walked Archie, in his spanking new khaki uniform. His face was reddened with training for hours in the sun.

"I came to say 'hello' and 'goodbye'," he said. They greeted each other with great warmth, each moved by the drama of the situation. The talk turned to the situation of the troops and the evacuation from Dunkirk. Edward turned on the radio, "They're going to broadcast Churchill's speech to the House of Commons, just about now. I want to hear it." They fell quiet as the growling voice of the Prime Minister came over the airwaves. The men paused with their whisky in their hands, and even the children sensed they should listen:

> "We shall defend our island, whatever the cost
> may be; we shall fight on the beaches, we shall
> fight on the landing grounds, we shall fight in the
> fields and in the streets, we shall fight in the hills.
> We shall never surrender."

Edward switched off the radio – no one knew how to follow such oratory. They were stunned. "What a speaker!" Edward broke the silence. "What a command of the language! And he has caught the mood of the country. If anyone can lead us out of this mess, he can. He's the man to stand up against those bloody German fascists." But he couldn't resist adding, "Old Tory bastard!"

"Well, with him in command, at least we've got a chance." It was Gilbert who spoke. "People will unite behind him. That's what we need. He's a wily old devil, but he's got the country's interests at heart." He raised his glass with the remains of his whisky. "Here's to you, Ned and Honor, and the end of the war." They rose and said their goodbyes, but Archie stayed behind after the others had left.

"Remember to write to Ned and me, Archie. We're your closest family, now that your mother's gone."

"And you write back to me, Honor. Tell me about the family. God knows what they'll do with me in the army. A bloody history teacher. I'm not cut out to be a soldier."

"They'll have you as a teacher, teaching other soldiers, in no time. That's what they always do with educated ones like you. Other than that, they'll commission you and put you in command."

"Command boys to go into battle. I couldn't do that. Never."

"Don't worry, Archie. We'll be thinking about you. Keep your head down, and never volunteer."

"Goodbye, then." He gathered up his hat and gloves.

"Goodbye, Archie. Take care of yourself." Honor kissed him affectionately.

"Tell Elsie I asked after her, as I was leaving," he forced himself to say.

"Aye, I'll tell her all right, Archie. You just come home safe, now. That's all we care about."

The two brothers shook hands, and Edward looked away to hide the tears in his eyes. And then Archie was gone. Honor picked up the glasses and emptied the ashtrays. "Put some more coal on the fire, Ned. It's quite cold, tonight. I'll see to the baby, and get the children undressed. It's time they were in their beds."

"Aye, Honor," Edward said as he placed the pieces of coal on the fire. "We had better put the children to bed."